"IN THE TRADITION OF THE BEST VINTAGE STUFF! BE PREPARED TO SHUT OFF THE PHONE OR THE FAX; YOU WON'T WANT ANY INTERRUPTIONS ONCE YOU START IT."
—*CBS RADIO NEWS*

"FAST-PACED ACTION!"   —*Kirkus Reviews*

"WITH HIS MASTERY FOR DETAILS AND HIS KEEN EYE FOR VIVID CHARACTERS, HALLINAN MAKES THE FAMILIAR FEEL FRESH, ORIGINAL AND EXCITING."
—*The Drood Review of Mystery*

"Hallinan writes with humor and insight into the Los Angeles scene. . . . The plotting is flawless, the clues fairly played, and the story well-told. Grist bears watching: he may turn out to be a modern successor to Raymond Chandler's Philip Marlowe."   —*Los Angeles Daily News*

A
SIMEON GRIST
SUSPENSE NOVEL

EVERYTHING BUT THE SQUEAL

BY

TIMOTHY HALLINAN

AN ONYX BOOK

ONYX
Published by the Penguin Group
Penguin Books USA Inc., 375 Hudson Street,
New York, New York 10014, U.S.A.
Penguin Books Ltd, 27 Wrights Lane,
London W8 5TZ, England
Penguin Books Australia Ltd, Ringwood,
Victoria, Australia
Penguin Books Canada Ltd, 2801 John Street,
Markham, Ontario, Canada L3R 1B4
Penguin Books (N.Z.) Ltd, 182-190 Wairau Road,
Auckland 10, New Zealand

Penguin Books Ltd, Registered Offices:
Harmondsworth, Middlesex, England

Published by Onyx, an imprint of New American Library,
a division of Penguin Books USA Inc.
Previously published in an NAL Books edition.

First Onyx Printing, July, 1991
10 9 8 7 6 5 4 3 2 1

ACKNOWLEDGMENTS
"She's Leaving Home" by John Lennon and Paul McCartney © 1967 Northern Songs Ltd.
All rights for the U.S., Canada and Mexico Controlled and Administered by SBK
Blackwood Music Inc. Under license from ATV Music (Maclen). All rights reserved.
International copyright secured. Used by permission.

Lyric from "Starmaker" by Ray Davies used by permission of Carlin Music, London.

 REGISTERED TRADEMARK—MARCA REGISTRADA

Printed in the United States of America

PUBLISHER'S NOTE

This one is for Constance Stone,
who gave me time, space, and encouragement,
and for Munyin Choy,
who gives me everything else.

The curious life cycle of the botfly begins with an egg laid on a mammal's lip or fur. When the egg is licked and swallowed, its coating dissolves and a voracious larva is freed to float in the juices of the stomach. Eventually it begins to eat its way out, gaining weight as it goes. When it reaches the surface, usually through a flat muscle, the baby fly leaves behind an exit wound about the size of a .22 caliber bullet.

—Frederick Wendt, *An Entomologist's Notebook*

Home is where you hang your head.
                              —Groucho Marx

Oh, the little chickie hollered,
And the little chickie begged,
And they poured hot water
Up and down his leg. . . .
                    —Traditional American
                    children's song

I

The Little Chickie Hollered

1

Looking for Aimee

"*Hey!* No, no, no, no, no. How many times I gotta tell you, huh? You gitouta here. Git*outa* here." The Mountain's wooden *geta* sandals clattered over the concrete as he grabbed the Guitar Player by the frayed strap of the unstrung, bogus Stratocaster guitar he toted up and down Santa Monica Boulevard day and night. The Guitar Player's eyes, which had been closed in temporary bliss, opened as wide as they could, which is to say halfway, as the Mountain—three hundred quivering pounds of food-stained plaid shirt, scrubby beard, and yellow fangs—yanked him to his feet and launched him toward the sidewalk. The neck of the guitar knocked to the floor the dingy plastic tray containing the Guitar Player's cardinal sin: a package of store-bought sliced ham that he'd been surreptitiously dipping into somebody else's side order of the special teriyaki sauce, the one that Tommy, the Mountain's Okinawan boss, used only for teriyaki tacos.

There was no house rule against leaving leftovers for others—not much ever made it back into the kitchen—but bringing in food from outside was tantamount to *kamikaze*.

The eighty-six, which was part of the nightly floor show at the Oki-Burger, caught people's attention as though it were something new. At the other end of the Guitar Player's picnic-type table, the Toothless Man—two missing in front, top and bottom, nodded his head. "Maximum force," he aspirated approvingly to the Young Old Woman, fourteen

3

years old from behind and fifty from in front. The Young Old Woman, the only one who could understand him most of the time, cackled. She translated his conversation for the others and made his alibis to the cops. His speaking-tongue dog was what the others called her. When she wasn't being his speaking-tongue dog she worked the darker doorways with her back to the street, giving unpleasant surprises to fools on the prowl for pubescence.

One of the *genuine* teenage girls, seated at a table strategically near the sidewalk where a glimpse of her might make a straight hit the brakes, paused in a heroin nod-out long enough to giggle as the Mountain dispassionately lobbed the Guitar Player across the sidewalk and onto the back of a concrete bus bench. At the last possible instant, as he did almost every night, the Guitar Player managed to twist his body so that his ribs, rather than the imitation Stratocaster, cracked against the edge of the bench. "Wuff," he said. He straightened up, wrapped himself in a tenuous shred of affronted dignity, and set off down the street toward the sheltering hedges of Plummer Park. The kids did a lot of business in Plummer Park.

The nodding girl continued to exceed the limits of her body's chemical tolerance long enough to giggle again and say something to an equally loaded friend through what sounded like a mouthful of highly glutinous mush. Me, I just took a sip on my very old Diet Coke and a sniff at my even older purple T-shirt and wondered how long it would be before everybody stopped thinking I was a cop.

It was three A.M. at Tommy's Oki-Burger, and all was as well as it was going to get. A little earlier the clatter of silverware two bright orange tables away had announced the fact that a skinhead in black leather had hit the bottom of the curve on downers. He'd bounced twice on the cement floor, and the Mountain had hauled him into the men's room to be treated to a refreshing dip in the toilet. A girl had broken out in bugs that no one else could see, and the Mountain had sprayed her with an imaginary can of Raid to calm her down. It worked. The LAPD cruised slowly by every fifteen minutes or so, one of them checking out the girls and trying to keep his tongue from hanging out the window while the other one drove. They switched seats and tongues on alternate passes.

"To protect and to serve," the Mountain read off the side of the squad car, mopping down the table with a malodorous rag that might have been a recycled mummy wrapping. "Who they protecting, you think?"

"Each other," I said. To my great relief, my Diet Coke had finally dried up. I pushed the empty cup away as though it had contained uranium.

"And who they serving?" The Mountain picked up the empty cup and rattled it and then snapped the rag at a fly guilty of being out after curfew. A vaguely cheesy and thoroughly unwholesome smell spread its leprous wings beneath my nose.

"They're not serving Diet Coke," I said, fanning the vapor away. "And you're not either, not if you've got any pity in your soul. God, there must be something else to drink in this dump."

The Mountain lowered his voice. "Don't spread it around," he said, narrowing his eyes conspiratorially, "but I could offer you Diet Pepsi. And anyway, what do plainclothes cops care?"

On the whole, I liked the Mountain. He eighty-sixed people with style and he rarely held a grudge. I'd been hanging around the Oki-Burger four days and I'd told him at least twelve times that I wasn't a cop. I told him again now, scratching at my chin. My carefully cultivated four-day beard itched.

The Mountain gave me a knowing look and wiped his face with the damp mummy-wrap, making my skin crawl. "Nobody as grungy as you isn't a cop," he said. "Whyn't you go to Jack's? They're not as sharp there. You might pass for a human."

I knew good advice when I heard it. I hauled my backside off the hardest wooden bench this side of bankruptcy court and headed for Jack's.

Jack's Triple-Burgers is on Hollywood, near La Brea, and Tommy's Oki-Burger is on Fountain, near Fairfax. It's easy to map the physical geography—they're about a mile and a half apart, and Jack's is farther north and east than Tommy's—but the emotional geography is more subtle. It had taken me a couple of days to figure out that Tommy's got the new runaways and Jack's got the Old Hands. The drugs of choice in Tommy's are downers, mainly codeine and other painkillers, but at Jack's nobody screws around with anything you don't enjoy at the sharp point of a needle. The occasional exceptions in both places are freebasers, folks whose idea of a day at the beach is a waterpipe filled with a brain-jolting mixture of cocaine and ether and, occasionally, PCP. The freebasers are rare in both establishments, though. Cocaine makes you alert and jumpy. By and large, both Tommy's and Jack's cater to a crowd that puts a high value on anesthesia.

The other difference is that the boys and girls at Tommy's sometimes say no to a straight. He has to be pretty repulsive and not very prosperous-looking, and he's probably asking for something that would stun the Marquis de Sade, but the kids will say no. The boys and girls at Jack's don't. At Jack's, "Just say no" is a punch line.

To get to Jack's, I took the streets no one knows are there. Between Santa Monica and Hollywood boulevards there runs a network of narrow, pinched little avenues, paved when cars were smaller, and lined on either side by small houses, mostly stucco, built in the thirties. They were dark now, most of them, tucked away behind weedy lawns, climbing roses, and chained dogs. Here and there light spilled through a window, and at one point I heard the sad strains of Brahms' Double Concerto. There were few families. Most of the children in these neighborhoods come and go with the night, passing back and forth between the boulevards where the money is, looking at the houses from the wrong side of the chain-link fences.

I'd parked Sweet Alice, my car, on Cherokee, about halfway between Tommy's and Jack's. I won her in a game of chance that had begun in Malibu, not far from where I live, and ended in Pacoima. Her flamboyantly mustachioed owner, one Jaime, had painted her an indelible shade of iridescent horsefly blue, lowered her so far in front that she would have bounced going over a pack of Luckies, and hung a surrealistically large pair of furry dice from her rearview mirror. I'd removed the dice by way of expressing my individuality. Other than that I'd kept her, as they say in the used-car trade, as is. I patted her on the fender as I passed her and headed on up to Jack's. The sodium lights of Hollywood Boulevard gleamed luridly against the low-hanging April clouds. Jack's and the Boulevard were up the street, and Easter was around the corner.

Jack's squats on what L.A. realtors call a corner lot. Hollywood Boulevard runs vaguely east-west, and Gardner, the north-south street, culminates to the north in what the same L.A. realtors call a cul-de-sac. In English, that's a dead end. Normally, a cul-de-sac is regarded as an especially safe configuration by couples with young children. There weren't many couples on that little stretch of Gardner, but for the children who patronized the place, it was a terrific place to shoot up.

A heaviness in the air told me that it was about to drizzle. The week's weather had been all over the map. Normally in L.A., the weather is as orderly, and about as interesting, as a family tree: warm blue day breeds warm blue day. But this April, counting down toward Easter, was made up of days that arrived like runaways from other climates. The week had begun as clear and cold as North Dakota and then turned warm as a mass of tropical air wheeled up from Baja. Wednesday was marked by a chilly rain that had obviously made a wrong turn on its way to San Francisco and then decided it liked L.A. long enough to hang around through Thursday.

The drizzle started as I hit the Boulevard. At this hour, probably eighty percent of the people in Hollywood were holding, loaded, on illegal errands, or all three. There was the usual complement of parked bikers sneering on their black-and-chrome hogs, surrounded by the usual flock of biker girls. They were there day and night.

"So?" said Muhammad, the counterman. Unlike Tommy's, where there is a Tommy, there's no Jack at Jack's. The place was bought by Koreans several years ago, and the help is all either Hispanic or generically Middle Eastern. Muhammad was a generic Iranian.

"Coffee," I said, sitting down. My back hurt. I was getting old for this stuff.

"How many sugars?" Muhammad said. Junkies eat a lot of sugar.

"Four," I said, trying to turn my wince into a smile.

"You want fudge, say so," Muhammad said. It was his standard rejoinder. I was too frayed for standard rejoinders, so I leaned across the counter and took his skinny black tie in my hand as he turned away. He jerked his head back to me, looking alarmed.

"If I want fudge," I said, "I'll mug the Good Humor man. Give me a coffee with four sugars, and clamp the stirrer between your teeth until I leave."

"Jesus," Muhammad said, tugging at his tie, "what's with you tonight?"

"Lip," I said, giving the tie a little yank. "There's too much lip on Hollywood Boulevard."

"So call the Lip Squad," he said. He wrapped the tie around his fist and pulled it free. Against my will, I laughed, and he gave me a bleak smile. "I'm tired too," he said. "If I rub my face one more time tonight I think I'll hit bone."

"Sorry," I said. "Make it a large coffee. And hold the sugar."

The smile went wise. "Knew you were a cop," he said.

I gave up and drank it. Five years ago, no one would have taken me for a cop. I was obviously getting older. Behind me a fifteen-year-old girl fought fuzzily with her pimp. "I left them in the jar by the bed," she said. "You didn't have to take them all."

"Girl," the pimp said, "there wasn't enough for both of us. You should be happy they made *me* happy."

"You're a pig," she said.

I heard a gagging, snuffling noise and turned to see the pimp push the girl's dish of soft ice cream into her face. He clamped the back of her head with one hand and held the dish over her nose and mouth with the other while she choked and kicked her feet under the table. "You want a extra mouth," he said, "open the one you already got one more time." He sat back and regarded her. Ice cream ran down her chin and neck, onto the lavender cloth of her cheap blouse. She began to cry.

I leaned forward onto the counter, rested my head on my arms, and listened to my heart beat in my ears. It almost drowned out the sound of the girl's sobbing. Once I might have wrapped the pimp's chair around his neck. That was a long time ago, four full days. After four days spending time with kids who had an average life expectancy of only three more years, all I wanted to do was drink my coffee and go home.

The girl kept on crying while the pimp finished her ice cream. I rubbed my chin bristle and felt sorry for myself. Four numbing days and nights, and not a glimpse or a whisper of Aimee Sorrell.

2

Over the Rainbow

They called each other Mommy and Daddy, but it was sheer force of habit. The tone of voice into which the marriage had finally settled was scratchy and raw, a couple of light-years on the wrong side of polite. Basically, they were restraining the impulse to begin their remarks to each other, Oki-Burger style, with "*HEY!*"

They'd showed up at the bottom of my driveway six days before I'd made my first unconvincing appearance at the Oki-Burger, and the weather had just begun its runaway act. It was gray and crappy outside, neither raining nor not raining. Wood snapped and sputtered optimistically in the stove that heats the place. Mommy and Daddy, faced with a slate-gray day and a private detective with dubious credentials, were both trying to be good. They were working overtime to project the public image of their marriage, the image that satisfied their country club in Kansas City, and it was obviously something of an effort.

She had the ironclad serenity that comes with years of putting up with things. He had the kind of enforced control that builds permanent knuckle-size muscles in the corners of the jaw. You sometimes see them in military men. The muscles were well on the way to being thumb-size, even though I'd cleaned up the place before they arrived. If I hadn't, they'd probably have stuck out like Boris Karloff's neck plugs. He also had wet-looking hair, a rawboned bunchy face, and a tiny disapproving mouth.

Mommy was smoother and probably tougher, although she didn't look it. She looked like hugging her would be like falling into a tub of very good butter. "Her name is Aimee," she said, spelling it just like that. No shortcuts here. They'd used all the vowels they could think of, and thrown in a couple extra for good measure.

"Ah," I'd said, wishing they would leave. "Coffee, anyone?" I was on my fifth cup. Three to fuel the effort of cleaning the living room and two to deal with Mommy and Daddy. Missing children are not my specialty, not by a long shot. If they want to stay missing, they will. And even if you hit enough dumb luck to find them, how do you know whether you should send them home? Home is a generic word. It can mean where the heart is or where the horror is. Looking at Daddy, I wasn't ready to guess which it had been for Aimee.

"No coffee," Mommy said, pushing down gently on my wrist. I put the cup back on the table, and she allowed her hand to remain on mine. "And don't blame me for the name." Despite the gentleness of her touch, as she turned her gaze to Daddy there was enough acid in her tone to etch glass. "*All* their names begin with A. His name is Alan, you see."

There were two boys, she said, and another girl. She spelled their names. Wherever possible, they all had extraneous vowels tucked here and there, sad little head starts on distinction. She finished the litany and looked over at him out of luminous blue eyes. "Isn't that cute?" she said to me. He concentrated on the bright squares of his plaid madras sport coat, paying particular attention to a kelly-green area on his right cuff.

"Aimee's the youngest," I said neutrally. It was Saturday, and I wanted to be out of the house.

"She's the baby," Mommy said. There wasn't an ounce of fat on her, just a slender, expensively maintained woman well-wrapped in a sleeveless dress, long delicate tendons in her forearms, a big sapphire glittering on one hand, as dry and bright as her eyes. "She's also the problem child."

Daddy grunted something that could have been a negative. It could also have been gas.

"How do you know she ran away?"

"Well, she's missing." She gave me the cool blue eyes full-bore. Daddy fidgeted impatiently in his chair, plucking at a button.

"As opposed to, well, foul play," I said. Inwardly I cursed Janie Gordon, whom I'd once brought kicking and screaming home to her mother, for telling her distant cousins the Sorrells where I lived and what a whiz I was.

"She left a note, of sorts," Mommy said. "Aimee's not much of a writer." She reached into the enormous Louis Vuitton purse on the floor at her feet and pulled out a much-creased piece of paper. *Mommy,* it read, *I always hated it when you played your farty old music. A bunch of old geezers acting like their Young. But there's one song I like. Push Play.*

"Play?" I said.

"This is pretty cute," Mommy said with obscure pride. "I have to give Aimee credit for it."

Out of the purse came a little chrome cassette player. She put it on the coffee table in front of me. "It's the big black button," she said. I pushed it.

Paul McCartney's voice, distorted by the small speaker, sang the opening verse of "She's Leaving Home." When he got to the words "stepping outside, she is free," there was a click, and a young girl's voice, too close to the microphone, said, "Here's another one." Four raucous, unmistakable guitar chords, and even before I heard the singer's voice, I knew it was the Kinks.

"I can make the most ordinary little man in the *world* into a star"—Ray Davies leered, all pinky rings and cigar-smoke flash, while his brother Dave chopped the air into fuzzy heavy-metal chords. Then there was another click, and the young girl was back, a little farther from the mike this time. "That's all, folks," she said. Then she giggled. And a bank of strings cut the giggle short, and Judy Garland sang "Over the Rainbow" all the way through. Then there was nothing.

Daddy cleared his throat in the silence. "She's crazy about *The Wizard of Oz*," he said, shaking his head. "Punk music and *The Wizard of Oz*."

"Why wouldn't she be?" Mommy said with a rasp you could have struck a match on. "Dorothy got out of Kansas."

"She wants to be an actress?" I asked.

"At her age, who doesn't?" Mommy said. "I sure as hell did."

"How old is she?"

"Thirteen." That was Daddy. "But she's mature for her age. She can take care of herself. I know she's okay."

Mommy and I looked at him in disbelief.

"Well, I have to believe that, don't I?" he said defensively. "Stop staring at me like that, Mommy. Otherwise, where would I be?" It was his longest speech to date.

"Where you should be, maybe," Mommy said. "Worrying about her instead of yourself."

Daddy subsided. He looked back down at the bold squares in his plaid coat, moving a finger from one to another like someone tracing the moves in a classic chess game. His bony face worked slightly.

"Got any pictures?" I asked.

"They're almost a year old." Mommy scooped out four little color shots taken for a yearbook: crumpled blue-paper background and the kind of lighting Joan Crawford made lifetime enemies to get. Daddy notwithstanding, Aimee was a young-looking twelve, a pretty little blond with a hopeful smile, but also with something knowing around the eyes, an expression that could have been either premature confidence or something much less attractive.

I let out a sigh. I didn't want any part of it. "How long has she been gone?"

"Six weeks," Mommy said.

"Any communication since she left?"

"One note." She pulled it out of the ubiquitous bag.

"The note is how you know she's in L.A.?" I asked, opening it.

"Yes."

"She's a good girl," Daddy said suddenly. He sat up, buffed a cufflink, and crossed his ankles. "She and Mommy don't always see eye to eye, like women don't sometimes, but she can always talk to me. Always. If she has homework trouble or gets a crush on some little jerk, she'll always come to me with it. The boys really like her, though. They really like her."

Mommy's foot tapped the carpet as I opened the note. If Aimee was on the loose in Hollywood, being attractive to the boys was going to be a mixed blessing at best.

The note was written in pencil on blue-lined paper. It said: *Over the Rainbow.* Then there was a telephone number.

"Have you called?"

"Five or six times," she said. "No one had ever heard of her. I think a different man answered every time I called. Some of them sounded, well, like they were drunk or something. There was loud music and people talking and laughing in the background. It sounded kind of noisy and frantic." She reached out and moved the tape recorder about a quarter of an inch to make it exactly parallel with the edge of the coffee table. Her hand shook very slightly. "It sounded awful," she said.

"Well," I said, "let's give it a try."

First I had to find my phone. It was wedged on one of the bookshelves, behind a warped and rippled copy of Gibbon's *Decline and Fall of the Roman Empire,* a casualty of the perpetual leak in the living-room ceiling. I'd opened it up and leaned it against the phone to dry it out. The phone cord is long enough to let you place a call from the bottom of the Marianas Trench, so I took it over to the couch and sat, giving Mommy a grimace that was intended as an encouraging smile as I dialed. She was looking at her fingernails. Daddy cracked his knuckles. It sounded like a ton of popcorn.

The phone rang two, three, four times, and then someone picked it up and dropped it. There was an interval of clattering and a thick male voice said something that sounded like "Yunh?"

"Hi," I said brightly. "Is Aimee there?"

Mommy was still looking at her fingernails, but she was as still as an insect in amber. Daddy was gazing intently at the opposite wall and he'd poked his tongue into his cheek, adding one more lump to an already lumpy face.

"Who?" the voice on the other end said. Head-banger music filtered through the wire. "Who the fuck you want, Jack?"

"Aimee," I said. "Aimee Sorrell. She gave me this number."

"I don't care if she gave you the clap, I never heard of her. Good-bye."

"Wait," I said. "Tell me one thing, okay?"

He paused. A woman made a sound in the background that could have been a laugh or a cry.

"Depends," he finally said.

"Where are you? Where's this phone?"

"It's a pay phone," he said reluctantly.

"Yeah, but where?" The woman in the background made that sound again. This time it sounded like a bray.

The guy at the other end breathed heavily. "It's the pay phone at the end of the world," he said. He hung up.

Mommy and Daddy were both staring at me. "It's a pay phone," I said, "with a single-digit IQ answering it. Sounds like a very public place, not '21' or Spago maybe, but not anyplace illegal either. It's a hangout." Neither of them looked very impressed. Well, it wasn't very impressive. It was so unimpressive that it nettled me, so I picked up the phone again and called Al Hammond at home.

Hammond is my pet cop. He'd kill me with his teeth if he knew I thought of him that way, but I can't help it. He's two hundred twenty-five pounds of whiskers, bass voice, and bigotry, tempered only by an uncontrollable desire to put the bad ones away and tuck the good ones safely into bed.

"Yeah?" Hammond belched into the phone.

"Jeez," I said, "sorry to interrupt the well-digging or log-splitting, but I was wondering if you could do me a favor."

"I was waxing the kitchen floor," Hammond said.

"Oh, Al," I crooned. "How domestic."

"Well, I haven't really gotten to the waxing yet. Right now I'm in the middle of skinning a sheep so I'll have something to buff it with."

"Can you get me an address to go with a phone number?"

"Could Einstein count to ten?"

"And some idea of what's at that address?"

"Some idea?" Hammond said. "Yeah, I guess I can manage to give you some idea."

"Five-five-five-one-four-two-four."

"Two-thirteen area?"

"Yes."

"You at home?"

"Just waiting for the sun to come out."

"Give me ten minutes. What do I get out of this?"

"How about a big chocolate Easter bunny with your name on it?"

"How about a drink at the Red Dog?"

"Only one?"

"Hold the phone." He hung up without saying good-bye. He always does. He learned it from the movies.

Mommy and Daddy were both watching me with a kind of repressed anticipation that made me feel like a broken TV set. It was time to disappoint them.

"Listen," I said. "I don't really think I can help you. This just isn't the kind of thing I do."

"I told you, Mommy," Daddy said with grim satisfaction.

"But Janie . . ." Mommy said. She wasn't going to give up.

I held up a hand. "Janie was a couple of years ago. I found her because she wanted to be found. Her mother, I hope this doesn't offend you because you're related to her somehow, her mother is a bucket of loose marbles. She'd driven everyone else in her life crazy enough to leave, so she aimed it all at Janie, and then Janie left too. I brought her home twice because she was living wrong when she was on her own. That's the end of my experience with missing children."

Daddy got up. "Let's go," he said.

"Sit down, Al," Mommy said. She pointed to his chair with an arm that was all muscle tone and electrical energy. Al sat.

"There are about twenty-five thousand missing kids in L.A. at any given time," I said. "I'm one man. The cops are better at this than I am. Have you gone to them?"

"They made us fill out a report," Mommy said. "As long as they have a report, they seemed to say, they'd done their job. They didn't even dial the number. At least you dialed the number."

"I'm going to get you an address, too," I said. "But I'm afraid that's it."

"That's it, all right," Daddy said, getting up again. "Look at this dump." He glanced around my living room. It looked okay to me, but I could see his point. He hadn't seen it the night before. "You can stay and waste your time if you want," he said without giving me a look. "I'll be in the car."

"I'll walk you down," Mommy said, "but I want to talk with Mr. Grist for a moment or two more." She took his arm and steered him to the door, throwing me a glance over her shoulder as she went. The glance said *wait*.

I used the time to drop the coffee cups into the sink and to put the copy of Gibbon under the woodburner where it would dry more quickly. Five minutes later I'd decided on a jog at the beach followed by a sauna at UCLA, and she was back.

"He's resting," she said.

"He looks like he could use it."

"Be quiet," she said. "Just clam up." She sat down again, reached into a pocket, and tossed onto the table three bright, hard little color Polaroids. I knew before I picked them up that I didn't want to. After I looked at them, I let out a slow, labored breath. "Oh," I said.

All three pictures showed Aimee, naked, standing up against a wall. There was a man's hand in the picture. The hand was reaching up, doing something obscene. Her eyelids in one of the shots drooped lopsidedly, one much lower than the other.

I knew that look. It was the blink of someone who's deeply stoned. The eyes come down at different rates of speed. She had bruises on her arms and an angry, swollen mark in her navel that looked like a burn. The man's hand was just a man's hand. No watch, no rings, no tattoos, just five nasty fingers sprouting from the end of a hairy forearm. The wall behind Aimee was white and featureless.

"He doesn't know about these," I said, meaning Daddy.

She held my eyes with hers. "No. They'd kill him. He had heart bypass surgery a few months ago. He weighed two-eighty then. There isn't enough of him left for something like this."

"When did they arrive?"

"Last week. I was home when the mailman came. I'm always home. I had to leave so I wouldn't be there when he got back. I drove around for hours before I could face him without giving it away."

"Was there a note with them?"

"It just said, 'Don't do anything stupid. I'll be in touch.' Nothing since."

"Have you got it?"

She pulled a wallet out of her purse and a piece of paper out of the wallet. It was a single line, printed on what looked like a cheap dot-matrix printer, the most anonymous of all printing media. No envelope.

"Who's seen the pictures?"

"No one."

"No cops?"

"Why would I show them to the cops in Kansas? She's here. And if I had showed them to the cops here, Daddy would have learned about them, wouldn't he?"

"So you're carrying this alone."

She flicked the edge of the top picture with a painted nail. It made a sharp click. "I'm stronger than I look."

"I guess you are." There didn't seem to be anything else to say.

"But I don't know for how long," she said. She made a sudden stab at her hair with her right hand, and her nails scraped her forehead. She was bleeding immediately. The phone rang.

"Go into the bathroom," I said, picking it up. "Press toilet paper to the cut until it stops. Hello?"

She walked toward the bathroom as though her spine were made of steel. She took very small steps. The blood ran in a thin red line down her cheek.

"Missing kid, huh?" Hammond said.

"Why?" I could barely understand him. I was fighting the ghost-image of the photographs.

"Tommy's Oki-Burger. Fountain, near Gardner. That's one of the places the kids go. It's a pay phone. And it's no place for somebody's baby. You plan to talk to your friendly neighborhood cop about this?"

"Later."

"Whatever you say, pal. Got to go. The sheep's bleating." He hung up again.

I stacked the Polaroids into a neat little pile and aligned their edges precisely. Then I picked up the top one and studied it. Aimee's hair, so meticulously unfashionable in the yearbook photos, was matted and greasy-looking. There were dirt smudges on her wrists and elbows and a scab on her knee. She'd traveled a long way from Kansas City.

After Mrs. Sorrell came out, tissue pressed to her forehead, I told her I'd do what I could. I forgot to ask about the fee. When she was gone, I studied the Polaroids again, trying to learn anything I could about Aimee's first starring role.

3

One After Thirty-nine

"The problem," Bernie Siegel was saying as he stood on one leg, closed his eyes, and tried to touch the tip of his nose with his index finger, "is that the amount of intelligence on the planet is a constant, and the population is increasing." Then he frowned in concentration and stuck his finger into his eye. He'd just failed the roadside sobriety test.

Neither the gesture nor the sentence was as precisely articulated as Bernie might have liked, but most of us were three or four notches beyond the point where we would have noticed. The one exception was Bernie's girlfriend and sole source of support, Joyce, who was pregnant. She was following her doctor's advice, or maybe it was her own advice, since she *was* a doctor, and not drinking. She had the glow that comes with early pregnancy. The rest of us had the glow that comes with advanced intoxication.

A fortieth birthday party is like trying to cut your wrists with an electric razor. It takes longer than you'd hoped it would, and there's no payoff. Although most of us had been doing our best, this evening was no exception.

The candles were burning in Wyatt and Annie's living room, just as they had in the late sixties and early seventies, and the food, most of it fearsomely healthy, smelled the same as it had then. The birthday cake was carob. Annie thought that carob tasted like chocolate. She also thought that near-beer tasted like beer. The cake was enormous and slightly lopsided, and it said FORTY IS BETTER THAN NOTHING. Most of us in attendance, if we'd been polled when Wyatt was twenty-five, wouldn't have put small amounts of money at favorable odds on his reaching twenty-six, much less forty. When Wyatt was twenty-five, any vampire sufficiently ill-advised to bite into his neck would have OD'd long before sunrise.

Of course, that was before Wyatt had married Annie and straightened out his act. It had been more than a decade since he'd sought either cosmic enlightenment or comic relief in anything that had to be snorted or injected. Jessica and Luke, the kids on whom he and Annie had collaborated, had a lot to do with that.

I was the least interesting person present. For one thing, I was drunker than Wyatt. For another, I was thick and stupid from lack of sleep. Even if I'd been at my best, though, I'd have thought twice, or at least one and a half times, before I opened my mouth. The folks who'd gathered to celebrate Wyatt's unlikely survival into his forties could be a critical bunch. Everybody had lived through something that emphatically did not have the Good Housekeeping Seal of Approval.

"Looking around this room," said Miles Brand, who'd been our graduate adviser when Wyatt and I had been taking our doctorates in English, "I feel like I'm with the survivors of the Children's Crusade." Miles, as ever, both glittered and soothed. The glitter was candlelight refracted off his steel-rimmed spectacles, and the soothe was the influence of yet another of his apparently infinite number of cashmere tweed sport coats. Miles was the only member of the UCLA faculty whose family owned a Texas bank, and the town that went with it. He made the most of it.

"The Children's Crusade?" asked Joyce as Bernie gave up trying to stand on one leg and collapsed to the floor beside her. "What was that?" Joyce, a gerontologist, had come relatively late into Bernie's life. Bernie had gone to college with Wyatt and me. The difference among us was that Bernie was still going to college, working on his fifth or sixth degree, and would probably stay until Gabriel blew the trumpet for the Great Matriculation. Thanks to Joyce, he now lived in an actual apartment. For years, the address for Bernie in the UCLA alumni handbook had been the gas station where they'd let him sleep in his car. At the moment, he looked like he was thinking about going to sleep on Joyce's shoulder.

"One of history's sadder footnotes," Miles said, a bit more dramatically than was probably necessary. "Twelve-twelve or thereabouts, wasn't it, Wyatt?" Miles believed in sharing the stage.

Wyatt looked up from pitching lengths of pine and oak imprecisely into the cast-iron stove. There were large pieces of wood on the floor. "Poor little buggers," he said. "A bunch of French and German kids, wandering around in the rain trying to find the Holy Land."

"Well," Bernie said, reviving, "at least they were foreigners."

"Pipe down, Bernie," Joyce said in the tone of one who paid the rent. She folded her arms across her swelling stomach. "What happened to them?"

"They were eaten alive. Not literally, or at least I don't think so." Wyatt looked over at Miles, who made a show of searching his cluttered mind and then shook his head no. "But that was about all they weren't. Betrayed by Christians and captured by infidels. No leadership except a couple of cracked kids."

"Sounds like the Democratic party," Bernie said in a melancholy tone. He closed his eyes.

"Steven the something or other," I said from what seemed like a great distance. I felt like I had to say something. After all, I'd been invited.

"Of Cloyes," Miles said. "That was the French one. And Nicholas of Cologne leading the Kraut column," he added, secure in the knowledge that there were no Germans in the room.

"Where were their parents?" Joyce said indignantly. "How come I've never heard of this?"

"You're a gerontologist," Bernie said. "If there'd been a senior citizens' crusade, you'd probably be dazzling the whole room now."

Wyatt slammed the door of the stove and looked to Annie for approval, but she'd gone into the kitchen in search of yet another bowl of her avocado-and-clam dip, with a bunch of mean little red chilies thrown into it as an unwelcome surprise. Two bowls had already turned brown at the edges and there was still no sign of dinner. I was almost hungry enough to attack the carob cake.

"But their families," said Joyce, who supported, in addition to Bernie, a happily idle mother and father. "There have always been families. Where were their families?"

"The family is largely a literary invention," Miles said cheerfully. He was a bachelor. "In the tenth century, painters depicted the children who were lucky enough to live as little adults, and that's what they were. They died so often in infancy that the Koreans, for example, held a birthday party on the child's hundredth day to celebrate its having survived so long. The Chinese did it at the end of the first month."

"They still do," I said. "I went to a one-month party with Eleanor a couple of weeks ago. There were lots of red eggs, sort of a Chinese Easter, except that the kids didn't have to die and get resurrected first."

"And where is Eleanor?" Miles asked. "I didn't want to intrude into what might be touchy territory."

"In China," I said, wishing I hadn't brought her up.

"Doing what? Seems rather a long way to go to escape your admittedly peculiar charm."

"Research on the extended family. Looking at ancestral shrines. She's going to write something," I added, both to change the subject and to forestall the question I saw forming in Miles's mind.

Joyce wasn't interested in China. She folded two hands defensively over her swelling stomach. "What do you mean, the family is a literary invention?" she demanded.

Miles held up his empty glass, sighted through it, and poured some more red wine into it. He'd brought four bottles with him. "In medieval times, the family was purely and simply a unit of economic survival. The more kids, the more hands for harvest or for work, the greater the chance of passing along whatever miserable property the family might have managed to accumulate. Otherwise, when papa passed on, the neighbors would divide it, or the local lord—which is to say the closest armed thug—might simply annex it, just as he was likely to annex the prettiest daughter. Except that he'd keep the land, whereas he'd return the daughter after he'd had his way with her. 'Had his way with her,' " he repeated, rolling the words and about twenty cc's of wine around in his mouth. "Such a delicious phrase."

Joyce was one of the few humans of either sex I'd met who could ruffle, and she ruffled now. "I guess it's delicious to some," she said.

"This is wonderful wine," Miles said, congratulating himself. "Where were we?"

"We were listening to you," Joyce said a trifle ungraciously.

Annie bustled in through the door, bowl in hand, looking domestic. "As the mother of two," she said to Miles with a disarming smile, "I'd like to hear the rest even if it *is* a bunch of shit."

"You were more respectful in college," Miles said.

"I hadn't had kids then," Annie said. "I thought the world was something real, and that people could explain it to you. I didn't know that it was something you invented as you went along."

"Anyway," Joyce said, "what about mother love? You can't tell me that mothers haven't always loved their children. It's the central fact of the female principle." Bernie put his hand possessively and approximately on her stomach, and she gave his wrist a pat. He lifted his glass to his mouth with his other hand. "I'm driving," she said.

"Of course they loved them," Miles said soothingly. "They just couldn't get too attached to them. They were too likely to die."

"Mine," Wyatt said, pulling the cork from a bottle of cognac, "are going to live forever. Sometimes I think Jessica already has." Jessica, his daughter, was thirteen years old and too pretty for her own good. Her little brother, Luke, was nine.

"Child mortality was fifty, sixty percent up through the seventeenth century," Miles said. "Visit any old European graveyard and look at all the little stones."

"No, thanks," Annie said.

"It wasn't just child mortality," Bernie said, surfacing from what had begun to look like a comfortable snooze. "Children were sacrificed, too. The archaeologists poking through the ruins of Carthage found the remains of more than twenty thousand children sacrificed to Baal and Tanit to avert bad fortune. In mitigation," he added as Joyce gave him the kind of stare that Benedict Arnold must have seen a lot of, "they sacrificed sheep instead when things weren't so rough—say, to ward off a bad weather forecast." Joyce got up, and Bernie, who had been leaning on her, toppled to the floor on his side. "Then there were the Polynesians," he continued from his new position, "ritually exposing kids on mountaintops or dropping them off cliffs every time the population reached overload, sort of Malthus as an active verb. Greek plays are full of children exposed on mountaintops. Oedipus, right?"

Joyce went into the bathroom and pulled the door closed sharply behind her.

"I'd sell my girl right now," Wyatt said, setting down a glass that had been full of cognac only moments earlier. "Anyone want to make an offer?"

"The point, if there is a point," Miles said, "is that the disintegration of the family that people make such a fuss about these days is highly misleading. It wasn't until the seventeenth century that the family as we know it took shape. That was the first time that children were treated as children, that they wore different kinds of clothing, that they began to be sentimentalized. The trend reached its zenith in Victorian England about the time of the invention of the Christmas card, when children were transformed into symbols of innocence and it became the responsibility of adults to protect them from the evils of the world. Of course, we're talking about upper-class children here. The children of the lower classes were on their own. Or at the mercy of their parents, which was sometimes worse. Not much sentimentalizing over the little angels among the gin-drinkers. Child prostitution was a boom industry in Victorian England, and no one wanted to know about it."

"They still don't," I said. "Go down to Santa Monica Boulevard in Hollywood any night, and they're out on the sidewalk. Boys, girls, and kids who haven't figured out what they are."

"Something tells me you're working again," Wyatt said.

"I wish I weren't," I said, meaning it.

"I still think it's a bunch of junk," said Joyce, coming back in from the bathroom. "What about all those fairy tales?"

"Exactly," Miles said with the air of someone who'd been waiting patiently for someone else to fall into a trap. "The most damning evidence of all. *Find* me a happy family in the fairy tales. They're about wicked stepmothers and children abandoned in the forest, boys and girls cooked for dinner, sisters separated from their brothers. Good Lord, they're a catalog of child abuse. No writers in history were ever more aptly named than the brothers Grimm."

"The family is the basic unit of society," Joyce said defiantly.

"It is these days," Miles said. "Back then, it was the village. What are you working on, Simeon?"

It was just one more thing I didn't want to think about. "A little girl," I said, wishing I were at home with all the doors locked, a safe distance from my friends. "She ran away."

"From what?" That was Joyce.

"How the hell do I know? Her father has a face that looks like he shaves by slamming himself with a two-by-four to drive the whiskers in so he can bite them off inside. Maybe she wanted to go somewhere where people had smooth faces."

"Well, Lordamighty, excuse me," Joyce said, lifting her eyebrows all the way into the southern reaches of her hairline.

"I'm apologizing a lot lately," I said. "I'm sorry. She found her way here from Kansas City. She seems to have settled in with a bunch of kids who think so little of themselves that they seek their common level at the point where the scum surfaces on the pool. They're killing themselves, right out there in front of everybody. What else can I say? What I want right now is a house in the woods, about three hundred miles from the nearest neon light. I'd also like a nice, stupid dog. A spayed dog."

"So excuse me," Joyce said, meaning it this time.

"I don't know," I said. "Maybe I should just go home and chew on the furniture."

Annie came into the room. I hadn't even seen her leave. "Dinner," she announced.

People made unsteady attempts to stand up. "Don't go home, Simeon," Wyatt said. "Otherwise, we'll just worry about you. This party is already weird enough without that."

"You're the birthday boy," I said. "I'll even cheer up, if that's what you want."

"Don't go overboard," Wyatt said, clutching his cognac bottle to his chest.

"Would you like to call your children?" Annie asked him.

"They're *my* children, if you noticed," Wyatt said. "That's a sure sign of how things are around here. If they get straight A's and they haven't killed anything lately, they're Annie's. If their mug shots are pinned to the telephone poles in the canyon, they're mine." He went to the foot of the stairs and bellowed, "Luke. Jessica. Dinner, believe it or not."

He turned away from the stairs and threw an arm around my shoulder. "Come on, Simeon. If you get to the table without saying anything else that's depressing, I'll share my cognac with you."

The table, which Annie waxed obsessively as an outlet for nervous energy, of which she had an abundance, glowed supernaturally. The fireplace crackled. "It's so nice to eat someplace where people don't say grace first," Miles was saying, ladling onto Joyce's plate something that looked disconcertingly like beef stew. "I never know what to do with my hands, not to mention my soul. And look, the salad has real lettuce in it, not arugula or radicchio or rocket, whatever that is. What in the world is rocket?" he said, looking up as we came in.

"The only lettuce that's not supposed to extinguish sexual desire," I said. "In the Middle Ages, lettuce was prescribed for nymphomaniacs. Sort of the edible equivalent of a flannel nightgown."

"I've known people who could eat their way through a flannel nightgown," Joyce said. "Of course, they're all in jail now."

"The Doctrine of Signatures," Miles said, slopping food onto Bernie's plate. "Lettuce is limp, you see. According to the Doctrine of Signatures, which was a very hot theory in the fourteenth century, the way food looked was supposed to be a key to what it was good for. Walnuts looked like little brains, so they were good for brain fever, whatever that actually was. Oysters, because you had to pry them open, were supposed to help women conceive. Asparagus was erect, so it was—"

"We get the point," Annie said. "Hello, Luke."

Luke came into the room wearing a Superman T-shirt and red shorts. His knobby little legs ended in a pair of incongruously large furry slippers.

"Everybody looks pretty happy," Luke said suspiciously. He was a well-known drug nihilist, a preadolescent Carrie Nation who had single-handedly reduced his father's marijuana habit from half an ounce a day, smoked in public, to a furtive joint or two snatched behind the woodpile when the little cop was in school.

"Happy?" Wyatt said as he surreptitiously put the cognac on the floor. "That's the first time this evening that anyone's used that word."

"Have you been smoking?" Luke said, pulling himself up

onto a chair. "Jesus," he added, looking at the serving dish, "beef stew?"

"It's *ropa vieja*," Annie said a little defensively.

"That's what I said," Luke insisted. "Beef stew. The Ochoas serve it all the time."

"Rachel Ochoa is his current girlfriend," Annie announced to the table at large.

"Rachel is my *only* girlfriend," Luke corrected her gravely.

"Yeah?" I said unwisely. "What happened to Ariel?"

"*Ariel?*" Miles said in tempered disbelief. Shakespeare was one of his specialties.

"Ancient history," Luke said, throwing him a mean little glance. "Just give me some salad."

"The kid is a born polygamist," Wyatt said as Miles put a couple of glops of salad onto Luke's plate. "With a career like yours in front of you, you want to be careful with all that lettuce," he added.

"Why?" Luke said, fork poised.

"Never mind," Annie said, "and I know you hate it when I say that. Too bad. I'm still bigger than you."

Wyatt took a slug off the cognac. "Where's your sister?"

Luke made a neat little pile of his salad, putting a piece of avocado on top like a green and suicidal skier poised for a run. His attention was focused entirely on his plate. Then he mashed the whole hill flat with his fork.

Annie had put down her silverware.

"Luke," she said. "Your father asked you a question. Where's Jessica?"

"She's at Blister's," Luke said in a small voice.

The silence in the room couldn't have been more profound if the moving finger had suddenly appeared and writ Luke's words large in letters of fire on the wall. Miles was carefully examining his salad. Bernie was leaning far back in his chair and gazing at the ceiling, on the final downhill stretch toward comatose, and Joyce was busy having second thoughts about parenthood.

"Blister," I said brightly. "What an interesting name."

"His real name is Lester," Luke said in an artificially high voice that I recognized as a parody of his sister's. "We call him Blister because he's so *hot*."

"That's enough," Annie said. "When did she go?"

"A while ago. She said she'd be back for dinner." Luke mashed his avocado into a puree fine enough to satisfy Wolfgang Puck.

"Well, she's not," Wyatt said, gouging long angry scratches into the table's polished surface with the tip of his knife. "And I've had enough." He pushed his chair back and stood up, then tossed the knife onto his plate, which promptly split in two. Luke looked down at his lap.

"Wyatt, don't," Annie said, tight-lipped.

"Like hell I won't." He grabbed a blue parka off a chair and started to put it on.

"Then take Simeon."

"What am I, the Big Bad Wolf?" Wyatt said. There were small pinched white lines at the wings of his nostrils.

"Please," Annie said. "Take him."

"Wouldn't miss it for the world," I said, rising. "I've never met anyone named Blister."

Wyatt glared at me as though he'd never seen me before. It's a very peculiar feeling when your oldest friend suddenly looks dangerous.

"Whatever you want," he said. "I'm going."

As I followed him out, I heard Annie say in her Perfect Hostess voice, "Please. Eat your dinner." Then I heard a chair slam to the floor, and Joyce said, "*Bernie*."

In the Jeep Wyatt slugged the steering wheel a couple of times before he turned the key. The horn coughed each time. "Son of a bitch," he said. "Son of a *bitch*." Then the motor caught and we jerked backward over the bridge across the creek. A Chevy van, heading north on Old Canyon Road, hit its brakes and slithered around us, its driver shouting one-syllable words with ancient Old English pedigrees that didn't make them sound any less rude.

"Double damn," Wyatt said, accelerating and raising the cognac bottle to his lips. I hadn't realized he'd brought it, and the new knowledge wasn't reassuring. "I can handle enemies. What do you do about your own kids?"

"I've never had any."

"So you're lucky. So shut up."

I shut up for three or four miles that would have made Wyatt's insurance agent, had he been there, give serious thought to a new career. After we'd passed everything in the vicinity, and after Wyatt had settled the bottle between his thighs, I crossed my fingers and said, "So who's Blister?"

"A dealer," Wyatt said, jerking the wheel to the right to avoid a plummet down to the creek, which was by then three hundred feet below us.

"Dealing what?"

"Mainly crack. Also regular old coke. Free-enterprise system, you know? Whatever the little kids want to buy."

"How old?"

"Twenty."

"*Twenty*?" I asked, shocked in spite of myself. "Jessica's only thirteen." She was, after all, my goddaughter. "How long has this been going on?"

"A month. Son of a *bitch*," he said again. This time he pounded the dashboard with a closed fist.

"What happens if you maim him?" I asked.

"My daughter hates me."

"Not for long."

Wyatt caught up with something with four wheels, a Starion or a Jetta or a Sentra or something else with a name that was chosen because it sounded good to someone with an accent, and passed it on the right. Gravel rattled beneath the fenderguards, and the horizon took a dizzy spin. The creek, with its ample complement of hard sharp rocks, yawned beneath us, and then we were on the road again.

"Not for long," I repeated when I could trust my voice.

"What? A week? Two weeks? Do you know how long that is when you're thirteen?"

At least he was conversing in whole sentences. Pushing my luck, I said, "Then let me be the heavy."

He glanced over at me, and I instantly wished he hadn't.

"Wyatt," I mewed. He looked back at the road, crooked the wheel, and somehow managed to navigate between a car that was turning right and another that was coming straight toward us. Various brakes screeched, and he laughed for the first time in five minutes. "Another coat of paint on any of us," he said, "and we'd be a memory."

He slowed to maybe seventy. "Anyway," he said, "we're almost there."

He wrenched the wheel to the right and we jolted up Entrada, a goat path that can be called a street only by courtesy of L.A. County, which marks it as such on its maps. By anyone else's standards, it is a treacherous, precipitous collection of gaping potholes, so narrow that kids on two-wheelers have frequent head-on collisions. The tops of eucalyptus trees waltzed overhead in the wind, and the stars were as cold and bright as Mrs. Sorrell's sapphire. The scent of sage filled the air. Cold or not, it was too nice a night to die.

Wyatt said, "We're here."

He pulled the car to the left side of the road. Sage scraped at the paint job and the tires squealed. Wyatt looked out his window and swore. Vegetation was pressed against the glass like man-eating plants that smelled blood. "I'll get out on your side," he said.

He waited, but I didn't reach for the door handle.

"Listen," I said. "I'm not going to tell you I know how you feel, but listen anyway. We're here to get Jessica. If anyone has to do anything unpleasant, let it be me. It's time to think about short-term goals. All we want is for her to come home with us. If you spread good old Blister's brains all over the wall, she might decide not to. If I do it, on the other hand, she'll just hate me for a while, and I think I can live with that."

"Open the door," he growled.

"Eat the big patootie," I said. "Are you going to behave?"

He lifted his shoulders almost to his ears and blew air out through his mouth. Then he shook his head several times as though he were clearing it, and when he looked at me he was Wyatt again.

"Okay," he said, "you're the tough guy."

"Good at heart, though."

"Whatever you say. Can we go? That bloodsucker could be on top of my daughter right now."

"If he is," I said, "you get her out from under, and I'll put him on top of something else. Like a broken aquarium, okay?"

He nodded, and I opened the door.

I was out and he was past me so fast that I barely saw him. He sprinted up a series of stone steps that put a permanent part in the sagebrush, and I followed as best I could. By the time I got to the top of the steps I was winded, and Wyatt was pounding at the door of a surprisingly nice house that commanded a panoramic view of hills and sky.

I grabbed his hand in mid-pound, and it was a good thing I did, because it opened at precisely that moment and Wyatt would have begun the negotiations by hitting his daughter in the face. He tried to jerk his hand away from me, then focused and let it drop to his side.

"Daddy," Jessica said coolly. "Is dinner ready?"

I hadn't seen her in a few months, and I wasn't prepared. Sure, she was still a baby to anyone who'd known her as long as I had, but she was a woman too. Most of the baby fat that makes children look so tentative had dropped away, revealing a face that had made up its mind to be beautiful. She wore a raggedly slashed T-shirt, shrunk bleached jeans, and a cloud of light brown hair with golden highlights. She sighted behind her father to look at me, and her hazel eyes narrowed slightly.

"Yes, it is," Wyatt said tightly. "In fact, it's getting cold."

"Mommy's *ropa vieja* never gets cold," she said. "Even when it's a week old, it'll blow your pants off."

"And I'm glad to see that yours are on," he said.

"Oh, please," she said. It was the wrong thing to say.

Wyatt grabbed her arm and gave her a shake that almost lifted her off her feet. "We're going," he said.

"So go," said a male voice from behind her, and a lanky young man pulled the door the rest of the way open. "Take her with you. She was going home anyway."

"I don't need your fucking permission to take my daughter home," Wyatt said.

Blister passed a hand through limp hair that dangled over a narrow forehead. He was wearing white drawstring pants and slippers, and his stomach muscles looked like something you wouldn't want to hit your head on. His eyebrows collided above his nose. The air from the room inside was overripe with cigarette smoke.

"This is boring," Blister said. "Oh, and happy birthday, Dad."

My hand was on Wyatt's shoulder, and I felt him tense to lunge at Blister, but Jessica defused the moment. Without turning around, she said, "Don't call him Dad." It was not a tone that invited discussion.

"So what am I supposed to call him?" Blister asked indolently.

"Call me Wyatt," Wyatt said after a massive effort.

"Yo, Blister," I said softly. Blister's eyes went to me for the first time. "Hi," I said. I made a small confidential pointing gesture at Wyatt. "Call him Mr. Wilmington."

"Who's this?" Blister asked the world in general.

"Nobody much," I said, smiling. "You can call me The Man with No Name."

Jessica looked from Wyatt to me and misjudged the degree to which the conversation had become civilized. "How about you give me half an hour, Daddy?" she asked. "Blister will drive me home."

Wyatt looked at me and exhaled slowly. Then he arranged his features into what might have passed for an open smile at a nuclear-disarmament conference, turned back to Jessica, and said, "In a pig's ass."

"Huh?" Jessica said, except that she didn't even have time to finish saying that. Wyatt crouched down, grabbed her knees, and straightened up without so much as a grunt of effort. Jessica dangled over his shoulder in a fireman's carry, her blue-clad bottom pointing at the sky. I stepped aside to let them go. Jessica was squealing and hitting at her father's back with her fists.

"*Hey*," Blister said, stepping all the way into the doorway. "Put her down, you jerk."

"Blister," I said, putting a hand gently on his chest. "Remember me?"

"Get out of my way, shithead," he said. "He can't do that." Jessica's squeals echoed up through the sagebrush. He pushed against my arm.

"Wrong on two counts," I said. "He can, and I'm not a shithead." I looked past him. "And how come there's another woman in your house?"

He looked confused. "There isn't . . ." he said, and then he turned his head to check. I hoisted a steel-toed cowboy boot and cracked him right below the kneecap. Blister made a gurgling sound and involuntarily grabbed his right knee and lifted it. As the gurgle turned into a moan I kicked his left knee, and it buckled beneath him, hitting the floor with a reassuring crack. He rolled on the floor, holding a knee in each hand and emitting high puppylike yelps.

He'd forgotten I was there, so I stretched out a foot and tapped his groin with the toe of my right boot.

"Have I got your attention?" I asked. He screwed his eyes up and nodded.

"For a couple of days you're going to walk like you're on stilts," I told him. "After that, you'll be fine. And remember, the next time you're screwing around with Jessica, or anybody less than sixteen years old, that The Man with No Name might be just outside the window." I wiggled my eyebrows for emphasis. "Got that?"

"You asshole," he said in a choked voice.

I lifted my right foot. He winced, and I looked down and examined the boot. "You've made me scuff it," I said. "Now say, 'Yes, sir.' "

He let his head slump to the floor. "Yes, sir," he said, squeezing back tears.

"Much better," I said. "Also, you might think about where else the boot might have landed. I don't think a scrotum with the word Frye permanently printed on it backward is much of a selling point. Anyway," I added, "for the future—and this is free advice, okay?—don't call anybody shithead unless you know where both his feet and both his hands are. And never, *never* look behind you." I bent down and chucked him under the chin with my index finger. " 'Bye, now."

I went down to the car, where Wyatt had dumped a sullen Jessica into the back seat. When we got to the Wilmingtons' house, I said good-bye. Neither of them had much to say to me.

Leaving Alice parked at the side of the road, I scaled the driveway to my house. It was cold and dark and empty. The light on the answering machine blinked a red semaphore while I uncapped a bottle of Singha beer from Thailand, a brew so sublimely lethal that it regularly loses its import privileges. With the first two gulps dizzily chasing each other down my esophagus, I pushed the Play button on the machine.

"One," the machine announced. It says that on the twelfth message too. I ignored it for the moment and looked around the living room. Eleanor's curtains, left over from the time when we'd lived together, still hung over the windows. Patches of damp glowered at me from the rug. Then the machine whirred and I finally got to the message.

"Out and about as usual, are you?" Hammond's voice said. "Well, we've got one, and she may be yours. Problem is, she's in the morgue."

4

Underground

Morgues are even colder than you'd think they'd be.

It was the next morning. I had a headache, and I was blowing on my hands as Hammond led me down a long linoleum stairway, our feet scuffing against steps that somehow managed to look as though they'd been washed every fifteen minutes since the tile was laid but were still gray. It was a gray that didn't have anything to do with dirt. If grief were a color, that was the gray it would be.

Hammond had his hands stuffed into his pockets. He heard me huffing and puffing away behind him, and said, "Brisk, isn't it?"

"Brisk?" I said. "An oyster could get chilblains."

"No oyster with any sense would be caught dead in here," he said with a flash of the wit that makes cops welcome additions to cocktail parties the world around. "Jesus, it's ten A.M. I usually try not to visit the morgue until after lunch."

"Not *soon* after lunch."

"No," he said, puffing on his cigar. "And not too close to dinner, either."

Hammond's cigar smoke, for once, smelled good. It momentarily elbowed aside an odor that suggested that all the frogs ever dissected by all the high-school kids in history had decided to hold a convention.

"I could get my ass in a sling for this," Hammond grumbled fragrantly, trailing a cloud of smoke. "You got no official status here, you know? You're just some dork from off the streets."

"Somehow," I said, "I don't think most of the folks here will care very much."

"The folks down here don't write reports," he said. "Not the majority of them, at least. But the guy you're going to meet does. What's the guy supposed to write?"

"That you assisted someone in an identification, and that that someone was assisting the police," I said patiently. It was all part of dealing with Hammond. If he didn't make a big production out of it, I might not share his view of how much I owed him.

"And are you going to assist the police? I mean, are you planning to talk to a cop at some point, or is this just between you and I?" We'd reached a corridor about twenty feet below street level. It was lighted by sickly fluorescent tubes, and emergency lines painted in different colors competed lividly with each other on the floor. There were no windows, which was just as well, since they would have opened onto dirt.

"I mean," Hammond said, without a pause, "I'm just a cop with a reason to be here, escorting someone with no reason to be here, and worrying about my future. What I'm getting at, in my uneducated way, is what're you going to say? That you're a relative of the deceased?" He slid a plastic card into a slot to the right of a metal door. "Just be careful what you say to the guy, huh?"

"Al," I said, "I'll be careful. If I'm not, just step on my foot."

"I'll fucking eat it for dinner," Hammond said as the door slid open. "Just be careful what you say to the guy."

The guy who stood behind the open door was a slightly overweight Asian female in her middle thirties whose hairdo looked like a cosmetic-surgery transplant; it had been teased and tossed and curled and back-combed and sprayed, shellacked and, probably, deep-fried. Somehow, it lifted my spirits. It was clearly the hairdo of someone who planned to leave the morgue and go someplace really *important* later. In a morgue, it looked pretty good.

"Hi," I said involuntarily.

"Hi, yourself," said the woman beneath the hairdo, which, despite all the teasing, didn't even come up to Hammond's red bow tie. "Hi, both of you, in fact. I'm Yoshino. Who are you?"

"Hammond," Hammond said, jabbing himself in the chest with a thumb to help her follow the conversation. "I called last night." He was doing his best to deal with the guy as though she were a real person.

"Lieutenant Hammond," she said neutrally. "You're visiting two-oh-eight, right? You look just like your voice."

"Is that a compliment?" Hammond asked.

Yoshino shrugged. "I guess it is, if you like hulking, oversize, red-faced, supermasculine men who smoke." She gave his cigar a glance that packed enough venom to stun a cobra. "It was two-oh-eight, wasn't it?"

"I'm not sure," Hammond said, yanking his cigar out of his mouth and holding it behind him. His ears turned bright red. "I haven't got the paper. She's about twelve."

"You haven't got the paper," Yoshino said. She'd heard it before. "Who's your boyfriend?"

"He represents the family."

"If it is the family," I added, moving the nearer of my feet away from Hammond's heavy shoes.

"Honey," Yoshino said to me, "for their sake let's hope it isn't. You a lawyer?"

"Something like that," Hammond said.

Yoshino took a step back and surveyed us. Her hairdo didn't even jiggle. "If she turns out to be the right one," she said, "you'll have to do better than that. We need something official, remember?"

"We both hope she won't be," I said.

"You don't know how much you hope it," Yoshino said.

She turned her back on us and led us into a large room with a bare cement floor with metallic drains in the center, and stacks of large file drawers, about three feet by two feet, set into the north-south walls. The tiny tips of Yoshino's black spike heels clacked on the floor. The gray gave way here to stark white, with a slightly bluish-green tint because of the fluorescent tubes buzzing overhead. It couldn't have been more than sixty degrees. The smell was stronger.

"Two-oh-eight, two-oh-eight, two-oh-eight," Yoshino said, reading little cards set into the file drawers. "Here we are." She slid the drawer open, tugged a white sheet halfway down, and stepped away.

My first reaction was surprise that the drawers had no sides. The dead were sharing the space on the other side of the wall, lying there next to each other on their metal tables, a little community in the cold. Hammond grunted inquisitively, and I looked down at the person on the table.

She was tiny. I hadn't been prepared for how tiny and still she would be. She was pathetically thin, and her skin was mottled, bruised and discolored. One hand clenched nothing. A red tag had been fastened with a twist of wire to the big toe on her right foot. It said JUVENILE JANE DOE.

Juvenile Jane Doe's eyes were open and startled-looking, and brown curls clustered around her head. Small perfect teeth gleamed below a slightly inverted upper lip. She must have had an enchanting smile. Twenty-four hours ago she had been pretty.

Hammond gave me a blank look. Yoshino was staring at the body as if sizing up the work that remained to be done on it, her face impassive under the hairdo.

"She's not the one," I said. My pulse was pounding in my ears.

Hammond made an abrupt gesture, and Yoshino began to cover her up. Without thinking, I put my hand on her wrist and stopped her. She snapped her head up at me, her eyes boring into mine with so much contained energy that Hammond took a step back and ashes tumbled from his cigar onto the sheet. Looking down, Yoshino brushed them away immediately, as though the girl on the slab might feel them.

"What happened?" I said. My voice could not have been more constricted if concrete had been poured into my throat.

"What happened? Or what killed her?" Yoshino said. She was back to being the perfect professional; all the rage or loathing, whatever it had been that had driven Hammond backward, was bottled up once more.

"Both."

She started to pass a hand through her hair, thought better of it, and threw Hammond a look. Hammond nodded.

"What happened was that she was given a massive injection of a painkiller called Demerol. It would have made her fuzzy about what was happening, screwed with her memory later. Demerol will do all those things. The world being what it is, God help us, Demerol is a very big drug right now." She toyed with a corner of the sheet that lay across the girl's rib cage. "Then she was used sexually, front and back. Probably in her mouth too, but he didn't get to finish there for reasons that will become apparent."

She looked up at both of us. Hammond had his cop face on, but my expression made her falter. "Are you sure you want to hear this?"

"Yes."

A kind of cold front dropped down behind her eyes. "Why?"

"He's okay," Hammond said. "He's looking for one this age that hung out in some of the same places."

"Up to you, Lieutenant. Whatever you say. Where were we?" She looked down at the little body. "At some point while she was alive her hands were tied behind her. There's still some lividity where the ropes pressed into the flesh. Look, you can see the way the rope was twisted. Here's where the knot was." She lifted the clenched hand to show us the wrist.

I didn't look. Hammond didn't either.

Yoshino put the hand back down gently. "What killed her was a sudden pressure on the neck. Broke it like a wishbone. Probably accidental." She swallowed. "This is really the *shits*, you know? God in heaven, I have a daughter."

"Why accidental?" I asked.

"The Demerol," she said as if it were the most obvious

thing in the world. "What else? The way it happened, it looks like he had his hand behind her head, gripping the base of her neck, like he was forcing her to go down on him. Jesus, she was a *baby*. Anyway, the break is simple and clean, like she jerked backward with so much force—that would have been the Demerol, numbing her, hiding the pain from her—and when he shoved down, the bones went and it was all over. The Demerol says it was probably accidental. If he'd planned to kill her, he wouldn't have given her the Demerol. It was to make the whole thing tougher to remember."

"Maybe the Demerol was supposed to dull the pain."

"Oh, no," Yoshino said in an entirely new tone of voice. "He *wanted* her to feel the pain. You haven't seen this." She pulled the sheet down to the girl's hips. There was a raw circular discoloration in the center of her abdomen.

"Look," she said tightly. "Before the Demerol, he put his cigar out in her navel."

Nobody looked. Hammond stared at the opposite wall, and Yoshino gazed at the two of us. I looked at a mental image of Aimee Sorrell, captured in a Polaroid with an angry burn where her belly button should have been.

"She's not the one," I said again.

"Well," Yoshino said, "whoever she was, I hope someone shoots him between the eyes before he gets to those fizzwits on the California Supreme Court."

She covered the girl again and slid the drawer closed before she led us to the sliding door and let us out.

"Where you going tonight, Yoshino?" I asked before the door could close.

"Out with my husband," she said. "It's our fifteenth anniversary." She looked from Hammond to me. "How'd you know I was going out?"

"Your hair," I said. "It looks terrific."

"No kidding?" Yoshino said, raising her hand to give it a proprietary pat. "I hope so. It took decades."

"It was worth it," I said. Hammond gave a snort and headed down the hallway.

I put my hand on the sliding door, and she looked up at me inquiringly.

"Call me if there's another one who's been burned that way," I said, slipping a card into her hand. "Anyone with a burned belly button."

"I only do official work," she said, sliding the door sharply closed. I barely got my fingers out in time.

Hammond was waiting for me halfway down the hall.

"What about *my* hair?" he asked, all tough guy again.

"The Red Dog tonight," I said. "Nine o'clock. Your hair will look perfect. You want me to talk to the cops? Bring me the right cop to talk to."

His mouth twisted. "That one's not so easy," he said.

"Do it, Al," I said. "Otherwise, I'm on my own."

5

Aurora

It was still only ten-forty-five, but I felt like I'd been awake for weeks. The world, as seen through the gritty glass of a downtown phone booth, was briefly bright. Even down here, directly across the street from police headquarters in Parker Center, traffic was light. The Saturday before Easter Sunday is usually a nice, peaceful day. I dialed my own number and listened to my answering machine go through its usual rigmarole.

"Hey, Simeon," Roxanne said, ever effervescent. I dated Roxanne occasionally, and now that Eleanor was in China I was seeing more of her than usual. "I have hidden eggs *everywhere*, and not even the big detective is going to find *one* of them. At least, not without a body search, which is a clue, I guess. What I mean is that I hope you haven't forgotten that you're supposed to be here tonight and that we're going to do eggs tomorrow morning. I'm tending bar at McGinty's until eleven, and I expect to see you there just before we close. If you're not, I've saved a dozen raw eggs and you'll find them in your bed when you get home. They'll be broken, like my heart. Be there, buster, and no excuses." She hung up.

I'd forgotten all about it. For the tenth time I resolved to get an appointment book and write things down in it. Other people showed up where they were supposed to be. Appointment books had to be the secret. Eleanor's appointment book was thicker than the *Oxford English Dictionary* and a lot worse organized, and she was always where she was supposed to be. At the moment, unfortunately, she was supposed to be in China.

The second call was from my mother. "Well, Billy be damned," she said, getting right to the point, "if I'd known I was going to spend my life talking to a machine, I'd have given birth to a battery, too. At least you'd be grateful. And speaking of you, I'm sure you remember that you promised to come by tomorrow. I'm sure you know how much your father and I are looking forward to it. Bring Eleanor, if she's speaking to you." I heard my father's voice in the background. "No," my mother said, "it's that damned machine again." Then there was a dial tone. That was how long it had been since I'd talked to my mother. Eleanor had left three weeks ago.

The machine had promised three messages, so I hung on, watching a little Mexican girl, decked prematurely in her Easter best, argue with her mother about something. Her plump brown sturdy legs beneath half a mile of white ruffled crinoline anchored themselves to the sidewalk as permanently as an Ice Age as she tugged her mother in the direction she wanted to go. In about eight years, she'd be the age of the girl on the slab.

"Mr. Grist?" It was a voice I didn't recognize. "This is Jane Sorrell. Something has happened. I'm at the Beverly Hills Hotel, and I need to see you. Please come. I don't know what I'm going to do."

I pressed my forehead against the glass of the telephone booth and watched the little Mexican girl, victorious, lead her mother down the street in the desired direction. Good for her. Somebody loved her.

To get to the hotel, I headed west on Olympic and then, after miles of stunted architecture and Korean neon signs, swung north on Doheny toward Beverly Hills. Alice was so sluggish and unresponsive that it felt as though she were reading my mind. I didn't want to see Mrs. Sorrell. I didn't want to see Mr. Sorrell. I wanted to go home and spend Easter with my mother and father and pretend that I sold aluminum siding or something that never rusted, never warped, and always looked shiny and new and hopeful. I didn't want anything to do with families that had rotted and turned brown at the edges like Annie's avocado-and-clam dip.

I was in a fine humor as I chugged up the driveway to the hotel. The clown who opened the driver's door, stuffed into a uniform that looked like something willed to him by the Philip Morris bellboy, didn't do much to raise my spirits.

"Yes, *sir*," he said with a bright smile as he estimated my income and looked Alice over. It was the smile a talent agent saves for a client who isn't working. "We don't get many of these, this far north of the border. We'll be real sure to park her where we can keep an eye on her."

"Park her on your chest," I said, climbing out. "I sure hope you don't have to live on your tips."

"I usually know what to expect," he said. He aimed Alice toward some unmapped area of the parking lot, the part they reserve for Volkswagen vans with psychedelic designs painted on them.

Mrs. Sorrell hadn't given me her room number, so I had to go through the formality of finding a house phone. As always these days, they were located behind a bouquet of eight-foot flowers that looked like Venus's-flytraps bred to eat airplanes.

"Yeah?" said a new voice, a sullen, young-sounding voice that I'd never heard before. It could have been a girl or a prepubescent boy.

"Is Mrs. Sorrell there, please?" I asked, yanking upward on the frayed bootstraps of whatever residue of courtesy I had left.

"No," the new voice said. Its owner hung up.

I resisted the urge to rip the phone out of the wall and feed it to the flowers, and once again requested the operator to connect me with the Sorrell suite.

"Listen," I said the moment the phone was lifted on the other end. "I've had to endure a lot of things today, not the least of which was a parking attendant so snotty that he should blow his nose into a parachute, and if you hang up one more time I'm going home, and you're going to have to deal with your mother, who will undoubtedly remove your skin in one-inch strips when she learns you sent me away. Do you understand?"

There was no response.

I squeezed my eyes shut until I saw little orange dots. "Is she coming back?"

"Sooner than I'd like."

"Fine. I'm in the lobby."

"Well, lucky you." It was a girl, no doubt about it. Boys don't learn to be that nasty until after their voices change.

"There's a bouquet here that wants to eat me," I said. "It's already got one of my buttons."

"Call me when it reaches your fly," she said. But she didn't hang up.

"That's the problem. It's a button fly."

She exhaled heavily, and I could imagine her rolling her eyes toward the ceiling, in the gesture of put-upon teenage girls everywhere. "I suppose you want to know our room number," she said. "It's eleven."

Number eleven was a pink stucco bungalow that squatted behind a hedge of birds of paradise that was obviously the pride and joy of a gardener who liked birds of paradise. I wondered where they'd found one. After I pressed the bell twelve or thirteen times I found myself looking at a trim little naiad of seventeen or so with the same pouty mouth that Aimee had pointed toward the camera in her yearbook pictures.

"Not bad," she said appraisingly. "A little old, but not bad."

She had her mother's careless, honey-colored hair, blue eyes, and the longest legs I'd ever seen, holding up a pair of creased white tennis shorts.

I pressed my fingers to my temples and closed my eyes. "Wait," I said, "it's coming to me. Your name . . . it begins with an A and it's got more vowels than a Hawaiian road map. It's . . . it's . . . Adelle."

"Fold your map and sit on it," she said. "Adelle's my older sister. I'm Aurora." She gave me something that might have passed for a smile in a lockjaw ward. "My mother's expecting you?"

"Your father calls her Mommy. How come you don't?"

"I don't know," she said. "It's a word I can't seem to wrap my mouth around."

"So what do you usually call her?"

"You. That is, when we're speaking."

"As long as she's gone, let me ask you some questions."

"Why should I?"

"Because your sister has gone thataway. Because she could be in some very deep trouble." She didn't drop to her knees or cry out helplessly, so I said, "Where is your mother, anyway?"

"Drinking," she said. "Me too."

She opened the door and I stepped into a carpet so deep that I nearly stumbled. The room was furnished in rattan and tropical prints. Palm trees waved balmily at me from the upholstery. There was a definite bite of whiskey in the air.

"You started without me," I said as she sat down on one end of a couch that looked like a great place to catch yellow fever, folded those legs, and picked up a half-full bottle of Johnnie Walker Black Label. Even with her legs crossed, her knees were perfect. Not a knobby patella or a skateboard scar in sight. Aurora slugged back an inch or so and handed the bottle to me, a challenge in her blue eyes. My mouth tasted like formaldehyde, so I took it. "Let's see if we can finish together," she said as I tilted it to my lips and drank.

It was like drinking smoke. I lowered it to take a breath, feeling something hot and red and alive burrowing down through the center of my chest, like an animated floor plan of hell. YOU ARE HERE, said the sign that had been posted at my mouth.

She reached out for the bottle. "Uh-uh," I said, pulling it away. "You can lose a hand that way." I drank again and then handed her the bottle. She tilted it upward and made a gurgling sound. When a girl looks good with a bottle of whiskey in her mouth, it's time to be careful.

"*Banzai,*" she said, wiping her lips with the back of her wrist. "The divine wind, right?"

"What's the divine wind?" I asked, taking the bottle back and drinking. Her eyes watched the level of the whiskey as I drank. With every gulp the girl on the slab grew smaller and farther away.

"I don't know," she said. "Those retards who flew their airplanes into the sides of aircraft carriers or whatever. They were the divine wind or something like that." She reached out a brown hand and grasped the bottle and chugged at it. A flush came into her cheeks.

"*Kamikaze,*" I said as the penny dropped. "*Kamikaze,* the divine wind."

"Yeah," she said, eyeing me over the mouth of the bottle, which was considerably emptier than it had been a moment ago. "What I want to know, when those guys finally got their orders and learned that they were supposed to go out and never come back, what I want to know is how come none of them ever said, 'Are you out of your fucking *mind*?' "

"The emperor was daddy," I said. A wisp of pale hair hung over her brow, and I leaned forward and brushed it back. She didn't move away from me, so I sublimated the next impulse and took the bottle from her hand and drank. "It was an ancestral society. They did what daddy said they should do."

"Hey, you," she said, her blue eyes level. "You're talking to me like I'm an adult now. Before, you talked to me like I was a kid."

"Before?" Before, as far as I was concerned, was the morgue.

"On the phone. Strips of skin, you talked about. Would you have said anything like that to an adult?"

"Um," I said.

"If adults talked to each other the way they talk to kids, what do you think would happen?" She retrieved the bottle and put away a slug that would have elicited cries of admiration on skid row.

I thought about it. "The homicide rate would zoom."

"The title of *War and Peace* would be *War and War*," she said.

"The neon signs at the corners," I said, "would read DON'T WALK, STUPID."

"Sometimes," she said, "I think I'd like to kidnap an adult and tie him up in the cellar and talk to him like he's a kid until he dies."

"How does anybody grow up?" I asked rhetorically.

She hoisted the whiskey and swallowed. "Don't ask me," she said. "I haven't done it yet. Bass—that's a fish, and I learned this in biology—bass parents spend days guarding the hole where their eggs have been laid. All they care about in the whole world is guarding those eggs. They drive away anything that comes close, no matter how big it is. Even snapping turtles, the ones that could take your thumb off like macaroni. They don't even take a break to eat. For all I know, they don't go to the john."

She took a more moderate sip. "Finally," she continued, "after four or five days, the eggs hatch. By then the parents are ravenous. When the baby bass swim up out of the hole, their mommy and daddy eat them. Just snap them up as fast as they can. So what's the difference between bass parents and human parents?"

"I give up."

"Bass parents eat the child all at once," she said. "Human parents take years."

"Some bass babies survive," I said. "If they didn't, there wouldn't be any more bass."

"So do some human babies," she said. "The ones who manage to swim away before they get eaten."

"Let's make a deal," I said.

"What?"

"I ask you questions about your family, questions about Aimee. You answer them."

She examined the level of the whiskey in the bottle, swinging her upper shin back and forth. It shone as if it had been polished. "Some deal," she said. "Why don't you wait for my mother?"

"You didn't let me finish. You get to talk to me as if I were a kid and you were an adult."

Abruptly she stopped swinging her leg and banged the bottle down onto the table. "Don't be idiotic," she said.

"Beg pardon?" I asked.

She flicked the bottle with a fingernail and I saw her mother snapping her nail against the edges of the Polaroids. "Aren't you listening?" she demanded. "How many times do I have to ask you? What's the matter, you got potatoes in your ears?"

"Oh," I said, "right. Did you have any idea Aimee was going to run away?"

"What a stupid question. Do you think I can read minds?"

"Did she ever say anything about it?"

"Oh, come on. *Think* for a change, would you? No, she didn't."

"Did she have a boyfriend?"

"That's none of your business." She raised the bottle and drank, and I watched her delicate throat work as she swallowed. "No," she said, wiping her lips again, "she didn't. Jesus, stupid, she's only twelve."

"Thirteen, I think."

"Christ on a crutch, what's that to me? You think I can remember a single year? Twelve, thirteen, what's the difference? I got things on my *mind*, you know?"

"The deal," I said, taking the bottle. "Remember?"

She gave me a narrow smile. "Just getting the flow going," she said.

"So no boyfriends?"

"Aimee doesn't have time for boys. She's going to be a movie star. Don't you know *anything*?"

"Were your parents brutal to her?" There was no other way to ask the question.

"Hey," she said, "we do the best we can. And by the way, did I tell you that I'm getting tired of the sound of your voice?"

"Did they hit her?"

"They didn't have to." She made a face. "Have you got a cigarette?"

"I don't smoke."

"Then what good are you?"

"Not much."

"What kind of kid are you, anyway? Kids talk back."

"Okay," I said lamely. "Stick it in your ear."

"It's no fun if you don't talk back." She sounded plaintive.

"It isn't much fun even if I do."

Aurora put a hand beneath the cushion of the couch and pulled out a slightly crushed pack of Marlboro Lights. "I guess it isn't," she said. Her shoulders sagged. "So why do they do it?"

"They don't know what else to do. They feel like kids themselves and they feel like they've got to hide it. Maybe they're afraid their kids will get frightened if Mommy and Daddy don't act like they know everything. It's probably easier for the fathers. At least their voices change. Mothers have it rougher. They always sound squeaky."

"Says you," Aurora said, lighting her cigarette. "My mother could handle my father, *his* father, and all his brothers without losing her place in the *Ladies' Home Journal*." She blew a cloud of smoke at me. "So, game over. What do you want to know?"

"What did Aimee run away from?"

"Well," she said, puffing away. "Kansas City, for one thing."

"Not enough," I said. "You said they never beat her."

"They don't have to *beat* us," she said. "They can *love* us to death." The right side of her mouth, the upwardly tilted, kissable side, turned up even farther. Her brown skin gleamed.

"That's not really fair," I said. "It's a cheap shot."

"Okay," she said. "Just for argument, let's say you're all right. I'll tell you an Aimee story. Just one out of hundreds."

"Shoot," I said, putting the bottle out of reach.

"She was eight, right? I mean, we're talking about a time of life when *anything* can kill you. Bad breath, ugly shoes. Buttercups are tough guys compared to an eight-year-old girl." She looked for the bottle, and I gave up and handed it to her.

"It was Halloween," she said. "Aimee wanted to be a princess. Well, I mean, who doesn't? She'd been asking for weeks for a princess costume to wear to this big party, this absolutely gigantic eight-year-olds' party, and the guy she had a crush on had even asked her to go with him. No prince was ever better-looking to Cinderella than this little eight-year-old creep—Jesus, his name was Arthur—was to Aimee. And *Arthur*, the wonderful Arthur, all of four feet tall, had asked Aimee to go to the party."

She lifted the bottle to her lips.

"You know what my father does for a living?" she asked when she'd finished swallowing.

"No," I said, realizing that I hadn't asked.

"He's a pork packer. 'Everything but the squeal,' that's his company's motto. When he's finished, that pig is *gone*. He was the first pork packer to advertise on the sides of barns. Farmer Al, he calls himself. To listen to his ads, you'd think Farmer Al owned every pig in America." She licked a drop of whiskey from her lower lip. "For all I know, he does."

I waited. "So?" I finally asked.

"So when Aimee goes upstairs to get into her costume, it's a pig costume. He can advertise on barns, so why not on his daughter? It was in a big cardboard box, and when she opened it, it was a bright pink pig's costume made out of rubber. It said 'Farmer Al, the Pig's Best Friend' on the side. Aimee took it out of the box and then sat on the floor, which people in our house just don't *do*, and started crying. She'd wanted a princess costume. Then, I'll give her credit, she got mad. She was still fighting with my parents when her date's father rang the doorbell."

"Holy Jesus," I said.

"So she didn't have any choice. She put on the costume, the fat little pink body with the sign on it and the little curlicue tail sticking out of its rear, and the pink rubber mask, and she walked down the stairs. I still don't know how she forced herself to walk down those stairs. I could hear her sobbing from the landing, where I was, but she had this pig mask on, you know? Nobody could see the tears. And down at the bottom of the stairs her date was waiting. He was dressed as a prince. Of *course* he was dressed as a prince. He had this dumb little sword at his side and this stupid little cape, and as he saw Aimee come down the stairs, his face dropped, and then, because he was a gentleman even at his age, he dredged up a smile. I'm still amazed that Aimee didn't die on the spot when she saw that smile.

"And they went off together, him smiling bravely, the prince who had chosen a pig, and her crying until she must have been soaked inside that rubber costume, and she won first prize at the party. All the other little girls were princesses, except the few who were ballerinas. And she came home with this big fat vulgar brass trophy, and my dad said, 'See? What was all the fuss about?' And to this day he doesn't understand why she threw the trophy through the picture window in the living room. He still doesn't know what he did to her." She remembered her cigarette and stared at it as though she'd never seen it before.

"He thinks he's her best friend," I said.

"There you are," she said. "Childhood is so much fun."

"Did that kind of thing happen often?"

"How often does it have to happen? It's not like they were belting us or hanging us up by our thumbs all the time. They've both just forgotten completely what it's like to be a kid. They take family votes to settle things, but their votes count for more than ours do. We're supposed to be little adults about it when they outvote us, two to four. Well, fuck that, we're not little adults. Aimee's still a baby. And two against four isn't a majority. Kids have a sense of justice, and you can't screw with it."

I retrieved the bottle and knocked back a swig. "Did you ever run away?"

"No," she said.

"Why not?"

"Aimee had all the guts," she said.

"Has," I said. Aurora looked at me, stricken by what she'd said.

The knob on the front door turned, and I snatched the cigarette away from her so that I was holding both the Marlboro and the bottle when Mrs. Sorrell came into the room.

"Rory," she said in a voice that was already furred by drink, "what in the world are you doing?"

Rory settled back onto the couch and crossed her arms. "I'm watching Mr. What's-his-name here drink and smoke," she said. "Just honing the skills I picked up at home."

Her mother swatted away some invisible gnats in front of her. "Well," she said, "go into the other room."

"Hey, don't worry," Rory said, glancing at me. "I've got potatoes in my ears."

"Is that supposed to be funny, miss?" Mrs. Sorrell said. "Don't you think I've got enough troubles without my own daughter turning into Henny Youngman?"

"Henny *who*?" Rory asked in honest bewilderment.

"Never you mind. Just make yourself scarce."

"Oink," Rory said, looking back at me as she stood up. Her elegant legs, brown below the white shorts, twinkled at me as though they had been dusted with Tinker Bell's goofus sparkles as she walked away. "Oink, oink," she said. "Everything but the squeal."

"What have you been *telling* him?" her mother demanded.

"Oh, Mother," Rory said. "The truth will out." She gave me another glance, walked very slowly to the door to what I supposed was the bedroom, and pulled it shut softly behind her. Mrs. Sorrell watched the door for a moment as though she expected it to open again, and then shook her head.

"We shouldn't have brought her," she said, "but we were afraid to leave her alone, after, well, after Aimee. And it's Easter vacation and she wanted to see L.A. And, I don't know, I thought if we found Aimee she might be more willing to come home if Rory were with us. If we found Aimee," she added bitterly. She rubbed at the bridge of her nose, stretching the skin tight over the fine bones of her face, and I could see Rory's face peeking out at me through her mother's. "So I'm drinking," she said. "The one thing I shouldn't be doing."

She was wearing a white blouse with little red cherries embroidered on the collar and a pair of navy-blue slacks with big safari-style pockets. There were three long scratches on her forehead from where she'd raked it with her nails, red, angry parallel lines. Hers wasn't the kind of face that should have had scratches on it. They made her look younger and softer than her daughter.

"Well," I said, hoisting the bottle, "at least you're not drinking alone."

"Put it down," she said in a tone that brooked no discussion. "One of us has to be clear-headed. I have something to show you, but first I have to know if you've learned anything."

"Not much," I said. I wasn't going to tell her about the girl on the slab and the burn in her navel. Not until I had to, at any rate. "I've been on the street for four days but I haven't found anyone who can put her there with certainty. That's where she was, though. There's a whole community of them out there."

"She's not there anymore," she said. "Come out on the terrace. I don't want Rory listening through the door."

I put down the bottle as she crossed the room to a big sliding glass door and pushed it open. I couldn't figure out what to do with the cigarette, so I carried it out onto the terrace and crushed it underfoot.

The terrace was enclosed by ten-foot pink walls and over-grown vegetation. A hummingbird that had been feeding on a big leathery *copa de oro* gave us an indignant midair stare and thrummed off over the wall.

"I hate those things," she said vaguely. "They're neither birds nor insects. They're like leftovers from some time when lizards flew and snakes swam. I always think they'll have dandruff."

I like hummingbirds, but I kept quiet. Mrs. Sorrell fished in the pocket of her slacks and pulled out a piece of paper. "We have to go home," she said wearily. "I guess I knew this was going to happen. I just hoped we'd find her before it did." I put out a hand and she put the paper into it. Then she sank onto a chaise and crossed her ankles, looking down at her hands resting in her lap. I opened the paper.

Same kind of paper, same dot-matrix printer as before. GET $20,000, it said, all in caps. BE HOME TUESDAY AFTERNOON. I'LL CALL.

I felt a sinking sensation in my stomach. "When did this arrive?"

"Here? Today. It got to Kansas City yesterday. The maid sends my mail out every day, Federal Express."

"Has he seen it?"

"He went home yesterday. I made him. I was worried about his heart."

"You're going to have to tell him now."

She looked up at me. "The hell I am," she said.

"But the money."

She lifted one hand from her lap and waved it away. "I've got money of my own," she said. "I'm richer than Daddy will ever be."

"You'll get the money, of course."

"Certainly I will. She's my little girl." She blinked twice, very quickly, and then drew both hands into fists. "The question," she said, after a moment, "is what you'll be doing."

"I've got two places to go today," I said with more

confidence than I felt. "One of them, I'm not so sure about. I'll get something at the other one."

She looked back down at her lap, at the two sharp little fists and the expanse of navy-blue cloth drawn tight over her childbearing hips. "Please," she said in a very small voice, "see that you do."

6

Jack's Redux

The place I wasn't sure about was Jack's Triple-Burgers,
but I had to go there anyway. Even if the note hadn't
arrived to speed things up, I'd realized when I was looking
at the little girl on the slab that I was finally too old to pass
as anything but an undercover cop. It was time to come out
from whatever meager cover I'd managed to establish, and
the place to do it was the place where I was less likely to
find anyone who knew Aimee. That way, if the approach
failed, at least I wouldn't have locked myself out of the
Oki-Burger.

It was pretty early for Jack's. Even after I'd killed a
couple of hours in the B. Dalton bookshop on Hollywood
Boulevard, ignoring the pointed stares of the clerks while I
read Philippe Aries' *Centuries of Childhood* and Gesell and
Ilg's *Child Development,* it was only five-thirty. Most of the
clientele at Jack's didn't even get up until five-thirty. I was
feeling the muzzy aftereffects of Aurora's whiskey. I was
also very tired, and once or twice I noticed that the book in
my hands was shaking slightly. The morning at the morgue
and the fact of the note had taken even more out of me than
I thought it had. I felt like I needed a soul transplant.

Figuring it couldn't get any worse, I headed for the
sidewalk.

As I emerged, blinking in the late sunlight, onto the Walk
of Fame, the first thing I saw was a woman walking two
little girls, aged ten or eleven. They might have been twins.

59

Although it was cold, the girls wore white T-shirts, knotted above their navels, identical green-and-white running shorts that ended several inches above the bottoms of their buttocks, and identical black patent-leather collars around their necks. Hooked into each of the collars was a short black leash, the end of which the woman held in her hand. She scanned the faces of the passersby, looking for takers. Well, I thought, at least now Jack's can't get to me.

I was wrong, as I had been so often since my first conversation with the Sorrells. The ice-cream pimp and his girl were there, and so was a Korean or Japanese teenager whom I'd seen several times before. The Oriental girl was tiny, impossibly fragile-looking, capable of ingesting vast amounts of drugs if her behavior on previous occasions was any indication, and heartbreakingly beautiful except for a ravaged coarseness in her skin that advertised bad acne in the past. She had her keeper with her, a skinny hardcase in his middle twenties whose mouth curved raggedly upward, courtesy of an old knife scar. He was sitting now, but on the move he walked like he was trying to slice his way through solid ice, elbows held away from his body, feet taking big stiff strides. His feet were encased in heavy scuffed black engineer boots, and his shirt, as always, was open to reveal his overdeveloped stomach muscles. He was smoking with jerky gestures and talking. When he wasn't hurting somebody he was always talking. Sometimes he talked when he hurt people. She, as usual, was looking down at the table. Given her probable condition, maybe her head was too heavy to lift.

"Hey, plainclothes," Muhammad said pleasantly as I sat down at the counter. "Coffee again? Hold the sugar?"

"Muhammad," I said. "This is a nice little place."

Muhammad looked around, his dark eyes unreadable. "You got a funny idea of nice," he said at last. "I don't know, sometimes I feel like I should go back home, except home is so crazy now. The Shi'ites, all the crazies." He wiped his hands on the damp towel that hung from his belt. "I guess maybe I don't know where home is anymore. Same like these kids." His eyes traveled over the tables and then came back to me. "You know what I mean?"

"What *I* mean," I said, "is that it's nicer open than it would be closed."

He put up both hands and waggled them. "Hey," he said, "no argument there."

"Open, it's a living," I said remorselessly. "Closed, it's just another Hollywood rathole."

"I'm listening," he said.

I took out one of the yearbook pictures of Aimee Sorrell and dropped it onto the counter. His eyes flicked down to it and then back up at me.

"So," I said, "have you seen her?"

"Cop," he said. "I knew you were a cop."

"You get an A," I said. "Seen her or not?"

"I don't know," he said. "There's twenty girls in here look like her. She's a blond, you know? How do you tell blonds apart?"

"Very carefully," I said. "Right now, you tell them apart very carefully."

He picked up the picture and squinted at it. "How old?" he said.

"Twelve, thirteen."

"How tall?"

"Four-eleven."

"This isn't fair," he said. "There shouldn't be such a world. Somebody should have this baby on his knee."

"Somebody does," I said. I pulled out one of the Polaroids and handed it to him. He went green, which is something Meryl Streep couldn't do on purpose.

"Ahhh," he said, losing another chunk of his innocence.

"Don't talk to me about there shouldn't be such a world," I said. "What are you doing here? Without you, where do these kids go? What's this place about, anyway?"

"Hamburgers," he said. "We make hamburgers."

"Throw the shit in another direction," I said. "I'm not catching. Have you seen her or not?"

He looked down at the Polaroid and then up at me. "I

don't think so," he said. I sat up and he took a step backward. "No, really, really, I don't think so. We get a lot of kids in here, right? But she's too pretty. I'd remember."

"Make an effort," I said as his eyes slid toward the ice-cream pimp. "Don't look around for help. If you're lying to me, there isn't any help. There's only me, Muhammad, and I'm not fucking around."

"No, no, me neither. You've always been straight with me, right?" He remembered that he thought I was plainclothes, and reconsidered. "Considering your job, I mean. You've always been straight. Now I'm being straight with you." He dropped the Polaroid onto the counter and wiped his hands again, more thoroughly this time. "What am I supposed to do?" he said. "I got a family to support."

"Any little girls?" I asked unnecessarily. I wanted to bite someone.

"Three," he said before he thought. Then his eyes dropped to the picture, and he said "Ahhh" again.

"Aside from the two specimens in here, and the guy with the Mohawk and the tattoos who was here on Thursday, how many regulars you got who deal in the little ones?"

He poured me some coffee to look busy, and I swiveled my chair around. The hardcase with the Japanese or Korean girl was looking at us. He was giving me what he probably thought of as his chain-saw look. I managed to get my metabolism back under control, nodded to him, and turned back to Muhammad.

"So," I said, "how many?"

"You don't want to mess with that one," Muhammad said without moving his mouth as he wiped the counter. "He's a knifer."

"I'm not messing with anybody. I asked you a question."

"You're messing with me," he said.

"You don't count."

He looked out the window at the freak parade, a uniquely Hollywood mixture of earnest tourists looking for glamour and sidewalk carnivores looking for tourists. An overweight man in greasy jeans, a white T-shirt, and a motorcycle jacket came in and grunted at Muhammad. There was enough oil in his hair to keep his bike running for weeks.

"Him, for instance?" I said, stirring my coffee. The fat man headed for a table at the back.

"You got a death wish, you know that?" Muhammad said, giving the fat man a terrified grin. "Anybody who can get them. Everybody wants the little ones now. Big business."

"Hey, fuckface," the fat man said behind me. "Coffee."

"Coming up," Muhammad said. He started to turn away, and I put my hand on his arm. He twitched galvanically but stopped.

"Him too?" I said.

"Sure. Sure, him too. Like I told you, anybody who can get them. Listen, is it legal to serve coffee?"

I lifted my hand, and he bustled around doing his job. When he put the cup on the saucer it jittered. He carried it to the fat man and put it on the table, and the fat man asked him a question, his eyes on me. Muhammad shook his head hurriedly and came back to the counter.

"Get out of here," he said quietly, pouring more coffee into my cup. "Don't come back unless you've got a platoon with you."

All the black, bitter bile I'd been holding back since the moment Yoshino had pulled down that white sheet rose into the back of my throat. I could hear my heart in my ears. "The hell with it," I said to Muhammad. "Nobody lives forever."

The stool squealed as I swiveled around so that my back was to the counter. The fat man looked directly at me and blew onto the surface of his coffee. His lips were thick, loose, and rubbery, and his sideburns ended in knife-sharp points that angled downward toward his fatty pudding of a mouth. His T-shirt said YOU CAN DIE LOOKING. The ice-cream pimp and his girl were in conversation, but the hardcase with the Japanese or Korean girl narrowed his eyes at me and turned the chain saw up to the setting marked Amputate. The girl, slower than her protector, gave me a tiny, stoned smile. Then she looked at him and stopped smiling.

I put my elbows up on the counter and stared back. "Oh, Jesus," Muhammad said behind me.

"Good evening, ladies and gentlemen," I said to the room as a whole.

The ice-cream pimp stopped talking and turned to face me. His girl looked at her feet.

"I hate to interrupt your sugar rush," I said pleasantly, "but I've got a problem. You see, I'm looking for somebody."

"Golly," the fat man said after a long moment. "Who would of thought it?" He looked beyond me at Muhammad, who produced the first audible cringe I'd ever heard.

"What's your name?" I said to the Japanese or Korean girl.

"Junko," she said. Japanese, then.

"Jennie," her protector corrected, taking her left hand and squeezing it until the knuckles turned white. "And Jennie doesn't know anybody."

Junko/Jennie sucked her breath in sharply. I heard her knuckles crack. "No," she said to him, and he sat upright in a jerky fashion, looking genuinely astonished, and bent her hand back sharply. "No," she said in a much higher voice, readdressing herself to me. "I don't know anybody."

"She doesn't," Muhammad said behind me. "She doesn't know anybody in the whole world." Junko emitted a thin squeal. The hardcase kept his eyes on me.

"Let go of her hand," I said to the hardcase. "Let go of her hand or I'll cut out your fucking tongue and feed it to the pigeons."

He dropped Junko's hand and lifted his own and displayed it, palm open and empty. "Hey," he said, "am I looking for an argument?"

"You?" the fat man said in disbelief. "Mr. Flower Power?"

"He *looks* like a nice guy," I said. I still hadn't gotten up, and Muhammad tugged at the back of my shirt. I sat forward and he let go with a long sigh.

"He is," the fat man said, sitting back in his chair. "What with his widowed mother and all."

"Am I a nice guy, Jennie?" the hardcase asked. The girl,

who had been tentatively flexing her fingers and wrist, looked up at him as though her head had been jerked on a string and nodded.

"Junko," I said, getting up. "Do you know her?"

I put the yearbook picture of Aimee on the table in front of her. She shook her head in the negative without glancing down.

"Look at it," I said.

She turned her eyes to the hardcase, and he lifted his eyebrows in a classic gesture of indifference. The only sound was the fat man slurping his coffee. Then she looked down at the picture, and a tiny jolt of electricity went through her shoulders.

"But she's—" she said.

The hardcase slapped his hand down over the photo and said, "Tssss." Junko sat back as though she'd been slapped, and gazed at him. "But she *is*," she said.

"Tsssss," he said again. Then he looked at me. "She doesn't know her," he said. The knife scar above his mouth twitched. It was a thin, curved, clean slice that traveled from the side of his nose right through his upper lip.

"I know you're a nice guy," I said. "Look at your character witnesses. But at the moment, I'm not talking to you. I'm talking to Junko."

"Junko's not talking to you," he said. He picked up his plastic cup of Coke and sipped at it. "So fuck off," he said.

"There's a bug in your Coke," I said.

He looked down at it, and I slapped him across the face. My hand caught the Coke and sent it flying. I slapped him again backhand just to let off some steam. His head rocketed back, and Junko let out a tiny scream. The ice-cream pimp's girl watched in fascination. The Coke had hit the wall and made a nice brown splash.

"I'd punch you," I explained, "but you're not worth it."

He got up slowly. There was a big red splotch heating up on each of his cheeks. The scar was white and livid.

"Oh," I said, "I'd *love* you to."

He had to step behind Junko to cross behind the table

and get to me. When he was standing directly behind her, he gave me a crooked smile, grabbed a knot of her hair in one hand, and yanked backward. Her head went back and her eyes rolled.

"Stick out your tongue, Jennie," he said to her. Her tongue came out all the way to the bottom of her chin, and his other hand appeared with a knife in it. It was a very shiny knife. He angled the blade down toward Junko's tongue and touched it against the pink surface. The edge was angled away from her face so that if she pulled her tongue back the knife would slice right through. "Don't move," he said to her. Then he looked back at me.

"So," he said, "you want to feed somebody's tongue to the pigeons?" He gave me the full chain-saw grin. "We got a tongue right here," he said. "Good as any deli." He let go of her throat and tugged at the tip of her tongue. "Don't suck it in, honey, or you'll lisp for life."

The girl had closed her eyes. Her fine black hair curled on her shoulders and her body was quivering, but her tongue was as still as if it had been carved from marble.

"Okay," I said, "she doesn't know her. Let her go."

One of his eyebrows arched upward. "Oh, don't worry," he said. "I'm going to let her go. Paul."

The fat man stood up and moved behind him. "May I be of service, my dear?" he asked in a courtly fashion.

"Hold her tongue," the hardcase said.

"A pleasure," Paul said. He reached two greasy fingers down and took the tip of Junko's tongue between them. A knife materialized in his other hand and came to rest where the hardcase's blade had been a moment before. Junko moaned.

"You and me," the hardcase said, stepping away from her. "Back to the pinballs."

"I don't play pinballs," I said, looking at the fat man's knife against Junko's tongue.

"You're not going to play," he said. "I am."

It didn't sound good, but there wasn't any alternative. Junko hadn't swallowed in half a minute.

"He's a cop," Muhammad said from behind me.

"Yeah," the hardcase said, "and I'm Cary Grant, you dumb immigrant. After you, jerkoff."

"You do anything to her," I said to the fat man, "and I'll come back for you."

"Careful," the hardcase said. "You might make his hand shake." The fat man let loose an explosive chuckle, and one of Junko's hands flew up in a gesture of pure desperation. I headed for the pinballs.

"Against the wall," the hardcase said, "facing me. Right between the machines."

I backed up until I felt a cold wall behind me and a pinball machine touching either hip. Even the most optimistic real-estate salesman couldn't have called it anything but a dead end. Cold sweat trickled its way down my sides.

"Hands behind your back," he said, glancing toward the big window that fronted onto Hollywood Boulevard. I followed his gaze and saw his point. From the street, anyone curious or stupid enough to look in would see the fat man's leather-clad back, between them and Junko, Muhammad polishing glasses, the ice-cream pimp and his lady enjoying their Cokes, and a couple of old friends having a chat between the pinball machines. I put my hands behind my back, feeling the rough texture of the stucco.

He lowered the hand with the knife in it. "Hope you hang left," he said. Then, very quickly, he stuck me through my jeans with the tip of the knife, just to the right of my fly. I felt a pinpoint of pain and my legs turned to water. "Move and you'll leave with her tongue in your pocket," he said. "Let's try a little lower." He stuck me again twice, jabbing the knife in and pulling it out so fast I could barely see it move.

"Three's the charm," he said, grinning lopsidedly at me. His teeth were rotted and brown; too much cocaine leaches away the calcium. I wished briefly that I were his dental hygienist, going after his tartar with a jackhammer. He must have seen something in my face, because he said, "But four's for fun," and he stuck me again, deeper this time. I had to fight to remain standing.

"What you're going to do now," he said, "you're going to go away. And you're not going to come back. *Are* you?" He gave me another little jab, in the hip this time.

"No," I said. "I'm gone."

He backed away, folding the knife and slipping it into his pocket. "Then get the fuck out of here, chickenshit," he said. He thought better of it. "No," he said, smiling with the half of his mouth that moved, "hold on."

With a little grunt, he dug deeper into the pockets of his jeans and came out with something that looked like an aqualung for a skin diver from Lilliput, a flat black tanklike affair with a nozzle at the end of it. The whole thing couldn't have been more than five inches long. Well, the anopheles mosquito is even smaller than that.

He did something to the end and a needlelike blue flame flicked its tongue at me. He brought it up under my nose.

"Ever do any welding?" he asked. He was having fun.

"No." The heat of the flame pricked against my upper lip.

"You ever want to, this'll do the job." He held it a little closer to my face, and I let out an involuntary moan.

"Knock it off," advised the fat man. "Or else hold it lower. People can see."

"Skin melts," the knife pimp said. "Next time you're back, we'll melt some. Understand?"

I nodded.

He gave me the half-grin again and lowered the flame. "Scram, pussy," he said.

I passed him as widely as possible, feeling like the Guitar Player being tossed out of the Oki-Burger. When I passed the fat man, he nodded at me, and I said, "You can put the knife away." I sounded shaky even to me.

"When you're all the way out," he said.

Muhammad was assiduously stacking cups and saucers as I passed the counter. Neon was blinking on up and down the Boulevard. When I reached the door the fat man stepped to one side and Junko sagged forward, all the way to the table.

"Listen, you guys," I said with the little bravado I could muster, "I'll see you."

The hardcase snickered. "Come back," he said. "We'll have a tongue sandwich." He got a laugh.

I'd been sitting in Alice for at least five minutes, bleeding through my jeans and waiting for my legs to stop shaking, before I heard again what he'd said to Junko when she'd started to answer my question about Aimee. It hadn't been "Sshh," as in "Be quiet." It had been "Tssss," as in a cigarette being put out in a bucket of water. Or a cigar in someone's navel.

7

The Red Dog

I was half-drunk and more than halfway to disorderly when Hammond and his friend walked into the Red Dog. I'd gone straight to the bathroom, tugged down my pants, and looked at the punctures, little purple-black slits that were already ringed with an angry red. Then I'd scrubbed the blood off my jeans with water and handfuls of paper towels and emerged into the bar looking like someone who couldn't hit the urinal even if the wind were right. I felt spent, incontinent, inadequate, and stupid.

I'd taken most of it out on Peppi, the aggressively lesbian barmaid, hassling her nastily about the quality of the whiskey she was foisting on me. I'd spent the rest of it on scorn for the burned-out cops in the bar who were trying to attain a level of intoxication at which they could shake off the fear and frustration of the day and kid themselves into thinking they were having a good time. Cop groupies, a scary bunch as a whole, were trying to help. I scorned them too. They didn't seem to notice. Scratchy sixties rock-and-roll screeched from the speakers. The Red Dog was a cop bar, and no compact discs were allowed.

Hammond, as usual, was heard before he was seen. I'd run out of scorn and I was gazing morosely at my drink, trying to remember why ice floated, when the patented Hammond Sonic Boom cut through the Buckinghams singing "Kind of a Drag." "Peppi," he bellowed, "upgrade that asshole and bring us a couple more. It's on him." He pulled out the chair opposite me and sat down, smiling around the room at no one in particular. "Jerks," he said through the smile. "No one above lieutenant. Sit down, Max."

The man who sat down was a slender little dandy with fine sandy-blond hair, blue eyes, a harpist's spidery hands, an air of permanent melancholy, a very good suit, and an impossibly long, droopy nose. He looked everywhere but at me as he sat, and he dusted the chair before he sank into it. More than anyone else, he reminded me of Leslie Howard as Ashley Wilkes in *Gone with the Wind*. He had the same air of overbred aristocratic uselessness. "Max Bruner," Hammond said, looking for Peppi. "Simeon Grist."

Peppi pulled my drink off the table with ill-concealed displeasure and put a new one down in front of me before serving doubles to Hammond and Bruner. When she plunked down Bruner's drink he pushed it toward Hammond with one hand and took Peppi's sleeve with the other. It looked casual except that it was so fast. He hadn't looked at either of them.

"Soda," he said quietly. "No ice." She strode back to the bar in her seven-league boots and her incongruous black mesh stockings. Peppi made black mesh look like chicken wire.

"Simeon here wants to know about the kids," Hammond said, putting the top half of his drink into the past tense. He burped and looked at Bruner expectantly.

Bruner turned flat blue eyes to me. "What's his interest?" he asked softly. So softly, in fact, that I wasn't sure I'd heard him right until Hammond said, "Interest? What do you mean, what's his interest? For Chrissakes, Max, he saw the kid with the belly-button." Bruner continued to gaze at him. "Which, by the way," Hammond said, "was earlier. Earlier than the broken neck, I mean. Scar was maybe a week old."

"He's not a cop," Bruner said without looking at me. His long thin nose drooped and twitched as he talked. I couldn't take my eyes off it. Hammond cleared his throat explosively and I realized I was staring. Peppi materialized and put a glass of plain bubbly soda in front of Bruner.

"I'm looking for a little girl," I said. When Bruner figured

out that I was through, he took a metallic-foil packet out of
the pocket of his immaculately tailored jacket, peeled it
back to free a couple of Maalox tablets, and chewed them
like they were potato chips.

"That's what I said," he said in the same quiet voice.
"You're not a cop."

"Al," I said, "I've had enough today without the Scarlet
Pimpernel here. What's with the gorgeous suit, anyway?
Working undercover at Bijan?"

Hammond threw back a pound of peanuts. "Shut up,
Simeon," he said, "and, Max, if you don't mind my saying
so, you shouldn't get all twisted. With your stomach you got
to be careful. I'm telling you, he's okay. Simeon helped me
out when they sent me to records."

"Is that so?" Bruner said neutrally.

"Max has been in records too," Hammond confided. "He
was taken off the street for trying to put a pimp's finger into
the fan belt of his squad car."

I thought about engines. "The fan belt?" I asked. "Didn't
the fan get in the way?"

Bruner sat back, distancing himself from the conversation. "Yes," he said. "It did."

"If it hadn't, he might not have wound up in records,"
Hammond said. "By the time they found the asshole's fin-
gertip they'd developed a bad case of witnesses. And then
the eleven-year-old veal chop on the pimp's string decided
to side with the pimp."

"Why'd she do that?" I asked.

"He," Bruner said.

A pall descended on the table. "Oh," I said. Bruner took
a sip of soda, his eyes on the middle distance. I found
myself warming to him. "Why a finger?" I asked, just to fill
the silence.

"He'd done something with it I couldn't condone," Bruner
said softly. Hammond's big heavy shoe caught me on the
shin, telling me to change the subject. "Max got out of
records," Hammond said, "but the doilies in charge wouldn't
put him back on the street. Gave him a desk job in the
underage vice task force."

"She's thirteen," I said. "From Kansas City. Gone about six weeks. Showed up briefly at the Oki-Burger." Bruner's blue eyes ignited briefly like a gas flame and then subsided. "She isn't there anymore."

"How do you know?"

"Because I've been sitting there for the last week."

"How'd you like it?" he asked.

"I preferred it to rectal cancer," I said, "but just barely."

He nodded about a sixteenth of an inch, the biggest reaction I'd provoked yet. "Is she pretty?"

I gave him one of the yearbook pictures. He looked at it and sighed. He sighed periodically. It added to his air of melancholy. "Too pretty," he said. "Haven't seen her, though."

"You girls drinking or just talking?" Peppi said, laying a gnarled hand on Hammond's shoulder. "They's people who'd like this table, you know?"

Hammond guiltily drained his drink and half of Bruner's. I had raised my glass to my lips when I caught Bruner's stare. He was looking up at Peppi, and his face was absolutely expressionless. She tried not to look as though she knew she was being stared at, but gave up after a beat and turned to face him.

"Peppi," he said in the same hushed voice. "Go away. Don't come back until we call you."

Two spots of color appeared on Peppi's cheeks. "What's with your friend, Hammond?" she asked, trying for a light touch. "Didn't he get lunch?"

Bruner reached over, lifted Peppi's hand from Hammond's shoulder, and let it drop. "Look at me, Peppi," Bruner said. She did.

"Are you tuned in?" She nodded. "Good," Bruner said. "Bring Lieutenant Hammond and his friend another drink and then leave us alone until one of us calls you over. If none of us calls you over, Peppi, stay the fuck behind the bar. If you don't, we're going to strain you through those stockings and use you to make chicken stock."

Peppi nodded slowly. "What I need," she said, "guys with balls you couldn't get through a basketball hoop."

Bruner gave her a gentlemanly smile. "Drinks coming up?" he said.

"On the way." She pivoted and marched to the bar, her legs muscular and bunched in the mesh stockings.

"Caliban in the net," I said to myself.

"Ah," Bruner said, " 'That's a brave god and bears celestial liquor. I will kneel to him.' " He raised his soda to his lips. "Or, in this case, her," he added.

" 'Him' will do," Hammond said. He was not noted for his sensitivity toward those who belonged to minority sexual genres.

" 'The liquor is not earthly,' " I quoted back at Bruner. I took a swallow. "In fact, it's demonic."

"Poor Caliban," Bruner sighed. "Running away from a stern father figure and falling into the clutches of a couple of drunks. It happens all the time."

"What are you guys talking about?" Hammond demanded.

"Who are the monsters?" Bruner asked. "The parents who make the kid run away, the ones who prey on the kid, or the thing the kid becomes?"

"Glad you guys are getting along," Hammond said, feeling left out.

"The pimps are the worst," I said, giving vent to my newest grudge.

"They get my vote," Hammond said.

"They're the easiest ones to hit," Bruner said, sipping again at his soda. "Who's going to file a complaint because you smacked some pimp? Nobody cares, or if they do, they'd just as soon hand you a bouquet. But who are the pimps? Half the time they're just the kids who were lucky enough to get old enough to get managerial. Being this kind of cop is like raising wolves. You try to protect the young ones from the old ones, and then when the young ones get old, you try to protect the new young ones from the ones you tried to save in the first place. There are times when you just want to let them eat each other."

"Wolves don't kill their young," I said.

"Sorry," Bruner said, sighing again. "It was a metaphor."

"What's a metaphor?" Hammond said.

"It's like an allegory," Bruner said as Peppi, acting huffy, put fresh drinks on the table.

"And what's an allegory?" Hammond asked stubbornly. He looked like a man who needed his blood pressure taken.

"A dangerous amphibian," Bruner said. "Like Caliban."

"Jesus," Hammond said, putting his glass down sharply. "Thanks for inviting me to the class reunion. I think I'll find someone who speaks English." He got up and went to the jukebox, parting the sea of dancers before him like a shark in a school of cod.

"Anyway," Bruner said, watching him go, "the pimps just fill the vacuum we've created. It's classic capitalism."

At the jukebox, Hammond fished around in his pockets and pulled out the roll of quarters that he usually saved for wrapping his fist around, opened it, and fed coins into the slot. He punched some buttons. When the machine didn't respond quickly enough, he kicked it.

"What do you mean, they fill the vacuum? Surely they help to create the vacuum in the first place."

Bruner shrugged his elegantly clad shoulders. "There are always going to be immature men who want immature sex partners," he said. "Whether they're straight or gay, they're not able to handle another adult. They need someone they can dominate, someone who's physically smaller, someone who makes them feel powerful for a change. Child prostitution is an international trade, like coffee or oil. But we make it worse here. We contribute to the vacuum."

"How?" I finished my drink and looked for Peppi. Hammond's invariable first choice, the Iron Butterfly's "Inna-Gadda-da-Vida," pumped through the loudspeakers.

"We're so very progressive," Bruner said. "Child labor? Unconstitutional. Cruel and unusual punishment. There's no legal work a kid can do without his or her parents' permission. So for a kid who's run away, what's left? *Il*legal work. And of all the illegal ways for a kid to make a living, none pays better than hustling." He picked up his soda water and sipped it distastefully, then chewed two more Maalox tablets. He had little flecks of yellow foam at the corners of his lips.

"They can't work at McDonald's," he continued. "They can't even sell their blood. So they wind up with their thumbs out on Santa Monica or Sunset, trying to make enough money to buy some anesthetic."

"Are most of them abused?" I asked, thinking of the knots of muscle at the corners of Daddy Sorrell's jaws.

"You mean sexually? Physically? It depends on what you mean by being abused. They almost all come from strict homes. Spare-the-rod-and-spoil-the-child stuff. This will hurt me more than it does you. Their parents say they love them, and they express their love by whaling the tar out of the kid every time the kid does something that isn't covered by the Ten Commandments. When we talk to them, they deny that they ever beat the kid. Just disciplined him for his own good. 'We spanked him, but we didn't *beat* him.' "

Hammond returned and sat down. He looked around the room. "Sure an exciting bunch of people," he said.

"You spank someone with your hands," Bruner said. "You beat someone with an object. Lamp cord, coat hanger, wooden spoon. Baseball bat."

I pushed the little picture of Aimee across at Bruner. "Aimee Sorrell," I said. "From Kansas City. Will you have your guys keep their eyes open?"

Bruner looked at the photo and chewed at the inside of his mouth. "Sure," he said, "but you want my guess? If she hasn't showed up at the Oki-Burger, the place she landed first, she's either left L.A. or she's dead."

"What do you know about this?" I handed him the Polaroid.

He studied it for a moment and then looked up at me, his eyes wearier than Ashley Wilkes's ever had been.

"I think she's dead," he said.

8

The Dog's Stratosphere

Easter Sunday was ninety minutes away as I lurched through the front door of the Red Dog into the drizzle and aimed myself unsteadily east, looking for Alice. As far as Hollywood Boulevard was concerned, it was just another Saturday night.

The Boulevard was bumper-to-bumper, and the sidewalks were packed wall-to-curb. Neon made little zetz sounds overhead. Drum machines accompanied amplified grunts from the rolled-down windows of wet cars jammed full of kids. The street and the sidewalk were slick with mist. A cop's blue and red lights flashed ahead of me and two patrolmen, one of them a patrolwoman, braced a couple of sagging Mexicans against the side of their dented Toyota. This was what we'd come to: a female patrolman under artificial daylight frisking a stoned Mexican against a Japanese car to the beat of synthesized music. The future had arrived while I wasn't looking.

My head was turned back, my eyes on Jack's, when I stepped up onto the curb and bumped into somebody who was very hard. "Excuse me," I said to whoever it was, and faced front to find myself looking at a phone kiosk. A skinny girl about Aimee Sorrell's age giggled wisely and said to her friend, "Scope *him* out. Talking to a pay phone."

"That's what they're for," I said with great precision. "They're less interesting than talking to you, but that's what they're for." The girls looked at each other uncertainly. I

attempted courtliness. "Does either of you have a breatha-
lyzer?"

"No," the friend said. "We don't." She said it very slowly,
as though she were talking to a tourist from *very* far away,
someone with several heads and suction cups at the tips of
his fingers. She wore a fringed buckskin jacket that had
probably been her father's pride and joy in the heyday of
the Buffalo Springfield.

"Pity," I said. "But you may go." Congratulating myself
on my gallantry, I picked up the phone and fumbled around
in my pocket for a quarter. "Hello, pay phone," I said.

Something touched the center of my back, and I snapped
around. The skinny one had stepped back but the fresh-faced
friend in the buckskin jacket stood her ground, looking up
at me with clear, brave eyes. "Um," she said, "you okay?"

To my bewilderment, my eyes filled with tears. "I'm
fine," I said. "What the hell are you doing on this street?"

"Nothing," the friend said. "You know, just messing
around. What's the matter with you?"

"The human condition," I said, for want of anything else.

"Well," the girl in the buckskin said, "as long as it's
nothing serious." She took her friend's arm and led her
away from me.

"He talks to *phones*," the skinny one hissed. "Leave him
alone."

"Chill out, Tabitha," the friend said, "relax, would you?"

"Tabitha's right," I called after them. "Leave me alone.
And get off the street. Here there be monsters."

"You're the one who's monstered," Tabitha said. Having
gotten in the last word, something she probably never did at
home, she led her friend away. The friend turned back to
look at me once and then both of them floated into the
crowd.

Since I had a phone in my hand, I dropped the quarter and
called my number. The machine happily played back two
hang-ups while I rested my forehead against the cold metal
of the kiosk. The third call wasn't a hang-up.

"Damn you," a girl's voice said. "Don't you ever go

home? Get over here right now, my mother's acting crazy and I don't blame her, considering what I found in her purse. Oh, yeah, this is Aurora Sorrell, and you know where I am."

When I stepped out of the kiosk the drizzle hit me in the face, but I didn't need it. I was as sober as Walter Cronkite. I sprinted for Alice, and people looked after me, hoping I might be something they'd see tomorrow on the news.

"Well, what a treat," Aurora said as she opened the door to the bungalow. "So glad you could find the time." Her mother was nowhere in sight.

"Where is she?" I said.

"Asleep. And it took long enough for you to get here."

"Honey," I said, "I've been working." She started to bridle, and I said, "Sorry, sorry, not 'honey.' Aurora. Miss Sorrell, if you like. I've been looking for Aimee."

"I've been calling you for hours." She stepped back to let me in. She was wearing a long white shirt that looked like it belonged to her father, and her legs were bare, as they'd been created to be. There were weepy little smudges under her eyes.

"What's happened? Can she get up to talk to me?"

"She took a sleeper," Aurora said. "She never takes a sleeper. She doesn't even take an *aspirin*. This is a woman who gets her teeth drilled without getting put out. It was one of my father's. He never packs right, you know what I mean? He left his whole overnight case here, razor and everything. I don't know how he stays in business." She turned her back to me and walked to the couch. Her shoulders were as straight as a T square and she moved as though she would break if she bumped into anything. When she sat down she crossed her long brown legs and said, "I hope you're good."

"I'm as good as I can be," I said, following. "What's happened?"

She pulled out the crumpled pack of Marlboro Lights and lit one, avoiding my eyes. "We've heard from Aimee," she said, fanning the smoke away with one hand. She made a sound that was midway between a sneeze and a laugh. " 'Heard' is the word, all right. My, oh my, have we heard from Aimee."

"What are we talking about?" I said. "What do you mean, you've heard from Aimee?"

"I didn't believe it," she said, drawing on the cigarette. "I didn't believe anything was wrong. They always worried more about Aimee than they did about me. Aimee's the baby. Aimee's the last thing left between my mother and menopause. Aimee's the pot of gold at the end of the hairbow. Sibling rivalry and then some."

"Stop acting like Tallulah Bankhead and tell me what happened."

She closed her eyes slowly and then opened them again. She was drunker than I was. "Who's Tallulah Bankhead?" she asked.

"A dangerous amphibian," I said. "Aurora. Tell me what happened."

Her chin crumpled up like aluminum foil and she dropped her head. Two wet spots fell onto the brown skin of her thigh and glistened up at me. Without having any idea what I was doing, I reached out and brushed them away. Her hair hung forward, masking her face.

"My mother's purse," she said in a muffled voice. "Over there, near the chair. Can you get it, please?"

Acting on automatic pilot, I got the purse and came back to the couch. I put the purse on the coffee table. "And?" I asked.

She took a shaky drag off the cigarette. "And open it, stupid," she said without looking up. "It's right on top."

I pulled the purse open and found myself looking at more stuff than the average man packs when he's going abroad for the rest of his life. "You've got to give me a hint," I said. "This is King Tut's tomb. This is a time capsule. Anybody who finds this purse a thousand years from now will know all there is to know about Western civilization."

"Western civilization is a joke," she said. "There's no such thing as civilization. There's just table manners."

She grabbed the purse and dug into it. "You want to see civilization?" she asked in a strangled tone. "You want to hear civilization?" She pulled out the little tape recorder and a cassette and fumbled around with them, trying to insert the tape into the player.

"I've heard this," I said.

"Just shut up. I'm so damned sick of people who know what's going to happen next. You don't know which way your rear end is pointed," she said, snapping the cassette player shut with a nasty little click. "Not that anyone cares."

"Slow down," I said. I touched her hand. "And before you play that thing, give me a drink."

She tilted her face toward me. It was wet and shiny. "Good idea," she said, wiping her cheeks with the back of her hand like she was trying to rub off a tattoo. "Oh, Jesus," she said, reaching to the floor behind her and coming up with a bottle. "We're both just kids."

"Who?"

She drank deeply. She'd graduated to cognac. "Everybody," she said, passing the bottle. "Aimee and me. You and me. Why would anyone think you could find anything? My mother and me. She's not so old either, you know." Her face wrinkled and she collapsed backward onto the couch. "Ohhhh, *foooey*," she wailed, covering her eyes with a forearm. "Fooey, fooey, fooey."

The cognac was rawer than scraped bark. I had to swallow twice to make sure it would stay down, and even then it reached up with little fingers of fume to chin itself on my uvula. After it subsided and went about the business of lighting up my stomach, I leaned forward and pressed the button that made the little black machine play whatever it was that needed playing.

There was nothing. Just a hiss like a long-distance phone wire. Aurora made a little choking sound and waved at the machine, and I pushed Rewind.

The tape snicked into place and I looked up to find Aurora staring at it as though it were something fanged and poisonous. "Do you want to go into the other room while I play it?" I asked.

She shook her head, her underlip caught between her teeth. Her face was a mask of taut muscle. "Play it," she said.

I did.

"Welcome to L.A.," a man's voice boomed. The voice had a hollow echo, like someone shouting in a bathroom. I snatched the machine up and fiddled frantically with the volume control. "Hope you like the hotel," the man said. "It's supposed to be *très chic*. I wouldn't know. I haven't got the money to stay there. But you're going to help me with that, aren't you?" His voice reverberated like a loudspeaker in a railroad station.

"Bastard," Aurora hissed.

"Of course, you're not supposed to *be* in L.A.," the man said. "You're supposed to be in Kansas City, waiting for my phone call. You're not taking me seriously. That's a mistake. You want to know how big a mistake it is? Yes, Johnny, as Ed would say, how big a mistake *is* it? Well, it's this big a mistake."

There was a rush of something that sounded like water. Aurora was chewing on her sleeve. Aimee's voice split the room.

"*Yaahhh*," she cried, "no, no, no, no. Please. Please, please. Anything you want. Please, anything, please God, I'll be good, I'll be, I'll be . . . Oh, don't. Please *don't*." Her voice soared through an octave of agony and into the stratosphere, into the range that only dogs are supposed to hear. Then the splashing sound stopped and there was nothing but sobbing.

I heard a muffled sound like someone picking up a microphone, and the man's voice said, "Once more, darling. With feeling this time," and we heard the splashing sound, and Aimee gabbled and hollered and gabbled and hollered and wept and snuffled and then gabbled and hollered again.

Aurora had her head down on the arm of the couch. She was making heaving sounds.

"Mommy," Aimee sobbed, "please come get me, please, please, please. I'll be good, I'll be so good, you and Daddy will . . . Oh, no, oh, no, please *don't* . . ." The voice trailed off into a ragged moan that sounded like the world being torn in two.

"I won't, this time," the man said. "Go home, Mommy. Go home tomorrow morning."

He said something else, but I didn't hear it. The door to the bedroom had opened and Jane Sorrell stood there, her eyes drugged and fuzzy, her hair hanging in disarranged, half-pinned loops around her neck.

"Aimee?" she said. "Aimee?" Then she looked at Aurora and me and let out a short raspy little breath and fell. She didn't bend her knees or sink gracefully or swoon. She went down like a redwood. Aurora got to her while I was still trying to turn off the tape recorder.

An hour later I pulled across the bridge leading to Wyatt and Annie's house. It was dark. I hammered on the door until Wyatt pulled it open, looking mussed and grumpy.

"Happy Easter," I said. "Is your daughter still for sale?"

II
The Little Chickie Begged

9

Easter

Jessica was sullen.

"You screwed up a perfectly good party, you know?" She assumed the offensive the moment I pulled Alice out onto Old Topanga Canyon. "Acting like an old fart. You and my father. And poor Blister, he's been walking like a cowboy ever since."

"He's lucky to be walking. If I had my way he'd be crawling on his belly like a reptile. That's from 'Little Egypt,' written by Lieber and Stoller, recorded by the Coasters. You wouldn't remember it."

"I certainly wouldn't," she said. "And if you weren't so goddamned old, you wouldn't either. What's it to you, anyway, what I do with Blister? When did you join the church?"

"He's too old for you."

"You and my father," she said again. "You know, I was raised like, um, my parents always went, sex is a normal, natural thing. People who didn't understand that were sick. Just a normal part of your life, right? So how come all of a sudden everybody's got their bowels in an uproar because I'm maybe going to bed with Blister? Why does everybody go so corny all of a sudden? You know why it is? It's because they're liberals. All liberals do is talk."

"And what are you?"

"Oh, leave me alone."

"He's too old for you. And he's a louse."

"And he's taking ad*va*ntage of me?" she said, drawing out the middle "aaaa" in "advantage" as though it were a word in itself. I was watching the road, but I knew her upper lip was curled. "What do you want, that I should do it with some little shrub who can't tell a condom from a condominium?"

"I don't want anything," I said. "I just don't like Blister."

"I don't like him all that much myself," she said unexpectedly. "But the pickings in Topanga aren't exactly world-class." Not knowing what to say, I shut up.

It was drizzling as we went down the hill toward the ocean. Alice was built in the fifties, the age of convenience, and both the passenger and the driver were thoughtfully equipped with shiny chrome buttons that operate all the windows in the car. After a snicker to let me know how corny I was, Jessica reached up and opened the windows on my side.

I endured the cold and the sting of the drizzle against my face until we made the turn. Then I used my own buttons to raise both windows on the driver's side and open the ones on hers. Jessica promptly slid them down again. I waited eight or ten minutes, until the Pacific, slate-gray and flatter than a razor's edge, slipped into sight between the hills and then raised the windows on my side, leaving hers open.

Jessica made a show of fanning her face with one hand, then closed her windows and opened mine. I closed all of them and pushed the button that locked all of them, the only button she didn't have. As I turned left onto the Pacific Coast Highway she fiddled unsuccessfully with the buttons and gave me a glance that must have cost her several grams of self-control. Then she turned her angelic face sweetly up to me, shifted delicately onto one haunch, and emitted a ladylike fart.

"Where'd all the fun go?" I said to no one in particular.

She gave me both barrels, a full-bore, hazel-eyed gaze. "Mommy says you're having an elastic adolescence," she said at last. "You've stretched it and stretched it, but one day it's going to snap back and leave you nowhere."

It sounded like something Annie might say. "I prefer to think of it as an escalator," I said, not very convincingly. "I'm enjoying the ride. When it's taken me high enough, I'll get off."

"And who will you be then?"

"Me. But older."

"*Older?*" she said nastily. "You must be joking." It was her second shot at the same target, and I figured she might be running out of bullets.

"People do get older," I said. "They even get older than I am. Someday you'll be older than I am now. Maybe you'll look back at this moment and say, 'Why wasn't I nicer to that poor kid?' "

"Fat chance." She took a satisfied sniff at the rotten-egg air and settled back, gazing through the windshield and daring me to do anything about it.

"Listen," I said, largely to prevent myself from giving in and opening the window, "the best thing that can happen to you is to get older. As someone once said, consider the alternative."

"Huh?"

I negotiated a curve in silence, waiting for her to get it. The Pacific slapped in disinterestedly to our right. When she didn't get it, I said, "Being dead."

"Oh," she said dismissively. "That."

"The dead can't fart," I said, losing points.

"They don't have to. They already smell bad."

We let a mile or so pass in malodorous silence. When I felt reasonably safe from scorn, I lowered my window.

"Chicken," she said, sounding pleased for the first time. She twirled a lock of hair around her finger and checked it for split ends. "I knew you were chicken. Blister should have farted at you. You would have fallen down the stairs headfirst." She gave up on her hair.

"What are you doing with a coke dealer?"

She emitted an exasperated little poof of air. "He's not just a dealer. He's a person too. Anyway, don't go figuring I hang around with him just so he can keep me high."

"Then what is it? His stomach muscles?"

"Oh, give me credit. I tried it. Why wouldn't I? But then I quit. Who wants to feel fast and stupid at the same time? It's like the Super Bowl, you know? There's always two guys talking: the big slow dumb guy and the little fast dumb guy. Who wants to be the little fast dumb guy?"

"Jessica," I said, turning to her. "How did you get this way? I knew you when you were one year old."

"You have the advantage of me," she said loftily. "And how about you keep your eyes on the road?"

I eyed the road, reflecting on the exchange between Wyatt, Annie, and me on the previous evening, when I'd asked them if I could have Jessica. First I'd reexplained the case I was working on.

"Are you kidding?" Annie had said. "She could get *killed*."

"She could get scared," I'd said. "Right now, she feels like she'll live forever, no matter what she does. Screw around with Blister? No problem. Run away? So what? All she has to do is come home and flash that old Jessica smile and you'll both be falling all over each other to make her bed and buy her school clothes."

"So what are you saying?" Wyatt had asked. He wasn't crazy about the fact that I'd been up at Blister's with him that night; he was, after all, Wyatt Wilmington the Third, even if he had decided to be a carpenter rather than a real-estate mogul like his father, and his family had always kept its problems to itself. It was the sacred WASP tradition: what matters is what people can see. Keep it secret, and maybe it can be fixed before it makes the papers.

"Wyatt," I said. He was my oldest friend, and Annie had been my girlfriend when I introduced her to Wyatt all those years ago when we were innocent students at UCLA. "Wyatt, I'm in the family. She's my goddaughter. I drove Annie to the hospital when she was going to be born, with the two of you in the back seat. You remember how smoothly I took the curves?"

Wyatt gave a grudging nod. He'd been too nervous to drive.

"Well, I'm going to do the same now. She's going to see that kids can't always go home again. She's going to realize for the first time that there are lines that we cross, or don't cross, that can't always be crossed in the other direction. She's going to see kids who can't hope to live more than another couple of years."

"And you're going to protect her?" That was Annie.

"You're protecting her now?" I said, without really thinking.

There was a long silence, and the two of them exchanged a glance from which I was profoundly excluded. I looked down at my coffee cup. It had coffee in it.

"Why do you want her?" Annie finally said. "What's she supposed to be?"

"She's my I.D. card," I said. "She'll make me fit in." Annie shuffled off one of her slippers and looked down at it as though it contained an answer. "Just my I.D. card," I repeated.

In the car, my I.D. card said, "I'm hungry. This is sure a weird way to spend Easter. Normally I'd be stealing pieces off the ham by now." It was two o'clock.

"Well, luckily for you, we're going to a restaurant."

"Will they have ham?"

"If they do, you probably won't recognize it."

"What restaurant?"

"It's called Tommy's Oki-Burger."

"Blister's been there," she said. "He told me something about it."

"It's Blister's kind of place. What'd he tell you?"

"That it was full of kids who'd split from home. And don't knock Blister. It's boring."

"Did he tell you what they were doing there?"

"Peddling their butts, he said."

"That's about it."

She thought about it for a while. "Why are we going?"

"You're going to help me find a little girl."

"Is she peddling her butt?"

"Where do you *hear* expressions like that?"

"Around," she said, sounding like a teenager for the first time. "Is she?"

"I don't know. For all I know, she's dead."

"Zowie," she said, half under her breath. "Is it going to be dangerous?"

"I don't think so. Not for you, at any rate."

"Hell," she said, clearly disappointed. After a moment she said, "Well, anyway, it sounds like fun."

"It does, huh?"

"More fun than Blister," she said.

Jessica started eating the moment we got to Tommy's. The place was largely empty at first; then, as the afternoon wore on into evening, it began to fill up with the usual highly checkered crowd. The Mountain had spent most of Easter Sunday out on the blacktop parking lot, practicing Sumo wrestling with some other fat guys inside a small circle painted on the asphalt. Jessica had stopped, fascinated, as the fat guys grunted and puffed inside the circle. Finally the Mountain had forced his opponent—a Japanese who couldn't have weighed less than three hundred pounds—outside the circle. He wiped his face with the malodorous cheesecloth and scanned the small crowd that had gathered to watch. He nodded pleasantly down at me, and then his eyes traveled down to Jessica. Cowed a bit by the sheer pleasure of all that sweating male flesh, she had slipped her hand into mine.

The Mountain's face dropped. When he looked back up at me, all semblance of good feeling was gone. He looked like an ill-considered cross between Charles Manson and the Pillsbury Doughboy. Elaborately, he spat at my feet and then he turned his back on us and stepped back into the ring.

"Friend of yours?" Jessica said.

"Not anymore, it seems." I was debating whether to tap the Mountain on the shoulder and try to explain, when he picked up a man who outweighed the average tractor-trailer semi and threw him out of the ring as though he'd been a

Q-Tip. That ended the debate. Jessica and I went back inside and she started to eat.

She'd gotten up to go to the bathroom when two regulars, a couple of pre-op transsexuals, greeted each other with the highest squeals I'd heard since the Beatles played the Bowl, and sat down at the table next to me.

"Dear," said the blond one, who was attired, despite the chill in the air, in a pair of gym shorts and a K-Mart blouse. "Dear, do you have any pants? Someone stole everything last night: my clothes, my cash, my makeup—even the good stuff, the Avon and the Clinique? Do you know what a girl has to go through to get Clinique? It's more expensive than *saf*fron." She lit a cigarette, ignoring the one that she'd just laid down in the ashtray.

"And almost as yellow," her friend said, snatching up the first cigarette with the air of someone stumbling over a canteen in Death Valley.

"Yellow, yellow, marshmallow. I wouldn't mind looking like the Dragon Lady, as long as I could look like *something*," the blond one said, exhaling a vehement cloud of smoke. "Look at me now, I'm so sallow. I've got circles under my eyes like the rings on a coaster, and I've got more pits than the full moon. Honey, they took *everything*."

"Your aura is intact," the other one said, scanning the street with practiced eyes.

"Beg pardon?"

"In fact, it could use a perm." A nice-looking teenager in the street let his gaze slide off the brunette's face and went back to checking out the traffic.

"What in the *world* are you talking about?"

Rejected by the teenager, the other one, the brunette one with nine earrings, squinted at the blond and said, "A little psychometric Kirlian photography tells me that your roots to the nether world are in place. I can see them shimmering."

"Well, what the hell good is that? Just look at me. Nothing on but these stupid gym shorts, loaned to me by a very active friend, and this awful blouse. Mamie *Eisenhower* wouldn't have worn this blouse. Honey, it's *April*. I'm freezing to death. I must say, I'd hoped for a bit more sympathy."

"I've got my own problems," the brunette said. He, or maybe she, pulled his or her tank top down to reveal two swollen nipples. "Six weeks," he or she said, "six fucking weeks of both shots *and* pills, and what have I got to show for it? Mosquito bites. At this rate, I'll be almost as old as you are before I can wear a B-cup."

"B-cup indeed," the blond one said. "Dream on. You're talking shot glasses."

"God, I hate Leos," said the one with the nine earrings. She turned suddenly to me. "What sign are you?"

"I'm a Chameleon," I said.

"In other words," the one with the earrings said, pouting, "fuck off."

"Not necessarily," the blond said. "I like people who don't believe in astrology."

"Then I'm your man," I said, sipping at my diet asphalt.

"Wouldn't that be nice?" the blond said, leaning toward me.

"What the hell do rabbits have to do with Easter?" Jessica said loudly, sitting down and fingering the cardboard bunny stapled to the pole at the head of our table. There were similar bunnies all over the place. Someone had drawn exaggerated genitalia on the one at our table.

"Oh, my God," the blond said, recoiling. "You're a *pervert*. My God, she's barely pubescent." Well, at least nobody thought I was a cop anymore.

"Are you talking about me?" Jessica demanded, sounding like the Grand Duchess of Fredonia. "Because if you are, I don't like your tone."

"Leave her to her sugar daddy," the one with the nine earrings said. The two of them shifted their weight and faced away from us, their surgically improved noses in the air.

"I know a guy in school who's going to end up like those two," Jessica said in a voice that would have penetrated a foot of lead. "Maybe I should bring him down here and give him a preview of coming attractions. It might straighten him up."

The blond started to turn back to us, and I could feel Jessica brace herself for the collision to come.

"The Easter Bunny," I said, plucking at the air. "That's a very interesting question. On the face of it, rabbits don't seem to have much to do with the Resurrection of Christ."

"No shit," Jessica said, watching the blond the way a mongoose watches a cobra.

"The, ah, the early Church took a very practical approach to the problem of getting started in places where other religions were already established. They built their churches right on top of the other religions' temples, and they did the same with their holidays."

"Yeah?" Jessica said, narrowing her eyes to meet the blond's gaze and picking up a fork from the tray in front of her. She tested it for balance, looking like Jim Bowie's granddaughter. The blond, relegated to the role of the cobra, hissed.

"They scheduled Christmas for the midwinter solstice, the most important festival of the year in the colder countries, when everybody feasted to celebrate having made it through the first half of the winter and started to look forward to surviving the second half." I leaned forward and removed the fork from her hand. "Easter was slotted at the time of the spring fertility rites, held to ensure good crops and big herds of cattle or sheep or whatever the hell they were herding. Rabbits are symbols of fertility, for what I hope are obvious reasons, because if they're not, I'm not going to explain them."

"Because they screw like minks," Jessica said in her piping treble. The blond, who probably hadn't been shocked since Halley's Comet, looked shocked. "And who's the genius who figured out that they lay eggs?" There was an Easter basket, lined with that terrible green cellophane grass, on the table—there was one on every table—and Jessica picked up the top egg in the basket and hefted it, evaluating its potential as a weapon. It had DOTTIE written on it in sparkles.

"Eggs are a fertility symbol too," I said, hoping she didn't plan to toss it at the blond.

"Well, duh," Jessica said scornfully. "They're also nice and heavy."

"But they've been layered over with Christian symbolism. They represent, among other things, the closed tomb from which Christ rose."

"Huh," Jessica said, looking down at the one in her hand.

"Um, listen," the blond said, "is all that true?"

"Sure," I said. "It's not what they teach you in Sunday school, but it's as true as anything else."

The blond looked from Jessica to me and then took a speculative leap. "You're her uncle."

"Sure, Tammy," the Mountain said, looming vast and horrible behind her. "Sure he is. And I'm her little sister." His greasy hair was captured behind his head with a bright pink rubber band, and his face was oiled with sweat. He gave me a look that made my sneakers itch.

It was a delicate situation: having dispelled the cop image, I wasn't inclined to explain the relationship between Jessica and me. I tugged the extremely heavy corners of my mouth up into a rictus that I was sure looked less like Easter than Halloween.

"Heh, heh," I said, appreciating his good-natured joke.

"He was telling us about Easter," the blond—Tammy—said.

"Was he?" the Mountain said ponderously. He wiped his hands on the cheesecloth as a prelude to spreading me over the table like margarine. "I didn't figure it," he said, reaching for my neck. "I didn't know what you were, but I didn't think you were a dink."

"Oh, boy," the blond said, happily changing sides. "Eighty-six."

I'd chosen the little finger of his left hand as the easiest one to break and was reaching up for it when Tommy, behind the counter, yelled: "*Mountain!*"

The Mountain, not one who was used to doing two things

at once, stumbled and looked up. "Nuh," he said. He swatted my hands from his pinky as though they'd been a couple of enervated houseflies and stared toward the counter. "What, huh?" he said to Tommy. "What?"

"Pakking lot," Tommy said in his best Okinawan English. He was the one who'd taught the Mountain sumo. "Fight. Inna pakking lot. Get 'em. Oddawise, cops."

"Balls," the Mountain said. He looked back down at me. I was shaking my hands in the air to relieve the sting. They felt like a locomotive had hit them. "You sit tight," he said, patting me on the cheek. The pat nearly dislocated my jaw. "I'll get to you." He lumbered off toward the fight inna pakking lot.

"He really likes you," Jessica said. "You know what? I think he thinks you're a dirty old man."

"Isn't he?" the blond asked with genuine interest.

For the next couple of hours the Mountain was too busy to bother with me. The place got full and then it got fuller. Kids who had been hustling in the drizzle came by to dry out and fill up, and the Mountain, after a long hiatus, returned from the general vicinity of the kitchen. Around his equator he wore something I hadn't seen before: a canvas change apron, like the ones worn by the ladies who work the slots in Las Vegas. On it were stenciled the words CALL HOME.

As each kid came in, the Mountain reached into one of the pockets of his apron and pulled out a slip of paper with a number on it. Some kids didn't want to take them, but the Mountain exercised his unique powers of persuasion, and almost all of the kids wound up tucking a number into a pocket. Then they went and checked the Easter baskets, usually pulling out an egg after painstakingly reading the names on all of them. The ones who didn't take one of the Mountain's slips of paper were eighty-sixed. I wouldn't say they were thrown out gently, but by the Mountain's standards it was an exercise in restraint.

"What in the *world* is going on?" Jessica said. By now Tammy and her friend, who called herself Velveeta, were sitting with us, sipping discreetly at beer from Diet Pepsi cups. They'd bought the beer at Glamour Liquors across the street, and I was sucking up the Glamour with them. Jessica hadn't asked for one, but every time I turned to watch the Mountain in action I found that the level in my cup had dropped an inch or two. She and Tammy were having a pretty good time.

"E.T. time," Tammy said. "Call home, get it? He does this every holiday. Sometimes he does it every Tuesday."

"Seven," the Mountain bellowed, and a frail, anorexic-looking blond girl with very sharp knees got up from her table, none too steadily, and advanced toward the pay phone. The Mountain ladled some change out of his apron and handed it to her more gently than I would have thought possible. I watched her whisper into the Mountain's ear, and then he took some of the change out of her hand, dialed the phone, and handed her the receiver. She hastily pocketed the rest of the change, and he let her. After a moment the girl said, "Hello? Mom?"

When I turned back, my beer cup was empty and Tammy and Jessica were giggling. Velveeta took the cup and filled it from a bottle held discreetly beneath the table. "Fountain of Truth," she said optimistically, batting her eyelashes at me.

While the girl was on the phone the Guitar Player came in, wet with rain, the imitation Stratocaster hanging from its frayed strap. His dark hair was dripping down into his eyes. He threw an anxious glance at the Mountain, who nodded him in as though nothing had ever happened, and then he was followed by a little girl, even younger than Jessica, who looked like she hadn't eaten in days. She stood in the doorway, surveying the scene with big starved eyes.

With new confidence, the Guitar Player took the Mountain by one arm and whispered something in his ear. The Mountain went back into the kitchen. A few minutes later he reappeared with an Easter egg in his hand. I couldn't read the name. The little girl looked at it in disbelief for a moment, her eyes going back and forth from the Guitar Player to the Mountain. Then she reached up and used the sleeve of her enormous sweater to wipe something away from her cheek. The Mountain pointed the Guitar Player to a table and gave him a slip of paper. The Guitar Player sat down and rummaged in the Easter basket that occupied its center. He fished out an egg labeled DONNIE. It sparkled at me across the room. The little girl sat down next to him and started to put the egg in her purse, being very careful not to knock off the sparkles.

"Eat it, stupid," the Guitar Player said. The anorexic girl hung up the phone and wobbled back to her table.

"Have you called home?" said the Mountain to the little girl who had come in with the Guitar Player.

The phone rang. The Mountain went to it and listened, waving an arm to quiet people down. The little girl started to peel her egg. A couple of new arrivals rifled through the basket on our table and pulled out eggs with their names on them. The Mountain said something into the phone and turned to survey the tables. "Donnie," he bellowed.

"Shit," the Guitar Player said. "Tell her I'm not here." The Mountain screwed up his little pink eyes and gave him a look that should have left an exit wound. Donnie unslung his guitar and went to the phone. All over the restaurant, people stopped talking and looked at him. A dull blush rose to his cheeks.

"Yeah," he said. "Hi, Mom. Listen, I'm kind of busy. Give me your number and I'll call you back." He started to hang up, but the Mountain clapped his hands over Donnie's ears, trapping the phone in place. Donnie struggled for a second, and the Mountain placed a size-twelve triple-E foot over both of Donnie's sneakers. The girl chewed on her egg with the dreamy concentration of the truly hungry.

"You know," Donnie said into the phone, "just working with the band." Somebody laughed, and the Mountain fixed her with a stare that transformed the laughter into a coughing fit. It was the Old Young Woman. She turned all her attention to peeling an egg for the Toothless Man. His egg said HERBIE. He put half of it in the back of his mouth and went to work. Egg white gathered at the corners of his mouth.

"Gross," Jessica said under her breath.

"Yeah, well, don't forget to floss," I said to her.

She gave me Parent Stare Number Twelve. "Give me a *break*," she said.

"No problem," Donnie said to the phone, rolling his eyes heavenward. "Really, doing great. Cold back there?" He nodded, glaring at everyone within earshot. "Sunny out here," he said, just as a bucket of rain hit the roof.

"And the band just got a gold record," the Old Young Woman said to the Toothless Man.

Donnie got through the call somehow and sat back down next to the little girl. He searched his pockets and came up with some coins, then went to the counter to order. The Mountain barked another number, and a thin guy with a lot of volcanic activity on his face went to the phone. The Mountain dropped change into his hands. Donnie came back with a burger and cut it into exact halves. He gave half to the little girl, who looked at it as though it were a whole Easter ham.

Jessica, who hadn't stopped chewing and drinking since we arrived, picked up the egg she had dropped back into the basket on our table. "Hey," she called to the Mountain, "can I eat this?" I tried to kick her under the table, but missed.

The Mountain hovered over me. Malevolence rose from him in fumes like heat off a road, but it was aimed at me, not her.

"Is your name Dottie?" he asked. Sure enough, that's what the egg said: DOTTIE.

"It's my middle name," Jessica said without turning a hair. "Jessica Dottie Wilmington." Her middle name was, and always had been, Jill.

The Mountain gave me another death stare, just to keep in shape, and then smiled at her. "Go to it, then," he said. "I guess she's not coming anyway."

Jessica picked it up. She started to crack the shell, and I looked at the name again and then took it from her hand.

"Hey," she said. "That's mine."

Her tone made the Mountain, who'd been lumbering back toward the pay phone, turn and stare. He'd had more than enough of me. "I gave it to her, shitbag," he said, advancing. "You can take her money if that's your angle, but goddammit, that's her egg."

"Dottie," I said, talking fast. He was on top of me. "As in Dorothy? Is she blond? About thirteen, looks a little younger?"

"What's it to you? You already got one, don't you? What are you, trying to build up a string?" He leaned over me and I smelled the cheesy odor of the mummy's wrap he used to swab the tables.

"Dottie—I mean, Dorothy—Gale?" I said. "From Kansas?"

He put a hand on my shoulder. "I think maybe you ought to get out of here. Maybe you should stay out of here. Otherwise, something might happen to your face, and then how would you scam the little chicklets?"

"We have to talk," I said.

"Eighty-six," he said, "and I'm going to love it." He grabbed the shoulder of my shirt and hauled me up.

"Jessica," I said, "tell him who I am."

She looked up at me through long blond lashes. "I don't really know who you are," she said. "You told me your name was George."

Tammy laughed. "They're all named George," she said, sipping at her cup.

"You asshole," the Mountain said. "I hope you can fly." He picked me up as though I were made of balsawood and toted me toward the sidewalk. Various mouths opened in expectation.

"Wait," Jessica said. "He's my—"

"Tell him in private," I said, trying to make hushing motions with my hands. The Mountain's arms were tight across my chest and I was beginning to see an interesting pattern of little black dots.

"Tell me what?" the Mountain said. He didn't ease the pressure of his arms. I tried to say something, and produced a postliterate wheeze.

"My godfather," Jessica said. "He's a detective."

A hush, the kind they call Angel's Flight, seized the restaurant. Tammy looked up at me, betrayal in her eyes. Donnie took the little girl by the hand as though to protect her.

I tried again. "Can we talk?" It sounded more like the jet stream than it did like English, but the Mountain relaxed enough to let me grab a few cubic centimeters of air. He looked at Jessica, who was nodding faster than a presidential yes-man, and then at me.

"I guess so," he said. Then, from a height of about two feet, he dropped me.

10

Solo for Guitar Player

"The one you want to talk to is Donnie," said the Mountain, sitting on the sink.

"Is he the cute one with the guitar?" Jessica asked. She was perched, cross-legged and precarious, on the edge of the urinal. The Mountain had chosen the men's room as the site of our private talk. Since all the seats were taken, I was standing.

"Cute?" I said, massaging my ribs. I felt like a collapsed accordion.

"Sure," she said. "You don't think he's cute?"

"Cute as a case of crabs," I said.

"What's crabs?" Jessica asked. "I mean, I know what a crab is, but what's a case of crabs?"

"Little girl," the Mountain said, "you don't need to know that yet."

"Or maybe ever," I added.

"Or maybe ever," the Mountain agreed. "Anyway, he's the one who was tightest with her. Goddamn, she was pretty. Like to break my heart when she came in. Poor little Dottie."

"So why do you think she didn't show up today?" I asked.

"Shit," the Mountain said. "She hasn't come around for weeks. I just put the egg in the basket because I was hoping she was okay. Like magic, you know? If the egg was here,

103

maybe she'd show up." He made a hopeless gesture with his big hands.

"How do you stand to work here?" I said.

"Well, once in a while I can make one of them call home. Then, maybe, I can make them go home. Anyway, Tommy's teaching me sumo."

"How often does one of them go home?"

"Never," he said.

"Why sumo?" Jessica said.

He looked from me to her. "I'm fat," he said.

"You're big," Jessica said, qualifying instantly for the United Nations. "Men are supposed to be big."

The Mountain looked at her sadly. "Honey, I'm not big. I'm fat." He looked back to me. "Is this joker really your godfather?"

"Ever since I was born."

The Mountain stared down at the little yearbook picture of Aimee cradled in his enormous hand. It looked like a microchip. "Poor little Dottie," he repeated.

"So how do I talk to Donnie?"

"I go get him, don't I?" He looked at the picture again, then sighed and hauled himself off the sink, which creaked gratefully. "I'll be back," he said, giving me the picture as he opened the door.

"You're sweet," Jessica said. The Mountain was blushing when he left. "I've never been in a men's room before."

"Glad to hear it."

"It's pretty seamy." She leaned forward to see if she could peer under the wall of the stall surrounding the toilet.

"All part of your education."

"Is this really what you do for a living?"

"I guess so." At the moment I was wishing that Eleanor weren't in China and trying to figure out what to tell my parents and Roxanne, all of whom had expected me. I had a feeling it was going to be a late night.

"Can we sleep in town?" Jessica said. "I'd love to sleep in town."

"Jessica," I said. "I borrowed you. I didn't buy you."

The door swung violently open, and Jessica lost her perch on the edge of the urinal. She went down, grabbing for support, and her hand splashed in the water. "Oh, no," she said, sitting on the floor and staring at her wet hand. "Cooties and then some."

"Wash it," I said. The Mountain blossomed horribly in the doorway, looking like the Masque of the Fat Death, if there is such a thing. "He's gone," he said.

"Thanks, Jessica," I said unsympathetically. "I should have worn a T-shirt that said DETECTIVE."

"I saved your life," she said, scrubbing her hands vigorously. "This nice man would have killed you."

"What about the little girl?" I asked the Mountain.

"Gone too."

"Well, heck," I said, editing my language unnecessarily for Jessica's benefit. "So what do we do now?"

The Mountain rubbed the back of his neck with the awful-smelling rag and screwed up his eyes. Then he pursed his lips and blew out noisily. He seemed to be undergoing some kind of crisis of conscience. "I guess I break the rules," he said at last. "I guess I take you to his squat."

"What's a squat?" Jessica whispered as we walked single file, the Mountain in the lead, down a dark block of Vista. Vista of what? I wondered. The only thing I could see was a tract house and a chain-link fence. "Where a runaway lives," I said.

"How romantic," she said. "Isn't there anywhere to lie down?"

"Two houses down," the Mountain said. "Across the street."

The house two down and across the street had burned down, some time back, from the look of it. Blackened timbers poked up at irregular angles in the fine mist. The front porch was untouched, but behind it something that had once been a house sagged, black and fractional. The remaining walls of the house were no higher than my shoulder, and the roof would have been something to look at the stars through, if there had been any stars. A little kid's bright plastic pedal car sat forlornly in the middle of the rectangular brown patch that should have been the lawn. A tiny sneaker lay next to it, dead-center in a coiled dog-chain with the collar still attached, as though the dog, deprived of its child, had wasted away into nothing. The entire doleful panorama was surrounded by the ubiquitous chain link, and a sharp smell of charred wood filled the air.

"He lives *there*?" Jessica said, disbelief coloring her voice.

"In the garage," the Mountain said. "In the back. It didn't burn."

The fence was eight feet high, topped by a long, lethal, lizardy spiral of razor-wire. "How do we get in?" I asked.

"*You*," the Mountain said. "You get in. I won't fit."

"You have an inferiority complex about your weight," Jessica informed him. "You're a very attractive man, actually."

"Honey," the Mountain said, "you have a sweet mouth. At times," he added after a moment's thought.

He parted some oleanders, poisonous and probably hallucinogenic if you could figure out how to use them; they're related to laurel, which was what the oracle at Delphi chewed before uttering her holy nonsense. From what I'd read of her advice, she was pretty stoned.

"Under there," the Mountain said.

I squinted into the dark. Hidden from view by the oleanders was a little hole that led under the fence, like the holes dogs dig to escape. Maybe it had been the dog that belonged to the little kid. Jessica could get through it. The Guitar Player, with his twenty-inch waist, could get through it. The Mountain certainly couldn't. For that matter, I wasn't sure I could.

"You're joking," I said.

"Oh, come on," Jessica said in her steeliest tone. "You're not going to quit now."

"You're not, are you?" said the Mountain. I might have imagined the menace in his voice, but it wasn't a theory I wanted to test.

"Of course not," I said immediately. "An involuntary ejaculation, devoid of meaning."

"I know about *those*," Jessica said.

"Well," I said, getting down on my hands and knees, "that's nothing to brag about."

Feeling fat and middle-aged, I started to wiggle under the fence. The smell of wet dirt was thick and heavy in my nostrils. Then the chain link grazed the back of my scalp, and I ducked. The taste of wet dirt made my nose superfluous. "Pfui," I said, feeling like Nero Wolfe. Jessica laughed. I found myself on the other side of the fence, looking out at them. "Come on," I said, looking at her. "If you're so smart, let's see you do it."

Well, of course, she did. "Piece of cake," she said, standing up and brushing herself off.

"Back there," the Mountain said, pointing. "Give him money. He'll tell you anything for money." He turned away and lumbered back up the street. Halfway up, he began to sing "Melancholy Baby."

"He's such a cutie," Jessica said as we skirted the remains of the blackened house. "I don't think all fat guys are unattractive."

"Oh, shut up," I whispered, recalling that one of the points of the exercise had been to scare her. She was less scared than I was.

Scraggly junipers lined the driveway on the left. To the right, ghost-ridden and black, was the skeleton of the house. The driveway was washing away from neglect, and I had turned my ankle twice by the time the garage rose in silhouette in front of us. Like the house, it was sagging. Unlike the house, it was intact. It was a two-car garage with a large single door. High in the door, two filthy panes of glass flickered in a jumpy fashion. Candles, I guessed, or maybe a kerosene lantern. Putting my finger to my lips to make sure that Jessica wasn't going to start a chat, I bent down, seized the handle in the center of the door, and yanked up.

The door shuddered, groaned metallically, and then jerked

itself upward, almost carrying me with it. "Ouch," I said, looking down at my scraped knuckle.

Inside the garage something scurried. It resolved itself into Donnie, traveling backward like a crab until his back hit a corner. "What the *fuck*," he said.

"You," I said, pointing at him. I spoiled some of the impact of the gesture by sucking on my knuckle. "Not a word until I say so. Where's the little girl?"

He sat crouched in the corner, rubbing his left forearm with his right hand. Closer up, his skin was sallow and no cleaner than it absolutely needed to be. There were half-moons of dirt beneath his fingernails. The nails on his right hand were longer than those on his left, and for the first time I realized that maybe he actually did play the guitar. After a moment he said, "Am I supposed to talk now?"

"I asked you a question, didn't I?"

He nodded.

"So talk."

"She got a trick," he said. "Some fat citizen in a Buick. He honked at us before we got off Santa Monica." His left eye had a minuscule twitch that made him look nervous and furtive.

"What's she going to do to him?" Jessica asked in a fascinated tone.

"I don't know," he said, noticing her for the first time. "Give him a blow-job, I suppose."

"Is that what the citizens usually want?" I said, closing the door behind us. With the door closed, the candles calmed down, and Donnie's multiple shadows gradually overlapped into one. It was a very skinny shadow.

"The easy ones," he said resentfully.

"Will he pay her?" Jessica asked.

"What are you, from Mars?" Donnie said. "Why do you think she does it, to keep her mouth in practice?"

"How much?" I said, for Jessica's benefit.

"Twenty, twenty-five. Maybe, if he's really stupid, fifty." He shifted his eyes from her to me. "You're the cop," he said accusingly.

"No, Donnie, I'm not a cop. I'm a private detective."

"Big difference," he said. But he sat up a little straighter. "How do you know my name?"

"*Twenty?*" Jessica said. Jessica spent twenty on gym shorts.

"It doesn't matter how I know your name," I said. "As long as you're straight with me, you've got no problem."

"Straight about what?"

"About her." I crossed the garage and held out the picture of Aimee. He ducked back as though he thought I was going to hit him, and then he slowly took the picture from my hand. He looked at it and then back at me, and something very much like a cash register clanged in his brain. His eyes slotted. "Never seen her," he said.

"How about a hundred dollars?" I said.

"How about five?" he said.

"Okay," I said. "Five dollars."

"Hold it," he said, standing up. "You said a hundred."

"And you bargained me down to five," I said. "Sit."

He sat. "Two hundred," he said sullenly.

"Fine," I said.

He looked startled and slightly regretful, as though he wished he'd asked for more. "Let me see the bread."

I took a couple of hundred-dollar bills out of my pocket and waved them around. The garage was lighted by only two candles, but they were bright enough for Donnie to register the denomination of the bills. He'd had practice seeing money in the dark. I handed them to Jessica, who looked vaguely alarmed. "She'll hold it," I said, "until we're through."

"Her name is Aimee," he said grudgingly, "but she calls herself Dorothy. Most of us call her Dottie."

"Good start," I said.

He gestured at Jessica. "Who's she?"

"You don't need to worry about that. She's obviously not a cop."

"She could make a fortune on the Boulevard," he said speculatively, every inch the young pimp in training.

"No, thanks," Jessica said at once.

He shrugged. "Up to you," he said.

I squatted down in front of him. "Listen, Donnie," I said. "You're going to tell me everything you know about her. If I find out later that anything you told me wasn't true, I'm going to sic the cops on you. After I break your nose and sit on your guitar. Are we clear?"

"Hey," he said, the picture of affronted innocence, "whatever you say."

I looked around the garage. It had been spray-painted black, and over the black, designs and graffiti had been sprayed freehand. One large graffito said FUCK THE CITIZENS (BUT NOT UNLESS YOU HAVE TO). Another one said HOME IS WHERE THE CHECK IS MAILED FROM. The ceiling was hazy with cobwebs and the air was sharp with the smell of mice.

The filthy, cracked concrete slab that served as a floor was largely bare, except for a cardboard box on which the candles guttered in motel ashtrays, a sleeping bag, and a rumpled heap of blankets. Donnie's imitation Stratocaster leaned upright in a corner. A plastic trash bag held a few items of girls' clothing and, on top of them, a small hair dryer.

"Tell me about Aimee," I said. Jessica sat on the sleeping bag, and I folded one of the blankets under me.

"Like what? What do you want to know?"

"Everything. Where'd you meet her? Where is she?"

"Can I smoke?"

"You can shoot speed for all I care."

"Got any?" He looked eager.

"Have a cigarette."

He lit up with a disappointed air. "I met her on the street," he said. "She'd hitched a ride with some truck driver."

"And?"

"And this faggot named Willie picked her up in the street and steered her to the Oki-Burger. You've seen Willie, he was there tonight. Real big and real black. Very popular with bankers."

"Skip Willie."

"You said to tell you everything."

"Everything about Aimee."

"Okay, okay. So Willie parked her in the Oki-Burger and I picked her up." He grinned at me, one male to another.

"You picked her up."

"Well, she needed somebody. She didn't know enough not to cross on the red."

"What did she tell you?"

"A whole bunch of shit at first, about how rich her father was and what a porker he was. Told me her name was Dorothy Gale. Well, come on, you know? I've seen *The Wizard of Oz*. We always watched it at Christmas when I was . . . when I was . . ." He faltered.

"When you were home," I said.

"Yeah," he said, glad to get past it. "Christmas TV dinner. Eat your crappy turkey and watch little Judy sing her heart out. What a dope. All she wanted to do was get away from home, and then all she wanted to do was get back. The only thing I liked—you know?—is when she opens the door of the house and it all turns to color. That's it."

"Merry Christmas," Jessica said.

"And a Happy Easter to you, too, sweetie," Donnie said. "I like the monkeys too. So anyways, Aimee didn't know anything. I had to show her which way was west."

"And you taught her how to hook," I said.

"Oh, skip it. What do you think she's going to do, be a chemist? She didn't want to, at first. Thought she was going to be a movie star. So I bought her a couple of burgers and then, the third time, I told her that it was on her. Well, she didn't have any money. Tough, I said. How do you think I get it? So I put her on the curb and took her wrist and stuck her thumb out, and a car stopped just like that. The guy wanted us both, so that made it easier for her. She had company, right?"

"Right," I said. "Company." Jessica shifted uneasily on her blanket but didn't say anything.

"So after that we were tight. Asshole only gave us twenty each. She cried for half an hour before I got her calmed down. Still, she never wanted to do it. Only when we didn't have anything, not a nickel. You can't even buy gum with a nickel." He took a drag from his cigarette.

"This is how long after she arrived?" I asked.

"Week, maybe ten days. But it was obvious that she wasn't sitting on no golden ass. Acted like she invented her tail and it was a military secret from the rest of the world. Nobody could buy a piece of it unless she was actually starving. And she could never learn to get the money first."

"That's important," I said.

"Bet your buns. Half the time some citizen in a Mercedes will pull in behind some supermarket or somewhere and let you do your job on him, and then when it's time to pay he pushes you out of the car and drives off, and there you are, on your ass on the asphalt. She had this problem asking for money. Very genteel chick. So after a while I gave up and taught her how to live in the mall."

"The mall?" I wasn't sure I'd heard him right.

"You know, the Centrum, over on Beverly."

"I know it."

"Well, it's perfect." He stubbed out his cigarette on the floor and looked at Jessica. "How about you give me one of the hundreds now?" he asked. "Since we been speaking of money, I mean."

"Give it to him," I said. She did, and he folded it into one-sixteenth squares and tucked it into his black leather rock-star jeans.

"The mall," he continued. "You know, it's heated and it's dry. And you move around from one store to another, hoping nobody looks at you too long. When they do, you move on. When it's time for everything to close, you roll under one of the rest benches and hope no guard finds you. If one does, you hope you can blow him and he'll leave you alone."

"And you usually can?"

"Sure. I mean, what are they? Bunch of rent-a-cops. For them, a blow-job is a passport to paradise."

"Tell me about the mall," I said.

"Well, for Queen Aimee it was the only place, what with her figuring her ass cost more per square inch than real estate at Malibu. They've got movies there, right? So that means it's open until midnight or later, and it means that the lower floors are pretty much empty after ten o'clock. So, like I said, you sleep under a bench until a guard finds you, and if you can't blow him you try to get into an elevator."

"An elevator," Jessica said.

"Sure. You can jam it between floors. So you bring an umbrella into a mall elevator and push the button for the top floor. Then, halfway between three and four or whatever, Aimee or somebody would shove the point of the umbrella in between the doors. Period. End of ride. The elevator sticks wherever you are, and we all go to sleep. Nice, clean, heated. Sometimes we'd spray something on the walls to make it ours."

"And this is what Aimee did?" I asked.

"Until she got her cop," he said.

I felt something that was doing a good imitation of fear roll over me. "Her cop?"

"Not a real cop, dummy. A rent-a-cop. Worked at the mall, at Robinson's. Little skinny guy with about as much life in him as a ham sandwich, but he was real horny. Guy would have fucked the crack of dawn if he could've reached it in time. Little guys are like that, you know?"

"Did he have a name?" I asked.

Donnie squinted. "Warner. Looked like a rope with clothes on. Like I said, though, horny."

"So Aimee met him," I prompted.

"Yeah, he wanted to throw us out. He found her and me under the bench outside Robinson's, I mean we figured we had it made for the night. Movies were out and everything.

Usually, if you can stay put until the movies are out, no problem. We'd even started to cuddle. Her and me loved to cuddle." He put up a hand. "Hey, you know," he said, "I'm no fag. I go with guys because it's usually guys who want me, but I loved Aimee. She was even more than family. I mean, even when she wouldn't trick, I helped her out."

"I'm sure you did," I said as gently as possible.

"Well, let's just keep things straight," he said with a little of his old bravado. "I ain't no faggot."

"Anyway," I said, "Warner didn't want you. He wanted her."

"Warner *loves* little girls. He just couldn't believe that Aimee was willing to do him. He looked so surprised while it was going on. I kept expecting him to pinch himself."

"You know Warner's last name?"

"That is his last name. He's the kind of guy always gets called by their last name. Probably his mother called him Warner. His first name," Donnie said, anticipating my question, "is Wayne. Wayne Warner. Is that lame or what?"

"Is he still working at Robinson's?"

"Naw." Donnie loosed a short, ugly laugh. "He got canned."

"Why?"

"Because of Aimee."

"What happened?"

"I'm getting to it. So that night, he wants to throw us out, but Aimee does him instead. She didn't want to, but she did. Right in the middle of Robinson's, in the Spanish Mediterranean living room. Big asshole couch with wooden feet. Real nice room. Better than the Sleep-Eze motel. That's where we stayed when we had the bread. They don't hassle you, or at least not much. Lot of coke dealers too. You know, they move in for a couple of nights, set up shop, and then move to another motel. Not the best neighbors, though."

"Why not?" That was Jessica.

"They got guns, and once in a while they like to shoot

them off. They got to shoot something off. Most of the time, they can't get it up."

Jessica sniffed in an offended fashion, defending Blister.

"All that blow," he continued, heedless. "Takes the life out of the old snake."

"Warner," I said.

"Sure. So he keeps her. Well, this is heaven for Aimee, you know? I mean, he's not Mr. Universe, but he's only one guy, and Aimee just doesn't like to do a lot of guys. And by then anyway she's not feeling so good. She's got stomach-aches and her hair is falling out a little bit. Maybe she's got the clap too, which would be pretty funny for old Warner, who's got a wife and eight or ten kids somewhere."

"She was sick?" I said.

"Sure. You can only live on catsup for so long, no matter what McDonald's says. She's got, like, you know, scurvy or something. All she wants is a bed and some oranges."

"What happened?" I said. "Did you split up?"

"What else could I do?" Donnie sat upright, spooked by something I hadn't heard, ready to run, and I started toward him. Then the garage door suddenly squealed open behind me, and I turned to see the little girl standing there, staring at me with frightened eyes. Before I could move, she backed away into the darkness.

"It's okay," Donnie called. "It's okay. They just want to know about Aimee. Look," he said, waving the hundred in the air. "They're even paying."

There was a long moment, and then she stepped back into the light. Her long matted hair hung in ropes over her oversize sweater. "Are you sure?" she said in a tiny voice.

Jessica got up. "Come in," she said. "I think I'm sitting on your bed, but there's room for both of us."

The two girls looked at each other and then Donnie's girl came slowly into the garage and shut the door behind her. Keeping her eyes fixed on me, she went to Donnie, fishing in the pockets of her sweater. "Look," she said, "fifty. We can go to the Sleep-Eze."

"We can go to the fucking Executive Suite," Donnie said. "You can take a two-hour bath and wash your hair. Hell, we can have room service. These guys are going to pay me two hundred."

"I don't have any shampoo." She lifted a tress of hair and sniffed at it.

"They got shampoo at the Executive Suite, stupid."

"Did you know Aimee?" I asked.

She turned the scared, luminous eyes to me. "No," she said, "but Donnie always talks about her."

"Apple knows all about Aimee," Donnie said proudly. "I told you I loved her."

"Apple?" Jessica said.

"It's Nora, really," Apple said. "But Donnie says I should never use my real name."

"Which you just did," Donnie said with some exasperation.

"But they're your friends," Apple said, bewildered. "Aren't they?"

"Yes," Jessica said, sitting down and plumping the sleeping bag with one hand. "Sit down."

"I didn't do anything wrong?" Apple asked Donnie.

"Forget it," Donnie said magnanimously. "Executive Suite, here we come."

Apple sat next to Jessica, giving her a microscopic smile. "The man was very nice," she said to Donnie.

"Listen," I said. "I know you two are anxious to get to the motel, so let's finish up. Tell me what happened with Warner."

"He got fired," Donnie said. "For about a week they slept every night in Robinson's. They chose a different room every night. They were all over the furniture department. Finally they had a party. He bought some red wine, and Aimee got drunk and spilled it all over this Santa Fe couch. It was white, naturally. It couldn't have been red, could it? That would have been too much to hope for. So he went to find something to clean it with, only it didn't work. He got real scared and threw her out. Next day he got fired. Aimee showed up at about four the next afternoon and slept here, and told me the whole thing. The day after that she packed up her stuff and left. And that was the last time I saw her."

I sat silent for a moment, trying to figure out the calendar.

"Can we go now?" Apple asked. "I'm all itchy." Jessica moved a fraction of an inch away from her.

"In a second," I said. "I don't suppose," I asked Donnie with no hope at all, "that you've got Warner's phone number?"

"Sure," Donnie said instantly. "When you meet a jerk that big, you get everything you can." He gazed at me, weighing his chances. "For another hundred," he said, "I'll send him to you."

11

The Sleep-Eze

The Sleep-Eze was a two-story stucco excrescence, air conditioners protruding from the windows of the rooms like technological tumors. Most of them were off, in deference to the wintry Easter climate, but a few pumped valiantly away. The motel was arranged in a U around the parking lot, and as we pulled Alice into a spot I looked up. Three of the twelve doors were open. In each of them, a very large man sat. Two of them were black and one was white. Dealers, waiting for business.

Jessica and I got out of the car and headed for the front office. You couldn't get into the front office. From behind a window made of about three inches of bulletproof Lucite, the old dame behind the counter accepted my credit card, took one look at Jessica, and demanded her I.D. I produced a twenty and handed it to her.

"Twenty," the old dame said, studying the bill. "She doesn't look that old."

"I've led a sheltered life," Jessica piped up.

The lady looked from her to me and back to her again, then made a clucking sound with her mouth. "Suit yourself, dearie," she said, "but I've had guys, they showed I.D.'s that said their girlfriend was a hundred. Name your price and get the cash first, if you know what's good for you, which I doubt."

"He's my godfather," Jessica said. "I trust him. Golly, he's friends with my daddy."

I summoned up a grin from some dim subterranean depth.

"And you," she said to me with a fearsome squint, "you oughta be ashamed of yourself." She was wearing what had to be the world's last muumuu.

"I'm going into therapy tomorrow. In the meantime, can I have a key?"

She shoved it through the little hole and snatched her hand back as though mine were Germ Warfare Central. "One-oh-five," she snarled, "all the way to the left." To Jessica she said, "If anyone knocks in the middle of the night, it'll be the cops."

Jessica wrapped both arms around herself. "Oh, good," she trilled. "I feel so safe."

I grabbed her by the sleeve of her blouse and yanked. "That's what I like," she said. "Forceful. Young guys are such wimps." She rolled her eyes. Lillian Gish couldn't have done it better.

"Someone's going to ask for her," I said to the old dame. "Her name is Aimee."

"Better and better," the gorgon said nastily.

"Just make sure he gets the right room," I said. I held up another twenty, and she started to reach under the plastic for it. I slapped her hand. "Ah-ah," I said. "Make sure the man finds her."

"That's what I mean," Jessica said to her, "he's so forceful."

When I had her outside, I pinched her arm. "You're overacting," I said.

"Yummy, yummy," she said, jerking her arm away, "another bruise." She lowered her voice. "How do you know no one's listening? Jeez-o-crips, look at all these windows."

"Just behave," I said in a whisper. "There are limits on how scummy I'm willing to feel."

"That's your problem. It wouldn't bother old Blister." I shut up.

The room was small, dirty, and painted that peculiar shade of pale green that's usually reserved for veterans' hospitals. Fluorescent tubes hummed, and a single queen-size bed offered shade for the cockroaches. Other than that, there was nothing but a chipped desk with a blotter, a ball-point pen, and a couple of dog-eared postcards advertising the glories of Hollywood.

"God," Jessica said, "it looks like they painted it with Linda Blair's leftover vomit." She surveyed the room critically. "That's got to be the john," she said, nodding at the far door, "and I get it first. Girls, you know. It has something to do with the relative length of the urethra. What do you think about the relative length of the urethra?"

"I think it means you go first," I said.

"I'm not real fast." She started to pull the door closed and then turned back to me. "I don't think this locks," she said.

"I'd be surprised if it did."

Fast she wasn't. Eight minutes later, when the knock sounded on the door, she was still inside. I went to the bathroom and rapped twice.

"Don't you *dare*," she said.

"Oh, for Christ's sake. He's here. You stay inside until he's gone."

"Okay," she said. "But if you get into trouble, I'm coming out."

"I can't tell you how much better that makes me feel." I tugged at the door once to make sure it was closed, and wiped my hands on my pants. They were wetter than I would have liked them to be. I hadn't counted on Jessica being around when I talked to someone who might have kidnapped Aimee Sorrell. On the way to the front door I stopped at the desk, picked up the ball-point pen in my left hand, and put it behind me.

He rapped at the door again, more urgently this time. A husky voice whispered, "Aimee?" I positioned myself on the hinged side, counted to three, and then pulled it open very fast.

"Yow," Wayne Warner said, stepping away. I reached out, grabbed his shoulder, and manhandled him into the room. Before he could say anything else, I slammed him

around, facefirst, into the wall—he didn't weigh very much—
and pushed the sharp end of the pen into his back, hard.

"Hey," he said. "Don't. Don't, please? I thought you
wanted to talk."

I pushed the pen a little harder into a spot just above his
left kidney and wiggled it. "I'm not a surgeon," I said, "but
I think I could get that kidney out if I had to. Can you get
along on one?"

"Holy Christ," he said. "I didn't do nothing. Holy Christ,
I can't stand knives."

"You didn't do nothing," I said. "You didn't do nothing
to Aimee Sorrell?"

"I gave her a hand."

"You gave her more than a hand, from what I've heard."

He was twitching. He was jiggling around like a bag of tics
held together by a belt, some buttons, and a zipper. I
wiggled the pen around some more.

"Hey, man," he said plaintively. "Don't do that. I'm
jumpier than a flea circus. I'm a nice guy, honest I am. She
was just too cute. There wasn't nothing I could do about it."

"Wayne," I said, "shut up. Now, put your arms above
your head, palms flat against the wall. Spread your fingers,
spread your legs. Not a word, now, you hear?"

He did as he was told, but his knees were shaking so
badly that I wasn't sure he could remain standing. He had a
breast pocket stuffed full of pens and, hanging from a loop
fastened through his belt, a pocketknife and a bunch of
keys. Other than that, the search told me nothing that I
didn't already know except that he wore knee-length white
socks, none too clean.

"Use your left hand," I said. "Reach down slowly and
unfasten the knife and give it to me."

"No problem," he said shakily. "No problem. Look, watch,
I'm doing it. You want cooperation? You got it."

"Good boy," I said as I heard the ring unsnap. "Now
hand it to me."

"You got it," he said breathlessly, extending his hand

behind him. I opened the knife and tossed the ball-point to the floor.

"Turn around," I said, "but slowly."

He did, trying to keep his hands up on the wall behind him. I heard one of his shoulder joints pop. "Relax," I said, waving the open knife under his nose. "No point in dislocating your shoulder."

"Thanks," he said, staring cross-eyed at the knife. "I do that from time to time. Hurts like a son of a bitch, too." He lowered his arms to his side and looked penitently up at me. I felt more like his confessor than his interrogator. He couldn't have weighed more than one hundred twenty pounds and he wore a wispy white little Ho Chi Minh goatee. An aging hipster: probably went home in the morning after work, smoked a little grass, played the Modern Jazz Quartet, and leafed through back issues of the *Evergreen Review*, looking for the juicy parts.

"Aren't you a sorry sight," I said.

"I used to be okay," he said.

"I'm sure you were," I said mercilessly. "I'm sure you used to be six-four, too."

"Aw, come on," he said, heartened by the fact that I hadn't killed him yet. "What kind of thing is that to say?"

"Sit on the bed," I said.

"Sure," he said. "I'll sit anywhere you like." He looked around the room. "Are we alone?"

"As alone as we're going to be." I pulled out the chair next to the desk and straddled it, facing him. I tapped for attention on the back of the chair with the knife blade. "Tell me about Aimee."

He swallowed, and his Adam's apple did a swan dive. "Why?"

"Wayne," I said, flourishing the knife. It was an improvement on the pen. "I can take out your kidney from the front too, you know."

"Yeah, sure," he said. "Aimee," he said. He was all jitters. His eyes shifted left to right and his knees bounced up and down. He seemed incapable of controlling the fluttering of his hands. They flew around him like demented butterflies. First they smoothed his hair, then they laid flat the wings of his collar, then they checked his buttons, and then they brushed the cloth of his trousers.

"The hands," I said. "Sit on them." I'd checked his hip pockets, but his hands were making me nervous.

"Sure," he said, following orders. "Look, I'm sitting on them."

With his hands imprisoned, the kinetic energy in his body jolted willfully through his other systems. His shoulders twitched as though they had an agenda of their own. He crossed his legs and then uncrossed them. His feet tapped on the floor.

"You're a very jumpy man," I said.

"Well, who wouldn't be?" he said with a pale attempt at defiance. "I get a call from some kid saying Aimee's here and then you stab me in the back, and all I was doing was having a good time."

"Wayne," I said. "You absolutely can't imagine what an asshole I think you are. Let's talk about your wife."

He retreated into himself, growing physically smaller, if possible, as he did so. "No," he said, "you win."

"Aimee," I prompted.

He sagged on the bed. With his hands under him he couldn't straighten himself. "She wanted it."

"She wanted someplace to sleep."

"Aaaah," he said, blinking. His eyelids were as thick as a lizard's. "She knew what she was doing."

"No, Wayne," I said. "You taught her what she was doing. You and some other respectable citizens. You know why she came to Hollywood? To become a star, that's why." I tested the edge of the knife against my thumb. "She really believed she could become a star. Isn't that a joke? To become a star."

"Well," he said, eyeing the knife, "maybe she will."

"What?" I said. "What does that mean?"

The bathroom door creaked.

"Hey," he said wildly. "I thought you said we were alone."

"I said we were as alone as we were going to be."

"Cops," he said, standing upright. "I don't have to be afraid of cops."

"Sit," I said.

"We're not cops," Jessica said.

He turned toward her and then to me. I was between him and the door, the knife in my hand. He gave her a long look, tried to make sense of it, and then gave up. "Who's she?" he said, pointing at Jessica.

"The Ghost of Christmas Past," I said. "Are you going to sit, or not?" He sat, doing a jitterbug of conflicting emotions. He pulled at the crease in his pants and he tugged at the wispy little beard. It stayed on.

"What do you mean, Aimee will be a star?" I asked.

"She got an agent," he said. He sat back down on the bed.

I didn't believe my ears. "An agent? What was his name?"

"I don't know," he said.

"What kind of an agent?"

"A kids' agent, what do you think?"

"How'd she find the agent?"

"Got the name from some kid, I guess. Jesus, I don't know."

"The name, Wayne."

"I told you. I don't remember." He brightened. "Some kind of vegetable."

"A vegetable?" I said, slicing through the air with the knife.

"A vegetable," Warner said. "Even if you cut me, I don't remember nothing more."

"That's good enough," Simeon," Jessica said.

"It's good enough when I say it's good enough. This little bedbug has a way to go yet." I got up from the chair. "This is going to hurt me more than it does you," I said, "although that's probably not true."

He squirmed back and finally fell full-length on the bed, his hands still trapped obediently behind him.

"Holy Jesus," he gasped. "I told you, I told you, I don't

remember. God, don't you think I'd tell you? I *hate* knives. What do you want from me?"

"Everything," I said.

"She was going to have her picture taken," he said with a burst of inspiration. "She told me she was going to have her picture taken."

"Did she tell you the photographer's name?"

"Yes. I mean, no. I mean, yes, but I'm no fucking good with names. Holy Jesus, I told you this much, why wouldn't I tell you the name?"

It was a good point. "I sure hope you keep this knife sharp, Wayne," I said. "Where was the photographer?"

"Somewhere on Melrose. She said Melrose. Near here, probably."

"And the agent?"

"I don't remember. Please, can I go home now?" He was wringing wet.

"The agent's name, Wayne."

"I told you. Holy Jesus, I told you. Some kind of vegetable."

I looked at Jessica, who was watching openmouthed, and closed the knife.

"Some kind of vegetable," I said.

12

The Halls of Academe

An hour later Jessica had talked to Annie and Wyatt, and I'd been hung up on by my parents and Roxanne. My mother had sworn at me with Irish creativity, and Roxanne had made me listen to a page being torn out of her phone book.

"You know my number by heart," I'd said unwisely.

"I didn't before," she said, "and now I won't again." That was when she'd hung up.

Jessica was sitting on the bed, regarding me as though I were someone new. The business with the knife had impressed her, and not in a way I'd hoped to impress her.

"Mad, huh?" she said.

"Madder than Qaddafi."

"Who?"

"Jessica, don't you know anything?"

She sat back, stung. "He's that greaser in the Gulf," she said. "I just needed to think for a second."

"Well, think for a minute more. When I get back, we'll have a quiz on the politics of the Mediterranean." I got up and went out the door.

"Hey," she said plaintively as the door closed, "don't leave me alone." It was a little late in the day for plaintive.

The old dame in the Lucite fortress stared up at me disbelievingly. It had only taken eight rings on the bell to get her to turn away from a late-night rerun of *Wheel of Fortune*, the last three minutes of which I'd watched over

126

her shoulder on a tiny black-and-white TV so old that it probably ran on steam.

"Another room?" she repeated as though I were crazy.

"Another," I said very slowly. "Room."

"You mean, two?" she said.

I sighed and held up two fingers. Verbal communication was getting me nowhere.

"Full up," she said, as pleased as her place in life made it possible for her to be. "Where's my twenty?" She grinned, showing me a raddled picket fence of decaying calcium with much potential for expensive dental work.

"Waiting for a room key."

"You already got a room key."

"Yes, I do," I said wearily, "and I need another."

"Can't have one," she snapped. "No vacancy."

"In this rathole?"

"My twenty," she said, looking over her shoulder at the TV. "I could rent your room too," she added. "Rent it five times by sunup. Rats or no rats." She gave me the ruined teeth again, like a preview of a mine collapse in West Virginia.

"But you'd have to stop watching Vanna," I said, tearing my gaze from the dental disaster area and up to her fierce little eyes.

"She's over in a few minutes. The twenty. I don't get it, I call the cops. They'd love the Little Woman." She infected both words with a kind of swampy, virulent meaning.

"What about a roll-away?" I said.

"The twenty."

I gave it to her. There was nothing else to do.

"Don't got no roll-aways," she said maliciously. "The kids we get here, they sleep with the adults." She went back to *The Wheel of Fortune*.

"It's 'To be or not to be,' " I said, to spoil the game. The only things missing were the vowels.

"Awww," she said, exhaling decay. "I was just about to get it."

I went back to the room. The prospect of a one-hour

drive to Topanga loomed unpromisingly before me. I needed an early start in the morning, and I wanted Jessica with me for at least the first half of the day.

The Little Woman was flat on her stomach on the bed, writing a postcard with the pen I'd used to terrorize Wayne Warner.

"Who's that to?" I said.

"Blister," she replied, none too clearly. Her tongue was wedged in the corner of her mouth.

"Well, forget it," I said. "Or finish it in the car. Anyway, I doubt that he can read."

She sat up. "The car? Where are we going?"

"Home."

"Oh, Simeon," she said, giving it an extra half-octave. "You promised we could sleep in town."

"That was a lie," I said. "We detectives lie a lot."

"But *why*?" She was working up to a daughterly wail. "Why can't we?"

"Because we can't get another room."

She wriggled fitfully around on the bed, grabbing fistfuls of fabric. Then she pulled herself up to a full sitting position and threw the bedspread at me. "No problem," she said. "Look, there's even another pillow." She threw that at me too. A corner of the pillow slip caught me in the eye.

"Peachy," I said, wiping away a tear.

"Take the towels from the bathroom," she said with the unemotional assurance of a hired expert. "You can sleep on top of them. They're pretty clean."

Considering the loss of time involved in going home, I got up and went into the bathroom for the pillows. "Don't be in there too long," she called. "I may need it again."

"What do you do, Jessica," I said, "draw moisture from the atmosphere? Have you got gills or something?"

"You just don't know anything about girls," she bellowed. I grabbed all the available linen, left the bathroom, and went into the other room, where I laid the towels on the floor, end to end. They had holes in them. I dropped the washcloths over the holes in the sad little arrangement I'd made, and put the pillow at the top. "If you did," she continued implacably, "you wouldn't have let that snotty one hang up on you."

"And what should I have done?" I asked, just for form's sake, getting up to turn off the lights.

There were contented little burrowing sounds from the bed. "I can't tell you," she said airily. "You either know or you don't."

Reflecting that I obviously didn't, I tried to get comfortable on the linoleum. My hip bones seemed determined to inflict internal injuries at the slightest provocation. If *I did* know anything about women, I thought, Eleanor and I might still be together. In what already promised to become an eternal quest for a comfortable position, I turned around so that I faced the window. The Sleep-Eze's extravagantly large neon sign blinked in my eyes. I was being bombarded by fuchsia photons and serenaded by sound waves from motorbikes. It was like trying to sleep in a microwave oven. Nevertheless, I dropped off into a Technicolor doze.

I had barely begun a bright tropical dream, based loosely on the upholstery in the Sorrells' hotel suite, when two very loud shots broke the night into splinters, and I found myself sitting bolt upright, grabbing for a gun that I didn't have. There was a rustle from the bed.

"It's the dealers," Jessica said. "Remember?"

"Swell," I said. "The walls in this place are made out of Saltines."

"Oh," she said dismissively, "don't be an old lady."

I lay down again and tried to get comfortable. A moment later I heard the bed rustle again.

"Simeon?" Jessica said, sitting up. "You know what? This is *fun*."

The next morning, after Jessica called Annie to assure her that she was alive and well, and I had brushed my teeth with my index finger and scratched at the whiskers sprouting in the folds of my neck, we drove Alice across town to UCLA. I introduced Jessica to the dragon who guarded the towels in the women's gym so she could take a sauna and a shower, and I slogged to the men's gym to tend to my own needs.

An hour later I was in the Powell Library, looking at the only book I could think of that might lead me to the name of Aimee's agent. Jessica, her hair still wet from her shower, was sublimating her impatience by breathing over my shoulder. "*He's* cute," she said, indicating a malnourished juvenile with a tennis racket over his shoulder. The book was the *Actors' Directory*, published by the same folks who impose the Academy Awards upon you each year.

"Don't you know any word but 'cute'?" I asked offensively. "He's cute, Donnie's cute, even the Mountain's cute. Try something different. 'Lissome,' maybe, or 'earthy.' If you use the same word to mean everything, it doesn't mean anything at all."

"He's cute," she said again. "*You're* earthy. I'm lissome," she added as an afterthought.

"Kale," I said.

"What?"

"Write it down. Homer Kale Agency, 9255 Sunset. He represents this little creep," I said, pointing at her cutie. I'd deputized her to take notes as a way to keep her fidgeting from distracting the scholars.

"Kale is a vegetable?"

"It's like okra. Or maybe not."

"Yuk," she said deep in her throat. "Okra is nauseating."

"Well, Mr. Kale may be too. Just write it down. And try not to stick your tongue out when you write."

"I don't stick my tongue out," she said, sticking her tongue out. She wrote his name and address on her pad. It was only the third entry on the page after half an hour of scanning the "Juveniles" section for agents whose names sounded like vegetables. We already had a Leaf and a Green.

"I think Green is stretching it," she said, referring to the second name on the pad.

"Jessica, there's no delicate way to say this, but I don't

really care what you think." I was flipping through the pages. I'd finally gotten to the section on girls.

"God, you wake up grumpy."

"And so would you, if you'd slept on the floor."

"The bed was no bargain. I think there was a pea under the mattress."

"At least it didn't have legs," I said. "I was the only one on the towels who didn't have an exoskeleton."

"Oh," she said, her impatience flowering, "speak English."

"Shhh," someone said near us. Jessica favored him with the glare that had wilted Tammy in the Oki-Burger. I turned to a new page.

"I don't believe this," I said.

"Shhh," the scholar said again.

"You must have no powers of concentration at all," Jessica said loudly. The scholar quailed visibly and retreated to his book. "You don't believe what?" she said to me.

"This," I said. "Marjorie Brussels."

"Brussels is a place," Jessica said.

"Her agency," I said. "It extends the threshold of the gag reflex. It's called Brussels' Sprouts."

"Skunks and cabbages," Jessica said, writing. "That's worse than okra."

13

Ten Percent for Starters

Mr. Leaf was wispy and tremulous and saturated with failures, Mrs. Green was large and black, and Mr. Kale was slimier than okra, and a lot greener. Mr. Leaf and Mrs. Green had been all too obviously on the up-and-up, mostly because they both insisted on seeing my bona fides. I didn't have any bona fides, which was part of the point. Mr. Leaf had thrown up his hands and Mrs. Green had ejected us in a rather forceful fashion. We'd moved on to Mr. Kale. The day, as they say, was still young, and three is popularly supposed to be the charm.

"My, my," Mr. Kale kept saying, glancing furtively at Jessica. "My, my. What a lovely child." Three notwithstanding, Mr. Kale was no charm. He was small and olive and balding and threadbare, and one of his nostrils was twice as large as the other. The small one was pretty big. He wore loafers without socks to capitalize on his resemblance, from the ankles down, to Don Johnson.

"What's your standard arrangement?" I said. He was awful enough to qualify for serious consideration.

"Your regular agent gets ten percent," he said, making a visible effort to wrench his eyes from Jessica to me. If it had made a noise it would have sounded like Velcro ripping. "But I'm not your regular agent. What we have here is a total package. Agent, manager, all in one. Image, training, preparation, representation, what-have-you. 'No representation without preparation,' that's our motto. Complete career guidance for the little thespian."

"*I beg* your pardon," Jessica said, straightening up as though she'd slipped her toe into a socket.

"*The*spian," I said correctively, "*thes*pian."

"She'll need head shots," Mr. Kale said, gazing longingly at her.

"Sounds like a fatal wound," Jessica said, her nose still out of joint.

"Can you recommend a photographer?"

"Best in the business," Mr. Kale said promptly. "Nothing but the best, that's our motto." The motto apparently didn't extend to his office, which was smaller than Blister's sinuses.

"So what's your percentage?" Jessica asked meanly.

"Twenty-five," he said with a negligent little hand gesture. "Plus expenses."

"Who's the photographer?" I said, putting my foot on top of Jessica's.

"Ah-ah," he said, chiding me in a leaden fashion. The relatively smaller of his nostrils flared unappealingly. "Papers first." Whimsy was not his strong suit. It was hard to imagine what might be. The room swam in front of me.

"Mr. Okra," I said, without thinking. Jessica made a snicking noise and spit her gum into her lap.

"Okra?" he said, looking bewildered. "Who's Okra? Kale's the name, Homer Kale."

"Mr. Kale," I amended. "We can't do business unless we know you're really top-notch. What's the photographer's name?"

He gave me a con man's look, full of honesty and candor. The man could have dealt three-card monte one-handed. "Fink," he said. "Norman Fink."

Jessica gave up searching her lap for her gum, threw up her hands, and just laughed. "This is the *pits*," she said.

"Jewel," I said, "shut up. On Melrose?" I asked Mr. Kale.

It was over for Jessica. *"Jewel?"* she said, choking. "Excuse me." She got up and left the office. I heard her laughter even after the door closed.

"Excitable little girl," Mr. Kale said, licking his lips with a tongue a Komodo Dragon would have envied. "But lovely." He wiped his brow. He was wearing more rings than I would have thought he could have lifted.

"On Melrose?" I said again.

"Naw," he said, waving the rings at me. "Way down. South. On Olympic."

I got up. "Mr. Kale," I said. "You'll hear from us."

"It *could* be on Melrose," Mr. Kale said, sounding surprised. "You want Melrose, maybe I could find one on Melrose." I let the door swing closed while he was still speaking. Outside, I grabbed Jessica by the elbow and marched her into the daylight.

Brussels' Sprouts was something else again. It occupied the entire lower floor of a two-story ersatz Greek building tucked just above Sunset on Sunset Plaza. Doric columns guarded the door like erect concrete watchdogs. The door whispered inward as we stepped on the mat in front of it. The mat had little blue and yellow puppies frisking on it.

"Shit," Jessica said, looking down at the mat. Air conditioning rolled over us through the open door.

"Try Jeez-o-crips," I suggested. "You're a little girl here."

She gave me an arch look. "I'm a little girl everywhere. Ask my mom."

"Yessss?" someone hissed. It sounded like Kaaa the Python in *The Jungle Book*.

"Where are you?" I said defensively. The sheer sibilance of it unnerved me.

"Over here," the someone said as I blinked into the dark. "Behind the desk."

"Jeez-o-crips," Jessica said obediently as the door closed behind us.

The waiting room was bigger than the *Niña* and the *Pinta* combined. As my eyes adjusted to the gloom I saw that its walls were lined with enormous black-and-white photographs, pictures of the kind of little kids who go through life just begging for a pie in the face. They had freckles. They had missing teeth. They had straw in their hair. They featured suspenders, gingham neckerchiefs, and catcher's mitts. One or two had a burnt-cork black eye. All in all, they were about as cute as an advanced case of bubonic plague, but less contagious.

"Oh, good, you've got the door closed. May I help you?" the voice said.

The voice belonged to a tiny man in the kind of pleated linen shirt that's been popular for inexplicable decades in the Philippines. He was seated behind a big desk at the far corner of the office. No, I decided, he was standing. He had a pinched little face, topped off by a widow's peak that was pronounced enough to symbolize all the wives bereaved by World War One. He also had very hairy forearms. Short as he was, he could have traded forearms with Bluto, and Bluto wouldn't have noticed the difference. On top of it all was the kind of haircut that a friend of mine had dubbed turban renewal: to cover the fact that he was balding on top, he'd grown the hair on the back of his head about a yard long and combed it forward. It sat on his forehead like a knickknack shelf from which someone had stolen the knickknacks.

"Help me?" I said. Jessica nudged me. "Of course you can help me. We'd like to see Miss Brussels."

"Mrs. Brussels," he hissed. The phrase offered a lot of opportunity for hissing.

"Well, sure," I said, feeling larger than I was by about two feet. His widow's peak hit me at the nipples. "That's what I said. Mrs. Brussels."

He gave me a bright, cockeyed little bird's stare. "You didn't, of course," he said. "What you said was *Miss*. Have you got an appointment?"

"Yes," Jessica said bravely.

"No," I said.

"Darlings," he said, "make up your *minds*. I always have a headache on Mondays. You could be a tumor or you could be an aspirin. Personally, of course, I'd rather you were an aspirin. For one thing, you can get a refund on aspirin."

"No," I said, taking the frank, honest approach. "We don't have an appointment."

"Well," he said, looking at a book in front of him, "of course you realize that Mondays are very busy."

"You'll be Birdie," I said, reading the nameplate on his desk. That's what it said, Birdie. Other than the nameplate and the appointment book, which was the size of the average aircraft carrier, the desk was nearly barren. At one end of it stood a computer terminal, swiveled so that the screen was turned away from us.

"I'll be Birdie when the headache fades," he said. "Until then I'll just be miserable. What would your business be with Mrs. Brussels?"

"This little darling here," I said. "We're looking for representation."

"Are we," he said. "You realize that the usual method is to make an appointment first."

"You couldn't see her on the phone," I said. "You might have said no. So we decided to take a chance. Make a dimple, darling," I said to Jessica.

Jessica put one finger to her cheek and smirked terribly. "My name is Jewel," she said in a passable imitation of a Chinese singsong girl.

"She sings and dances," I said. "Acts, too. Acts up a storm."

"Not here, *please*," Birdie said. "Save it for Mrs. B. If you'll just take a seat, I'll inquire as to the state of her calendar."

"It's in California," Jessica said.

"Quick-witted, too," Birdie said acidly. "Just what Johnny Carson is looking for." He pushed a button under his desk and the door behind him slid open. "It's *so* Flash Gordon, isn't it?" he said, leaving us. He couldn't have been more than five-four, and he waddled.

"Put you in your place, didn't he, Jewel?" Jewel collapsed resentfully onto a couch, and I took a closer look at Birdie's desk. It was empty of any personal touches except for a Lucite frame holding a color picture of a little Yorkshire terrier, a breed I've always despised. "Purse dogs," a friend of mine calls them, "society ladies put them in their purses to bite anyone who tries to steal their wallet." There was also a little plaster-of-paris paperweight with the impression of a tiny dog's paw pressed into it. Below the paw, it said in shaky pencil, "Woofers, June 1988."

I swiveled the computer workscreen toward me. I was looking at some kind of data base, a single record. IDAHO, it said, and then the date. FINGERS: 2000 ORDERS. Then there were a couple of names, followed by five-digit numbers. LAST REQUEST: the screen said: FINGERS: 1200 ORDERS. SPECIAL ORDERS: it said: PAGE DOWN. Lacking the nerve to push PAGE DOWN because I wasn't sure I could get back to the first record, I swiveled the screen back into its original position. "Fingers are a boom market in Idaho," I said.

"They've got a lot to give the finger to in Idaho," Jessica said from a maroon plush couch where she was staring in dismay at a copy of *Jack and Jill* magazine. " 'PeeWee to Marry,' " she read aloud. "Who the hell is PeeWee?"

I ignored her. Most of the furniture in the waiting room was half-size, perfect for children. Toys glimmered in the corners like the refuse of an overenthusiastic Christmas. There were wooden ducks with pull-ropes for the newly mobile and, at the other end of the spectrum, electronic baseball games and computerized time-wasters that were *Star Wars* ripoffs. Most of the books and magazines were profusely illustrated with pictures of squirrels and other sanctioned rodents wearing hairbows and bow ties.

"Well," I said, folding myself into a chair so small that my knees hit my chin, "isn't this nice?"

"Simeon," Jessica said, "you look like a paper clip."

"Call me Dwight," I said. "You Jewel, me Dwight, okay?"

"You ridiculous," she said, giving up on *Jack and Jill*. "Can't you find someplace else to sit?"

"Jewel. Try to behave. This could be the place."

She sat up, looking apprehensive. "Really? Why?"

The room didn't seem to be miked, and I couldn't see a hidden camera, but that didn't mean there wasn't one. Anyway, I wasn't sure I could explain why. I reached over affectionately and pinched her wrist, hard enough to get her attention. "For your career, Jewel," I said, between my teeth, "this looks like the big time."

"Bug time, you mean," she said. I pinched her harder. *"Yowk,"* she said. "Okay, okay. If it looks good to you, Dwight, it looks good to me."

We passed what seemed like a decade in silence, if you didn't count the electronic beeps of a *Star Wars* game, which Jessica beat the bejesus out of in three consecutive passes. The phone blinked eight or nine times, but it was answered from inside. "They design these for cretins," Jessica said, tossing the game aside.

"There's nothing wrong with Crete, honey," Birdie said, coming back into the room. The door sighed closed behind him. "Very lovely, all mountains and ocean and fishermen."

"Oceans and fishermen usually go together," Jessica said sourly.

"Well," Birdie said archly, seating himself, "there are fishermen and fishermen."

"They all smell like fish," Jessica said.

"What're you, a lactovegetarian?" Birdie asked, exposing a nasty streak and half an inch of swollen gum.

"Will she see us?" I asked.

"A few minutes," he said, pulling himself up to the computer and tapping a couple of keys. "She's on the phone now." He looked over at the instrument on his desk. "She's on *three* phones," he said proudly.

"She must have a lot of ears," Jessica said.

"Witty child," Birdie said, staring at the computer screen. "Perhaps you'll excuse me."

With my face partially hidden by Jessica's discarded edition of *Jack and Jill*, I watched Birdie futzing around with the computer. What I saw was a middle-aged male secretary, a homosexual member of the lost generation, the last generation that was uncomfortable with the idea of coming out of the closet. I saw a prissy, probably obsessively neat little man who went through life feeling short-sheeted, a man who counted his change in supermarkets and felt grieved when it was right, a man who doubted the advertised beef content of wieners. Presented with a bill in a restaurant, he would have added it twice and then fudged on the tip. His party lost the election. His disposable razors wore out too soon. He never had enough money. Handed the daughter of the Pork King, he might have looked on her as a one-way airline ticket to Crete. The question was, who the hell was Mrs. Brussels?

He caught me staring twice and smiled in happy misunderstanding. I smiled back. We were getting along great. The phone rang a few more times, and he weeded out the unwanted from the wanted callers in a voice that had all the regret of a funeral director learning that the client was dead. Finally, his phone buzzed discreetly, and he rose the four inches that marked the difference between his sitting and standing heights and rubbed his hands in the best Uriah Heep imitation I'd seen in months.

"She'll see you now," he said.

"Just don't tell us to walk this way," Jessica said unwisely. "I don't think I could do it."

"Honey," Birdie said, but this time he said it to me, "you're going to earn your money." We followed him through the Flash Gordon door.

Mrs. Brussels stood up to greet us. Her suit was brilliantly tailored, but it had nothing on her manner. "Mr. Ward," she said, echoing the name I'd given to Birdie, "and this is Jewel. Jewel Ward?" she asked.

"Not actually," I said, choosing the larger of the two chairs in front of her desk. The other was sized for a child, and Jessica climbed grumpily into it. "Jewel Smith," I said.

"Smith," she said, sitting down. "Jewel Smith. We'll have to do something about that. If we come to an arrangement, of course." She gave me a radiant smile, and I gave her the best I had in return.

"How did you get my name, if you don't mind my asking?" she asked, beaming with democratic impartiality on both Jessica and me.

"Through the *Actors' Directory*."

The smile went a little rigid and her gaze wavered. "How ingenious. How did you ever think of doing that?" She was sitting up straighter than she had been a moment earlier.

"A friend suggested it."

"A friend," she said with the same smile fixed in place. It did nothing to her eyes. "Is he in the business?"

"He's a teacher," I said.

"What level does he teach?" It was a question I hadn't anticipated.

"College," I improvised.

She blinked at me. For the first time since we'd entered the room I felt that she was at a loss for words. Something, for her, didn't add up, and she didn't know where to go next.

"It makes good sense," I said, to fill the silence. "Where else could you go through pages of kids and get their agents' names and addresses?"

"At least," she said, relaxing slightly, "you can find out who's active." I still had the feeling that she was watching me, but I had no idea why.

"And you can see what kinds of kids they've got and how good the photographs are," I said, trying to figure out what was going on. "You can see whether you've heard of any of their clients. It can tell you a lot."

She sat back in her chair. "I suppose it can," she said noncommittally. "Of course, many of my clients are featured in the directory. Most of them are doing very well indeed. I must say, fortune has looked favorably on our little enterprise in the last three or four years." Whatever had caused the uncomfortable moment, it had passed.

"That's why we're here," I said. I had placed the emotionless smile. She had something of the third-grade teacher about her, the one who could smile at you while she was explaining why you weren't going to see fourth grade within your expected lifetime.

"It's unusual," she continued, as though I hadn't spoken, "for me to see anyone who hasn't made an appointment.

But Birdie explained your reasoning to me, and he also told me what a remarkably beautiful little lady you've brought with you." She glimmered at Jessica, who gave her a cool nod. Jessica, as I was beginning to realize, had good taste. Dismissing her lack of responsiveness, Mrs. Brussels said, "She reminds me of the young Margaret O'Brien."

"She has skills," I said, "that Margaret O'Brien never heard of." Jessica gave me a quick, evil look.

"I'll stipulate that she's talented," Mrs. Brussels said comfortably.

"What's 'stipulate'?" Jessica said suspiciously. She still hadn't gotten over being called a thespian.

"It's lawyer talk, sweetie," Mrs. Brussels said. "It means that I'm willing to believe that you've got talent."

"You haven't seen me do anything," Jessica said, dimpling again. It had been her least attractive skill at the age of four. I hadn't seen it since.

"Mind of her own," Mrs. Brussels observed.

"You don't know the half of it," I replied.

"At any rate, talent is mainly a matter of training. It can be learned. What can't be learned, what's much rarer, is beauty and, of course, presence. This little girl has a great deal of presence." She gave Jessica a look that dared her to voice a contradiction. Mrs. Brussels had practiced little mid-forties laugh crinkles around her eyes, fine bones, a full lower lip, all topped off by a mass of auburn hair held up by a few pins arranged in an oddly Victorian fashion. Wisps of fine hair framed her face. She looked like Colleen Dewhurst playing Colleen Dewhurst. There was a little too much flesh under the skin, but not so much that it kept swinging back and forth after she'd finished shaking her head. Once I got past the image of the terrible third-grade teacher, she reminded me of nothing so much as the prettiest of all my elementary school friends' mothers. I had gone to his house largely to see her.

Jessica acknowledged the challenge with a disdainful sniff. Maybe she just resented being called a little girl.

"She's very special," I said. I paused before the word "special."

"And you're her what?"

"She's my ward," I said.

"Like your name," she said brightly. "Ward."

"Exactly," I said. "Isn't that a coincidence?"

"It certainly is," she said, watching me with an entirely new expression.

Jessica, feeling excluded, began to fidget.

"You're legal?" Mrs. Brussels said.

"Well, Mommy and Daddy aren't here."

"They could show up," she said, one hand under her chin. "Where are they, anyway?"

Jessica heard her cue. "They're dead," she said.

"Is that so?" Mrs. Brussels said, her face turning into a postcard of sympathy. "That's terrible."

"Oh, golly," Jessica said, "you don't know how I cried." I was proud of her; she resisted the impulse to wring her hands.

"And now"—Mrs. Brussels in her most motherly tones—"you have no one but Mr. Ward, here." Her eyes, when she turned them to me, were older than rocks.

Jessica looked at me proudly. "He's all I need," she said. "He's wonderful."

"They died in Idaho," I said. "A car wreck."

"What a sad story," Mrs. Brussels said perfunctorily. "And you said you were her legal guardian?"

"Legal enough," I said.

"Because there are contracts," she said.

I looked at Jessica, who had withdrawn into herself. She was sitting on her hands like Wayne Warner.

"And are you willing for her to travel?" Mrs. Brussels said in the tone I would have used to ask if it were sunny. And why not? If I was right about her, and I was sure I was, all we were talking about was the Mann Act.

"I'm a frequent flier," Jessica said remotely.

"What a delightful child," Mrs. Brussels said. Her voice sounded like a knife being sharpened on a whetstone. "So precocious. I'm sure we can work something out, Mr. Ward. There are the standard papers, of course. Nothing special, all to your benefit and little Jewel's. Perhaps we could draw them up overnight and you could come in tomorrow and sign them. You and Jewel, I mean."

"Sure," I said. "Be delighted. Call me Dwight."

"And where are you staying? Since you've just come here from Idaho, I mean."

"The Sleep-Eze Motel," I said, "on Melrose."

She gave me the crinkly smile. "Nice place," she said. She directed a glance toward the computer terminal on her desk, which had just whirred and beeped. Eyes on the screen, she tucked a wisp of hair behind her ear. "And now," she added, "I have work to do." Without looking up from the computer, she extended a hand to me, ignoring Jessica completely. "We're going to do just fine," she said. "Great career. Come tomorrow, tennish? Birdie will show you out."

"Tennish," I said.

Birdie showed us out.

In the parking lot, Jessica tugged at my hand. "That woman is a snake," she said. "What was the big deal about the *Actors' Directory*? She acted like you'd goosed her."

"Jessica," I said, "I think you've got a future in this line of work."

She got into the car, sat back, and glowed.

14

Through the Keyhole

"What's the name this time?" asked the old bat at the Sleep-Eze as she took my money. I had told her that we'd be expecting phone calls.

"Ward," I said, "Dwight Ward. And this is my little ward, Jewel."

She glared down at Jessica. "There ought to be a law," she said, dropping the bills into a drawer.

"There is," I said, "and you're breaking it."

Jessica had stopped glowing by the time she got home. I dropped her, figuratively kicking and squealing, at her parents' house. Annie leaned in through the car window long enough to ask whether she was okay.

Jessica dispelled whatever doubt there might have been. "Hey, Mom," she said, stomping toward the house as though she weighed a thousand pounds, "count my arms and legs, would you?" She didn't want me to go anywhere without her.

At home, I spent several damp hours making notes on the Sleep-Eze's purloined stationery and then painstakingly tapping them into my computer. The roof was leaking. There was something about the sight of my notes on paper that reawakened my collegiate faith in the much-vaunted and probably overrated human ability to solve problems. I flipped off the computer, tossed the stationery onto the floor, and went out and watered the garden, which didn't need it. Time passed slowly. I was waiting for dark.

On the drive into town, I indulged my latest crankiness by dialing from station to station to listen to what the traffic reporters were doing to the English language. Where, I wondered, was the linguistic equivalent of the antivivisectionist league? Motorists who were "transitioning" from the Hollywood Freeway onto the Five would find an accident "working" in the right lanes. Working at what? I'd seen accidents, and as far as I could tell, they were just accidenting. CHP was "rolling," and the whole mess would, I was told, cause slowing "for you." And only for you, apparently. Who says we live in an impersonal world?

I got off the freeway and cut north into Hollywood. Even on a Monday night Santa Monica Boulevard was cramped and crawling, due largely to scavenger driving as solo male motorists eyed the kids on the street. I angled up onto Fountain so I could pass the Oki-Burger, and slowed down, along with most of the other male drivers, to take a look. No Aimee.

I hadn't expected her to be there, of course, or on the curb near Jack's either, although that's where Junko was. Her black hair spilled over her white blouse as she divided her attention between a parked and bearded biker and the oncoming traffic. Keeping her eye on the main chance, wherever it might come from. She looked jumpy, trying for alluring. Her pimp was nowhere in sight.

I stopped at Computerland and bought a bag full of blank disks, both the five-and-a-quarter-inch versions and the little three-and-a-half-inch ones. I had no way of knowing which I would need. I hadn't paid enough attention. I also bought a DOS diskette, just in case I couldn't find Birdie's. Then, to kill time, I drove past both Jack's and the Oki-Burger again. No Aimee this time either, and no Junko. She'd gotten a customer.

At precisely nine-fifteen I walked briskly into the lobby of Mr. Kale's building, nodded in a businesslike fashion at the night guard, an undersize specimen with a telltale scarlet nose that Jim-Beamed up at me beneath the visor on his cap, and headed for the elevator.

Some years back, when I decided to ignore everyone's advice and go into this line of work, I did something that many a smart crook has done before and since: I apprenticed myself to a locksmith, a lovely old guy named Zack Withers. In four months I'd learned that most locks aren't worth the space they take up in a door, and that the bigger and more massive they are, the less they're usually worth.

Mr. Kale's were worse than most. A careful man, he'd installed three. I could have unlocked, relocked, and unlocked them again all evening long without being able to decide which was the most worthless. I felt like the Big Bad Wolf. Even if I hadn't quit smoking, I could have blown the door down.

Once inside, I closed the door behind me and took off the World War One aviator's scarf I had draped jauntily around my neck. I stuffed it against the crack at the bottom of the door and then turned on the lights.

Except for the fact that I had no real idea what I was looking for, I was in fine shape. The office, without a little sunlight shouldering its way through the two dirty windows, was even tinier and more depressing than I remembered it. I started with the desk and had gotten through most of it when the phone rang. I watched it with the attention I usually reserve for poisonous snakes until, on the fifth ring, a cheap machine on the desk emitted a click, and Mr. Kale's voice wormed forth.

"You've reached the headquarters of Kale International," it said. "We're sorry, but all our offices are closed. Please leave a message at the tone. If this is urgent, call 555-1366." So I had Mr. Kale's home phone. As I wrote it down I listened to a disgruntled parent complain that when his little Jeannie went to her audition that afternoon she'd been told that it had been held a week ago. "I could have read *Drama-Logue*," the man said, "and learned that. What are we paying you for, anyway?" Wondering what *Drama-Logue* was, I finished with the desk and went to the files.

The files were an archaeological theme park of pederasty, *Kiddie World*, full of bits and pieces of the curling fringes of twentieth-century life, the disconnected fragments and potsherds of a peculiarly twisted version of the American dream. It was like F.A.O. Schwarz in reverse; for more than two hundred years people had been coming to America to make it big, but not until recently had they hoped to make it big on the backs of their children. Before I opened the second drawer, I went to the photocopier and turned it on. I copied the most perverse documents and photographs out of sheer acquisitiveness, even though they contained nothing about Aimee Sorrell. By the time I left, I was carrying a stack of photocopies that was thicker than the West Hollywood Yellow Pages' section on florists.

There was a burglar alarm at Brussels' Sprouts, but it was junkier than Kale's locks. It required a short walk to a Seven-Eleven on Sunset, run by a family of Thais, for a little Scotch tape to keep the terminals together. The youngest daughter of the Thai family sold me the tape with a blinding smile. If an Anglo tried to duplicate that smile, he'd sprain both cheeks.

The tape was older and less sticky than I might have wanted it to be, but it, plus about two feet of copper wire out of Alice's trunk, did the job. With the alarm silenced, I opened the door in less time than it takes a twelve-year-old to shave. Stuffing my scarf under the door and feeling like I'd just won the lottery, I fumbled around in the darkness for the light switch and failed to find it. Using a flashlight instead, I went to Birdie's desk and pressed the button on its underside that opened the Flash Gordon door.

No deal. No access to Mrs. Ming the Merciless.

So why was it no deal? There had to be a master switch somewhere, and it had to be on my side of the door. Otherwise, Mrs. Brussels, whoever she might actually be, couldn't have gotten in in the morning.

I looked everywhere. Squinting along the flashlight's beam, I lifted the cushions of the couch. I pried up the corners of the rug. I even risked going back outside and peeling up the doormat. Then I ran my hands over the wallpaper, looking for a little bulge. The one or two I found, I pressed without any payoff. Probably cockroaches caught in the glue.

When you can't get what you want, I reasoned, settle for what you can get. I went to Birdie's desk and looked at his phone. It was a technological miracle, full of what the people who sell you phones like to refer to as "extra features." Down its right-hand side were sixteen auto-redial buttons. In other words, jackpot.

Touch-tone technology has turned the telephone system into music: every number that you press sounds a different note. A phone number is like a musical snowflake, in that no two are alike. I pressed a pocket tape recorder against the earpiece of the phone and pushed each of the redial buttons in turn. When the beep pattern had sounded, I hung up and went to the next button. After about a minute I had them all on tape. Then I turned my attention to the reason I had come in the first place.

The computer was nothing special, an IBM clone. I pulled it around so I could fool with the keys and switched it on. A little bit late, I thought about disks. NONSYSTEM DISK OR DRIVE ERROR, the screen signaled me. INSERT SYSTEM DISK AND PRESS ANY KEY.

A disk holder was stashed in the third drawer down on the right. I pulled out the DOS diskette I'd bought and put it in. When the A Prompt blinked at me, I put another of the disks into the B drive. DIR B: I typed.

The machine whirred and the screen lit up with a long list of meaningless file names. I pulled the DOS disk out of drive A and inserted one of my own, one of the ones I'd bought at Computerland, in its place. Then I typed COPY B:*.* A:. In human talk, that meant copy everything on the disk in the B drive onto the disk in the A drive.

After some whirring and some beeping, the machine told me that the disk I'd inserted wasn't formatted. I should have known that. A computer disk is like a long-playing record without any grooves until you format it. Only then can it figure out into which grooves it should place the information you're copying onto it. I put the DOS diskette back into drive A and formatted all the disks I'd bought at Computer-land. Then I repeated the steps that told the machine to copy everything on disk A onto disk B.

It took nine of the ten disks I'd bought to copy the contents of Birdie's diskette file. Then, just to make sure, I copied his DOS diskette, which I found in the back of the holder, as well. DOS doesn't take up an entire diskette, and who knew what else he had hidden there? I finished up by labeling all the diskettes. Birdie had just numbered them, one through nine plus DOS, so I copied his system. Then I put back everything I'd touched.

With the diskettes tucked back into the box I'd bought them in, a thick square of cold hard cardboard pressing up against my stomach beneath the belt of my jeans, I went over the office again in search of the secret passkey to the Flash Gordon door. Still no deal. Feeling defeated, I went back out through the front and into the fog of the evening.

L.A. glittered at me like the jewels in the Seven Dwarfs' mine as I drove back west toward the ocean. Somewhere out there, socked away among the semiprecious stones, was Aimee Sorrell. Or maybe not. What had Mrs. Brussels asked me about Jessica? Was she free to travel? Something like that. Travel how far? I wondered. Rio? Japan? Saudi Arabia? The white slave trade, I knew, extended into all the black, brown, yellow, and coffee-colored countries. And into the white countries as well.

Great, I thought as I killed Alice at the foot of my driveway and climbed up the hill, I'd eliminated none of the world's continents except Antarctica. And if anyone lived on Antarctica, it would still be on my list. Good work.

When I opened the door of my house, it was just as I'd left it, only colder. I pulled a sixteen-ounce bottle of Singha out of the refrigerator, and sat down in my only chair, feeling sorry for Aimee, and a little sorry for myself. Coyotes howled in the distance, and I went out onto the deck and howled back. The clouds had cleared briefly and the full moon shone down like a cue for Lon Chaney Jr. to appear and start mumbling. I was *absolutely* getting a little old for all this, I thought. I'd gone back inside to put the diskettes into the computer when I noticed that the light on the answering machine was blinking. If Eleanor had been in America, or anyplace closer than Nanjing, China, I would have noticed it earlier. I always checked the machine when Eleanor was around.

I pushed the button marked Replay. First came some garbage: a tape-recorded voice asking me whether I had ever thought about gold futures, followed by a kid who asked me if my refrigerator were running. I skipped the part where he (or she) told me that I'd better go out into the street and chase it, and got Mrs. Sorrell's voice.

"Mr. Grist?" it said. "Are you home?" The voice waited, and in the background I could hear horns honking. "If not," she said, "just listen to me. Stop looking for Aimee. Don't do anything more. Just forget it. Send me a bill. If you have to talk to me about this, don't call at night. And don't do *anything*, do you hear me? It's all going to be all right. I've paid the ransom, and it's all going to be all right."

She hung up. I took the plastic box of diskettes out of the front of my pants and tossed it onto the floor, next to the wadded-up motel stationery. So she'd paid the ransom, I thought, knocking back about three inches of Singha. So it's going to be all right.

Somehow, I didn't think so.

15

Perfect Pitch

"Don't you listen?" she snapped, long-distance from Kansas City. She sounded like Aurora's imitation of an adult talking to a child. "I said that you weren't to do anything." I'd awakened late, but even in Kansas it was only noon, so it was safe for me to call: the Pork King couldn't be home.

"You paid the ransom," I said. "What does that mean?"

"It means that I mailed the money. Please, Mr. Grist, just send me a bill and forget about it."

"Mailed it?" I asked. I was pretty sure that she was speaking English, but to me it didn't make any more cognitive sense than running water. "Mailed it where?"

"To an address he gave me. In Los Angeles. Now, please, leave us alone."

"Hold it, hold it," I said. "Park and idle for a minute. He gave you an *address*?"

"Yes."

"In Los Angeles."

"I believe I just said so."

"Mrs. Sorrell," I said. I was developing a headache. "Kidnappers don't give out their addresses."

"This one did," she said in the tone of a threatened child. "Ask Aurora."

"I don't want to ask Aurora. Aurora's a kid and Aimee's her sister. What do you mean, he gave you an address? Was it a he?" I asked, backtracking.

151

"You heard him on the tape. And when I say he gave me an address, I mean a number and a street and a zip code, all the things that usually make up an address."

"What is it?"

"I'm not going to tell you that," she said. "Just send me a bill."

"How long are you supposed to wait?"

"Four days. Aimee will be home in four days."

"She won't," I said, without thinking.

"Oh, yes she will. And listen, you, don't do anything. This is my daughter's life you're fooling around with." She hung up. When I called back there was no answer. I noodled around with the phone for a few minutes, dialing numbers at random and hanging up when they started to ring. I didn't like any of it, and I needed to do something meaningless while my subconscious sorted it out and came up with something for me to do.

So I didn't have a client anymore. So bill the client. I made out a bill for a few days' work, addressed it, remembered to add the receipts from the Sleep-Eze, and slogged down the unpaved muddy driveway to the mailbox. I raised the red flag to get the attention of my brain-damaged mailman. Then I stuck the letter halfway out and closed the mailbox on it to get a little more of his attention. After twenty years of sizzling his neurons with anything he could buy cheap, his attention needed a lot of getting.

So, there. I'd done something.

The house, as usual, was a mess. I sort of cleaned it, wondering how Eleanor was, all those watery miles away in China. Then I went outside and sort of weeded my root garden. The radishes looked good; you can't discourage a radish. The onions were up, and the potatoes were probably rotting after the cold snap and the rain. I dug one out, and it looked fine. Little, but fine. It wasn't something you could put back, so I went inside and washed and sliced it. Then I fried it in butter for a few minutes and wrapped it into the center of a nice breakfast omelet. Then I threw the omelet away. I hate breakfast.

So *now* what was I supposed to do? I made some more coffee that I didn't want and sat around, counting my toes through my shoes. When I got to ten for the second time, I remembered that I was scheduled to see Mrs. Brussels at ten, or tennish, or something. I called to cancel.

"We've been trying and *trying* to reach you at the motel," Birdie said waspishly. "They said you weren't there."

"And we're not," I said. "We're at the Free Clinic. Jewel has the flu."

"Oh, my God," Birdie gasped, "and she was in here only yesterday."

"She's okay," I said.

"Who cares about *her*?" Birdie said. "She was probably absolutely redolent with germs. That's why the flu spreads, you know, because you're most contagious before the symptoms appear. I hope it's not one that dogs can get."

"In fact," I said spitefully, "it is. It's called the Bowser flu. It's decimated the canine population of Hong Kong."

"Oh, heavens. Poor Woofers. I'll have to wear a surgical mask when I get home. That *will* upset her. She loves to see me smile."

"Whatever you do, don't smile. This virus coats the surface of the teeth. A smile could be lethal. You'll know she's got it if her tail starts to droop."

"My baby," he said. "I'll tell Mrs. B. that you won't be in." He hung up.

The moment I hung up, Jessica called. I told her nothing was doing. She sounded disappointed, but she mastered it. Youth is resilient. I'm not sure what's supposed to be so great about being resilient.

There was a time in my life when I enjoyed having nothing to do. There was also a time in my life when I smoked two packs a day and my idea of exercise was reading a digital watch. It was the only thing I did that took two hands. In those days, I'd weighed more than two hundred pounds. Eleanor had changed all that. She'd gotten my beer consumption under control, helped me to cut out the cigarettes, and gotten me running. My first quarter of a mile had been sheer agony, wheezing and limping behind her while she encouraged me in a bright and completely stress-less voice. "Positive reinforcement," she called it. It was only the view of the back of her gym shorts that kept me going. Six months later I weighed one-eighty and was doing six or seven miles at a time. I had actual muscles. I bought new clothes. Women smiled at me on the street.

Unfortunately, with health came energy. I could no longer sit still. So here I was with a day, or four, on my hands. An hour in, and both my feet were tapping.

Jessica called again. "Maybe we could *make* something happen," she said brightly.

"No way. We're on hold for four days."

"There must be something I can do. I'm going crazy sitting here. Simeon, if we don't do *something*, this is going to be the longest Easter vacation of my life."

"Can you vacuum?"

"What's that, a joke?"

"We can clean house," I said. "They didn't say anything about cleaning house."

"Heck," she said before she hung up. "I'd rather do my math."

I sort of washed the dishes. Then, probably in order to avoid sort of drying them, I realized that there was actually quite a lot I could do, without Aimee's kidnapper knowing anything about it.

I cleared a space on the living-room floor and went through Mr. Kale's files, a sheet of paper at a time, without much hope. My pessimism was rewarded. There were many good reasons why he should never be elected president of the Girls' Club of America, but there wasn't anything that linked him to Aimee. I made a note to turn the files over to Hammond and then dumped them into a box.

Okay, concentrate on Mrs. Brussels. I got the little tape recorder I'd taken with me when I broke into her office and played back the tones of the phone numbers I'd lifted off Birdie's auto-redial telephone. I listened to all of them about ten times but they went by too fast to do anything about, so I scrounged around in a closet until I came up with an old semiprofessional reel-to-reel that an aspiring rock singer had left there after she and I stopped seeing each other and she decided that being a secretary was steadier. I recorded the tones at three and three-quarters inches per second and played them back at seven and a half. They still went by too fast, but at least now there was some tape space between them.

Using a pair of rusty scissors and the roll of Scotch tape I'd bought to silence Mrs. Brussels' alarm, I cut into each of the spaces between the tones and inserted a few inches of blank recording tape. Manual dexterity is not my strong point, but eventually I had a nice long pause after each tone. I had also invented a few profane expressions that I could use later to please and impress my friends. Hauling the contraption over to the phone, I went to work.

The procedure was simple: One, crank the recorder back down to three and three-quarters, then play a tone and stop the recorder. Two, hit a number on the touch-pad of the phone. Three, when it didn't sound right, rewind, play the tone again, and hit the next number. When I found the matching tone on the telephone at last, I wrote down the number on a pad and went on to the next tone on the tape. After three or four hours of mind-numbing boredom, I'd developed perfect pitch for all the tones from one to zero, I had a blister on my index finger, and sixteen phone numbers were scribbled on my pad. Three of them were outside the 213 area code. Hot damn, I thought, I really am a detective.

By then I was on my eighth cup of coffee and more wired than a marionette. I switched to beer to calm down and dialed the first of the numbers.

"Doggies Do," said a fey voice on the other end of the line.

I coughed a little beer onto the mouthpiece of the phone. "I beg your pardon?"

"Doggies Do," the voice said, sounding a tad peevish. I'd have been peevish too, if I'd had to say it twice.

I took a wild conjectural leap. "I'm calling about a dog," I said.

"I certainly hope so. If you're not, I'm wasting my time. What is it you want?"

"Well, I was hoping you'd tell me about your services."

"Wash, dry, curl, manicure, dip," he said automatically. "Perms require advance notice."

"Perms."

"Permanents, you know? Permanent *waves*, silly. If your dog needs a permanets, you've got to call forty-eight hours in advance. Got it?"

"Thanks," I said. "She's a Mexican hairless, but I'll keep it in mind." I hung up. The next number on the pad was a veterinarian's office. The one after that was a dog hotel, the Bark 'n Wag. Woofers had more appointments than a producer's wife. What I had burgled, apparently, was a Yorkshire terrier's Rolodex.

The fourth number rang forever. The fifth was a disconnect. The sixth was Birdie's colonic therapist. I was not on a hot streak. I worked on the beer for a while and then went back to the phone.

The seventh, just maybe, was something. It rang twice and then a gruff male voice said, "Cap'n's."

For lack of anything better, I asked, "Is the captain there?"

There was a long pause, and then the man said, "You've got the wrong number," and hung up. When I called back, the phone was off the hook. On the whole, I thought, a very odd exchange.

One more disconnect. Then no answer. Then, on number ten, one of the ones with an out-of-state area code, I got a different man, but the same greeting.

"Cap'n's," he said.

"Which captain?"

I listened to the cosmic whistle of long distance. "Who is this, anyway?" the man asked.

This time I was ready. "I'm calling for the National Naval Census. We've gotten up to captains."

"How did you get this number?"

"I told you, I'm calling—"

He disconnected. I tried another out-of-state number. "Cap'n's," a new man said. This time *I* hung up. A small revenge, but mine own.

My, my, my, I thought. I may even have said it out loud. Captains, or, rather, Cap'ns, all over the landscape. Where were all the people who answered the phones when I punched up these numbers? Hammond could have given me addresses, but I figured that calling the cops was out of bounds until Mrs. Sorrell said it was okay. However remote I thought Aimee's chances of getting home standing up might be, I didn't want to do anything to jeopardize them.

What I could do, though, was check the area codes with the operator. One of the Captains was in Arizona, one was in Idaho, and the third was in L.A. It was beginning to sound like the First Interstate Bank.

"Your phone has been busy *forever*," Jessica complained when I picked it up on the third ring. "Are you working?" She sounded aggrieved and suspicious.

"Looking for a job," I said.

"You *have* a job."

"Jessica," I said, "this has been a memorable partnership, but for the moment it's over."

"*Treat* me like a baby," she said bitterly. "I thought we were getting to be friends."

"As soon as there's anything you can help me with, I'll let you know."

"In other words, don't call me, I'll call you."

"Something like that."

"Yeah, well, maybe I'll be at Blister's."

"Great idea," I said. "You can bench-press his nose."

"You are totally gross," she said, hanging up.

I tried the remaining numbers and got nothing. There was something else I wanted to do, but it would have to wait until Hollywood's nocturnal population crawled out from under their paving stones. In the meantime, there were the computer disks.

The disks, unfortunately, seemed to be garbage. Every time I tried to find my way into them, I got a bunch of mathematical symbols that looked like a physicist's guess at the perfect universal symmetry that might or might not have existed a millisecond or so before the Big Bang. They booted up okay, but after one or two keystrokes I found myself looking at all that garbled math.

A computer whiz is something I've never claimed to be. I bought the Korean-made micro that takes up most of my desk in a misguidedly upbeat moment after a client had overpaid me almost to the point of sarcasm. That was a couple of years ago, when everybody who claimed to be an expert on the future was talking about the electronic world: people working at home and shooting messages and data back and forth like a bunch of wash hung on a line that traveled at the speed of light. Well, that hadn't happened. Despite the experts, people still wrote in longhand and talked on the phone. The U.S. postal service was still in business. And me, I'd learned to work a simple word-processing program to the point where I could type in my case notes and print them out, and I'd mastered Flight Simulator. I could now land an imaginary airplane at an imaginary airport. Neither of these accomplishments had prepared me for the mathematically coded chaos of Birdie's disks.

Nevertheless, I went through all ten of them, including the one I'd labeled DOS. DOS is short for disk operating system, and it's what you feed the computer first. Until it's digested DOS, you might as well stick your fingers in the drive and ask for a readout on your prints. In short, without DOS, the computer is just something you have to dust. It can't do anything.

Birdie's DOS diskette was the first clue that something was intentionally wrong. You're supposed to put DOS in and then turn the goddamned machine on. After some beeping and some blinking, the screen gives you an enigmatic symbol that looks like this: A>. Then you can load whatever program you want and tell the computer what to do. If you're lucky and if you know what you're doing, it'll behave.

I'd used my own DOS diskette to look at the disks numbered one through nine, and I'd gotten the mathematical salad. In a flash of inspiration, I shut the computer off and slipped in Birdie's DOS diskette. Maybe it was a different DOS, I reasoned. Maybe it could make sense of numbers one through nine.

But when I turned the computer on and hit Enter twice, as I'd learned to do, the reassuring A> was nowhere in sight. Instead, I got a message that said: DISK ERROR OR NONSYSTEM DISK. INSERT SYSTEM DISK AND PRESS ANY KEY.

I'd seen that before, and recently: on the screen of Birdie's computer, when I'd forgotten to put a DOS diskette in before firing up the computer. When I'd worked on Birdie's computer I'd used the DOS I'd bought. And that meant that Birdie's DOS diskette wasn't really DOS. Like the other nine disks, it was written in some kind of computer code.

There was nothing to do but try my own DOS diskette again. As before, I got a few words of English before the screen dissolved into the kind of mathematics that gives high-school kids zits. But this time, I noticed the message at the bottom of the screen. It said: DISK FULL.

Well, that was peculiar, because I'd already done a directory on that disk, and the computer had told me that there was lots of space left. When you do a directory, you just type DIR, and the screen fills up with the names of the files or documents that are taking up space on the disk, and at the bottom is a number that tells you how much space remains. I did it again now. According to the directory, there was enough space left on the disk for a biography of Leo Tolstoy. Tolstoy lived to be eighty-two.

But when I went back into the English and tried to type a word or two, I got the DISK FULL message again. What that meant, in plain English, was that I was in over my head. Whatever the hell was on the disk had been hidden somehow, and it would require someone a lot more conversant with the perverse ways of computers to figure out what was going on.

The problem was, I didn't know anyone more conversant with computers than I was. Most of my friends said a cheerful good-bye to technology in the early seventies, about the time they noticed that most airplanes didn't have propellers anymore. They regarded computers as Big Brother's uncle.

I had just discovered a new use for mine—resting my head on the keyboard—when the phone rang. It was, for the ninth or tenth time that day, Jessica.

"Any progress?" she said, making an easy assumption that I'd been lying to her since morning.

It seemed pointless to tell another one. "What I am," I said, "is stonewalled. Find a new godfather."

"I like the one I've got," she said a trifle shyly. "What's the problem?"

"The information revolution."

"Computers?" she said promptly.

"Exactly."

"You need help with computers?"

"You've grasped the challenge."

"What time is it?"

"Around seven."

"Come over," she said. "Bring your problem. Have I got a boy for you."

16

Slipped Disks

Coyotes were beginning to wow and flutter at the rising moon when we pulled off Old Topanga Canyon and up a driveway that was almost as vertical as mine. This one, though, was wide and graded and nicely paved, with stone Japanese lanterns blinking every ten feet to tell you when you were about to drive off the cliff.

"New money," I said. Topanga has been a freaks' refuge for decades, and anyone with *any* kind of money is new money.

"Pull to the right at the top of the hill," Jessica said. "There's room for a hundred cars."

The house was cedar and pine, a rambling affair that had a view of the lights of the San Fernando Valley off to the northeast. The door was opened by a nice-looking woman in her middle thirties in blue jeans and a man's ruffled tuxedo shirt. She had a glass of red wine in her hand, and her feet were bare. One of the Mozart horn concerti made its way, sweetly geometrical, from speakers somewhere in the house.

"Hello, Jessica," she said, blowing back a lock of hair.

"Hi, Mrs. Gurstein," Jessica said. "Morris knows we're coming."

Mrs. Gurstein gave me a politely inquisitive glance, and Jessica said, "This is my godfather, Simeon. He's too old to understand computers. Morris is going to help him out."

"Elise Gurstein," Elise Gurstein said, holding out a hand and stepping aside to let us in. I took the hand. "If Morris

161

can't help you, no one can. Would you like a glass of wine?"

"Wouldn't I?" I said.

"You're the detective," she said. "Ho, and then ho again. I know Annie. We're both on the PTA. She's told me more about you than you'd like to have in the papers. Coke, Jessica? Are you hungry?"

"Mom," a little girl's voice said from around the corner. "They're not hungry. They've got things to do."

The little girl hove into view behind her mother and turned into a little boy, maybe Jessica's age chronologically. Boys, as I learned in excruciating slow motion in junior high school, mature more slowly than girls. Also more awkwardly. This little boy had made it all the way into awkward hyperspace. He had a long, narrow head, carrot-colored hair with an unmanageable cowlick that seemed to bring his skull to a point, a fringe of fine, pale eyelashes, and thin, high shoulders. His shirt was buttoned at the neck and his khaki pants had a crease in them that was straighter than a plumb line. He gave Jessica what was supposed to be a casual glance and blushed to the roots of his hair. "Hi, Jessica," he said. He barely got it out.

"Hey, Morris," Jessica said negligently. "Ready to go?"

Morris swallowed. "All set up," he said, trying for her casual air. He gave me a red little glance that reeked of jealousy.

"No food, then," Elise Gurstein said. "I'll bring you some wine in a minute. All I've got is cabernet."

"Cabernet is fine."

"And a Coke for little Jessica."

"Mom," Morris squealed in an agony of embarrassment.

"Fine, fine. Then I'll leave you to Morris."

Morris, his hands thrust deep into his pockets, led us broodingly through a living room filled with modern, or maybe postmodern, shapes: hard-looking rectangles of white that probably posed as furniture as long as people were awake and then turned into giant sugar cubes. Mozart winged its way around the room, and what looked like copies of

Klee and Kathe Kollwitz hung coolly on the wall. Thirties art and eighties furniture. Jessica touched my arm and pointed at Morris' rear end: he had a patch on the rump of his pants that featured a bright red apple and the legend TAKE A BYTE. He led us down a flight of stairs.

At the bottom, Morris—who hadn't looked back at either of us—threw open a door, and we entered a room that was lit by the shade of green they painted Margaret Hamilton's face in *The Wizard of Oz*. The light, as I saw when I entered, came from three computer screens, all up and glowing.

The screens were only part of the picture. Computers, or parts of computers, were everywhere: on the floor, in the middle of the mussed-up single bed, on the big desk that had been made from a door and two sawhorses, and stacked on top of the filing closets that lined one wall.

"Floppies or flippies?" Morris asked, gazing in a preoccupied fashion at one of the screens. It was tossing up a frantic jumble of data, scrolling past far too fast to read.

"Beg pardon?" I asked.

"Floppies," Morris said, closing his eyes with the air of a man whose patience is being tried, "or flippies?"

"These," I said, holding up the disks.

"Floppies," Morris said with modulated disdain. "Nobody uses them anymore."

"I stole them," I said defensively. "I just want to know what's on them."

"What's all this stuff?" Jessica asked, watching the screen with the flying data.

"The Yellow Pages," Morris said in a completely different tone. If it was possible to say the words "The Yellow Pages" in a tone of abject adoration, Morris had just managed it.

"You copied the Yellow Pages into a *computer*?" Jessica sounded like she doubted her ears.

"It's a test," Morris said, licking nervously at his lower lip. "I've been working with a scanner—you know, it reads a page and feeds it into the system?—and I thought I'd try to link it up with a data base. So I scanned about two hundred pages of the Yellow Pages, and reworked them into the data-base language and told the data base to rearrange them, by length of entry instead of alphabetically. I'll know in an hour or so whether it works."

"Why bother?" Jessica said, moving on to the next screen.

"Just to see if I can do it," Morris said, giving a tiny shrug. He looked at the flashing screen with new doubt. "I'll work out an application later."

"Even if you can do it, what good is it?" Jessica said loftily. "Who wants a phone book arranged by the length of the name? You know, Morris, that's one of the things that's wrong with you. There's enough junk to learn without making up new stuff." She sat down on the edge of the bed, pushing aside something that was probably vital to some computer in the room, and looked around her with the disinterested air of a deaf person who'd been dragged to a concert.

Morris swallowed the rebuke in silence, but then he reached down and twisted a knob that plunged the offending screen into darkness. He chewed on his lip as the silence lengthened.

"My, my," I said heartily, looking at a large pair of apparently extraterrestrial landscapes on the wall, an oddly colorless mountain and a shoreline, jumbles of rocks and natural forms, as lifeless as the moon. "Where are these?"

Morris wasn't buying peacemaking from anyone he was jealous of. "To the extent that they're anywhere," he said tartly, "they're in Benoit Mandelbrot's frontal lobe."

"Old Bennie," I said. "I knew they looked familiar."

"They're fractal landscapes," Morris continued, ignoring me, "computer-generated mathematical pictures that approximate the natural world. Only less sloppy."

"I like the world 'sloppy,' " Jessica said. "I don't want some egghead turning it into a bunch of numbers. What *good* is it?"

"It helps us to understand the world," Morris said doggedly, looking everywhere but at her.

"Ah, we've gotten to fractals," Elise Gurstein said, coming into the room with a glass of red wine in one hand and a Coke in the other.

"I don't know why everybody has to *understand* everything," Jessica said defiantly. "Why can't we just leave things alone? Can't I like a blue sky without someone like you explaining to me that it's because the air scatters the light waves? When I go body-surfing, do you think I need some schnook in goggles swimming along next to me telling me about the movement of liquids?"

"But you don't understand *anything*," Morris insisted, holding his ground. His color had heightened, making his eyes even paler. "Don't you want to know how things work?"

"See you," Elise Gurstein said, leaving the room. "I've heard all this."

"I can start a car," Jessica said silkily, turning her hazel eyes on Morris. "I can go shopping. I can read a map and use a calculator and turn on a television set. I can find something in a library if I need to. What else do I need to know?"

Morris gave an exaggerated Gilbert-and-Sullivan shrug, as though he were rolling the weight of the entire globe from one shoulder to another. "Nothing," he said with a finality that would have been impressive in anything but a soprano. "Just nothing. You're doing great."

"There are *already* people who know all the stuff you're talking about. That's their job. Haven't you heard, Morris? It's called specialization."

"You want to know what's wrong with the world?" Morris said to me. "Attitudes like that."

"Oh, talk to each other," Jessica snarled. "You're both so much smarter than me." She lay back on the bed, rolled over, and faced the wall.

"Than I," Morris said, looking longingly at her back.

"Find the appropriate orifice, Morris," Jessica said, plumping one of Morris' wrinkled pillows and curling herself around the computer.

"Listen," I said, "this could go on all night." I waved the disks in the air. "The floppies."

"I'm not sure Morris is interested in the floppies," Jessica said to the wall.

"Of course I'm interested," Morris said, shamefaced.

"Then do something, Morris," Jessica said in a voice that was pure saccharine. "Show us what a genius you are. Who knows, maybe you'll inspire me to learn something myself."

Morris wedged his hands back into his pockets and then realized that I was holding the disks out. He pulled out one hand with some difficulty and took them from me. "What are they?" he said.

"Some kind of code. It looks like algorithms or something. Lots of numbers and calculus signs. Some stuff that looks like Greek."

"Hmmm," Morris said, slipping one disk into the drive of the nearest computer. He sat down on a stool and peered at the screen. "You don't know what language they're in?"

"The beginning is English," I said.

He was tapping the keys. "What computer language, I mean."

"Well," I said, feeling dumb again, "no."

"There are only so many," he said. He banged at the keys faster than Horowitz doing scales and looked at the result on the screen. It was the same junk I'd seen.

"Who knows?" he said to himself. Seated at the keyboard, he was back in his element. He yanked out the first one and slid in the next. "What are these numbers on the labels?" he asked.

"I don't know. I just copied the numbers on the originals."

He looked up at me. "These aren't the originals?"

"I told you, I stole them," I said. "If I'd taken the originals, they'd have missed them."

I heard Jessica draw in her breath behind me. "Simeon," she said, "you mean, they're—"

"It doesn't matter where they came from," I said quickly. "Morris doesn't need to know where I got them to figure out what they are."

Morris gave me a glance that was full of curiosity. "That depends," he said. "Are they from some kind of scientific facility?"

"No."

"Math? Computer specialists?"

"Nothing like that."

"Well," he said, looking back to the screen, "they're specialized somehow. Are they all like this?"

"I don't know if they're identical. All I know is that they all come up in English when you boot them, and then they turn into gibberish. Also, they seem to have lots of space on them when you do a directory, but after you type a few words into the English part they come up with a DISK FULL message."

"Very interesting," Morris said. "Very, *very* interesting. Some kind of hidden files, then. Or else somebody's just balled them up."

"I don't think so," I said. "I think whoever created them knew exactly what he was doing."

"Or she," Jessica said. She was sitting up on the bed now, staring at the screen as Morris tried some more wizardry.

"Let's assume you're right," he said, tapping away. "Let's assume that somebody has hidden information on these things. What do you think it is?"

"Illegal," Jessica said.

"No, I mean, what kind of application? Is it language, or math, or what?"

"I think it's some kind of data base," I said.

"Well," Morris said, looking at me as though I were a performing monkey who wasn't performing very well, "why didn't you say so?" He moved crablike across the room on the stool, which, I saw, had wheels, and pulled open a drawer in one of the filing cabinets. "Data bases," he said, gesturing at the drawer.

It was absolutely jammed with bootlegged software, stacks of photocopied manuals wedged in every which way, sandwiched between disks. He grabbed a handful of disks and wheeled back to the computer. "This could take a while," he said.

I sat down on the bed, next to Jessica. For forty-five minutes or so, Morris tried one program after another, humming happily to himself. It was like watching submarine races. I had absolutely no idea what was happening. Jessica dozed off, emitting zippery little snores.

"This is pretty neat," Morris said at last.

Jessica started and opened her eyes. "What is it?" I asked.

"That's what's neat," Morris said. "I haven't got the faintest idea." Jessica made a small groaning sound. "It's pretty cute, though, whatever it is," Morris said, his eyes glued to the screen.

I looked at my watch. It was almost nine, and I had somewhere to go. "Can I leave them with you?" I asked.

"Sure, sure," Morris said without looking around at me. "I'll call you when I figure it out. Maybe tomorrow sometime."

I stood up, and Jessica stood next to me, yawning. "Don't bother leaving your number," Morris said. "I'll get it from Jessica when I need it." He darted an anxious look at her and then turned back to the screen. He was clacking away at the keys when we left the room.

"Nice guy," I said as I started the car.

"You and my mother," Jessica said. "He'd be great if his voice didn't break windows. He makes me feel like I'm singing bass."

"Women," I said. "Lift up, would you?"

She hoisted her bottom from the seat and I grabbed the army blanket she'd been sitting on and threw it into the back. I'd brought it down from the house when I left. I planned to use it later in the evening.

"What's that for?" Jessica asked, looking back at it.

"It's an army blanket," I said, shifting into reverse. "I'm thinking about joining the army."

"Are you going somewhere?" She settled back down into the seat as Alice's headlights illuminated the driveway.

"Yes," I said.

"Something to do with all this?"

"Yes."

"Can I go?"

"No." We turned right onto Old Canyon.

"Why?"

"It might be dangerous."

"Okay," she said sweetly. "So you like old Morris, do you?"

"He likes you."

"He likes anything that can wear a dress without getting arrested."

"He's got a good head."

"Except for the point."

We pulled into her driveway in silence. She kissed me demurely on the cheek and said, "You'll call when I can do something, right?"

"Right," I said.

"I think Dad and Mom would like to see you for a few minutes."

"Fine," I said, killing the motor. I probably couldn't accomplish anything for an hour or so anyway.

I followed her into the house and she told Annie and Wyatt where we'd been and went up the stairs. "I've got to work on my math," she said.

Annie watched her go, openmouthed. "I don't believe it," she said, when Jessica was gone.

"Maybe it's Morris' influence," I said.

They didn't particularly want to see me, but we talked for a while anyway, and then I went out and started Alice up and headed for the great department store of flesh called Hollywood.

17

A Bad Case of Gas

I know now that what I meant to do that night was a mistake. I suppose I even knew it then, as I got off the freeway and headed north on La Cienega.

I told myself that I wanted information. I told myself that it couldn't hurt Aimee. I told myself that I didn't want to lose four days while Mrs. Sorrell was waiting for the results of her useless ransom payment. I told myself a lot of things and they were all bullshit. I didn't really want information. I wanted revenge.

What I was relying on was fear. I figured I was mad enough to make someone really afraid, and I figured that he was already afraid. Add the two up, I thought, waiting for a red light to turn green, and he'd keep his mouth shut and behave. I was wrong.

Because I was wrong, somebody got killed.

Half a block east of Jack's, Junko stood on the curb and trolled the traffic in a little white middie blouse like the ones Japanese schoolgirls wear. She had a wad of chewing gum in her cheek. She'd chosen this corner, I figured, because of the pay phone. I was parked across the street when the first john picked her up. She was cute enough that it didn't take long. As I'd guessed she'd do, when she finished leaning in through the car window and outlining her deal, she went to the pay phone—the one I'd used when I'd talked to Tabitha and her friend—and dialed a number. She said two or three words, hung up, and got into the car. Now Mr. Wonderful knew she was employed. Groceries tomorrow.

Almost exactly thirty minutes later she was back, smoothing her blouse and running her fingers through her hair. She bought a Pepsi at Jack's, like any kid, and resumed her stance at the curb. By then I was checking my rearview mirror every few seconds, but I was wasting my time. The change was still too small to bother about.

Junko got into two more cars while I sat there growing progressively more irritable. He had to come sooner or later. It wasn't smart to leave your walking meat on the street with too much money. Somebody might take it away from her. Or, less likely, she might figure she finally had enough in her purse to go home to Mommy. I wondered briefly about Mommy.

It was almost eleven when he showed up. He cruised to the curb, concentrated cool, in a vintage '67 Chevy convertible with the top up against the weather. Junko handed the money in through the window and went back to eyeing the traffic.

If it hadn't been for the old Chevy's distinctive vertical taillights, I would have lost him. He passed Jack's, weaving in and out of traffic, swung up onto Franklin, and then cut left toward Sunset. I ran a light to keep up with him and then followed him onto Sunset, heading west, and then south onto a nothing little street called Sierra Bonita. I killed the lights as he made the turn so he wouldn't spot me. He pulled in to the curb halfway down the block, in front of the last of the old double-decker apartment houses, now flanked by four-story stucco affairs with balconies that were edged by waist-high hollow pipe railings that looked like the railings on an ocean liner. All that was missing were the life preservers. They wouldn't have worked in Hollywood anyway.

His car sat there at the curb, still dark, so he hadn't cracked open either of the doors. I took a repulsive-looking little .32 automatic, eight shots, out of the glove compartment and climbed out the door on the passenger side. I didn't have to worry about Alice's interior light: it had burned out decades ago.

I landed on my knees on the parking strip, feeling dried grass and weeds crackle underneath me. There was also an empty tin can, which collapsed with a squelching sound. Someone had thoughtfully parked a van behind the man's car, so I could stand up as I passed behind it. A carload of black kids careened by, Prince blaring from the radio. They shouted something at me in Urban Black. I used the noise as cover as I came up behind his left-rear fender.

I waited. I heard a sharp sniffing noise through the open window on the driver's side of his car. In another thirty seconds or so I heard the beginning of another sniff. I was at his window before it was over.

"Don't breathe," I said, sticking the barrel of the gun up his left nostril. "Not in, not out. Otherwise, this thing might go off."

"Yurk," he said, glancing frantically up at me. The knife scar at the corner of his mouth twitched, a thin white line with a life of its own. He was holding a girl's pocket mirror just below his chin, and on it was a generous quantity of white powder. I leaned forward and blew the powder off the mirror. It settled, like the snow in one of those water-filled balls you shake up, onto the front of his greasy jeans.

"Remember me?" I said, pushing the gun another centimeter into his nostril. He started to shake his head, but I shoved the gun barrel a little further and he began to nod. "I thought so." I looked past him at the old two-story building. "This is where you live?"

He started to shake his head again and thought better of it. Very carefully he nodded.

"Good," I said. "We're going in. Get out slowly and sweetly. Pretend your mother's watching and you want her to be proud of you." I opened the door and pulled the gun back, aiming at his left eye. He climbed out very slowly, staring into the barrel of the gun like a man who sees his future unfolding before him and doesn't like the look of it.

When he was standing, I took his arm, pushed the gun into his neck, and turned him gently toward the curb.

"Sure hope you cleaned the house," I said. "I get real edgy when things aren't just right." He caught the toe of his shoe on the edge of the curb and stumbled slightly.

"Look out for the dog-doo," I said. When he looked down, I reversed the gun and slammed him with the handle, just beneath the base of the skull. His legs collapsed beneath him and his forehead cracked on the sidewalk with a pleasing sound. Just to make sure, I clipped him again with the handle of the gun. He let out a wet little sigh and his legs twitched.

I tucked my fingers under his thick leather belt and lifted him, and he folded at the waist, knees and elbows dragging on the sidewalk. I hauled him like a badly packed garment bag up the block to Alice.

There she was, looking even dirtier than usual in the blue glare of the streetlights. I dropped Prince Charming on the grass in the parking strip, opened the back door, and yanked on the edge of the army blanket. A human being rose up from the floor of the car. I almost put a bullet through it.

"Hi," Jessica said. "Where are we?"

I leaned my forehead against Alice's roof and listened to my pulse pounding in my ears. "You *idiot*," I said. I'd nearly killed my own goddaughter.

"You can't talk to me like that," she said indignantly.

"You're in Hollywood," I said, straightening up and trying to catch my breath. "The next bus home is leaving in about ten seconds. Up there." I gestured with the gun toward Sunset.

"Who's the basket case?" she asked.

"He's a guy who likes to use knives on little girls. How did you get here, anyway?"

"I went upstairs and then came down the back way and got into your car," she said, looking at the pimp with the kind of fascination most of us save for scorpions and tarantulas. The pimp moaned and started to move. "Um," Jessica said uncertainly, backing up.

"The tape on the seat," I said. "Give it to me."

She felt around for a moment and then handed me a roll of electrician's tape. I took it, put the gun on Alice's roof, and bent down over the pimp, who had begun to turn his head from side to side. I yanked his hands behind him and taped his wrists together. I taped them tightly enough to cause gangrene.

"Do you do this a lot?" she asked, watching.

"You're lucky I'm not doing it to you."

"You're weirder than Blister. I don't really have to take the bus home, do I? Daddy says it's dangerous."

I almost laughed. "No. But you ever do this again, and I'll have the goddamn bus run over you. Also, you're explaining this to your parents."

"That's another day," she said with the nearsighted assurance of youth. I was getting heartily sick of youth.

"Get out. Bring the blanket with you. No, no, on the other side. Come on, make it quick. He won't be out forever."

Grumbling, she climbed out and came around to my side, dragging the blanket behind her. I lifted the pimp by his belt and heaved him into the back seat. He emitted a reflexive sigh as his midsection hit the edge of the seat. Lifting my right leg, I kicked him down onto the floor behind the front seat. He was on his stomach, hands taped behind him. I gave him a once-over, feeling like I'd forgotten something, and then tossed the blanket over him.

"Let's go," I said. "Into the front seat."

Alice started with unusual self-assurance, and we made a U-turn back onto Sunset. At Highland I turned left, heading up toward the reservoir.

"He's a bad guy, huh?" Jessica was as high as a kite, loving every moment of it.

"He's the lowest form of life since the slime molds," I said. "Have you ever cleaned out the refrigerator and found stuff with green, smelly hair growing all over it, and it dissolved in your fingers when you picked it up?"

"Yuck," she said. "Yes. Mommy made me do it the second time I went out with Blister."

"Well," I said, steering left, "on the Great Chain of Being, he's two steps below that."

"Just above yellow snow," she said.

"Right about there."

"So what are we going to do?"

"You're going to stay in the car," I said. "I'm going to have a campfire."

"I was a Campfire Girl."

"You're still going to stay in the car."

"What kind of a campfire?"

"You'll see."

We'd made a right off Cahuenga when I smelled something. It could have been Alice's brakes, but I hadn't braked lately. I'd worked most of the way through the litany of automotive malfunctions before I realized what it was. At the same time, I realized what I'd forgotten.

"Oh, balls," I said, pulling over. We were on a quiet little winding street. "Damn you, Jessica."

"Damn me? I didn't do anything."

"You're here," I said, getting out. "If you hadn't been here I'd have remembered to tape his goddamned fingers." I ran around to the passenger side, threw the door open, and yanked back the blanket. The pimp glared at me over his shoulder. He'd worked the little butane torch out of his pocket and was holding it to the tape at his wrists. What I'd smelled was burning tape and singed blanket.

"Ah-ah," I said, taking the little blowtorch from his hands. "Creativity is not always rewarded. Mustn't use up the gas. I've got plans for it." I got the tape and passed it around his fingers and his thumbs for insurance. Then I rifled his pockets and came up with a couple hundred dollars—Junko's take for the evening—and his switchblade.

"Much better," I said, slamming the door on his feet. The door swung back open, and he moaned. "Pull the feet in or lose them," I said. He pulled them in, and I slammed the door again.

Five minutes later, we were there.

At that late hour, the reservoir was the picture of placidity. Moonlight gleamed from its surface, and no joggers plodded around it, chasing the waistlines of their youth. Except for the electrical carpet of L.A., spread out and glittering between us and the ocean, we might have been in the Donner Pass.

"Remember the Donner party?" I said, hauling the pimp out of the car by his belt. His elbows cracked against the ground and he made a mushy sound. "I didn't think so. Guys like you have no frame of reference. The Donner party ran out of mules or horses or whatever pulled their wagon train in a pass some miles northeast of here. Then the snows came." I dragged him up against an oak tree, substantial but not too thick, and slammed his back against it. He grunted.

"Jessica," I called, "the battery cables. They're in the trunk. Use the ignition key and bring them here." To pass the time I slapped his face a couple of times. "After a while, the people in the Donner party did the only thing they could do," I said. "They ate each other."

"Big fucking deal," he said. His forehead was bleeding where it had hit the pavement, and it hadn't done his disposition any good. He was still nobody you'd like to be seated next to at dinner.

"It was to the Donner party," I said. Jessica brought the cables and I wound them around his chest and waist and passed them around the oak. He took a halfhearted kick at me, but his heart wasn't in it. He knew it wasn't going to do him any good. "You see," I said, "they didn't have any matches. They had to eat each other raw. Imagine the emotional trauma it must have caused. In the twentieth century it would have kept a squadron of psychiatrists fat for years."

"Fuck you," he said. The sliced side of his mouth twitched in the moonlight.

"Hey, this is serious," I said, tying a double square knot. "For you, anyway. She and I are going home when it's over. You're not."

"What do you think you're doing?"

"Well," I said, "for one thing, I'm getting even. But we've got another agenda here as well. At an earlier point in our thus-far unsatisfactory relationship, you said 'Tssss.' I want to know what 'Tssss' means."

"Like I said, fuck you."

"*As*, I said. Jesus, is it really harder to speak good English than bad? It doesn't take any more words. Do your hands hurt?"

"Yes."

"Well, here's something to take your mind off it. Pull in your tongue." He did, and I slammed him under the jaw with my fist. "See?" I said as his knees sagged, "if I hadn't told you to pull in your tongue, you'd be standing here bleeding to death and pleading with us in broken English. Your problem is that you don't know who your friends are."

"Your problem is that you're an asshole and you don't know what you're fucking around with." He was sweating, and his tongue came out to lick off a drop that was rolling past the corner of his mouth. Then he looked at me and yanked his tongue back in as though it were the retractable cord on a vacuum cleaner.

"Well, tell me," I said reasonably.

He looked away for a moment, thinking about it. Then he gazed over my shoulder at Jessica. "Who's the pretty little thing?"

I hit him in the stomach. "As I mentioned, there's an agenda here," I said, flexing my knuckles to make sure they were okay, "and my job is to see that we stick to it."

He made windy huffing sounds and then straightened up and gave me the worst look he could manage. "Man," he said, "you can talk to me all night and you're not going to learn nothing."

"Anything," I corrected automatically. "And you're laboring under a delusion. You don't talk, and you're the steak for the evening. Unlike the Donner party, we've got fire. Jessica."

"Yeah?"

"Go back to the car. Get the gasoline can and the tool kit and bring them back."

"The gaso*line* can?"

"Do as you're told."

Muttering, "Yes, massa," she went and got them. The pimp looked at the can with some skepticism.

"You wouldn't dare," he said.

"I don't think I'll have to," I said, pulling my belt out of my pants.

"I'm scared to death," he said.

"Wait," I advised him. "Tell me a little later."

I took the can from Jessica and used my belt to fasten it to the tree above his head. Then I opened the tool kit, took out a ten-penny nail, and punched a hole in the bottom of the can. A couple of drops of gasoline hit him on the right shoulder.

"God." He sneered. "I've never been so frightened."

"I don't suppose you did much physics in high school."

"I didn't do high school," he said with some pride.

"Jessica, explain to this little beast the effect of atmospheric pressure on the flow of a liquid."

"Huh?" Jessica said, safely behind me. Her eyes were enormous.

"I have to do everything myself," I complained. "The flow of the gasoline is slow right now because the top on the can is tight. But when I loosen it, like this," I said, going on tiptoe and giving it a twist, "the weight of the atmosphere—which is fourteen pounds per square inch, by the way—pushes down on the gasoline and the flow increases."

Sure enough, the gasoline began to drip steadily onto his shoulder.

"So?" he asked, but with less certainty.

"So," I said, "do an experiment. Find a measuring device, anything that's more or less steady. Your heartbeat would do if it weren't about to speed up, which it is. Find something that doesn't give a shit about you. The crickets will work. Listen."

I held up a scholarly finger and all three of us listened.

The crickets shrilled in the trees with monotonous regularity. "Count the pulses of the cricket noise and then count the drops of gasoline. The crickets don't care if you live or die. Count the pulses as I open the top a little further."

We all stood there as the crickets rubbed their hind legs together. "Three drops to a pulse," I said. I gave the top of the can a twist or two. "Now we've got five. Atmospheric pressure, you see."

"Big deal," he said.

"What does 'Tssss' mean?"

"Nothing. Fuck yourself with a fire hydrant."

"Ah, vivid speech. Good for you. Spunk is so appealing. But I'm afraid you don't fully understand your position. You see, the gas is only one problem. Here's the other. Think what it would have meant to the Donner party."

I pulled his miniature butane torch out of my pocket and thumbed it. A blue lizard's tongue of flame flickered forth. He drew in his breath with a sound like ripping silk.

"I don't believe it," he said.

"And you shouldn't. I'm not going to set you on fire. You are. Here's the plan. Jessica, the tape."

She got the roll of electrician's tape, and I taped the butane torch open. The flame licked at the air. I built up a mound of loose earth and put the torch on it, pointed at his ankle. "Okay," I said. "We're going to talk. Just to cut through the bullshit, I'm going to take the top off the can." I leaned up and did it. The dripping turned into a trickle.

"The laws of physics are in charge," I said. "When the gasoline saturates the cuff of your pants, we're going to roast our marshmallows and go home. You're not. You're going to spend eternity, or at least as much of it as you need to worry about, against this tree."

He mumbled something, his eyes on the flame. The reek of gasoline was overwhelming.

"Your shirt's getting wet," I said. "What do you know about Aimee Sorrell?"

"Nothing."

"You recognized her picture."

"No, I didn't. I'd never seen her before." He was blinking his eyes against the fumes, and tears were beginning to run down his cheeks.

"You recognized her and you said 'Tssss.' "

"I said shhhh. I wanted Jennie to shut up."

"Let's try something," I said. I took his knife out of my pocket and crouched at his feet. "Kick me and I'll cut your nuts off," I said. I made five or six little slices in the cuff of his right pants leg and tore upward, creating a ragged fringe that hung from the knee. It reminded me of Ben Gunn in *Treasure Island*. I cut off a strip from the back of his jeans and rolled it up in my hand where he couldn't see it.

"What are you doing?" Jessica asked.

"More physics," I said. "I'll explain in a minute." I got up and looked at him. "Wet to the waist," I said.

He had his head pulled as far to the left as possible to get away from the steady trickle of gasoline, and his eyes kept going down to his body and then farther down to the flame. His focus was none too steady, and I guessed that the fumes were beginning to make him dizzy.

"Aimee Sorrell," I said. "Where'd you meet her?"

He licked his lips and looked down at himself again. The gasoline was seeping down onto the front of his pants. "Oki-Burger, the Oki-Burger."

"You tried to put her on the string?"

"Sure."

"When was this?"

"A few months ago."

"She wouldn't do it?"

"She had some geek rent-a-cop."

"Poor Wayne," Jessica said. The pimp gave her a startled glance.

"Then what?"

"Then she was back on the street."

"Who got her then?"

"Don't know."

"Oh, but you do. And you know why somebody put out a cigar in her belly button, too."

He closed his eyes. I went nearer to him and put up my hand as if to lean on the tree. "Fumes getting to you?" I asked. The gasoline trickled onto the strip of cloth wadded up in my hand.

He nodded.

"Tough. Who got her? Who hurt her?"

He shook his head.

"Why did they hurt her?" The strip of cloth in my hand was soaked. I took my hand away and put it behind me. "How did you know they hurt her?"

"I'm getting sick," he said. He looked a little green.

"You're getting wet, too. It's almost to your knees. Who hurt her?"

He summoned up all his bravado and spit at me.

"Physics lesson number two," I said, kneeling at his feet again—to the side this time, to make it harder for him to kick me. "Gasoline actually is not very flammable. It's almost impossible to get liquid gasoline to burn. You need extremely high temperatures." I fluffed up the ragged strips hanging over his ankles. "Gasoline *fumes*, on the other hand, are flammable as hell. Mix those gasoline molecules with oxygen, and you've got the recipe that runs the world." I got up, and his eyes followed me. He wasn't quite as woozy as I'd thought. "What I've just done to your trouser leg, aside from having a kind of rakish charm, has the effect of increasing the surface area of the denim. More surface area, more fumes. Like raising a wick on an air freshener. I'd say that that ankle is where you'll explode first."

"Don't stand so close to him, Simeon," Jessica warned. "You don't want to be there when he goes off."

"Why did they hurt her?" I asked. Behind my back I let the saturated strip of cloth in my hand dangle free. The torch flickered blue on the ground, its sharp little tongue darting at the fringed ankle. The smell of gasoline was almost unendurable. "Down to mid-calf," I observed. "My least favorite length for a skirt."

"Don't," he said suddenly.

"Let's just give it a little fluff," I said, kneeling down.

"No, no. Don't."

"Why did they hurt her?" I loosened up the strips of trouser leg and waved them around a little. I let the end of the fabric in my hand touch the flame, and when it ignited I pushed out breath all the way from my diaphragm and said, "Fwoooosh."

Jessica screamed. I jumped back, and the pimp tried to rip himself away from the tree, eyes jammed closed, shouting, *"Obedience school."* He shouted it twice, and it echoed from the hillsides opposite. A long moment passed. Then he realized that he wasn't on fire and he opened his eyes to see the strip of cloth burning on the ground. He sagged bonelessly against the cables, closed his eyes again, and emitted a high-pitched noise that was halfway between a giggle and a sob.

"That was dress rehearsal," I said. "What's obedience school?"

At first he just hung there against the cables, his head down, a white caricature of a lynching. Then he said, "It's where they scare the kids before they put them out."

Jessica started to say something, and I put up a hand. "What happens?"

"They get knocked around. They get put in a cage for a while, whipped or locked in a closet if they do anything wrong. They get left in the dark a lot. They're not allowed to wear clothes. Ever. Different people fuck them. Different ways. Everything that's going to happen to them when they're out." He took a deep, fume-laden breath. "Once in a while, they kill someone in front of you. Someone who fucked up."

"Tell me about the belly button."

"That's like graduation. That's the last thing they do to you. They tie you to a table, faceup, and the guy smokes a cigar and then they put it out in your navel."

"The guy," I said. "Is there someone who isn't a guy?"

The pimp shook his head. "Don't ask."

"How do you know about all of this?"

"Junko."

"How does she know?"

He looked down at his feet. The fringed cuff was beginning to grow damp. "Could you move the torch?"

I didn't stir. "How does she know?"

"She went through it," he said, his eyes on the flame. "They did it to her." He sucked in a breath, full of gasoline, and leaned back against the tree. He was beginning to turn olive drab, and his face glistened with sweat.

"Tell me about when they kill somebody."

"They get as many kids together as possible and do in whoever done wrong. Like a lesson, right? Keeps people on a pretty short leash."

"Junko told you this?"

"Sure. Move the fucking torch."

"Who'd they kill?"

"That's why she'll never leave me." I took hold of his chin, and he rolled his eyes wildly to keep the flame in view.

"Who?" I said.

"One of them, one of the ones in Junko's group, was a Mongoloid, you know, one of those idiot kids who looks like an Oriental? God only knows where they found her. I mean, that kid wasn't going to tell anybody anything, but they put her through obedience school anyway. And when she made a mistake, like the little dope was bound to do sooner or later, they offed her. Junko was watching, with a bunch of other kids. Said she threw up all over the floor. Right up to the point where they cut the little dummy, she figured they were only fooling, even after what they'd done to her. They made her clean up the mess, I mean both messes, hers and the dummy's. So, see? I look like a pretty nice guy."

"How did you get her?" I felt like throwing up myself.

"They used her up," he said with an obvious effort. "Please move it."

Jessica started toward it but I waved her off. "Don't touch it. He's got a minute or two, unless the fumes kill him. What do you mean, they used her up?"

"They got tired of her. They passed her around to everyone a few times and then nobody wanted her anymore. They always need new ones. New babies."

"How old is she?"

"Now?" He looked at the horizon and tried to focus his eyes. "Sixteen. Then, she was twelve."

"Four *years*? They've been at this four years?"

"Just about. She was one of the first ones." He kicked out feebly at the torch and missed. "Please," he said, "I'm talking to you. I'm talking to you, right?"

I reached down and picked it up. "They just let her go?" I asked.

"Sure. What's she going to do? She came to me." He kept his eyes glued to the torch as though he thought I was going to touch the flame to him.

"How long ago?" I asked.

"About a month." *Bingo*, I thought.

"Why wouldn't she go to the police?" Jessica said.

"That's the first thing they teach you," he said. He sounded like he'd run a marathon. "Don't trust the cops."

"Why not?" she asked.

"Money," he said. "These people are making lots of money. Cops like money, same as everyone else. You go to a cop, it might be the wrong one. Then you'd be dead, just as simple as that."

"She didn't come to you," I said. "You bought her."

"Wrong," he said.

"You bought her. You're connected with them. That's how you know they had Aimee. In fact, you gave them Aimee, didn't you? A month ago. And they gave you Junko."

"Please," he said, sounding very young. "I'm getting real sick." I realized for the first time how young he was, realized for the first time that I didn't even know his name.

"Sick, schmick," I said. "You can still die. You took Aimee to her 'agent.' "

"No way," he said weakly. He was on the verge of tears.

"I want names."

For the first time in several minutes he looked directly at me. "No," he said. "I don't know any names."

"Let's change tack," I said. I went right up to him, and his eyes followed the flame in my hand. The gasoline fumes poured off him in waves. He didn't even see his knife in my other hand.

I stuck it through the fabric of his denim jacket and sliced down. The knife went through it like margarine. His skinny chest, slick with gasoline, gleamed at me. "We can start with skin instead," I said. Behind me, I heard Jessica step back.

"Don't matter," he said, looking at me again. "I'd rather die this way."

"Well," I said, "I don't think you know what's involved."

"Fuck off," he said. He closed his eyes again. "Just kill me."

"We'll open with a nipple," I said.

He shook his head, his eyes closed now. "So do it," he said.

I turned around and saw Jessica looking at me with eyes bigger than Bambi's. I looked down at the torch in my hand, and then turned and walked away and tossed it into the reservoir. It hit the water with a hissing sound and disappeared.

"Untie the cables," I said to Jessica, turning back from the water. When she did, he fell forward onto his face. His hands were still tied behind him. Then he turned his head and retched.

He retched for longer than I would have believed possible, until his stomach was empty, and then he retched air.

I put my fingers into his hair, lifted his head, and rubbed his face into the vomit. "This is for Junko's tongue," I said. When I pulled him upright, he was covered in dirt and vomit.

"Don't move," I said. I went behind him and cut the tape binding his wrists. I left intact the tape over his fingers and thumbs. Then I took the money and cigarettes out of my pocket and shoved them into the front of his trousers.

"For Christ's sake," I said, "don't try to light up." I threw the knife into the reservoir and then undid my belt from the tree and dropped the gas can to the ground. "Come on, Jessica," I said, walking toward the car.

"Wait," he half-sobbed. "What about me?"

"Oh, I haven't forgotten about you," I said, still walking. "You'll be on my mind for quite some time."

"How am I supposed to get home?"

I reached back and pulled Jessica along behind me. He yelled after us as we walked, but I tuned it out. At the car, all the violence and ugliness came up into my throat, and I had to turn and spit it out. When I got into Alice, my throat hurt and my mouth was sour and foul. I started the car. Jessica sat against her door, small and self-contained and silent.

As I hit the lights and shifted into drive, I said, "I'm afraid you're not seeing me at my best."

"You're fine," she said. She was quiet until we'd bumped all the way down the road and made the turn that would lead us onto the Ventura Freeway.

Then she shifted in her seat and faced me. "Do you really think he gave them that little girl?"

"Maybe. He got Junko at just about the right time."

She turned and cracked her window and breathed the fresh air, getting the gasoline out of her lungs. After a moment she turned back to me. "If he hadn't told you anything," she said, "not anything at all, would you have let him catch fire?"

"No," I said. A mile or so passed in silence.

"Softy," she said.

18

Mountain

Upon returning home, as Annie told me later, Jessica received the first spanking she'd had since the age of four. When she was four, Jessica cried. At thirteen, she responded by running away.

"She's not going to come here," I'd said the first and second time Wyatt and Annie called me. "After last night, I'm the last person she'd want to see. Try Blister's. Maybe she's gone up there to punish you."

They *had* tried Blister's. There was no one there. Wyatt had broken in through a window on the assumption that they were both inside, hiding. They weren't.

"I'm afraid they've run away together," he said on phone call number four.

"She'll be back," I said. "She knows that Blister is a walking abscess. And she's not going anywhere alone. After what she's seen, the street doesn't look any better than the Seventh Level of Hell."

I wasn't in the best of shape. I'd awakened twice in the night, escaping the dream vision of Junko's pimp on fire. My mouth tasted as though I'd been gargling with gasoline. After the second time I'd cajoled myself back into sleep, I had a nightmare about someone in a pig costume. It was one of those peculiar dreams where nothing frightening happens but the air is charged with the kind of low-voltage electrical hum that makes the hair on your arms stand on end before an electrical storm. The person in the pig costume slowly walked up a flight of stairs and into a room. I followed, and the pig stood with his—her—back to me, and that was when the hum started. Then the pig mask came off. When the big pink pig started to turn around, I woke up. I was wringing wet, and cold to the center of my bones.

By then the sky was beginning to pale, and some L.A. birds were coughing in the trees. I got up, thankful to have awakened alive, and made a quart of coffee. Half an hour later, Wyatt called for the first time.

In addition to the fact that I felt sleepy and lousy, I was pretty much out of things to do. It was only Wednesday, the second day of the four-day ransom period, and I'd done just about everything I could think of that wouldn't directly endanger Aimee, on the remote chance that her kidnapper actually intended to release her after he picked up the ransom that had been mailed—*mailed*?—to him. I didn't believe for a second that he would. I had to wait, but I felt like I was waiting for the second coming of a deity whose first coming I had never accepted.

So I sort of cleaned the house again and hoped that Morris would call to announce that he'd broken the code on Birdie's disks. He didn't, and I couldn't call him: I didn't have his number, and there were no Gursteins listed in Topanga. Since I was sitting by the phone, I called once more the three numbers that had been answered by some guy saying "Cap'n's." On the first two, I got the same response. I hung up. The third, the one in my area code, just kept ringing. Well, that meant that the various Cap'ns kept something like business hours, so I hadn't entirely wasted my time.

But I still didn't know what the Cap'ns' business was. What do Cap'ns do, anyway? The one in California might possibly have been a nautical man, but it seemed unlikely that the Cap'ns in Arizona and Idaho discharged their duties on the breast of the briny deep.

I staved off my identity crisis for a few hours by pulling on my shorts and a pair of battered shoes and running about six miles on the softest Pacific sand I could find. The clouds were back and there was a chill in the air that was the meteorological equivalent of a horse laugh at the idea of spring. My calves were on the verge of cramping permanently when I headed Alice into the main entrance of UCLA, still clean and empty because of Easter break, and headed for the saunas. When I got back to Alice, whom I'd parked in one of the dim underground lots that the state built for the convenience of rapists, it was ten-thirty, and I was showered, gleaming, and as pink as the pig in my nightmare.

Well, I thought, since I'm in town anyway, let's drive the streets and soak up the atmosphere. Maybe it would provoke an idea. What it provoked was an almost suicidal sense of futility. Even at that hour, even in the cold, the kids were out on Sunset and Santa Monica, both boys and girls, their thumbs extended to snag twenty dollars, a beating, or a nice case of AIDS. Without thinking about what I was doing, I pulled into the Oki-Burger. Since I was no longer under cover, I parked in the lot.

"You're kidding," the Mountain said, using his nauseating cheesecloth to swab at one of the many spots on Alice's fender as I got out of the car. He'd been standing forlornly in the center of the asphalt sumo ring, waiting for a fat guy to come along and challenge him. All the fat guys were still in bed, tucked warmly away in the gray morning, and he'd come over to the car the moment I drove in. "I haven't seen one of these since I rented *La Bamba*."

"I wish I were kidding," I said. I assuaged the twinge of disloyalty I felt by patting Alice on the driver's door. "She drives okay."

"One of the players drives an old Chevy, too," he said, wiping a headlight. "He's a real jerkoff." I suddenly remembered Junko's pimp's car.

"Hey, Mountain," I said in my best Wednesday-morning voice, which wasn't much, "how about I buy us both a burger?"

The Mountain lived on burgers, and he always wanted one or, more usually, two. Two it was. He set mine down in front of me and both of his in front of him, gave me a big yellow smile, and took the first burger like an aspirin.

"So?" he said around a mouthful of beef, bread, and onions. It actually sounded more like "Fo?" Some mustard landed on his plaid shirt, adding a nice touch to the edible Jackson Pollock that decorated it.

"What's his name?" I asked.

"Mark Intveld. A knife boy. Likes to call himself Marco. Got a little Okinawan girl. Tommy just about shit, first time he saw her."

"Junko."

The Mountain raised his eyebrows in acknowledgment.

"He's scared," I said.

"Marco? Good. Hope he gets scared to death. He ever comes around here, I'll turn him inside out and use him for rubber gloves." He amputated half his second burger in a single bite. "What's he scared of?"

"Me," I said, "and this is between us."

"Muumph," he said, chewing.

"I'm serious. I'm not supposed to be talking to anybody. The truth is, I think I may need some help pretty soon."

The Mountain made a gesture like he was zipping his lips closed and then realized that his mouth was wide open to take another bite. He lowered the hamburger with a supreme act of will and completed the gesture.

Although the place was empty, I leaned toward him and lowered my voice. "There's a bunch of people who are dealing in kids. Not street pimps. This is a real business, not a cottage industry. They put the kids through something called obedience school to break them, and then they pass the kids around somehow. Whatever they do at obedience school, it scares the shit out of the kids. They also mark them by burning them with a cigar."

The hamburger remained in his lowered hand. His little pig eyes glowed. I could have seen them across a dark room. "Who are they?"

"I don't know, exactly. I mean, I think I know, but I can't

prove anything. They've got the little girl I was looking for."

"The little blondie?"

"That's the one." The Mountain started to say something and then looked up.

"Whoops," said a throaty contralto behind me. "El copperino."

I turned to see Velveeta and Tammy. Tammy had finally gotten something warmer to wear, a ratty thrift-shop chinchilla that had probably begun life as a small herd of muskrats. They were out pretty early, for them, and they both looked like they'd had a bad night.

The Mountain got up. It was like Mount Fuji taking wing. "What do you two want to be called today?" he asked. "Boys or girls?"

"Girls," Tammy said primly.

"Well, girls, scram. We're closed to pre-ops until four. New health rule."

"Jeez," Tammy said. "Not even coffee?"

"To go," the Mountain said.

"Come on, Tammy," Velveeta said, tugging at the fur. Some of it came away in her fingers. "We'll take our trade elsewhere. Who wants to eat with cops anyway?" The two of them wobbled on their high heels back into the parking lot. The Mountain turned his attention back to the remainder of his burger.

"I think they pretend to be talent agents," I said. "They tell the kids they're going to make stars out of them, take their pictures, fill their heads full of stuff. Then, I guess, they put them through obedience school and use the pictures to sell the kids to whoever's on the circuit. Listen, do you remember a little Mongoloid girl on the streets a few years ago?"

"Anita," he said promptly. Something like pain squeezed his features. "Sheeze. Hispanic, but everybody thought she was Oriental. She was only here a few days. I got her to go home, but her parents didn't want her, can you believe it?

She was back in a week. Kid was seriously mental. Couldn't even get dressed right without help."

"They got her too," I said. "She did something wrong, and they killed her."

The Mountain sat back and blinked heavily. He looked around at the empty tables as though he was trying to remember where Anita had sat. Then he picked up the remaining half-burger and threw it across the room. It hit another table with a flat, splatting sound.

"Fuckers," he said. He reached up behind him, grabbed his greasy pigtail, and gave it a savage tug. The action seemed to center him. "You want help," he said, "you got it. Anytime."

"What do you know about the cops?"

"Like what?" His eyes were watchful.

"I've heard something about some of them being on the take. Do you know anything about that?"

"Not exactly."

"What does that mean?"

"Kids talk. You know. I figured it was just an excuse not to get anywhere near them. Kids don't like cops."

"What did they say?"

"That there were cops who weren't straight. You know, who were in the game."

"Maybe they were right."

"According to who?"

"Marco."

"So you talked to old Marco." He almost smiled. It wasn't a pretty sight. "You get his knife?"

"He'll get another one."

"Yeah. Asshole can't pick his teeth with anything smaller than a bayonet."

"I want to know if you hear anything else about the police."

"That the help you wanted?" He looked disappointed.

"Only part of it. I may need you to kill some guys." I was only half-joking.

"That's more like it."

"So, now," I said, "you've got something to look forward to."

The Mountain put several chins on top of a massive palm and regarded me. "You're worried about the cops. That's why you're not going to them."

"You got it," I said.

"Hey," a girl's voice said.

Apple hovered uncertainly over the Mountain's shoulder. "Hey, honey," the Mountain said in an entirely new tone of voice.

"Have you seen Donnie?" Her enormous sweater was wrapped around her, but her lips were purple with the cold. She couldn't have weighed ninety pounds. Her hair looked better for the washing in the Executive Suites, but not much.

"Not since last night. He was in here last night."

"He didn't come home." She had a bruise on her cheek that hadn't been there the last time I saw her.

The hair on my arms prickled. "Was he supposed to?" I asked.

"He always does. This was the first night I slept alone."

"Where did he say he was going?"

She spread thin, empty hands. "He didn't."

"You had anything?" the Mountain asked.

"Couple of ups."

"I meant food, Apple," he said.

She looked gravely at him for a moment. "I don't think I could," she said. "You can call me Nora, but it's a secret."

"Jesus," the Mountain said, mopping himself with the rag. "What happened to your face?"

"I fell down," she said, too promptly.

"Under anybody I know?" the Mountain asked, looking grim.

"No," she said.

"Well, you're going to have an orange smoothie whether you want it or not." He got up to fetch it.

"He's sweet," Apple said, watching him.

"Sit down, Nora." She did, looking around as though she

were afraid someone would tell her to get up again. "You don't know anything about where Donnie went?"

"He never tells me."

"He didn't have any routines?"

"No. When there's a customer, there's a customer."

"But he always comes home."

She started to say something, and her chin suddenly broke out in a random pattern of dimples. She swallowed and, instead of speaking, she nodded her head. She turned one palm up and rubbed at it with the other as though she were trying to erase her lifeline. For the first time I saw the narrow gold ring, too big for her, on her index finger.

"Where'd you get that?"

She looked nervous. "I didn't steal it," she whispered.

"Of course you didn't. It's very pretty, that's all. I was just wondering where you got it."

"My mother's," she said. "It was hers."

"Was she pretty?"

"I don't know." She looked at me, trying to figure out where the question had come from. "They say she looked like me."

"Then she was pretty," I said. Apple ducked her head as though I'd hit her and looked at the table. "Who do you live with, Nora?"

"Donnie," she said in a very small voice. She didn't look up.

"I meant before."

"Nobody," she said. "They're all dead. Or they should be."

"*Aiya,*" I said in an unconscious Cantonese imitation of Eleanor.

Apple looked at me, her eyes bright. "That's a funny thing to say."

"It's a funny world."

"No kidding," she said, sounding fifty.

"Here," the Mountain said, slamming down a cup that must have held a quart. It was filled to the brim with a thick, viscous, slightly orangish fluid. "You're going to drink it if it takes all day."

"Okay," Apple said submissively. She looked relieved to have someone giving the orders. It took both hands, but she lifted it and started to sip.

"Don't worry about Donnie," I said. "He'll come here sooner or later." I pumped my voice full of an assurance I didn't feel. For a moment I imagined myself as one of the idiots in a werewolf movie who are always telling the other idiots that there's nothing to worry about: go ahead, go outside and take a leak under the full moon. We'll keep your nice Middle European food warm until you come back.

"Anyway," the Mountain said, watching her drink, "you're staying here." He reached out a hand the size of a Smithfield ham and touched the bruise on her cheek, so gently that she didn't seem to feel it. She kept her eyes on the surface of her smoothie, now dropping almost imperceptibly in the cup.

"Jesus," he said. "Dorothy was like this, you know?"

"Aimee," I said.

"Aimee," he corrected himself. "Just like her."

Apple turned her dark eyes first to him and then to me. "Aimee," she said in her little girl's voice.

"Anytime," the Mountain said flatly to me. "Anytime you need help. Any kind of help. Anytime."

19

The Steel Table

"**D**amn you," Hammond said into the phone. He sounded as though he meant it. It was getting dark, and I'd just arrived home. Two messages on my answering machine had told me that Jessica hadn't come home yet. Hammond was number three.

"Damn me? Why? Is it something I've done recently, or some kind of general principle?"

"Yoshino," he said.

I squinted into the past. "Who's Yoshino?"

"That's hilarious," he said.

"Oh, *Yoshino*," I said. "What happened?"

"More important," he said, "what the fuck are you up to?"

"Al, I told you. Kansas City. I showed you her picture."

"That was one girl. Kidnapping, I think you said. You didn't say anything about a serial murderer."

"You've got another one?" A sense of futility, familiar by now, swept over me. "Don't say you've got another one."

"Don't tell me what not to say. And you better get your ass in here. Some people in this here building are hopping."

"*Have* you got another one?"

"Yes."

I looked around the living room. I'd lighted a fire in the wood-burning stove, and the Mozart horn concerto I'd heard at the Gursteins' was giving the room's acoustics a workout.

The computer was on and blinking at me, its dinky little fan whirring in a comfortable fashion.

"Blond?" I said.

"That'll wait until you get to the morgue."

"I'm in the car."

Rush hour had congealed on the freeways. The gods of weather had decided that a little sprinkle would grease the roads and slow the traffic, so Alice's useless windshield wipers were sweeping sarcastically back and forth when I turned into the neon-lighted parking lot under Parker Center, the cops' home base. I went straight to the morgue.

Yoshino let me in, looking slightly shamefaced. "Thanks," I said nastily as she closed the door behind me.

The morgue was cold, but a lot warmer than Max Bruner's voice when he said, "She was doing what she was supposed to do."

"Well, hey," I said, "whatever happened to individual initiative?"

"It went out with the frontier," Bruner said. He was wearing a cashmere jacket that would have made Miles Brand goggle with envy and a pair of fawn-colored wool slacks that proclaimed some kind of fashion statement with an Italian accent. I was almost afraid to look at his shoes. They were certain to be made of the skin of an unborn calf or something else you could wear only once without saying hello to your toenails.

"Looking good, Max," I said, thinking about bad cops.

"Because of Al," he said with an air of sorely tried patience, "I've agreed to let you see the body before we have our talk. Like I said, that's because of Al. If I'd had my way, we'd have put you up overnight with a bunch of vomiting DUI's before we even said hello." He reached into the pocket of his elegant jacket, pulled out a handful of loose Maalox, and tossed them back like popcorn.

"That's white of you," I said. To Yoshino I said, "Figure of speech."

"Four-one-two," Bruner said to Yoshino as he chewed.

Her hair looked messed up, and I hoped her anniversary party had been a success. She tossed him an icy glance that said she already knew the number and went over to the wall, pulled out a drawer, and peeled back the sheet.

The stainless steel gleamed under the fluorescent tubes, but not enough to outshine Junko's face. She'd been opened from her throat to her hipbones.

"No," I said. I looked for someplace to sit. Precise as an atomic clock, Yoshino pressed a chair against the backs of my knees and I folded into it. Big black butterflies performed a mating dance in front of my eyes, and my pulse threatened to burst out of my wrists. I thought I was going to black out.

"You know her?" Bruner asked. He was bending over me. Over his shoulder, Hammond looked concerned.

"Junko," I said through lips that felt as dry and parched as the pages of a Gutenberg Bible. I knew I shouldn't start to cry, but I wasn't sure I could avoid it.

"Furuta," Bruner said. "Junko Furuta. Sixteen. From Gardena. Middle-class parents, father an executive with an automobile dealership. She was a methadone junkie. On the street about a year."

She'd been on the street about a month, I thought. I shook my head, not to disagree with Bruner, but to deny that she was dead. After all, I was the reason she was dead.

"You okay, Simeon?" Hammond asked.

I ignored him. Probably I couldn't have responded if I'd wanted to. I was trying to find another reason for her to be dead. I couldn't. She'd been killed because her pimp was afraid that I'd get to her and that she'd talk to me.

"I don't give a fuck if he's okay," Bruner said. "What I want to know is what he knows about it." His stomach emitted a painful little growl.

"Max," Hammond said, "ease up."

I looked up at Hammond. Was he playing good-cop, bad-cop? Or was he on my side? He caught my eye and stared at his feet. He was playing good-cop, bad-cop.

"I want to look at her," I said. I didn't, but I had to.

I got up, shaking off Yoshino's attempt to place a steadying hand under my elbow, and walked very slowly to the drawer. Junko's hair hung over her shoulders, limp and wet as seaweed. Her eyes were wide open. They didn't make her look alive. They had the same expression of dusty surprise you see in the eyes of stuffed fish. I could see the glistening white of her sternum, dead cartilage peeping through the top of the long gash that ended just above her pubic hair. I noted with something like dispassion that the gash divided her scarred navel, turning it into a pair of surprised-looking parentheses.

"This one really *could* be my daughter," Yoshino said.

"She's Okinawan," I said. I was startled by the sound of my voice. It sounded like a gravel avalanche. "You're not Okinawan."

"How do you know that?" Bruner demanded.

"Yoshino's Japanese," I said. "There's a difference."

"How do you know that this one is Okinawan?" Bruner's eyes narrowed. "I didn't know that."

I leaned against the drawer, defeating an urge to reach out and close Junko's eyes. After all, what did it matter to her? I fought off a surge of weariness. "That's the trouble with L.A. cops," I said. "They're racists. Can't tell the difference between a Japanese and an Okinawan."

"Simeon," Hammond said, "this isn't the way to go."

I lifted the tag on Junko's toe. It said JUNKO FURUTA. "You knew she was on the street," I said to Bruner. "What else did you know?"

"Lockup," Bruner said. "I know you're going to the lockup."

"Great," I said. "That'll do her a lot of good. Do you a lot of good too. Do you know who her pimp was?"

"Marco," he said. "Some crustacean named Marco."

"But you're not interested in that," I said to Bruner. I had to blink to fight down tears. "Well, fuck off."

"I'm interested," Bruner said. He looked down at Junko and then up at me and held up one hand, palm outward. It was meant to be a placating gesture, but it just made him look like a Teutonic Smoky the Bear. "There's a lot of kids out there. She's already dead. I have to be interested in the rest of them. Which means that I'm interested in you."

"So put me in the lockup."

"There's room to negotiate here," Bruner said, backing off. He reached out and pushed the drawer shut. Junko rolled into the dark. "You know Marco's name, you know Junko's name. Question is, what else do you know? Hammond says you're all right."

Hammond muttered something.

"So," Bruner continued, "what else do you know? That can help us, I mean."

"Nothing," I said.

"Wrong answer," Bruner said tightly.

"Max, if it hasn't gotten to you yet, I told you a while ago to fuck off."

Bruner smoothed a hand down the seam of his four-hundred-dollar jacket. Then he lifted his wrist and checked his watch. When he looked back up to me, his face was open and guileless. "Let's be specific," he said.

"Be as specific as you like," I said, reseating myself in the chair.

"You'll answer my questions?"

"As long as they're specific."

"How do you know about Junko?"

"I was looking for Aimee Sorrell. I was hired by her parents to find her. They thought she was in Los Angeles."

He nodded as though I were a slow pupil who had just gotten his first right answer. "Did you find her?"

"No."

"Do you know where she is?"

"No."

"Have you got any idea who's got her?"

That was the big one. "No," I said. "In fact, last night I got fired."

"What's the connection between her and Junko?"

"Oh, come on. The belly button," I said. I wasn't telling Bruner anything new.

"Why did you ask Yoshino to call you if anyone else came in with a scarred belly button?"

"Max," I said, "you saw the picture of Aimee. After I saw the picture, I told Hammond to call me if a little girl came in with a burned belly button. He did. It was the wrong girl. I asked Yoshino to call me if another one came in." He kept staring at me. "In case it was Aimee," I said.

"You're not trying to figure out who's burning all these little girls."

"I'm looking for Aimee. If figuring that out would help me, I'd try to figure that out. Same as you would."

"That's very specific," he said.

"I'm a very specific kind of guy."

"And why do you know Junko's name?"

"Are you looking for the pimp?"

Bruner made a sound that was a lot like spitting.

"He's not on the street," Hammond said. Bruner gave him an angry glance.

"So where is he?"

"You," Bruner said to Yoshino. "Go do something."

"Well," she said, "there's the records." She shuffled off toward the door. Her heels clacked indignantly on the concrete floor.

"Gosh, you dress nice, Max," I said.

Bruner pulled up another chair and straddled it, facing me. "We can lift your license, you know," he said. He pried some Maalox loose from his back teeth with his tongue and chewed it.

"No shit," I said, looking around wildly. "Stop the car."

Bruner slowly leaned forward until his head was resting on the back of the chair. His acidic stomach rumbled. He had a bald spot the size of a mature tarantula that I hadn't noticed before.

"I know Junko's name," I said, "because I spent more than a week on the street. I know Marco because I know

Junko. You can learn a lot sitting around in the wrong restaurants. You should try it sometime."

"I'm not allowed to work the street anymore," Bruner said without lifting his head. "We're looking for the pimp. Who else should we be looking for?"

I took it as a rhetorical question and didn't bother to answer. "What do we do now?" I asked.

"I don't know," Bruner said, lifting his head. His face was wan and sour and exhausted. "Listen," he said, "I spent years of my life out there, whether you like my clothes or not. You've been there for a week, and it's practically killing you. I saw you when you looked at her." He jerked his chin in the direction of Junko's drawer. "Do you know how many I've seen come and go? Do you know how many greasy little perps I've questioned? How many corpses I've had to look at? Most of them babies. Have you got any idea what a shitty job this is?"

"I think I do," I said. "So, to get back to business, what do we do now?"

Bruner looked at Hammond, and Hammond nodded.

"You don't do anything," Bruner said. "But if anything happens, anything at all, you'll give me a call, right?"

"Max," I said, "you have my personal word of honor." I may have laid it on a little thick, because he gave me a mean little squint, but then he got up.

They followed me to the parking lot, both of them, but they let me go. As Alice chugged dutifully up the ramp and into the drizzle, I asked myself whether I'd just eliminated my main source of information. I knew Hammond was okay, but could I or couldn't I trust Bruner? I couldn't answer the question, so I just kept driving. When in doubt, I'd learned at a relatively early age, just keep doing what you're already doing. If you do, at least you're doing *something*. To this rule I'd long ago added a codicil: don't change your mind before sundown.

Sundown had long come and gone by the time I reached home again. According to my answering machine, Wyatt and Annie had called three more times about Jessica.

"She's not here," I said, calling back. I'd run out of sympathy.

"Do you know what this is doing to Annie?" Wyatt demanded. "She's been in bed with a sick headache since three."

"Wyatt," I said, "it'll be okay."

"Where is she? I should go get her."

"So go get her," I said unkindly. I hung up. Then I popped open a bottle of Singha and drank it in one long chug. I drank seven more before I finally passed out, trying to wash the image of Junko Furuta from my memory.

20

Cracking the Code

The telephone clanged and whirred like a chain saw poised above my forehead. I opened my eyes, saw four of everything, and closed them again. When I reopened them they had uncrossed, and the phone was still ringing.

No wonder it had sounded like it was poised above my forehead. It was. I was flat on my back on the living-room floor, looking up at the rickety wooden orange crate that supported the answering machine and the phone. I used an arm that seemed to outweigh the rest of my body to reach up and grab the receiver.

"Unghh," I said, registering that my tongue didn't work.

"Mr. Grist?" said a voice that could have belonged only to Yma Sumac in her top register or to Morris Gurstein. Since Yma Sumac didn't have my phone number, I said, "Hlo, Mrrs." My voice was furrier than Tammy's chinchilla.

"I've got it," he squeaked. "It's *very* interesting."

"What is?" I asked, trying without success to sit up.

"This code. I've never seen anything like it before."

"Morris," I said, managing it better this time. "What's on the disks?"

"Data base, like you said." He sounded less excited. "Maybe some kind of bulletin board. Bunch of junk, if you ask me."

"Where are you?"

"What do you mean, where am I? I'm a kid. I'm at home."

"Yeah, right." An alien was trying to chew its way into the world via a route that led through the center of my forehead. "I'll be right over." I was straining my back to get the receiver anchored again when a shrill sound told me that he was still talking.

"What is it?" I said, slamming the receiver painfully against my right ear.

"Bring Jessica," he said.

"Morris," I said through clenched teeth as my ear throbbed, "don't be coy."

I took a hot shower, a cold shower, and a second hot shower while the coffee brewed. I drank two cups as quickly as I could pour them, standing stark naked and dripping wet at the kitchen counter, and then took another cold shower. Then, still wet, I took four aspirin. When I climbed into Alice, a third cup of cooling coffee quaking in my hand, it was about eight A.M. outside, and grayer than the Confederate army.

Elise Gurstein, in a flowing housecoat, handed me yet another cup of coffee as I came through the door. She seemed always to be handing me things. "I didn't know," she said apologetically. "I had no idea. I never go into Morris' part of the house."

"Skip it," I said around gulps. "Kids are smarter than we are. Just give me a refill." She did, splashing some hot coffee on my wrist, and I descended into Morris' lair, rubbing alternately at my sore ear and my wrist. I took some encouragement from the fact that my head remained on my shoulders all the way down the stairs. I still had it on when I used what seemed like somebody else's hand to open Morris' door.

"What *took* you so long?" Morris demanded. The computer screens were on and glowing, and Jessica peered at me over Morris' shoulder. She gave me an excited grin.

"Tell you in a second," I said, reaching over his shoulder and slapping Jessica on the cheek. I hit her harder than I'd intended to, and she toppled to the left and landed on

Morris' rumpled bed, on top of a heap of school books that I recognized as hers. Somebody else's hand tingled from the force of the blow.

"Hey," Morris said protectively, assuming the half-assed karate stance of wimps the world over. Jessica looked at me in sheer disbelief, then looked at Morris, and started to bawl. I brushed aside Morris, who was trying to figure out which fist should point palm-up, and stood over her.

"You self-centered little shit," I snarled. My forehead was wet and aching and probably green with sweat. "I saw a dead girl last night. That was my second in a few days. Another one is still missing, and maybe she's dead too. How do you think *their* parents feel? You've had enough to do with this that you should know better. Annie and Wyatt are my friends, and they're your friends too, even if you're too dumb to know it. How dare you do this to them?"

"We didn't do *any*thing," she sniffled. "I slept in Morris' data room."

"She did," Morris said, abandoning his lethal pose after one last futile pass at getting it right.

"Shut up, Morris." I wiped my forehead with the hand that had the coffee in it and poured some on my nose. "I don't care if you slept on a bed of nails," I said to Jessica. "Your parents didn't know where you were."

"They hit me."

"My golly, my gosh. The brutes. Well, now I've hit you too. Maybe we know something you don't."

She turned over on her stomach and cried into Morris' pillow, abandoning logic in favor of something that usually worked. I wiped the coffee off my nose, gave her rear a thwack with the back of my hand, and turned to Morris.

"You're a jerk too," I said. "What did you think you were doing, guarding the ideal of justice?" He gave me a startled look that told me that that was exactly what he'd thought he'd been doing. "Listen," I said, trying for a tone of sanity and taking one of his hands in mine as I sat on the bed next to Jessica's heaving back. I balanced the coffee against her thigh. "I'm here this morning because there are people in the world who think that kids like you and Jessica are merchandise. Some of the kids they sell are dead. Some of the others probably wish they were. Your parents, hers and yours, Morris, aren't monsters. They're trying to help you get to the point where you can tell the monsters from the human beings. That's all. They know they can't make you happy for your whole lives. They know you're going to fuck up and make mistakes."

Morris made a dismissive gesture with his free hand, and I caught it. Now I had both of them, and he looked faintly uneasy. "You're going to marry some twit who beats you or cheats on you or takes everything you've earned," I said. "You're going to vote for the wrong presidential candidate and go to work at some job that grinds your soul to dust. You're going to wake up some morning when you're forty-five and look around you and realize that you're living someone else's life by mistake and that it's too late to change your mind. Those are things they can't do anything about. But they *can* protect you from monsters while you're still too young and dumb to see them for yourselves, and you have to let them do it. Hell," I said, "give them a break, okay? It's not like they think they're going to get anything out of it. They do it, even though they'll probably fail, because they love you."

Morris looked down at Jessica on the bed. He looked like a man watching a sparrow fall. She'd given up on crying. I let go of his hands.

"I told her she should go home," he said to her back.

"You've got to take love where you find it," I said to Jessica. "There's not so much of it in the world that you can turn your nose up at it."

"They hit me," she said again, her face buried in the pillow.

"You're breaking my heart," I said.

"Well," she said, rolling onto her back and wiping her eyes on her sleeve, "they shouldn't have." The coffee cup tilted over and made a brown stain on Morris' bed. There were a lot of stains on Morris' bed, so I gave up on it.

"You're going home with me. Your home, not mine."

She looked at Morris, who immediately focused on one of the computer screens. She swallowed and then nodded. "But you can't let them hit me."

"I'll see to it." I looked up at Morris, hovering over us. "And you," I said, "you have to promise not to kill me with a flying fist when my back is turned."

He considered it in all seriousness. "Okay," he said.

"Good," I said. "Let's look at the disks."

As Morris busied himself with the computers, Jessica pulled herself up to a sitting position, took one last wipe at her face, wiped the coffee off her jeans, and tucked her knees under her arms. "Do you know what's on these?" I asked.

"I've *seen* them," she said. "I don't have any idea what they mean."

"I figured it out about six," Morris said, doing something esoteric to a keyboard. "I woke her up and we looked at it, and then we called you."

"Six? You mean, in the morning? What time did you get up?"

"He didn't," Jessica said with a note of concealed pride. "He got me started on my math at about ten last night and then came in here. The next thing I knew, he woke me up to tell me that he'd busted it."

"You worked all night?" I said. I wanted to hug him.

"I'm a kid," Morris said. "Kids don't need as much sleep as old people."

"You win," I said. "Let's look at them."

"Hold on," he commanded, back in his element, "let me bring the first one up."

Keys clacked, and then he grunted. I patted Jessica on the head in a paternal, old person's fashion, picked up the empty cup, and peeked over his shoulder. Morris was looking at a screen full of words. I'd seen it before.

"Morris," I said, feeling disappointed, "I got that far." I was considering a new career.

"This is real cute," Morris said, gazing at the screen as

though it were *The Last Supper* and he'd just bought it to hang on his wall among the fractals or whatever they were. "It looks just like word processing. In fact, it is, it's Wordstar, one of the later upgrades. Now watch." He typed a few words and a warning came up at the bottom of the screen: DISK FULL.

"I've gotten that far too." Maybe I should go back to teaching, I thought. Tenure, pretty young students, regular office hours. It all looked a lot better to me than it had while I was doing it.

"But you haven't gotten *this* far," Morris said triumphantly. He typed the word AND, and added a question mark.

"My sentiments exactly," I said.

He hit Enter.

The words fell away, and instead of a bunch of impenetrable math I found myself looking at a data-base entry just like the one I'd seen on Birdie's console. It read like this:

RECORD 1. (186–486)

1. 3088 Compton Blvd., Bellflower, CA 90266 (213) 555-1296

2. 4 yrs

3. Turkey

4. CURRENT

5. ORDERS

    a. Fingers, 1200 orders, last order 1000 (913)

    b. Parts, 2800 orders, last order 2300 (913)

    c. Paper, 4000 orders, last order 3300 (913)

    d. Drinks, "A" category (no change) (911)

6. SPECIAL ORDERS

    a. 188, u.r., 188 (422–427) JX6

    b. 217, c.r., 188 (517–522) CP1

    c. 217, c.r., 188 (523–529) UI

    d. 202, u.l., 687 (unavailable) BX

    e. 226, u.r., 188 (74–711) BX

    f. 226, u.r., 188 (712–718) UI

    g. 193, l.c., 188 (1001–1010) BX

We sat there, all three of us, and stared at it. Nobody said anything.

"Turkey?" Jessica finally said.

"It still looks like garbage," Morris said in his soprano, "but it can't be. Look at the trouble they went to to hide it."

"Page down," I said. "I think there's more."

There was. There were five more records on the disk. They all consisted of similar gobbledygook. It was a classic data-base form, the same from screen to screen. All that changed was the data, and we didn't have any idea what it meant.

"Fingers," Morris said, flipping through the forms. "Parts. Paper. Drinks." He shrugged. "All the disks are more or less the same."

"Let me sit down," I said.

He gave me a look full of deep misgiving. "Which keys are you going to touch? I haven't backed these up and I don't want you to trash them."

"I'll touch the keys you tell me to touch. Now get up." He did, and I sat. "Page down, right?" I asked. "That moves me to the next screen."

"Right," Morris said, "but be careful."

The next screen, even upon closer examination, looked pretty much like the last screen. So did the others.

"Concentrate on one field," Morris suggested.

"What's a field?" Jessica asked.

"The little answers after the periods. Each one of those answers is a field. The whole thing is called a record."

"Let's look at the first disk," I said, pulling out the floppy that Morris had put in and inserting the one I'd labeled ONE, in imitation of Birdie. The top of the screen read: RECORD 1. (186–486). "Since we haven't got anything else to do, let's look for numerical sequences."

There weren't any. The numbers were the same at the top of every record. They all read: (186–486).

"That's real productive," I said. "Let's look at the other numbers."

We did. We flipped from record to record. Some numbers seemed to have a logical sequence and some didn't. One thing did change: the words after the period following the number three. I wrote them down as we paged through the records, and then we all sat and looked at the page I'd written on.

"Turkey," Jessica read. "Inthe. Straw. Hollered. Begged. Hotwater." She looked at both of us and shrugged.

"They're code words," Morris said. "If this is a bulletin board, which I think it is, these are the words people use to access the board. All the users have secret words. Without them, they can't get into the data base."

"What's a bulletin board?" Jessica said.

"It's just a data base that people reach by telephone. See all the phone numbers? You use the modem in your computer to dial a number and then you've got to give a code to get to the information. If you use the wrong code, the bulletin board disconnects. There are dating services that work like that," Morris said, blushing becomingly. "The people who called this board probably typed in these names, and that was their code."

"Look at the other disks," I said, getting up.

Morris dealt disks into the slots like an old Vegas hand playing a new form of computer poker. Each of the other disks contained six records, just like the first. The same six words, or combinations of words, came after number three on each disk.

"They're duplicates," I said, feeling disappointed.

"Turkey in the Straw," Morris said suddenly, looking at the page. "That's a kind of folk song, some kind of hillbilly music."

"Yeah?" I said, grasping literally at straws. "How does it go?"

"*Mom,*" Morris bellowed. I quailed nervously, and Jessica retreated a step. "She'll know," Morris said in explanation. "She and my dad are into hayseed music. They're old-fashioned liberals."

"Poor you," Jessica said with the new conservatism of the American teenager.

Elise Gurstein came to the door. "More coffee?" she asked.

"Sing, Mom," Morris commanded. " 'Turkey in the Straw.' "

"Morris," Elise Gurstein said, looking flustered. "Surely you jest. It's nine-fifteen. I can barely talk at this hour."

"Then get Dad."

"He's asleep. They shot until three last night. Morris' father is in television," she said to me.

"You get the part, then," Morris said mercilessly. " 'Turkey in the Straw.' You and Dad know all those chestnuts."

"This is more than a trifle embarrassing," Elise Gurstein said to me. "Especially since I don't know the words."

"Just 'deedle, deedle,' " Morris said. "This could be important."

"It had better be," said his mother. "Okay, but all of you have to turn your backs." We did, and I heard her draw a deep breath. "Ohhh," she sang in a pure soprano, "de deedle deedle deedle and de deedle deedle de. And de deedle deedle deedle, deedle de de de."

"Again," Morris commanded.

"I know the words," Jessica said, cutting Elise off in mid-deedle. "My dad used to sing it sometimes when he was carrying Luke and me around on his back." She looked down at the pad. "Oh, Jesus," she said.

"What?" I asked. "What is it?"

"They're here, sort of," she said. Then she sang:

> Oh, the little chickie hollered
> And the little chickie begged,
> And they poured hot water
> Up and down his leg.

"That's pretty morbid," Elise Gurstein said reprovingly. Words like those weren't in the Liberals' Children's Songbook.

"It's a children's song," Jessica said. "Or that's what Daddy says."

"Hot water," I said. Something connected in my mind, with the force of a bolt lock being shot home. I heard the gush of water echoing on a tape cassette, almost drowning out Aimee Sorrell's screams.

"They've left out Chickie," Jessica observed, scanning the words I'd written.

"Is the concert finished?" Elise Gurstein asked. "Can I go back upstairs now?"

"I guess so," I said. She left.

"So that's it," Morris said. "Maybe they're all folk singers. Maybe this is a folk singers' bulletin board. They all get together on Saturday nights and clog-dance."

"They're not anything that dull," I said. "Look, we've got one sequence already. The words occur in the song in the same order as the records. One is 'Turkey,' two is 'Inthe,' and so forth. Let's look for other sequences, numbers, this time."

"There aren't any," Jessica said. "We already did that."

"Not on a single disk, there aren't. But what about if we look from disk to disk?"

"Wait," Morris said. "I'll load them onto the hard disk and then we can look at them all without having to change disks all the time." He did some magic at the keyboard, and two minutes later we were able to page from disk to disk as well as from record to record.

"Look at the numbers at the top," I said, "the ones we were looking at before."

After five minutes we'd found the progression.

The disk I'd labeled ONE had in parentheses the numbers (186–486). There were similar numbers in parentheses on each of the records on the disk. The disk I'd numbered TWO identified all the records on it as spanning (586–986). THREE began with (1086–187). Morris hadn't copied them to the hard disk in numerical order, so it took a little longer than it would have otherwise.

"They're dates," I said conjecturally. "One-eighty-six means January 1986. Look at them all. They're a continuous record. Disk one ends with April 1986, and disk two begins with May 1986. They're not duplicates, they're some sort of chronological record."

We all looked at the screen.

"Yes," Morris said, rubbing his chin with an oddly middle-aged gesture. "Yes."

"Yes, what?" Jessica demanded, sounding like her old self.

"Then some of the numbers following the orders and the special orders are dates too," Morris said. "Just put a slash in between the first or second number and the last two. Look, all the numbers to the right are sequential top to bottom. Special order A lasted from April 22 to April 27. Special order B goes from May 17 to May 22, and special order C is May 23 to May 29. I think you're right."

"It's Simeon's job to be right," Jessica said.

"Why no years in those fields?" I asked, thinking out loud.

"Because the year is at the top," Morris said in the patient tone of one who had to break the news to a half-wit. "This disk covers January 1988 to October 1988."

"Wooey," Jessica said, staring at the screen.

"There's another sequence," Morris announced to the room at large, paging through the records and the disks. "Look: 1200 orders of fingers, 2800 orders of parts: 4,000 orders of paper. So fingers and parts equal paper. See? The amount of paper equals the number of parts and fingers added together."

"Son of a bitch," I said, moderating my awe at Morris' expertise. Addition had never been a comfortable subject. "Can you print this one out?"

"Sure," Morris said confidently, "no prob."

"Before you do, type in the dates."

Humming to himself, Morris typed for a few minutes, then hit a couple of keys, and said, "Here it comes."

Something behind me panted and then whirred. I turned to see a laser printer. After a moment it stuck out a tongue of white paper at us.

"This is really *neat*," Jessica said, grabbing the sheet. She put it on the desk and we all gathered around it. Now it looked like this:

RECORD 1. (April 88–October 88)
1. 3088 Compton Blvd., Bellflower, CA 90266 (213) 555–1296
2. 4 yrs
3. Turkey
4. CURRENT
5. ORDERS
    a. Fingers, 1200 orders, last order 1000 (September 13)
    b. Parts, 2800 orders, last order 2300 (September 13)
    c. Paper, 4000 orders, last order 3300 (September 13)
    d. Drinks, "A" category (no change) (September 11)
6. SPECIAL ORDERS
    a. 188, u.r., January 88 (April 22–April 27) JX6
    b. 217, c.r., January 88 (May 17–May 22) CP1
    c. 217, c.r., January 88 (May 23–May 29) UI
    d. 202, u.l., June 87 (unavailable) BX
    e. 226, u.r., January 88 (July 4–July 11) BX
    f. 226, u.r., January 88 (July 12–July 18) UI
    g. 193, l.c., January 88 (October 1–October 10) BX

"What the hell happens only in January or June? And what are the numbers on the left? What's u.l.? What's u.r.?" I asked. There was a long silence, followed by a mutual shrug.

"Look at the other disks," I said, and Jessica and I looked over Morris' shoulder as he toggled some key or another to bring disk after disk to the screen. As he did so, a number caught my eye.

"Back up," I said. "No, not that one, the one before it."

The record I wanted came obediently back to the screen

and sat there glowing a comfortable green. "Well, I'll be damned," I said.

"Which number?" Morris said, eyeing the screen intently.

"The phone number," I said. "At the top."

"What about it?" That was Jessica.

"I picked it up off Birdie's memory dialing buttons. I called it a couple of times."

"And?" Morris said, popping his knuckles in his eagerness.

"The guy who answered it said 'Captain's.' When I asked him Captain who, he hung up. Find me a number with an L.A. area code."

Morris found two. "That one," I said, stopping him at the Bellflower screen. "I got the same answer there."

Morris did something, and I found myself looking at another screen with an L.A. address and area code.

"I didn't have that number."

"You've got it now," he said. "Fingers, parts, paper, drinks. The Captain." Suddenly he giggled. "*Chickie*. Oh, my gosh, chickie. Come on, Jessica," he said. "What's there? Sixty-one-sixty Sunset. Fingers, parts, paper, drinks, chickie, the Captain. What's there? Think single-digit I.Q."

"How should I know?" she said defensively.

"Full of idiots. Wearing masks. The most bogus place to eat in the whole wide world. *Fingers*, Jessica."

"Morris," she said reverently. It was a tone I hadn't heard from her since Wyatt explained how the world was round, when she was six. "That's brilliant."

Morris glowed modestly while I sat there feeling like a floor lamp. "Listen," I said after they'd simpered at one another for a few moments, "I hate to intrude on the communing of true spirits, but what's there?"

"The Captain's," Morris said. Then he extended a hand, vaudeville-style, to Jessica, and said, "Ta-*da*."

"Cap'n Cluckbucket's," she said, slapping his palm. "The world's corniest fast-food restaurant." She gave Morris a blinding smile, and he ducked back toward the keyboard as if he were afraid her smile would blow his head off.

"Cap'n Cluckbucket's," I repeated in complete incomprehension, but even before I breathed in I knew what they meant. "Chicken," I said. "Chicken fingers. Chicken parts. Drinks. Paper for serving all that crap on. Guys in chicken suits."

"Paper masks. Cute little beaks and rooster combs," Morris said.

I got up. "Listen, Morris," I said, "can you get into this data base and screw around with it? Change it around, make it do things?"

"Probably." He looked at Jessica for approval. "Why?"

"I don't know yet. I just need to know that you can do it."

He hesitated and then decided on bravado. "Sure I can," he said.

"Where are you going?" Jessica said.

"I'm hungry," I said, going through the door and up the stairs and into the nonfractal world. As I'd promised, I dropped Jessica at home. As a bonus I fended off her ferocious parents before heading Alice into Hollywood.

21

At the Cap'n's

Considering that it was Hollywood, absolutely nothing was going on. Anywhere else, the big guy in the chicken suit would have been news.

Cap'n Cluckbucket's hunkered down on a littered square of asphalt in the 6100 block of Sunset, between a new coppery-glass office building and a once-elegant 1930's apartment house with paper trash from Cap'n Cluckbucket's heaped against its walls like a postindustrial snowdrift. Even for a detective who had to have his work done for him by a teenage kid with a voice like Minnie Pearl's, it was easy to tell which building was Cap'n Cluckbucket's: it was the one with the eighteen-foot-high yellow chicken on the roof and the 270-pound chicken walking around outside.

I'd been in the vicinity for a few hours, mostly watching and trying not to attract attention. First, I'd parked across the street until the occupants of an LAPD cruiser had checked me out twice. Then I'd driven around the block ten or twelve times. Finally I'd abandoned the car out of sight in the Starlite Bagels parking lot down the street, hiked to the restaurant, and sat under the interior neon, cheek to jowl with a rain forest of plastic ferns, eating greasy fried chicken from an orange tray until my cholesterol count zoomed into the red zone. I also took the "Chicken Trivia Quiz" that was printed on my napkin. I scored in the Big Cluck range.

A beefy individual in a gaudy rooster outfit stood at the curb outside and waved the cars in. And in they came, drawn from the flow of Sunset by the promise of noise and company and a quick meal on a day that probably already seemed too long. The cars were full of Mommies and Daddies and Kiddies. Many of them, more than you see in any other country on earth, were overweight. And no wonder. The chicken breasts I'd ordered were so puffed up with batter and oil that they could have been dinosaur thighs. From a very greasy dinosaur.

Cops ate there too. The occasional black-and-white pulled in and two guys, or a guy and a girl, dressed in blue and packing iron, jingled in through the crush of families and named their poison. I didn't see any of them pay. Fast-food joints are cash-intensive businesses, and they like to have the cops on their side. That was worrisome.

The seed of cop paranoia had been planted by good old Marco and watered by the Mountain. On the whole, it seemed to me that there were more cops patronizing the Cap'n's than the Cap'n's food warranted, even given that it was free. If the restaurant was involved in child prostitution, it was possible that some of the folks in uniform were too. I kept my eyes on my food and wallowed in anxiety.

The bunch behind the counter was the usual L.A. minimum-wage mixture of legal and illegal Hispanic immigrants, none of them much over high-school age. They took the orders and punched them up on forbiddingly complicated cash registers. The registers totaled the price, calculated the sales tax, and printed out a receipt that itemized every dreadful thing you'd ordered. THREE-PAK, mine said, meaning three pieces of something that might have begun life as a chicken. BISCUIT. LG. SOFT DRINK. And to the right were the prices, and at the bottom, the total, followed by HAVE A NICE DAY. Fat chance, I thought. Fat, polysaturated chance.

The registers, I mused, might also be feeding data into the console on Birdie's desk.

The manager, an obese, untidy Anglo with skin the color of pancake batter, moved back and forth frantically behind the counter, clapping his hands together like a demented cheerleader to spur on his tropically indolent staff. He wore a chicken costume like the one on the outsize bruiser who was working the curb, and every time he clapped his hands the rubber rooster comb on top of his head quivered. His face was uncovered so we could all see his smile. It was a pretty ghastly smile. The sign on his chest, or, rather, breast, since he was masquerading as a fowl, said MARTY.

I was sure that I didn't want to talk to Marty. In addition to the bustling kitchen crew, who didn't have time to talk to anybody, there were three young Hispanic women who took the orders, largely ignoring Marty. I might have spoken to them, but didn't: it was only Thursday, the third day since Mrs. Sorrell had paid the ransom for Aimee, and I couldn't risk starting anything. I had a full day to go.

So I choked down my LG. SOFT DRINK and picked at my THREE-PAK and hefted my BISCUIT, which might have been made out of reconstituted iron filings, and tried to figure out what, if anything, was going on.

At the table across from me a family of four, Vietnamese immigrants from the look and sound of them, were working their way through a meal that at least some of them would surely regret. The mother and father, both of them brown and delicate, stared dolefully at their plates, obviously missing their noodles and their odorous but delicious fish sauce, but the kids tucked in with the gleeful appetites of new Americans. They were, as near as I could tell, a boy and a girl. Both of the children had come back from the counter wearing paper chicken masks that terminated in little yellow beaks just below their noses and paper chicken bibs decorated with printed feathers. I was trying to determine how old they were when I realized that the mother was staring at me. As a rule, Vietnamese don't stare. It's considered impolite. I smiled at her, and saw that the father was staring at me too. I'd been looking too long at their children.

"Beautiful kids," I said.

The father glanced at the mother and then returned my

smile. "How you knowing?" he asked. "Them look like bird."

"A boy and a girl, right?"

"This one girl," he said, pulling at the mask on the child nearer to me. A pert little face peeked brownly out at me and then the child reached up a hand made of fragile bird-bones and firmly replaced her mask. "Other one boy," the father said. He looked happy not to have to eat. "Boy number one."

"Firstborn?" I asked. The boy, who was gnawing at a wing that could have come off a pterodactyl, was marginally larger.

"Number one," the father repeated. "Born Vietnam."

"Where in Vietnam?"

The father grew watchful. For all he knew I was a Viet-nam burnout with an Uzi under my shirt. "You been Viet-nam?" he asked carefully.

"No," I said, "but I hear it is very beautiful."

"Was," he said, still on guard. "Near Hue."

"Hue." I had no idea where that was.

"Farm," he said. "Cows and chickens. Chickens not like this." He gestured at his plate.

"No chicken was ever like this," I said.

"American chicken no good," said his wife with the air of one who was testing her English. She sat back at the end of the sentence and allowed herself a private smile. She'd talked to an American. She had a story to tell when she got back to the Vietnamese enclave in what used to be Chinatown. It was now one of several Little Saigons. The Chinese had moved to Monterey Park.

"I like it," the boy said from behind his mask. His English was as unaccented as mine. "Hell, I think it's great."

"Language," his father said reprovingly. "Watching lan-guage, please."

"Let me see your face," I said to the boy. He pulled up his mask and let it rest on his forehead. A lock of straight black hair was captured beneath it. Two dark eyes winked out at me like raisins in a rice pudding. He was about nine.

"You like this better than Vietnamese chicken?" I asked.

"Vietnamese chicken stinks," he said. "I'm an American. My name is Tony."

Tony's parents looked at him with loss in their eyes. His mother said something in Vietnamese. Even his sister stared at him, her paper beak turning in his direction.

"Um," I said, and then the conversation was interrupted by a high-pitched squabble from the counter.

Two boys were fighting. The one parent with them, the mother, tossed out pleading smiles in all directions as the boys threw looping roundhouse punches at each other. At issue, it would seem, was a torn, brightly colored piece of paper. Each of them had approximately half of it in his hand. The smaller of the two fell to the floor in self-defense and clutched his half of the trophy to his stomach. The larger boy administered what looked like a persuasive kick to the smaller one's backside.

"Whoa," said an adult male's voice, and I saw the big rooster named Marty wade into the fray. "What's the problem here?"

"Willie took my mask," said the little one, still hunched over. Outraged righteousness rang in his voice.

"Forget it," Marty said gruffly from under his rubber rooster's comb.

"But it's *mine*," the little one said. "Willie is a dork."

"Ho, ho, ho," Marty laughed with all the rich and hearty sincerity of a Macy's Santa. "We got lots of them." He snapped his fingers in the direction of the nearest of the Hispanic girls, and she reached under the counter and came up with what looked like fifty chicken masks.

"Two," Marty said with a new note of command in his voice. "Two, stupid." He apparently couldn't be bothered with remembering her name, even though it said ALICIA on her name tag.

Blushing in anger, Alicia dropped all but two of the masks under the counter and handed the pair to the big rooster. Then, biting her underlip, she turned to the soft-drink machine and yanked the handle down, filling a cup that no one had ordered. Rooster Marty kept a watchful eye on her as he handed the masks to the two boys, giving each of them an awkward, ham-handed pat on the head. Then he turned his head and looked at me. He'd looked at me before.

"Sorry," I said to the Vietnamese couple, "I think I've had enough chicken." I got up and headed for the sidewalk.

Watery sunlight sparkled off leftover Easter decorations in the shops as I walked east, toward Western Boulevard. Western, as its name suggests, used to be the western edge of L.A.; now it's somewhere in the middle. The foot traffic here was made up of the class of Los Angeles residents who don't own cars: bus stops were crowded with stolid, fatalistic-looking Hispanic women going to, or coming home from, domestic jobs, and street crazies mumbled and jabbered their messages to the world, walking as though they were propelled by a system of contradictory and overwound springs. Out-of-work men sat on the low wall surrounding a parking lot, talking and smoking cigarettes. Women and children went in and out of a discount shoe store or stared longingly at the large-screen color television sets in the windows of an appliance-rental center. It was the kind of neighborhood where people rented things. Several children who had either been parked in front of the window by their mothers or had gathered of their own accord gazed gravely at the images on the screen.

This was a neighborhood in its last throes. Above the little run-down thrift shops and *clinicas medicas* and four-story apartments, the new office building next to the Cap'n's loomed like a coppery finger pointing toward the future. The neighborhood in which these people lived and worked and raised children was a tax deduction for incorporated dentists on some business manager's books in Beverly Hills, and somewhere some computer was running a rentals-versus-land-values equation that would eventually bring in the bull-dozers and then the architects and steelworkers and concrete pourers, and, penultimately, the interior decorators. Then would come the executives and junior executives in their BMW's and Cherokees, most of them white, and the old brown neighborhood would recede north and south, away from the Boulevard and into the decaying side streets, and finally it would pull up stakes completely and reroot itself somewhere farther east and south, wherever the accountants' equation translated into Let the Neighborhood Go. I preferred this one the way it was, full of noisy, sloppy life spilling onto the sidewalks, quarreling and laughing and spending and dreaming and falling in love and shooting each other on occasion.

The thought of BMW's made me stop walking. Children were expensive merchandise. People didn't pick up expensive merchandise in dumped, primered Plymouths from the mid-sixties. The place to be was Cap'n Cluckbucket's parking lot. I went the long way around the block and retrieved Alice. Then I changed my shirt, put on my Jerry Lewis glasses, black horn-rims with white adhesive tape over the nose, combed my hair forward, and drove Alice into the Cap'n's lot.

With a tray of chicken so oily that Saudi Arabia would have gone to war for the mineral rights and yet another LG. SOFT DRINK, I sat and watched the traffic go in and out of the Cap'n's lot. There was a system, of sorts. After the rooster on the curb waved them in, cars went either into a parking slot or into the drive-through lane. Once in a while a kid would get out of a car in the drive-through lane and go into the bathroom, but he or she always came back in due time, so I figured the cars to watch were the fancy ones whose occupants went into the restaurant.

I was there an hour, which was as long as I dared to stay. I saw only four expensive cars the whole time I was there. A

Cadillac convertible with a male in it who arrived solo, ate solo, and left solo; a big Jeep Cherokee with a family of six who left without ordering because the place was too busy and they didn't want to wait in line; a Maserati driven by a man who had a little boy in tow and who left twenty minutes later with him still in tow; and a Buick Reatta containing a man and a little girl of twelve. When the man came out alone, I sat up so jerkily that I spilled part of the drink into my lap, adding to the already plentiful scars and stains of the day, but a moment later the little girl came running out of the rest room and climbed into the Buick and the two of them drove away. With a lump in my stomach that was compounded equally of disappointment and indigestible chicken, I headed into the rush-hour traffic and pointed Alice toward Topanga. The sun, as I drove west, glared through the clouds like a luminescent bottle of milk.

I wanted to call the Sorrells when I got home, but I couldn't. Daddy would be there. I wanted to call Hammond and ask whether they'd found Marco, but I couldn't. It might have endangered Aimee. I wanted to find out where Mrs. Brussels lived and break into her house, but I couldn't, for the same reason. In all, there wasn't a hell of a lot I *could* do.

So I called Roxanne. She was chilly and distant, nursing the grit of her grudge from Easter into a fine pearl of resentment. I called my parents to apologize, and my mother hung up on me, telling me they were watching something on television. I knew they never watched television.

For want of anything better to do, I put Elvis Costello on the stereo and built a fire in the woodburner, congratulating myself on having had the foresight to buy beer on the way home, and thought about dinner. Then the lump in my stomach reasserted itself and I stopped thinking about dinner and thought about beer instead.

Elvis Costello was singing about watching the detectives, and I was on my fourth Singha and wishing I still smoked, when someone knocked on the door. By the time I got up, Roxanne had opened it with her key and was standing there, all soft and milky and looking, as always, like she'd just sent herself out to be dry-cleaned. Her fine auburn hair hung down her back, fastened at the top by what seemed to be a red plastic clothespin. She'd ruined yet another pair of pants by pouring bleach directly into the washing machine instead of into the bleach dispenser. Roxanne is a fool for bleach.

"I'm a creep," she said without a prelude, "but you are too."

"I've never denied that I was a creep," I said, delighted to see her. "But I have a certain *je ne sais quoi*."

"Oh, God," she said, mimicking a swoon, "I go all buttery when you speak French. Is there any more beer?"

"Does the pope wear suspenders?" I asked.

She uncapped one for me and one for her, and I finished mine while she did it, and rolled the empty under the old mahogany sideboard. Roxanne curled up on the couch with her head on my lap and breathed into the front of my jeans. It felt warm and damp and healthy. Two beers later, she said, "Let's do something awful."

We went to bed and did something awful. When we'd caught our breath, we fell asleep.

I was once again in the watching place above the stairs, the place Aurora had told me about, looking down through the slats in the banister. Without knowing why, I knew that everyone else in the house was asleep. The front door opened, and Aimee-the-pig came in. She climbed the stairs just a little more slowly than was natural, sobbing inside the pink plastic costume.

When she passed me, making soft snuffling noises, I got up and followed. I seemed to be enormously heavy, and it took all I had to lift my legs, like I was trying to run through water. Aimee went into her room, her back to me, and stood at the foot of a little white bed decorated with frolicking pigs. Without turning around, she shed the obscene little skirt, with the hole in the back for the curlicue tail, and then the polka-dot blouse. The air in the room began to hum and I felt the hair on my arms bristle. I tried to say something, but all that came out was a croak. She didn't hear it. As I stood there, wanting to run away but unable to make my legs work, she reached up and popped off the snaps that fastened the pig head to the pig body and then she pulled the head off and shook her yellow hair free and turned slowly around to face me, and the air hummed more frantically, like a thousand imprisoned hummingbirds, and I saw her tear-streaked face, and it wasn't Aimee at all.

I sat up in the darkness, grabbing a fistful of blanket in each hand. Roxanne moaned and threw an arm across her face. Moonlight poured in through the window. I knew what was happening in Cap'n Cluckbucket's.

III

Hot Water

22

The Root of "Secretary"

"It's like every other fast-food restaurant in the world," I said into the phone. "They come in with kids and they go out with kids. But at Cap'n Cluckbucket's they're not always the same kids."

I could hear traffic wheezing and hooting on the other end of the line while the Mountain thought. A motorbike snarled by with a long, tearing fart. Then he grunted. "How?"

It was after ten on Friday morning. Roxanne was long gone, off to an aerobics class where she was purchasing a perfect stomach on the installment plan. She'd left a pot full of perfect coffee.

I took a grateful hit off my third cup. "Who notices the kids with an adult in a restaurant?" I asked. "And if they're worried that someone might, there are those chicken masks. I saw two males go in and out, and when one of them left, the kid with him was masked. How do I know that she was the kid he arrived with? They were the same size, but that's all I could testify to. Hell, the one family I talked to, I could barely tell the difference between a boy and a girl."

"I know the place," the Mountain said. He didn't sound very surprised, but then, I'd never seen him act surprised. "Good chicken," he added.

I put a hand to my throat to block the upward progress of the lump I'd ingested on the previous day. The Mountain could have digested Disney World without so much as a burp around Mickey's ears. "Mountain," I said, "there are

231

six of them, that I know of. Six Cap'n Cluckbucket's, maybe more, all dispensing children over the counter, so to speak, without a license. How many kids is that?"

"Hold it," the Mountain said. He put his hand over the mouthpiece and barked something at someone, and I suddenly felt a surge of paranoia wash over me. Suppose I was wrong? Suppose the cops were okay and the Mountain wasn't? Suppose I was talking to someone with a line to Aimee's kidnapper? After all, he was perfectly placed to nab little kids off the streets and stick their parents up for ransom. Worst of all, the kids trusted him. And why wouldn't they? *I* had.

"And?" he said, coming back on the line. Now it sounded as though his mouth were full.

"And nothing," I said, backtracking. "Just steer your kids away from Cap'n Cluckbucket's." I drew a series of interconnected boxes on my pad—a symbol, Eleanor always said, of spiritual imprisonment—and wished I hadn't made the call.

"Hey," he said, "I can't even get them to leave the Oki-Burger. And I can't keep the ones I want to stay. Little girl yesterday, I had her parents all set up to come by, and when they showed up, she was long gone."

"Yeah," I said, "well, that's the breaks."

"You okay?" he asked. "You sound kind of funny."

"Me?" I was perspiring. "I'm swell."

"You still think you'll need help?"

"If I do, I'll call."

"Do that." He yelled at somebody and then hung up.

I had the jitters. Trying to calm my doubts, I poured another cup of Roxanne's coffee and promptly poured it down the sink. What I didn't need was the jitters.

That day, Friday, was the fourth day of Aimee's ransom period, the day she was supposed to come home safe and sound. I'd resigned myself to a day of inactivity, maybe two days: Mrs. Sorrell might give it an extra twenty-four hours before calling for help. For want of anything else to do, I turned on the computer and began to enter notes on the case. Sometimes the act of typing out my thoughts clarified them. Sometimes I just wound up with a bunch of useless high-tech typing.

An hour later, I'd resigned myself to the latter. I felt like I was writing somebody else's novel, like a literary medium doing automatic typing for some second-rate mystery writer in the sky. I had no idea how it was going to turn out.

With a resigned sigh I turned on the printer and churned out what I'd written so far. After several minutes of irritating zipping sounds, five pages lay in the tray. Reading over them, I realized that I'd left somebody out.

Back to the keyboard. I'd never learn to handle it the way Morris did. For him it was a musical instrument, full of mysterious chords and unexpected progressions, modulations, and tone clusters. For me it was an expensive alternative to the ball-point pen. For approximately the thousandth time I wondered why I'd bought the damn thing.

Then, partway through a word, I stopped and stared at the screen. I was writing about Birdie, and the word I was writing was SECRETARY. The first six letters were a word in themselves, and the word was SECRET.

A secretary, in the original meaning of the word, was one who kept someone else's secrets. Birdie, with his terrible hairdo, his Philippine shirt, and his brutal forearms, materialized front and center in my mind's eye and grinned at me. Birdie knew the secrets of the data base. Birdie kept the day-to-day secrets of Mrs. Brussels' appointment book. What other secrets did Birdie keep?

Without thinking about what I was doing, I got up and poured another cup of coffee. It tasted like battery acid; the pot had been on the warmer for hours. I spit it out and rinsed the pot. I even washed my cup, something I usually don't do until all six cups have been used up. I would *really*, I thought, like to take a look inside Birdie's house.

But, as usual, there was a problem or, rather, two problems. The first problem was that it might endanger Aimee. Playing by the rules, I should have waited until the next day, and that was the second problem. The next day was

Saturday, and on Saturday Birdie would probably be home. There's a very good reason why most domestic burglaries, particularly in this age of two-family paychecks, happen on weekdays. Victims observe the work ethic. Burglars don't. There are almost no burglaries during the daylight hours on weekends.

As usual, when faced with something I wanted to do and a good reason not to do it, I rationalized. It's one of the patterns of my life. On a different level, it was the mental trait that had allowed me to talk myself into being unfaithful to Eleanor: she'd never find out about it, I told myself, and it couldn't really hurt her as long as I was clear about whom I actually loved. And, of course, she always found out about it and it always hurt her. Eventually it hurt her to the point where she decided it would be less painful to live without me. And now she was in China investigating extended families and I was floundering around L.A. looking for lost children.

My rationalization about Birdie's house was simple. Don't touch anything, and no one will know. Leave no traces. Just look around and come home. It'll be a head start, I said to myself in my most convincing interior-monologue tone, something I'll have to do anyway when Mrs. Sorrell calls to say that Aimee hasn't been returned. If I didn't do it on Friday, I'd have to wait until Monday. Three lost days, days that might either kill Aimee or save her life. At the time, it seemed like a powerful argument.

Powerful or not, I had the self-control to wait until afternoon. For all I knew, Birdie went home for lunch. I didn't want to walk in on him while he was forking his quiche or gnawing on his cigars or whatever it was that had stunted his growth.

In the meantime, I didn't know where he lived. I didn't even know his last name. I went back to the pad on which I'd written everything I'd learned about the numbers on his auto-redial buttons.

"Doggies Do," said the same peevish voice. He had to do

that five days a week. It was a miracle that he wasn't in a straitjacket.

"I want to make an appointment for a perm," I said flutingly. I made airy little hand gestures to get into the mode. "And a nail clip too. You should *see* what she's doing to the shantung on my couch."

"Your name?"

"Dorfenbecker," I said, gambling that there wasn't another one.

"Hmmmm," he said. Pages flapped. "Have you been in before, Mr. Dorfenbecker?"

"No. It's my very first time."

"How did you learn about us? Yellow Pages? One of our ads in the *Times* or the *Herald Examiner* or *Dog Digest*?"

"Oh, no, no, no. A very sweet man on my block recommended you. He said you were just marvelous. Birdie something; I'm afraid I don't remember his last name."

"That would be Mr. Skinker."

"Yes, of course, Mr. Skinker."

"Such a cute nickname, Birdie. When would you like to come in?"

"Tuesday?" By Tuesday it would be over one way or the other.

"Fine. And what kind of a dog is it, Mr. Dorfenbecker?"

I tried to think of a breed. "A Shetland," I said.

There was a pause. I could hear a pencil tapping on a desk. "A Shetland is a pony," he said. "We don't do horses."

"Well, of *course* you don't," I said. "And Shetlands don't claw couches, at least not unless you keep them in the house. I didn't say Shetland. I said *sheltie*."

"Silly me," he said. "Tuesday at two?"

"Peachy."

"Your phone number?"

I gave him Roxanne's. Roxanne was never home and she didn't have an answering machine. And if he did get her and she said she'd never heard of Mr. Dorfenbecker, he'd just think he'd transposed a digit.

"See you Tuesday at two," he said. *"Ciao."*

"Ciao yourself," I said, hanging up and going back to my pad.

"Holistic Pet Clinic," said the next voice on the third ring. "A holistically healthy pet is a happy pet." The voice belonged to a female.

"This is Mr. Simon, Animal Regulation," I said.

"Mr. Simon," she said, all business. "What can we do for you?"

"I've got an application for license renewal in front of me," I said, "and the man who filled it out neglected to give us his address. You're listed as the veterinarian who gave his dog her booster shots."

"Yes?" she said.

"Well, I can't send him his license tags without an address," I said. Dogs whooped in the background.

"How thoughtful of you," she said. To someone else she said, "Your dog is really terrorizing that kitty. Could you keep him closer to you, please?"

Another job I was glad I didn't have. "His name is Skinker. The dog is a Yorkshire terrier, it says here."

"Just a moment." She dropped the phone to the counter, and I listened to various quadrupeds making their trademark noises as I regretted pouring the battery acid down the sink. A little battery acid was just what I needed.

"Bertram Skinker," she said, "1310 Janet Drive, West Hollywood 90068."

"Thank you," I said, writing it down.

"Don't mention it. Ah, *ah,"* she said, "not on the floor."

At two o'clock I was driving Alice up and down Janet Drive. Janet was a quiet, curving street just barely on the wrong side of Doheny, within envy distance of Beverly Hills. West of Doheny was the Land of Oz, distinguished by desirable zip codes and real-estate values that were accelerating at the speed of light.

Janet Drive was short and almost unpleasantly sweet. There were only twelve houses on each side, mostly small one-story affairs hiding behind privacy walls and growths of nitrogen-rich bougainvillea. They probably cost five thousand dollars to build in the forties, and they were now going in the high threes, as in three hundred thousand. All the houses were painted one of the two current decorator colors, either clamshell white or industrial gray. Thirteen-ten was out of sight behind the full battlement, both an eight-foot-high privacy wall and a flourishing hedge of champagne-colored bougainvillea. I parked, climbed out, and wished for cheap locks.

Inside the privacy wall, one glance at the door reaffirmed my worst fears. Birdie knew about locks. There were three, and only one of them was junk. The one that worried me most was a Medeco double dead bolt, anchored both in the wall to the left of the door and in the concrete slab on which the house had been built. It worried me so much that I walked around the house to check out the back door.

I couldn't get to the back door. Both sides of the house were surrounded by yet another wall, this one more than ten feet tall, and on the right the wall was gated. The gate was as tall as the wall and secured by a heavy combination lock. I knew nothing about combination locks.

So I went back to the front door. Something, presumably Woofers, yapped in a dog version of Morris Gurstein's voice as I worked on the first two locks. They went without too much trouble, leaving me confronted with the Medeco. The Medeco took me almost forty minutes, while Woofers shrilled at me and I wondered whether Birdie worked banker's hours on Fridays. If he did, if he came home and caught me, I might literally be killing Aimee. That is, if she weren't already dead and buried.

Finally the lock groaned and turned to the right, and the arms of the dead bolt shuddered out of position. I realized that I was perspiring profusely. I pushed the door inward and looked down, braced for Woofers' onslaught. Even a little dog can lacerate an ankle, and I didn't want to leave blood on Birdie's floor.

What I was looking at was expensive fuchsia-colored wall-to-wall carpet. Woofers, once the door had creaked open, had beaten a hasty retreat. I went in with new courage and closed the door behind me.

"Wh*oo*-oo," I said in a falsetto that rose and fell like a graph of the Doppler effect. "Wh*oo*-oo, Woofers."

Woofers declined to appear. Instead, something that sounded like a fly being unzipped issued from the room at the end of the entrance hall. It took me a moment to place it as an attempt at a growl. I mustered up my courage and looked around.

Mounted high on the walls, antique masks from Bali or someplace else in Indonesia stuck faded tongues out at me. All the other art in sight was Japanese, mostly celebrating the suicidal spirit of the samurai. In between the bloody prints—decapitations and Japanese swords being swung against invincible ghosts—the walls were covered in a rough, nubby silk of a neutral beige that brought into bright relief the colors of the silk flowers, perfectly arranged, that sprouted from hammered brass vases on the long mahogany table against the right-hand wall. To the left was a door that led into a yellow kitchen with accents of blue in the tiles above the sink, accents that were picked up by the decorator rug on the floor.

The little zipper sound came from underneath a white sectional couch in the living room. Its sections were arranged artfully around a beveled-glass-and-wrought-iron coffee table, and in the center of the coffee table was a beautifully carved wooden head from Java, a graceful girl, or perhaps a boy, wearing an ornate headdress. Her/his features were round and smooth and as impassive as a diplomat's. There was no way to know what that face had seen.

I sat on the couch, and the growling stopped. Propping my feet on top of the coffee table as ankle insurance, I said, "Woofers. Hello, Woofers. Good doggie." The growling began again, but it sounded questioning. "Good old Woofers," I said, "the guardian of the castle. Best dog in the world. *What* a good dog."

Now there was a tiny thumping against the bottom of the couch. She'd traded ends, going from the larynx to the tail, always a positive sign. Still talking, I got up and headed for the kitchen, stepping around an area rug from China that must have cost two thousand dollars, and the tempo of the thumping accelerated.

When I opened the refrigerator the thumping turned into a positive thwacking. Birdie lived on bran, celery, and wheat germ, but there were three speckled brown eggs standing in line in a military fashion inside the refrigerator door. I found a saucer in one of the immaculate cupboards and broke an egg into it, and put the saucer on the floor. "Woofers," I said, "food for the good dog."

I held my breath, and then she trotted in, her nails clicking on the tile like a tiny parody of Yoshino's high heels. She was a perfect Yorkie, her hair shampooed and polished and layered and cut, two little fuchsia ribbons tied in bows through the fur above her ears. She stopped and cocked her head at me with a last twinge of uncertainty. At a certain point, the only thing to do with dogs is to stop trying. "Up to you," I said negligently, going back into the entrance hall. The sound of a lapping tongue followed me.

Birdie's bedroom was virginally perfect. The plum-colored sheets on his queen-size bed were linen, and a dust ruffle shimmered to the floor. The floor in here was bleached oak. Scattered here and there was an occasional area rug, each the result of a year's work in some third-world country. A Yoshitoshi print of a would-be shogun having his head lopped off faced a David Hockney of a boy diving into a pool that was bluer than Paul Newman's eyes. By the time I'd looked at it closely enough to realize that the Hockney was an original, Woofers was at my heels. There was a small Sam Francis over the bed, also an original. For a secretary, Birdie was doing okay.

Entrance hall, kitchen, living room, two little bathrooms, the bedroom. A dining nook off the kitchen. A tiny library with a computer on a pine desk just beyond the bedroom. That seemed to be it. Woofers followed me slavishly from room to room, a hummingbird's tongue hanging out one side of her mouth.

The house, the decorations, the dog: everything was perfect. And yet, that couldn't be the whole story, not unless I was radically wrong about everything. I went through the drawers in the kitchen and then the ones in the bedroom, discovering only that Birdie preferred Henckel cutlery and silk underwear, and then I sat on the bed. I'd been sitting there a minute or more when I realized that I was looking at the door to his closet.

Birdie had a great many Philippine shirts, all of them smaller than the rag I use to polish Alice once a year, and more shoes than a millipede. There were also some antique Japanese kimonos. His clothes hung in color-coordinated glory, like customized color bars on some tailor's television screen. I was reluctant to disturb anything, which was why it took me so long to push the clothing aside and find the door on the other side of the closet. The outside of the door, the side facing me, was extravagantly bolted and barred, but all the bolts and bars were open.

I reached for the doorknob. Behind me, Woofers whimpered.

The door opened inward, away from me, revealing a dim and narrow flight of stairs. They led down. I reached inside and found a light switch.

It was very cool, almost cold, going down. The stairs were oddly proportioned, narrow and awkwardly deep, with a curve to the left. The walls were unpainted plaster, slightly damp to the touch. When I rounded the curve, I saw a small door that might have been taken from a submarine. It was rounded and seemed to be made of iron, and it had a tiny window in it. A sliding metal bar, sufficient to lock it from outside, was pushed to one side.

From some rarely visited corner of my memory an image floated up. Something from first grade, something that brought back a sense of pressure on my knees and something hard over my head, a memory that was full of fear and also a kind of excitement. I reached for the iron door and pulled it open, and as it creaked on its hinges I remembered that the thing under my knees was the floor and the thing above my head was a school desk, and the memory was the vestige of a "drop" drill. What I was entering was a bomb shelter.

You still find them here and there in California, underground temples to the nuclear paranoia of the fifties. Absolutely secure, absolutely soundproof. And even before I found the light switch and looked at the blank white walls, I knew where I was. I was in obedience school.

The room was little, as it would have to have been: its whitewashed walls were concrete, at least four feet thick, and it had been built inside what had originally been a not-very-large basement. The floor was a cold concrete slab. The temperature couldn't have been more than fifty. It was colder than the morgue.

Woofers let out a questioning whine above me. "Come on," I said, suddenly wanting company. After a moment I heard her nails on the stairs.

The room was close to empty. There was a long cheap Formica table against one wall, entirely bare. Each of its four metal legs stood in the center of one-half of a pair of handcuffs. The cuffs circling the table legs were snapped shut but the other cuff in each pair was open. The table was certainly the podium on which Birdie held his graduation ceremonies. Near the opposite wall stood a Polaroid Spectra System camera on an expensive tripod. Aside from the table there was no furniture.

Set into the wall next to the door were three sets of recessed shelves, probably originally intended to hold canned goods and bottled water but now stacked with cardboard cartons full of odds and ends. One of them held Christmas decorations, little lights to make Birdie's house twinkle, and wrapping paper and ribbons. There were also old athletic shoes, garden supplies, extra detergent, and other homely junk that Birdie had stowed down here now that most people acknowledged that the threat of atomic attack was less pressing than the need to wrap presents, wash dishes, and prune roses.

There were also two doors.

The first led to a closet, no more than four feet by four

feet. There were no shelves in it; it was just a tiny room. The door had the same kind of metal bar across its outside, and a small grate had been positioned just above the floor, probably to let in air. A perfect place to lock people in the dark. The children had usually been naked, Marco had said. Naked and freezing in a lightless, comfortless concrete room.

The second door opened into a small bathroom with the kind of awkward plastic toilet they put on boats, and a tiled shower. This was where Aimee had hit high C for the tape recorder while scalding water flowed over her body.

I reclosed the bathroom door and the door to the closet and took a long last look at the room, trying to remember whether I'd moved or changed anything else. Woofers, who had been trembling slightly and keeping very close to me, sat on my right foot. She looked up at me anxiously, ready to go back upstairs.

As I leaned down to pick her up, she got off my foot and stood on her hind legs, doing an eager little dance. She was absurdly light. I wrapped an arm around her and she licked my chin as I headed toward the door.

On impulse, I reached out as I passed the Polaroid and pushed the shutter button. A flash bounced off the white walls and as I strained to get my iris open again the camera went *nnnnzzzet* and a picture slid out of it. A negative image of my retina slid across the picture's surface as I waited for it to develop, and Woofers squirmed in my arms. Thirty seconds later I was looking at an absolutely white Polaroid except for a hard brown edge running along the bottom of the photo: the white was the wall, and the brown edge was the top of the Formica table.

I stopped worrying about Birdie coming home. The boxes on the shelves beckoned to me, and I put the dog down and rifled through them. Christmas lights, Christmas wrappings, Christmas paper; an old set of silver-backed hairbrushes, odds and ends, decorator trinkets that had outlived their appeal on the tabletops upstairs, a wooden box about eight inches square, with an inlaid lid. Inside the wooden box, cigars.

The bows on Woofers' ears came loose with a single tug on each and dangled forlornly on either side of her face. I found a bright preglued red wrapping bow that clashed nicely with the ribbons on her ears, peeled off the backing, and pressed the square of adhesive onto her nose. It held. The transformation was amazing. In a few seconds she'd gone from being Molly Ringwald in *Pretty in Pink* to Bette Davis in *Whatever Happened to Baby Jane?* She had the grace to look embarrassed.

When I mussed up her hair, she seemed to enjoy it. She took a couple of passes at the bow on her nose with her front paws, but stopped when I said, "No, Woofers." By then I was looking at the Polaroid camera. It had everything I wanted, which is to say two more pictures and a time-release button.

I put Woofers on the table, told her to stay, and positioned the lever on the time release. Then I took a cigar out of Birdie's box, pushed the shutter, and went to the table. I patted Woofers on the head as the time release whirred away, lifted her front paws, turned my head away, and pushed the unlit cigar into the middle of her belly. "Coochy-coo," I said. She was wagging her tail, enjoying the game, when the flash went off.

It hadn't been necessary to turn my head because I was cut off at the shoulders. The image was perfect, a bedraggled, drunk-looking little dog with a big cigar pointed squarely at her lower intestine. I put everything back the way it was, tucked Woofers into my jacket, and left.

Bertram Skinker was going to sweat.

23

The Neutron Bomb

"**S**he's so *cute*," Jessica trilled. "Where did you get her?" Morris stood in the doorway behind her, slightly spectral in the daylight. I'd never seen him before without a green glow on his face. He seemed to have brought some of it with him. Jessica or someone had gotten him to wear a shirt with only one pocket for a change, but the one pocket bristled with esoteric writing implements. He held a big white book tucked under his sharp elbow. From where I sat, on the floor playing with Woofers, it looked like an upscale Yellow Pages—the one-hundred-percent-white pages, perhaps, designed for neighborhoods where no one who was yellow—or brown or black, for that matter—lived.

"I'm taking care of her for a friend," I lied. Woofers pranced from me to Jessica and back, groomed and immaculate in the morning light, the perfect dog for the perfect neighborhood where everything could be found in the white pages, and happy to be the center of attention. I found myself hoping that Birdie missed her more than she missed him.

"Jessica," I said, "I don't mean to be rude, but I don't actually recall asking you to come over. And do Annie and Wyatt know where you are?"

"Oh, don't be a grump. Of course they do. And wait until you see why we've come. When you write the story of your life, I want credit. Jesus, Morris, come *in*, won't you? You can't spend your whole life hovering. And close the door."

244

Morris did what he was told, muttering something when he turned his back to pull the door shut.

"Say what?" Jessica said. "And tuck in your shirt."

"I said I get some credit too," Morris said, blushing horribly and fiddling behind his back. At least the blush filled in his zits.

"Fine, fine," Jessica said dismissively. "But me first. What's her name?"

"Woofers."

She wrinkled her nose. "That's terrible. Can't we give her a different name?"

"You can call her Gladys for all I care. What's everybody claiming credit for?"

Jessica looked slyly at Morris and then back at me. "This," she said, pulling a creased and slightly damp piece of paper out of her belt. She opened it and smoothed it on the floor in front of me, and Woofers, sensing my attention the way a cat can, sat on it. I picked her up and dropped her to one side, eliciting a compassionate squeal from Jessica.

I'd seen the printout before, but not quite in this form. It now looked like this:

RECORD 1. (April 88–October 88)
1. 3088 Compton Blvd., Bellflower, CA 90266 (213) 555-1296
2. 4 yrs
3. Turkey (code name?)
4. CURRENT

5. ORDERS

a. Fingers, 1200 orders, last order 1000 (September 13)
b. Parts, 2800 orders, last order 2300 (September 13)
c. Paper, 4000 orders, last order 3300 (September 13)
d. Drinks, "A" category (no change) (September 11)

6. SPECIAL ORDERS

a. Page 188, upper right, January 88 (April 22–April 27) JX6

b. Page 217, center right, June 87 (May 17–May 22) CP1

c. Page 217, center right, January 88 (May 23–May 29) UI

d. Page 202, upper left, June 87 (unavailable) BX

e. Page 226, upper right, January 88 (July 4–July 11) BX

f. Page 226, upper right, January 88 (July 12–July 18) UI

g. Page 217, center left, January 88 (October 1–October 10) BX

"Page numbers?" I asked. "Says who?"

"It's a book," Jessica said triumphantly. "They're all in a book. It comes out every six months." Morris took a tentative step forward, eager to put in an introvert's one cent's worth.

"What book?" I asked.

The phone rang.

I waved them into silence and picked it up. "Hello?"

"Mr. Grist?" It was Jane Sorrell. She was trying to push beyond a whisper, but without much success.

"Mrs. Sorrell. What's happening?"

"She's not back," Jane Sorrell said in a rigid monotone. "She's not back and no one has phoned. She was supposed to . . . she was supposed to be back last . . ." A ring clacked against the mouthpiece, and she made a sound like a retch. "No one has . . . has . . ."

"Please, Mrs. Sorrell. Hang on to yourself. It isn't over yet."

"Oh, yes," she said, "yes, it is. They've got her, they've killed her, I'll never see—"

"I don't think they've killed her," I said. She made crumpled, wispy little sounds into the other end of the line. "She's too valuable to them. They're not going to kill her unless they have to."

Jessica and Morris exchanged wide-eyed stares. Even Woofers was watching me, her brown eyes alert and sympathetic.

"Valuable?" said a new voice, a tougher voice. "What do you mean, valuable?"

"Aurora, is that you?"

"Who else would it be, Donder and Blitzen?"

"Aurora, take care of your mother. I think I know where Aimee is." I didn't, but I knew how to find out.

"You do?" she said skeptically. "I'll believe it when you bring her home. So what's so valuable?"

"Listen," I said, gesturing toward Jessica to give me the pad and pencil next to the computer, "give me the address where you sent the money."

"Mom?" Aurora said. Jessica grabbed the pad and handed it to me, yanking a pen out of the bouquet in the pocket of Morris' shirt. He had about eight left.

"I don't know," Jane Sorrell said. She sounded wet.

"Of course you do," Aurora said authoritatively. "You wrote it down."

"Where is she?" her mother asked me.

"Here. Here in L.A. Have you got the address?" I clicked Morris' pen a few times. Different-colored tips kept coming out.

"We know she's in L.A.," Aurora said. "Haven't you got anything new?"

"That'll have to wait," I said. "What's the address?"

"I don't know why we shouldn't just call the cops," Aurora said.

My hands were perspiring, and I tucked the phone between neck and shoulder and wiped my palms on my pants. "Don't. Believe me, don't."

"Why not?" Aurora's voice was challenging.

I tossed a mental coin. Like most mental coins, it landed on its edge. "Because some of them may be in on it," I said.

There was a long, tense silence.

"How do we know that?" Aurora finally asked.

"You don't. You can't. Hang up," I said. "Hang up and call them. But if you do, don't ever call me again. And whatever you do, don't give them my name."

"You could be manufacturing business," Aurora said. "We call the cops, we don't need you."

"Aurora. You don't really believe that."

She exhaled noisily into the phone. She could have been blowing her nose. I remembered that she was just a little girl. "Mom," she said after drawing a deep sigh, "give him the address."

"I've got it," Jane Sorrell said shakily. "Do you have a pencil?"

"Go." I'd decided on the red point.

"Eleven-six-eighty-six Altham Street. Los Angeles."

"Zip?" The red point wrote blue.

"Nine-oh-three-five-two."

"Airport," I said.

"What?" I couldn't tell which one it was.

"That's near the airport. I'll call you."

"When?" Aurora said.

"When I've got something worth telling you. Good-bye." I hung up. Airport. That was a long way from Hollywood.

Morris was regarding me as though I were some newly ambitious life form that had just crawled ashore. Anything with the word "killed" in it was outside his frame of reference, as it should have been. Jessica was trying to look nonchalant. "People are dying," I said. "What's the book?"

Jessica looked at Morris. "Remember in Mrs. Brussels' office?" she began.

"You already won the laurel wreath," I said. "Spare me the play-by-play. Wait," I said, suddenly recalling the agent's agitation. In my excitement I snapped Morris' pen in half and four ball-point-pen barrels scattered to the points of the compass like a literary multiple-warhead missile. *The Actors' Directory.*"

"U.r.," said Jessica, beckoning to Morris, "means upper right." He handed her the book and she pried it open. "Recognize him?"

She put the book on the floor and pointed to a photo in the upper right. It was her tennis player, the one she'd described as "cute."

"Yeah," I said. "So?"

"Mr. Kale, right?"

"Right," I said, suppressing an urge to strangle her.

"So he's middle left, in the center of the left-hand page. Look upper right."

A little girl beamed up at me. KIMBERLY WINTER, it said under the photo. AGE: 11. "Oh, Jesus," I said. "Sure. I should have thought of it."

"She's her agent," Jessica said. "Mrs. Brussels. I was the one who figured it out, but Morris had the book. His father is in TV."

"And the others?"

"This is the January 1988 book," Morris said. "All the ones that say one-eighty-eight are here, right where they should be, and she's the agent for all of them. Check it out. We've already folded down the pages."

I went down the printout. If u.r. and c.r. meant upper right and center right, they'd figured it out. All the kids whose pictures were printed in those positions, both boys and girls, listed Brussels' Sprouts as their agency. One of them was the curly-haired little girl I'd seen the first time I went to the morgue. Her name was Lizabeth Worthy.

"Have you got the earlier books?"

"Only one," Morris said. "It's from 1987. It's got the entry that was marked 'unavailable.' "

"From June?" I asked, checking the printout.

"Yeah. I didn't bring it, but I brought a copy of the page they asked for." He put it down in front of me and I stared at it. It had been digitized and scanned, and it was pretty high-contrast, but the bright, star-struck face in the photo was definitely Junko's. She wasn't hard to recognize, even minus a hard year and a lot of drugs and misuse. She stared up at me, wearing a lopsided baseball cap and grinning a hopeful smile that I'd never seen while she was alive.

I had to wait a moment while my blood pressure subsided. I also had to blink a couple of times to clear my eyes. Then I said, "Good." My voice was forced and my face felt like a brass funeral mask from ancient Greece. "I'll need that other book," I said.

"There's more," Jessica said.

"More?" I looked down at Junko's lost, open face, trying to

imagine what more there could be. Woofers, feeling neglected, lifted a leg to wash an intimate portion of her anatomy.

"The next issue," Jessica said proudly. "It isn't out yet."

"What about it?"

"Morris called the publishers, acting like his father, to find out which of Mrs. Brussels' clients would be listed in the June issue," she said. Then all of it hit her, the reality of it, and her excitement faded. She looked away from me and out the window at the changeless mountains. "Page 281," she said, "lower left. It's a girl named Dorothy Gale."

The eleven thousand block of Altham Street was the Southern California equivalent of a ghost town. Directly beneath the approach of westbound jets from Chicago and points east, the block was battered twenty times each hour by the roar of Boeing and Lockheed engines being throttled back for a landing.

The noise from LAX had killed everything. The lawns were parched and brown, even in April, and the windows of most of the houses were covered with thick rectangles of plywood nailed directly into the external walls. No one was home, and no one was coming home. But the mailboxes were functional, and the mailboxes were all I cared about.

Eleven-six-eighty-six was a cramped single-decker the color of spoiled Dijon mustard. Casement windows, framed in aluminum, bravely faced the streets without the benefit of plywood to shield them from the thunder. The lawn was relatively green, and two hardy hibiscus plants framed the front door, their flowers cocked upward with wide, orange-lipsticked mouths, gobbling the gathering dusk as though straining it for sunlight. Compared to the other houses on the street, 11686 looked almost inhabited. I could understand the mailman's mistake.

Saturday afternoon was waning as I approached the front door. It wasn't daylight-saving time yet. The sun was most of the way down, and Alice was parked bravely in front. The remaining light was richly fertilized with airplane exhaust. A jumbo jet ripped through the clouds overhead as I knocked, laying down a footprint of noise so loud that it wiped out the sound of my knuckles on the wood. Either no one answered, or else I couldn't hear them. I chose the former and tried the knob. It turned easily, and the door swung open.

The first thing that came to mind—prompted, perhaps, by Birdie's shelter—was the neutron bomb, the miraculous technological advance that eliminates everything living and leaves only objects behind. The living room was cramped and dingy and linoleum-floored, and still furnished. The smell of urine hovered above the floor like a cloud of flies. A brown couch, frozen in the act of exploding, shed cotton stuffing and steel springs. Over it, a standing lamp swayed at a drunken angle. A coffee table with three unbroken legs sagged in front of the couch, and a false fireplace, jammed full of wadded-up newspaper, made a shallow dent in one wall.

My foot hit a ball of crumpled newsprint, sending it skittering across the floor. There was a closed door at the other end of the living room, and I thought I heard something move on the other side of it before another jet plowed through the turbulent air above the roof.

My heart was pounding, but this time, for once, I had a gun.

It felt heavy and cold and reassuring in my hand. It felt as reassuring as the remote control for a couch potato's TV set. If something dangerous was on the other side of the door, maybe I could change the channel.

Crumpled newspaper was an old trick. It was the hoodlum's burglar alarm. Stepped on in the dark, a crumpled newspaper could be the difference between dying and staying alive.

Even though my boots had soft crepe soles, I eased them off. I turned them around with my toes and left them facing the door with the precision of a character in a cartoon who thought he might need to jump into them for a sudden exit. Then, my footsteps cushioned by thick white athletic socks, I headed for the door.

There was no more sound from the other side. Not a shuffle, not a breath. I hefted the gun, took a few deep breaths, and tried the knob. It turned easily.

There was no one there, I told myself while I counted slowly to fifty. And if I were wrong, if there *were* someone there, it wasn't anyone I wanted. It just didn't make sense.

While I reasoned, I checked the gun to make sure that the bright coppery hollow-points were in position, ready to eviscerate anyone on the wrong end of the barrel.

They were. Good. At least I didn't have to make the piercing clicking sound that announces an automatic being snapped into killing position.

And then another jet roared overhead, and I lifted my right leg and kicked the door open.

It didn't open very far. It hit something and bounced back toward me, and someone moaned into the noise of the receding jet, and I kicked the door again and this time somebody yelled, the sound carrying over the *whoosh* of the plane, and whoever it was fell backward heavily, and the door went past him and slammed against the wall.

I had the gun pointed at his forehead even as I caught the flash of someone else moving away from us, and it took all my strength to overpower the impulse to pull the trigger. On its back in front of me was something that might once have been a person, as a person is defined by the state, which is to say a human being with clothes that belong to him, paper with his name on it, and someplace to go whenever what's happening is finished. The one who had flashed down the hallway had been smaller.

"Tell her to come back," I said, the gun up in marksman's position and aimed at the bridge of his nose. He looked up at me. He couldn't have been more than eighteen, and his face was very dirty.

Flat on his back, he waved his hands in front of his face as though the hands could deflect bullets. "No one," he said, "there's no one."

"Get her out here," I said. "Do it or you're dead." I gave the gun a little up-and-down wiggle for emphasis.

"Holy Mother of God," he said, rolling onto his stomach. "Mother of God, protect me."

There was a flurry of motion to my left, and a small figure darted through the door, looking down at the one on the floor. "You son of a bitch," the small figure said to me. It was wearing two green plastic trashbags, sweat pants, and a brave hat that said DODGER BLUE above its brim. "You leave him alone." The one on the floor moaned.

"Move and I'll shoot you," I said, just for insurance. I looked at the two of them. Probably they were part of the new community on this abandoned block, human hermit crabs who had hoped to shrug the deserted homes onto their backs as protection against a rolling tide of social indifference. "Put your arms over your head," I said to her. She seemed the more dangerous of the two, if only because of her fierce determination to protect him. She looked at the gun and then down at him, and raised her hands.

"Whatever you want," she said, "we haven't got it. Except if you want us to move, we'll move."

"I don't want you to move," I said. "I don't really want much of anything. It's just that you scared me." I held the gun up, away from both of them, and gave it a little shake. Then I tucked it into my pants. She crouched down next to him, still distrustful. The smell of fear and failure rolled off the two of them.

I held up my empty hands and gave them a hearty politician's smile. "I don't suppose," I said, sitting down on the floor, "that either of you got twenty thousand dollars in the mail recently."

When everyone had finished laughing, I gave them each ten bucks and they told me what time the mailman came and gave me a remarkably accurate description of the person who'd checked the mailbox for the last couple of days. We shook hands all around and I got back into Alice and drove home. At home I could drink Singha until the image of Junko floated away. At home I could finish making friends with Woofers. And at home I could finally tuck myself away into the warm dark until the start of business hours on Monday, until the time I could twist thumbscrews through the nails of Birdie Skinker.

24

Making Birdie Sing

The kid who carried the envelope to Birdie was skinny, eager, and as fraudulent as a campaign slogan. I'd found him jingling a fat tin can half-full of change up and down the sidewalks of Sunset, inspiring guilt in the patrons of the expensive shops just east of Tower Records and west of Mrs. Brussels', demanding donations to send nonexistent children to a nonexistent camp. It was the usual social scenario: the right money in the wrong place. When I'd offered him twenty bucks to carry an envelope to an address half a block away, his face had lit up like a Borscht Belt comic being booked into Caesar's Palace.

"Twenty bucks?" he'd said. Then, squinting with the ready suspicion of the deeply dishonest, he'd added, "I only gotta deliver one?"

"For now." I waved another twenty in front of him, and his eyes followed it like a lizard homing in on a mosquito. "There's a parking lot behind this building," I said. "Come back and tell me how he reacted, and you'll get this too." I palmed the twenty and made it disappear for effect and then materialized a ten in my other hand. "Come back in five minutes, and you'll also get this." It had taken me hours with the *Houdini Handbook* to learn to do that when I was a kid, and I'd finally found a use for it.

His eyes widened and he stared at my hands. Then he nodded, folded the first twenty four times, tucked it into the tin can, and sped away.

254

I put all the money back into my pocket. It wasn't that I didn't trust him. Well, yes, it *was* that I didn't trust him. Maybe I was souring on teenagers. The parking lot I'd chosen was on two levels, the upper a good twenty feet above the lower, offering a fine view of a smog- and cloud-socked Los Angeles. Far to the west was the dismal, squall-soaked gray line of the Pacific, bad weather all the way to Japan.

I'd parked Alice on the edge of the upper lot, and now I climbed the hill through the new spring growth, chanting Iranian-style wishes of death to the foxtails and puncher-weeds that were penetrating my socks and gouging my ankles. By the time I reached the top, I was equipped to carry a balanced biosphere of bothersome plant life to a newborn volcanic island. I climbed into Alice and started yanking the sharp little seeds out of my socks, keeping my head low and my eye on the parking lot below.

He was back in four minutes and twenty-two seconds, just enough time to have cut a fevered deal. He was smart enough to have told Birdie to wait before making an appearance, but not smart enough to avoid forfeiting the extra thirty bucks. After a minute, which the kid spent searching frantically for me, Birdie rounded the corner.

Birdie looked like a man ready to explode. His blue Philippine shirt provided a vivid contrast to his bright red face. Clenched fists hung like deadweights at the ends of the forearms he'd borrowed from Bluto, and the veins on his forehead were thicker than the transatlantic cable. He glanced frantically around the parking lot, but he didn't look up. People never look up. You'd think they'd learn. After exhausting the limited possibilities of right and left, he grabbed the kid by his shoulders and shook him like a terrier shakes a rat. I could hear the change in the kid's can rattling all the way up the hill.

But it was no go. The kid didn't know where I was, and Birdie had nothing but the kid. After a few additional shakes, more out of sheer frustration than because he thought they'd get him anywhere, Birdie let go of the kid's shoulders and stepped back, the ridiculous shelf of hair that was usually glued across his forehead drooping almost to his chin. The moment Birdie released him, the kid was gone. He jingled around the corner and onto the street, already sniffing out the next sucker.

Birdie stood alone in the parking lot, shoulders slumped, watching the kid's sneakers twinkle as they carried him around the corner. He wiped his face with a forearm as furry as a sheepskin seat cover, and then his legs buckled. He collapsed clumsily onto the asphalt of the parking lot, dead center in a space stenciled COMPACT. Well, if there was anything Birdie was, it was compact.

Like a pauper in a Rilke poem, he buried his face in his hands, but I wasn't in danger of developing any sympathetic worry wrinkles. I just sat in Alice, feeling remote and Olympian and godlike, and watched him cry. I would have felt more godlike if I hadn't been pulling foxtails out of my socks. After a good fifteen minutes, during which several people parked their cars, got out, and walked past him without giving him a glance, Birdie hauled himself upright and headed for the sidewalk. His feet were dragging so heavily that they should have left gouges in the asphalt. It was only nine-thirty, and if I had my way, Birdie had a long day ahead of him.

After two false starts I got Alice running and drove two blocks east to Ben Frank's, Sunset Boulevard's eternal coffee shop, to eat my version of breakfast—some acidic coffee, a glass of orange juice, and a liberal portion of curled lip from a waitress who took it personally when I didn't order a five-course meal topped off with baked Alaska. Other people were scarfing down two-pound slices of ham and half a dozen brutalized eggs. I forced myself to sip slowly at my coffee until practically everybody else was finished, partly to annoy my waitress, and partly to let Birdie work up a good lather. That was the absolute least that the little shit had coming to him.

There was a phone booth just outside of Ben Frank's. I dialed the number and waited.

"Brussels' Sprouts," Birdie snapped.

"Listen," I said, striving for an intensity of regret that would have put the Mock Turtle to shame, "I'm sorry about the picture."

"What? What?" he asked a bit wildly.

"She's much better-looking than that. I should have fixed her ribbons. God, she hates having her ribbons messed up. Of course, that's not news to you."

"Who are you?" he asked. "Oh, God. *Where* are you? Is she all right?"

I looked down at my watch. Barely ten-fifteen. "How do you like it?" I could barely restrain myself from taking a bite out of the mouthpiece.

He paused. "How do I like what?" He sounded simultaneously frantic and careful.

"Getting the picture for a change, you dreadful little half-pint. Instead of sending it."

"I don't know what you're talking about," he said slowly. He wasn't about to rise to anything as trivial as an insult.

"Well, cutie," I said, "aren't we cautious? Is someone there?"

"No. What do you want? How much? Damn you, is she alive?"

"Ah-ah," I said, "not so fast. Let's consider the implications."

It took him a few seconds to gather his bravado. "What implications?" he asked. "You've got my dog, that's all."

"Please. Don't insult my intelligence, it makes me nervous. I've got a lot more than your dog. What about the cigar?"

He didn't say anything, but I could hear him breathing. It sounded like a blacksmith's bellows.

"And where did we take the picture?" I said, mimicking Mrs. Brussels' imitation of a third-grade teacher.

"My house," he said after a moment. "You broke into my house. You took it in the basement."

"I took it in obedience school," I said.

Some clown on a Harley roared by, but it didn't matter: Birdie wasn't talking. The silence on the other end of the line lasted so long that I thought the line had gone dead. "Remember obedience school?" I asked. "The cigars in the belly buttons? Tsssss?"

"Oh, heavens," he said at last. He said it very faintly.

"I don't think heaven's on your itinerary. Even if it is, we have to talk first."

He swallowed twice. I heard him lick his lips. Then he said, "Skip it." He hung up.

The man needed a little more time. I walked up the block and loitered skillfully in front of Mrs. Brussels' building for a few minutes. A lady with unattractive identical twin girls went in. Forty-five seconds later she came back out, hauling them behind her. Her face was white with anger. Birdie must have scorched her to the roots of her hair.

Well and good. I strolled back down to Ben Frank's and ordered another orange juice from the same waitress. I'd tipped her before, so she brought the juice with a cheerful good-morning grimace that would have frightened a pumpkin. She even asked if I'd like a cup of coffee on the house. I declined more hastily than was strictly polite. The place was full of out-of-work actors and screenwriters wishfully discussing deal memos. Many of them wore long knit scarves carelessly knotted around their necks. When I'd drained the juice I went back to the booth and dialed him again.

"Brussels'—" he began.

"Hey, Birdie," I interrupted. "Do you want Woofers back?"

"Not enough to talk to you," he said. But he didn't hang up.

"Give me thirty seconds," I said. "You can count out loud if you like. Let's see if I can't come up with some things you *might* want. In fact, I'll count for you. One, obedience school. Two, ransom letters. Three, twenty thousand dollars. Four, Kansas City. Five, cigar burns. And, six, how about no cops or FBI?"

"FBI?" he said.

"As in using the mail to commit a crime. Remember that?"

"I never did." He didn't sound very sure of himself.

"You mailed the note and the cassette. Nice cassette, by the way. Terrific fidelity. Leonard Bernstein quality. Burnstein," I added. "That's a pun."

"Fuck you," he said weakly.

"Only if you'll print my picture in the *Actors' Directory*." He drew in his breath with a sharp hiss. "Birdie," I said, "I've got it all."

"I still don't know what you're talking about," he said with an edge of desperation.

"Think about it," I said. "It'll come to you." I hung up the phone.

In Ben Frank's, the maîtresse d', a spidery young woman with deep-black-dyed hair and fingernails she could have pruned fruit trees with, dug two talons into my arm as I walked past her and said, "Table, sir?"

"Just the bathroom."

"Sorry," she said with virtuous satisfaction. "Rest rooms are for customers only."

"I'm a customer. Ask Martha." Martha was the waitress I'd come to think of as mine.

Martha cut no ice with her. She gave me something that would have been a smile if it had happened an inch or two lower. As it was, it flared her nostrils. "I'm afraid you'll have to order something."

"Okay," I said. "I order you to remove your hand from my arm. I'm full up on your poisonous coffee, and I'm either going to unload it in the men's room or right here. Want to bet a buck I can't hit the counter?"

She pulled her hand back and gave me a reptilian blink. There weren't any rules to cover this. "I'll make a deal," I said. "I use the bathroom and *you* drink the coffee. My kidneys will be eternally grateful." I put a dollar into her hand for the coffee and threaded my way through the genteel unemployed of Hollywood to the men's room.

"Yeah?" Birdie said into the phone five minutes later. He'd given up on playing secretary.

"To pick up where we left off," I said, "let's try the Mann Act. Let's try interstate transport of minors for immoral purposes. Let's try Cap'n Cluckbucket's."

"Ahhh," he said. "I knew it. Sooner or later, I knew it. It was such a dumb idea."

"Whose idea was it?"

"My dog," he said, mustering his strength. The little creep was tough. "Let's talk about my dog."

"The topics aren't mutually exclusive," I said. "If you do everything exactly right in the next two minutes you can get your dog back and you can maybe avoid going to jail for the rest of your life too."

"It's all *her* fault," he said bitterly. "It was her idea. I told her it was stupid."

"That means you're ready to talk?"

"Depends," he said, trying for cagey.

"On what?"

"Talk about what, precisely?" In some part of his soul he was counting his change.

I thought about obedience school and clutched the receiver a little more tightly. "Remember what you said to me last time I called?"

"Refresh my memory," he said.

"Fuck you," I said, hanging up.

Wishing I had the Rolaids concession at the Thai market down the street from Mrs. Brussels, I walked back up the block and worked on my loitering. Nothing happened for the thirty minutes I skulked there. I couldn't tap the phone line, so I couldn't know who he might be talking to, but at least he wasn't going anywhere. Anyway, as far as I could figure, there wasn't anyone he could be talking to.

At one-thirty I called him back. By then I was home and Woofers was chewing happily on one of the shoes I'd kicked off. My answering machine had told me that Mrs. Sorrell had called once and Aurora twice. Mockingbirds were exercising their vocal cords outside the windows, and the sun had finally muscled through the clouds to create the fourth false spring in as many days.

"In addition to the Mann Act, how about white slavery and pandering in minors?" I said when he picked up the phone. "And let's not forget that we're also talking about this." I gave one of Woofers' ribbon-wrapped ears a mean tweak. She yelped gratifyingly, gave me a token snap, and regarded me with an expression that was pregnant with betrayal.

"*Yiiiiiy,*" Birdie exclaimed in anguish. He had a longer rope than most, but he sounded like he was at the end of it.

"*And* we're talking about Junko Furuta," I added, "and Lizabeth Worthy and Anita Morales and a bunch of other kids. And those are only the ones who are dead. Birdie, you couldn't dig your way out of all this shit if you hired a skiploader. You've got one chance, and I'm it." Anita Morales had been the Mongoloid, and I'd found her picture in the 1987 *Actors' Directory* that Morris had given me, the same issue that had marked Junko's debut.

"It's not my racket," he said, his nails beating a military tattoo on the phone.

"Of course not. You haven't got anything to do with it. All you do is take them down into your bomb shelter and turn them into zombies."

"Who are you, anyway?"

"I'm the Man with No Name," I said. "Or, if you prefer, you can call me the Masked Avenger. What I am is the end of the road unless you get a lot more helpful real quickly."

"Just tell me what you want."

"Well, for one thing, I want to know why it's not your racket."

"I could die for this," he said.

"Woofers could die in the next fifteen seconds. While you're listening. And even after you hear her die I could still put you in jail forever. Wanna hear another yelp?"

"She did it all," he said.

"Who, Woofers? That's hard to believe."

"Mrs. B.," he said. "It was Mrs. B."

"Then how come so much of it happened in your basement?"

"Hold on," he said. "I've got another call."

I apologized to Woofers for pulling her ear while the newscast from some radio station droned global desperation through the line. I was learning that a remote subcontinent was largely underwater when a click announced that Birdie was back.

"I got stuck with it," he said, so promptly that I immediately suspected that he'd put me on hold in order to think for a minute. "None of it was my idea. It all started with Mister."

"Mister," I said, ruffling Woofers' fur.

"We have to strike a deal," he said. Now I was sure: no one had called. He'd been thinking.

"Tell me about the deal."

"You're right about most of it. You're right about the Cap'n's and obedience school. But there's still something you don't know."

"Is that so?" I said.

He drew a shaky breath, hoping he was right. "You don't know where they are."

He was right. "I could always go to the cops," I said. "They'd be a lot less gentle."

"Oh," he said, "give me a *break*. If you wanted to go to the cops, you wouldn't be on the phone now."

"Then why am I on the phone?"

"Am I going to get Woofers back?"

"On a platter," I said. The line crackled. "Alive and well, of course," I added.

"You're on the phone because you expect to get something out of it," he said, "and if you talk to the cops you won't get it. Maybe you just figured it out, I don't know, or maybe someone hired you to find one of the little shits. But if you talk to the cops, you can kiss it all good-bye."

"Like I said, you can get Woofers back."

"How about protection?"

"For whom?"

"For me, for heaven's sake."

"I can try," I said. "Depending on what you tell me."

"I can tell you where they are. Which one are you interested in? Would you settle for one?"

"No." I thought about the kids I'd seen at the Oki-Burger. "It's all or nothing."

"Then I can tell you where they all are. Or, at least, where they'll all be eventually."

I waited. When he didn't say anything, I asked, "Are they all in Los Angeles?"

"Most of them."

"Are there any other dead ones?"

"Ella Moss," he said promptly. "She was ten. It wasn't my idea." He sounded desperate.

"I believe you. Where are the ones who are alive?"

"Tell Woofers to speak."

"Like how?"

"Just say, 'Speak, Woofers.' "

"Speak, Woofers," I said. Woofers barked.

He made a sobbing sound. "Please," he said, "take care of her."

"That's up to you. Screw up, and she could be the main course in some Korean restaurant on Olympic Boulevard."

"You want to know where they are. Don't you want to know how I got involved?"

Never interfere with the flow of a confession. "That'll do for a start."

"It was Mister," Birdie said.

"You've mentioned Mister twice. Who is he?"

"Mr. Brussels, of course," he said waspishly. "He liked the little ones. He was crazy about Ella. That's why he got into this business in the first place. Being a kiddie agent is a pederast's paradise. All those pretty little girls with their ambitious mommies."

"The agency was legit at first?"

"Of course," he said. "Do you think I would have taken the job if it wasn't?" I let it pass. "It's still legit, for that matter, or at least part of it is."

"When did it go sour?"

"When he realized that he could peddle the ones he got tired of. And then kids started running away from home and all the little babies hit the streets, and that was perfection, wasn't it? No parents, no guardians, nothing but profit."

"And if they disappeared for good?"

"Well, they'd *already* disappeared, hadn't they? Most of them were hooking anyway. You wouldn't believe what you can buy on Santa Monica Boulevard if you know where to look."

"Birdie," I said, "right now there isn't much I wouldn't believe."

"Yeah, yeah," he said impatiently. "We already know how smart you are."

"So you were working for Mr. Brussels."

He let half a minute slide by. "How do I know you're going to protect me?"

"You don't," I said. "Listen, Birdie, let's look at the score. I know ninety percent of it, enough to put you somewhere where absolutely everyone is going to be bigger than you, where you can't buy shirts from the Philippines, and they don't take kindly to people who traffic in kids. In a month, no one will be able to tell you from a bean bag. And I've got Woofers. I'm holding out an olive branch to you. If I were you I'd take it even if it were only a twig."

"Just asking," he said.

"Well, don't ask again."

"Can't we do this in person? My life is at stake."

"Respectively, no, and tough shit. I might be able to protect you from the cops, but I can't do anything about your business associates."

"You could kill them," he said promptly.

"Yes," I said, thinking about it, "there's that."

"But *will* you?"

"Get me mad at them. We were talking about Mr. Brussels. Speaking of which, where's the missus?"

"With a legitimate client. She won't be back until later."

"Mister," I prompted.

"Mister started setting up his leftovers, renting them to producers and directors who like them little. There are lots of them. He was also doing a profitable line in video."

"And you?"

"I was keeping the books," he said defensively. "That's all."

I didn't contradict him. "Only the books? What about the data base?"

"That was later. That was her."

"When did she come on the scene?"

"He had a heart attack on top of some twelve-year-old. I managed to keep it out of the papers, and then they read the will and she found out she was bankrupt."

"She was out of it until he died?"

"Was she ever. Helen Housewife, that's what she was."

"And why was she bankrupt?"

"The agency account was empty. Twelve-year-olds are expensive. He'd been eating the profits, so to speak. And then, he had a weakness for cocaine."

"Sounds like a nice guy."

"*You* would have liked him," Birdie said bitterly. "A guy who could kidnap a dog."

"What about the money from the sideline? All those producers and directors?"

"Ahhh," Birdie said, stalling.

I waited. "Maybe you'd like me to hang up again," I finally said.

"No. Wait. It was in a secret account, one that had nothing to do with the real business. She came in and tried to run the agency, or what was left of it, and finally I told her about the other account."

"And you explained where it came from?"

"That too."

"Why didn't you just take the money and say bye-bye?"

"I couldn't," he said in a grating voice. "She was the only authorized co-signer."

"I thought you said she didn't know about it."

"In those days, she didn't know shit from shirt buttons. She's a fast learner. He'd given her a bunch of papers to sign, and the signature cards from the account were among them. She would have signed a declaration of independence for the state of Alabama if he'd put it in front of her."

"So you were stuck," I said, trying to sound sympathetic. "You couldn't get out because you couldn't get your hands on the money. How much was it?"

He hesitated. "Half a mil." I was willing to bet it had been more.

"And how did she react when you told her about it?"

"You mean did she rend her clothes and tear her hair out? No. She didn't age before my eyes, either. She went home for two or three days and then she came back and announced we were back in business."

"Birdie," I said. The sun went back behind a cloud and Woofers cocked her head and looked up at the window. "She couldn't have done it without you."

"Don't you think *I* know that?"

"You knew where the money was. You knew where the kids were. You knew the names of the customers. What did she know?"

"She couldn't keep track of which hand her rings were on."

"So you were in the driver's seat."

"Ummm," he said. I could feel him retreat. "But she had access to the bank account."

"What did she give you?"

He weighed the odds, so slowly that I could almost hear the mental subtraction. "I'm not sure I know what you mean."

"The next sound you hear," I said, "will be Woofers' last yelp." I hung up.

It was well past lunchtime, but I wasn't hungry. I gave Woofers the cold hamburger I'd bought on the way home, by way of making up for the tug on her ear, and spent the next hour pacing and thinking things through. There was a delicate balance in play: not enough pressure, and he'd clam up. Too much, and he'd break. Broken, he'd be useless. Unless I wanted to start from scratch with Mrs. Brussels, who was a much tougher customer, Birdie was all I had.

At three I called him back. "Talk or listen," I said. "You won't like what you hear if you decide to listen."

"She gave me twenty-five percent," he said, "and she took over the books. So how do I know what's really twenty-five percent? And she made me responsible for obedience school."

And you enjoyed it, too, I thought. But what I said was, "It doesn't sound like enough."

"Fifty percent wouldn't have been enough."

"So why did you accept?"

"She had these big ideas," he said. "Go interstate. Find a new distribution system. Stop dealing in Hollywood, where you might get busted, and expand your horizons. That was her phrase, expand your horizons. Get the kids here and send them there."

"The Cap'n's," I said.

"This was a year later," he said. "Like I said, she's a fast learner. The chain was going bust, and she bought six franchises. They were happy to get rid of them. They sold them for the cost of the structures and real estate only, and agreed to keep them supplied with that vile chicken."

"The chicken orders are part of the data base," I said.

"Sure they are. It's a smokescreen in case anyone ever plugs into it by mistake. They call the orders to us and we dump it into the computer. All she had to do was staff the joints and buy a few trucks. By then she could have bought a whole fleet of trucks."

"So who do the customers call?"

"They call the local Cap'n's."

"And who do the stooges at the Cap'n's call?"

"That's cute," he said in a tone that made me sure it had been his idea. "They call a local number, and there's a call-forwarding mechanism that plugs it into one of our lines."

"Which line?"

He hesitated.

"Counting down," I said. "Five, four, three—"

"Oh-six-four-five," he said. "Same prefix, same everything, except no one ever answers it except the computer. If someone dials a wrong number, they just get this whine as the modem connects."

"Smart," I said. "So no one knows the real number."

"You do," he said. "You do now."

"And you weren't getting enough of what she was making."

"*Gornischt,*" he said, "I was getting *gornischt.*"

"You were getting ripped off. So you decided to talk to the kids while you were putting them through obedience school and find out everything you could about them. I'll bet you made them eager to tell you. I'll bet they were very talkative. And then you used what you'd learned to send ransom notes to their parents."

"Off base," he said. "Way off base."

"The notes were her idea?"

"Of course they were. You don't think that *I* could think of anything like that." Somewhere in his heart of hearts, Birdie still thought he was a nice guy. So does everyone. Emil Kemper, probably the most horrible of the recent rash of serial killers—a man who stored severed heads in his closet and cooked and ate intimate portions of his victims' anatomies—had described himself to the police as "too sensitive."

"So she pocketed the ransoms?" I asked, not believing a word of it. With what Mrs. Brussels was putting away, it didn't make any sense.

"Every penny," Birdie said virtuously. If I could have

reached through the phone and torn out the little liar's larynx, I would have done it, except for one thing. I still didn't know where the kids were.

"Fine, Birdie," I said. "I've got it. Mister started the whole thing going, he died, she came in and refined it, and you're getting cheated. If anyone is relatively innocent, you're it."

"Amen," he said.

"And I've still got Woofers." He didn't say anything. "Here's the trade. You tell me where the babies are, and I'll give Woofers back to you. Deal?"

"And you'll protect me."

"Look at it from my perspective," I said, recalling something he'd said earlier. "If I don't protect you—if I turn you over to the cops, for example—how do I get my money?"

"You don't," he said quickly. "You're planning to get it from their parents. Without me, you can't do it."

"So where are they?"

"Which one are you looking for? The new one? Aimee?"

"That doesn't matter. Where are they?"

"Here," he said, "in Los Angeles."

"Birdie, that doesn't qualify as a bulletin."

"Oh, golly," he said hastily. "She's coming. Mrs., I mean. I heard her car. Come to my house tonight at seven. Bring Woofers. I'll take you to them. You're going to need a guide anyway."

I weighed my options as rapidly as possible. "This conversation is on tape," I said. "If anything happens to me tonight, the tape goes to the police. Got it?"

"Just be there," he said. "Good Lord," he added, "don't you trust me?" He hung up.

Woofers started to whimper when we were still two blocks away. When we turned onto Birdie's street she began to claw at the window, her tail wagging back and forth like a metronome gone mad.

"Slow down," I said. "You'll see the little bedbug soon enough." She ignored me completely, bouncing up and down onto her rear paws and scrabbling with her nails at the nearest solid surface. I guess my mother was right: there's someone to love everybody.

Janet Drive was as deserted as an abandoned landing strip. The clouds had broken, giving the moon a chance to caw triumphantly at the earth until the clouds gathered again to seal off its light. In the meantime, the houses were lighted with a cold, chalky glow. When I'd been a kid and my family had lived for a year on the east coast, I'd filled a jar full of fireflies and read by their light under the covers so my parents wouldn't know that I was still awake. Janet Drive was bathed in the same icy, slightly greenish light.

I pulled Alice up to the curb opposite Birdie's house and snapped open the glove compartment. The little .32 I'd brandished in the house near the airport slipped into my hand as though a surgeon had reconstructed my joints just to fit around the handle. It didn't make me feel much braver, but it was better than nothing. Woofers was standing on my lap and emitting little breathless yelps. I looked both ways and grabbed her collar before I opened the door, possessed by images of a two-ton semi squashing her into the pavement.

"You go when I tell you to," I said. "Yorkshire terrier or not, I've grown to like you."

All the lights in Birdie's house were gleaming in welcome. For all I knew, he might have laid out a platter full of French bread and Brie to welcome his child home. He might also have been waiting with a Thompson submachine gun. When I was sure that the street was empty I opened the door and clambered out, Woofers straining eagerly. She was making a peculiar gasping sound. After I realized that she was in danger of strangling against her collar, I let her go. She made it across the street in Olympic time and paused at the end of the lawn, looking back at me.

"Beauty before age," I grumbled. "Just keep your mouth shut." One of the many things I didn't need was a howl of canine enthusiasm alerting whoever might be in the house that the detective had arrived.

"Stay," I whispered, crossing the street. Miracle of miracles, she stayed. I gave the little gun an experimental heft, and then, having managed to cross Janet Drive without being run down by a speeding bus, I reached down and took hold of Woofers' collar again.

"We're in this together," I told her. She looked up at me wisely, but her manic tail was a dead giveaway. The kid was not in control.

Walking bent over, one hand on the collar and the other on the gun, I negotiated the lawn. I looked like Rip Van Winkle before the kinks wore off. No one shot at me from the house before I reached the front door. No large men in chicken outfits bled through the bougainvillea to cut me into fingers, whatever they were.

The front door was ajar.

"Go," I said, letting go of Woofers' collar.

She went. She shouldered her way through the door with more strength than it was possible for her to possess, and I snapped a bullet into position in the gun and prepared to follow. I had my foot against the door when she began to cry.

She was making rapid little high-pitched sounds. I pushed the door open, and she came out. Her ears were flat against her head, and her tail was between her legs. She went past me and onto the lawn without looking back.

"Woofers," I said. "Come here, Woofers."

She sat down with her back to me and threw a mournful yelp at the moon. The sound of it sent shivers down my back.

"Birdie?" I said, pushing the door open with my foot.

The place was immaculate. It had been clean before, but someone had gone over it with the ultimate dust rag. Surfaces shone as though they were newly minted. The masks on the wall had had their tongues polished.

He was in the bedroom, sitting doubled over on the bed.

The bed was a terrible reddish-brown, covered with crinkly little coils of gift-wrap ribbon. Birdie was wearing an ancient silk kimono that once might have been yellow. Now it was reddish-brown, like the bed. His awful hairdo hung limply over his face, turban renewal gone permanently awry. One hand grasped something long and silvery, an antique Japanese sword.

He'd committed *seppuku*, Japanese ritual disembowelment, one of the world's most painful means of suicide. The gift-wrap ribbon spread over the bedspread was his intestines.

The little shit had had more guts than I'd thought. He'd also had the last laugh.

On the pillow next to his head was a piece of paper with a ragged top edge, torn from a secretary's steno pad. As Woofers mourned at the moon outside, I picked it up and read what he'd written.

FIND THEM YOURSELF, it read. AND WHILE YOU'RE AT IT, FUCK YOU.

I was nowhere again.

25

Ones and Zeros

"Tell me about the scanner," I said. It hadn't been much of a drive, but I felt like I'd run a triathlon. Woofers skulked next to me, keeping very close to my feet. She'd begun to cry when I'd tried to leave her in the car.

Morris looked down at her, blinking in semaphore, obviously rattled by my unannounced appearance at nine P.M., obviously wishing Jessica were there. Unless a good woman straightened him out, Morris was always going to be the kind of guy who needed moral support.

"The scanner?" he asked Woofers. He pronounced it as though it were a word he'd memorized phonetically from a foreign language.

"That gizmo," I said impatiently, "that doodad that you were fooling around with the first day I was here. The Yellow Pages, remember?"

"The *scanner*," he said. "Why didn't you say so?" His room was the usual technological mare's nest. Upstairs his mother was working on a full-size loom to the accompaniment of Dvorak's *New World Symphony*. It was a family whose members kept to themselves.

"Morris," I said gently, "forgive me. I'm not a technical whiz like you."

He scratched the back of his head while he mentally replayed the conversation. There was a child's scrabbled drawing of grass above the pocket of his shirt where he'd repeatedly put away his pens without retracting the points. "You *did* say scanner, didn't you?"

"Just tell me about the goddamn thing." I was desperate enough to be slightly menacing.

"It's very simple," he said, not noticing. "It just absorbs graphic information, digitizes it, and then inputs it onto disk. It has to interface with your software, of course. And your EGA board, if you're not scanning print."

Wondering what it was about teenagers that made people want to find the ones who disappeared, I drew back my hands—which had stretched involuntarily toward his neck—and said, "Morris. Morris, we're both going to make an effort now. I'm going to try to speak plain old English and you're going to try to understand it. Are we together so far?" I cracked my knuckles.

He started to say something and then looked at me more closely. Then he looked down at my hands, which, I was surprised to see, had moved again and grasped the points of his shirt collar. He shut his mouth and nodded. His Adam's apple did a little bob.

"Good," I said, pulling my hands back and forcing them into my pockets. "Good beginning. Now, using the scanner, if I follow you, you can take a picture off a piece of paper, put it into a computer, and then print it out again. Is that right?"

"That girl," he said nervously. "That Japanese girl who was on that lady's client list. The picture I showed you at your house was a scanned image. It was kind of low-res, remember?"

"Morris," I said threateningly, pulling out my right hand. It balled itself into a fist as we both watched.

He took a step back. "Low resolution. Like, dotty, you know?"

"It was good enough," I said.

"Good enough for what?"

"Okay," I said, ignoring his question. "Now, can you send these pictures around somehow, or do they have to be on a piece of paper?"

"I'm not sure I know what you mean. Do you want some coffee?"

"Your mother already offered me some coffee. Thanks, anyway."

"So what do you mean, send them?" he asked.

I tried to think of a way to explain what I meant. My train of thought was chugging slowly uphill when Morris derailed it.

"How about some wine?" Morris had the makings of a good host, in the unlikely eventuality that he'd live long enough to have a house of his own.

"The picture, Morris. Is there some way of sending it, like over the phone?"

"A modem," he said. He held up a hasty hand. "That's a digital decoder that works over a phone line. It reads the disk and then sends out the little ones and zeros—that's all a computer deals in, you know, ones and zeros—and the modem at the other end puts the code back together and stores the picture in the computer."

It sounded right to me. "I asked you before if you could get into that data base and fool around with it."

"Piece of cake," he said. "I could screw it up so bad that they'd never be able to figure out what hit them. By the time I was finished, they'd think they'd ordered four thousand girls' fingers to use as Coke stirrers, and no chicken." He made a dry, twiggy little sound in appreciation of his own wit.

"You can fool with the records," I said. "But what about the whaddyacallit, the interface?"

He furrowed his brow. "You mean could I change what happens when they call in?"

"Exactly," I said, almost weak with gratitude that we hadn't hit another semantic stone wall.

"That's more complicated," he said, dashing my hopes. "I mean, to do that I'd have to get inside the bulletin board."

I sat down on his bed and closed my eyes. Woofers sat on

my left foot. An image of Birdie, his intestines coiled around him, bled into my consciousness.

"I'm not trying to be difficult," Morris said, shifting from foot to foot and twisting his fingers apologetically. "I mean, let's talk about the bulletin board, which is what this program is. A bulletin board is just, you know, data by phone. People call in and make requests or whatever, and the program answers them and then stores the dialogue in the data base. Well, the first thing that comes up on the screen when the person calls in is something called a menu. The interface, like you said."

"You said there were dating services that work that way."

"Um," he said, blushing again. "They're more like an electronic post office. You know, you call in and leave a message for some type of person and wait for an answer. Not that they ever answer."

Poor Morris. "You can specify what type of person?"

"Well, sure," he said, looking like someone on the verge of pleading the Fifth Amendment.

"Like how?"

He scratched the back of his neck again. "Like, you know, what sex, what age. Like, for example, you can rule out a rhinoceros in its forties, right?"

"Right. Got it. And that's the menu?"

"Sure. That's the program going through its tricks. It takes your request and searches the data base. And it's harder to screw with."

"Why?"

"Because you have to rewrite the program."

"I don't have any doubt that it's hard. But you *could* do it?"

He chewed on an already ragged thumbnail. "Sure," he finally said. "I could do it on these disks."

"Then we're in business."

"But that's not going to do you any good."

"Why not?"

"Because it would only be here. To make a difference in the way the *real* bulletin board works, I'd have to be able to upload it to the original computer and overwrite the applications program."

"Why is that hard?"

"Jeez," he said, "how do I find the original computer?"

"Well," I said, "is that so difficult? I know where it is."

"You mean you want me to go there?" His eyes were wide.

"No," I said. "I certainly don't."

"Then I'd have to call it," he said. "You know, on the modem? And I haven't got the phone number."

I sat up and pulled a piece of paper out of my pocket. Birdie had given me something, after all. On the paper it said: 555-0645. "Morris," I said, "how about that wine?"

He got the wine from his mother and gave it to me, and I drank part of it, and then he climbed onto his stool and fed the phone number into his modem and we both waited. There was some high-speed beeping as the modem dialed the number, and then a sustained shrill pitch. Some text appeared on the screen.

"We're in," Morris announced.

The screen said: HOPE EVERY LITTLE THING IS OKAY. Y/N?

"What's Y/N?" I asked.

"Yes or no," Morris said.

"Hit Y," I said.

He did. The screen cleared, and new words appeared.

ENTER CODE, it said. The cursor blinked in front of a row of dashes waiting to be filled in.

"Now it gets dicey," Morris said.

"We know some codes," I said. "Try TURKEY."

Morris typed TURKEY. The computer beeped again and one of the disk drives whirred. "Look," Morris said. "It's writing to our computer."

"So?" I asked. "What does that mean?"

"It means that we've got a carbon-copy system going. Whatever we ask for gets bounced back onto our b:drive, right after it goes into their system."

"Why would they do that?"

"They must have some sort of automatic callback to confirm an order." He was chewing on the inside of his cheek. "Like if Turkey, whoever that is, orders something special, the computer on the other end calls back as soon as Turkey rings off to make sure that the order is legit."

"Don't touch any keys," I said.

He rubbed his wrists. "Why not?"

"Because you're not Turkey. If we place an order and their machine calls Turkey back, the order won't be on his computer."

"Whoopsy-daisy," Morris said softly, his hands poised above the keyboard like someone about to attack a Chopin polonaise. "So how the hell do we get out?"

"You're asking *me*?"

"I've only fooled with this bulletin-board stuff," he said. "You know, blond girl, long legs, wants to meet short dark guy? Not that there's ever anything like that, but that's what you always hope for."

"Why long legs?" I asked, curious in spite of myself.

"Awww," he said, "you don't have to ask that."

"Okay," I said. "Suppose there's only short-legged dark-haired girls?" Actually that would probably have been my preference, but it didn't seem important at the moment. "How do you get out?"

"Ummm," Morris said.

"Without leaving a fingerprint, so to speak."

"You hang up." He sounded reluctant.

"So hang up."

"But we just got *in*," he said doggedly.

"The wrong way. Hang up."

He gave me a stubborn glance. "Jeez," he said.

"Hang up."

He did something to the keyboard, and we were looking at a blank screen again.

"I don't know," he said, pushing the wheeled stool back from the computer. He scratched his head.

"Me too. Do you think anyone knows we dialed the number?"

His mouth twitched to the left and he transferred the chewing operation to the inside of his lower lip. "Well, we didn't place an order. Probably not, unless the sysop was on-line."

My fingers began to itch again. "What's the sysop?"

"System operator," he said. "We probably didn't write to the disk on the other end because we didn't ask for anything, but if the sysop was on the line, you know, sitting there watching the computer, he knows that someone calling himself Turkey tried to get in."

I got up off the bed, shoved my hands into the rear pockets of my jeans, and paced the messy little room. Woofers followed anxiously, cocking her head up at me to see where I was going next. Unless I was badly mistaken, the sysop was sitting in West Hollywood in the center of a baroque coil of intestines. "So there's something missing," I said.

"I wasn't thinking." Morris looked shamefaced. "We need the sysop's code name. Without it, we're just some schmuck trying to place an unauthorized order."

"And with it?"

"Are you kidding? With it, we can fool around with everything. The computer on the other end will think we're the boss."

"Morris," I said, "let's assume we can solve the problem. Here's what I want. I want everyone who dials his computer into the data base to get something other than the menu. First thing when they connect, I want them to get the picture we're going to put into your scanner. What's more, I want a message to go with the picture you're going to scan. And I don't want just one picture, I want four, and I want them to follow each other at twenty-second intervals, with a different written message under each one. Now, tell me, can you do it or not?"

"Piece of cake," he said. It was one of his favorite phrases. "But only on these disks."

"You've got the phone number," I said. "With the phone number you could do it on the other end."

"But I haven't got the sysop's code name."

"If you had the code, you could do it?"

"Sure. Like I said, if I had that, the system would be open to me. I could rewrite the whole applications system."

"I think you've got it," I said.

"The sysop's code name?"

"Think about it," I said. "I could be wrong, but think about it."

He concentrated hard enough to look middle-aged. "I don't know," he finally said. "I don't know what it could be."

"What was missing?" I asked.

He had looked puzzled before; now he looked bewildered. "Missing from what?"

"The lyric. The lyric to 'Turkey in the Straw.' "

He squinted at the ceiling. "We had 'Turkey,' " he said. "We had 'Inthe.' We had 'Straw.' "

"Jessica's lyric," I said.

He hummed for a moment, and then, for the first time in my hearing, he said, "Oh, shit." He looked down at the keyboard and said, "Worth a try. Should I dial the number?"

"Code name?" I said.

He gave me a big teenage grin.

"Chickie," he said.

26

The Last Picture Show

Morris was at his house writing code and working on the scanner, and I was at home fighting down the impulse to dive into a bottle of Singha. Woofers was under the couch worrying at a flea. As tempting as the Singha sounded, some tiny vestigial Puritan remnant of conscience was suggesting that I needed a clear mind to make sure that what I was doing wasn't just plain crazy.

On the face of it, the problem was simple. With Birdie dead, I needed someone else to take me to Aimee. That part was easy. Where we began to get into trouble was the fact that the only remaining possibility was Mrs. Brussels.

Unless I'd read her completely wrong, Mrs. Brussels wasn't going to open up the way that Birdie had. She'd just deny everything I confronted her with and then, as soon as she could, she'd cut her losses, pull money out of the bank, and disappear. Judging from what Birdie had told me and from the volume of orders in the data base, she had enough money to disappear to someplace very far away.

And whatever I did couldn't point directly at Aimee. If it did, she'd be dead in a minute—assuming that she wasn't dead already. As far as I could see, there was no reason why she should be dead; the kidnap note and the ransom had been Birdie's idea, his endearing way of getting some of what he saw as his by right. The little weasel wouldn't have told Mrs. Brussels anything about it.

So I was looking at a teenage sidekick who blew his nose

in polysyllables and a plan that was technical and complicated, and I distrusted it for both reasons. But I couldn't think of anything else, so I was stuck with it.

I gave up and went to bed. The moment I turned the light off, Woofers climbed up on the bed and nestled on my chest. Swell. I couldn't even turn over. This was going to be the longest night's sleep I'd had in months, and I was going to spend it flat on my back with a Yorkshire terrier listening slavishly to my heartbeat. To my surprise, I fell asleep instantly.

I forced myself to doze until eleven the next morning. Upon arising I made and actually choked down about a pound of pasta covered with tomato sauce. Eleanor would have called it carbo-loading. I ate it anyway because I had a feeling I might need endurance. Woofers ate the leftovers. She liked them better than I did.

At one, I made my first call.

She answered herself, as I'd anticipated she would. "Brussels' Sprouts," she said, sounding harried and snappish.

"Mrs. Brussels?" I said. "This is Dwight Ward."

"Mr. Ward," she said, warming slightly. "You certainly dropped from sight, didn't you?" There was a trilling sound from the other end of the phone. "Damn," she said, "there's my other line. Will you hold on for a moment?"

I said I would.

"Mr. Ward?" she said less than a minute later. "Excuse me. I'm handling the phones myself. My secretary seems to have decided to take the day off. How's our sweet little Jewel?"

"She's fine."

"Her flu is better?" Her voice was full of matronly concern. "She's such a pretty little girl." She paused.

"Well," I said into the silence, "that's why I'm calling. I'm ready to sign those papers."

"Wonderful. I think I can put her right to work. Did you say you objected to her traveling?"

"No," I said.

"We've got a lot to do," she said. "You and I have to

have a good talk first, of course, and then if we come to an agreement we'll have to get some pictures taken. I'm sure she'll photograph beautifully."

"We'll come to an agreement," I said. "Don't worry about that."

"That's grand, just grand. Can you come today?"

"Is fourish all right?" It would begin to get dark at five.

"Let me check my book." I held on, regulating my breathing, as she left the line again. Four had to be all right. By tomorrow she might know Birdie was dead.

The line clicked. "Four's fine," she said.

"Swell," I said heartily, "that's great. See you then."

The pay phone at the Oki-Burger was busy. Five minutes later it was still busy. At ten till two I was ready to get into Alice and drive down there, but I dialed the number one more time as I went out the door, and this time the Mountain answered.

"Christ," I said, "what the hell have you got, a party line?"

"I got one of them to call home," he said proudly. "Guess which one."

"I don't want to guess," I said. "I haven't got time."

"Apple," he said.

To my surprise, I found myself grinning. "I'll be damned," I said. "How'd you do it?"

"Donnie didn't come back," he said. "She was scared to death."

"But she was afraid to go home."

"She's got some aunt in Utah. They talked for two hours. Apple was a mess, you should've seen her, crying and laughing at the same time. I got her nose blown and her face dried and loaned her the money for a bus ticket and got her into a cab, and she's gone."

"You're just fine, Mountain."

"She kissed me good-bye."

"Hell," I said, "if I'd been there I'd have kissed you myself."

"Then I'm glad you weren't here."

"Remember when I told you I might need help?"

"Sure."

"How about I pick you up a little after three behind the Thrifty at Sunset and Fairfax? I don't want anyone to see you get into my car. And, Mountain," I said, "bring a gun if you can get one."

He considered it. "I can't," he said. "Anyway, I hate the goddamn things. But I don't need one."

Three hours later, I was early and Mountain was late. I used the time to go into the Thrifty and call Morris to synchronize our watches. It wasn't necessary, but I knew it would thrill him.

"They look great," he said, meaning the pictures. "You should see them on the screen."

"And the message?"

"All in caps, like you said. I found this really fancy font. They look like they came out of the Bible."

"That's great, Morris. I'm going to buy dinner for you and your parents if this works. Someplace fancy."

"Just not Cap'n Cluckbucket's," he said. I realized that Morris had made a joke, and I was so nonplussed that I laughed. "And Jessica," he added, sounding gratified. "Can Jessica come too?"

"Morris," I said, "you're on your way to being a *mensch*."

The Mountain was waiting in the parking lot, red-faced, sweaty, and fetid, when I came out of the store. A tight little band of Japanese tourists was giving him a wide berth, trying desperately to pretend he wasn't there. Once they were safely behind him, one of them, a shrunken old man in loud plaid slacks, lifted a little camera to one eye and snapped a picture. *They got people there who look like this,* he would say as his neighbors in Osaka registered thrilled disbelief.

"So," the Mountain said, lumbering toward me as the tourists climbed hurriedly into their van, "what's the skinnies?"

"You go with me to Sunset Plaza," I said, maneuvering upwind. "I go into an office and you wait in the car. Then I come out and we see what happens."

"And?"

"And maybe all hell breaks loose."

He gave me the kind of gargoyle's smile that you sometimes see in cognac-fueled dreams. If you're lucky, it wakes you up. The last time I'd seen one, I'd sworn off cognac. Temporarily. "Here's hoping it does," he said.

It was almost four when we rolled into the parking lot at Brussels' Sprouts. The weather was obliging us: an oppressive lead-gray layer of clouds had rolled in from the Pacific, and senior-citizen drivers, alert to any impending emergency, were driving dead center in the street with their headlights on full bright. The lights were on in the stores of Sunset Plaza too, picking out the spangles and bugle beads sprinkled across the fronts of overpriced dresses and the gleam of silk in handmade men's shirts. None of the little spotlights, I noticed, was focused on a price tag.

"Nice neighborhood," the Mountain said. "How much per breath?"

"If you have to ask, you can't afford it," I said, quoting J. P. Morgan. "Exhale only." I opened Alice's door. "You're going to stay right here, right? When I come out we may have to move in a hurry. I don't want to have to go looking for you."

"What a shame," the Mountain said, gazing with exaggerated longing at a beauty parlor. "I'm overdue for a facial."

"If this works out," I said, "I'll buy you a new face." I closed the door and started across the parking lot. A muffled rapping sound made me turn back. The Mountain had been knocking on the passenger window. Now he held up two crossed fingers and shook them at me. I returned the salute and went around to the front of the building, checking my watch as I went. It was 4:03.

Morris was supposed to start sending at ten after four.

The doors into Mrs. Brussels' waiting room whispered open. Birdie's desk was empty, and the Flash Gordon door leading into the inner sanctum gaped at me. One of the lines on the phone was blazing away. Woofers' plaster-of-paris pawprint still sat on the desk, but the appointment book was missing. Presumably she'd taken it inside. It was 4:04.

I could hear her voice from the other room. She sounded normal, sane, persuasive. If I hadn't seen obedience school and if Jessica and Morris hadn't figured out the code identifying the pictures in the *Actors' Directory*, I would have begun to wonder whether I were right.

The voice stopped.

"Mrs. Brussels," I called. "Mrs. Brussels, I'm here."

My pulse was hammering against my wrists. It was pounding with such urgency that I thought it might show, so I jammed my hands into my pockets and waited. After a moment she came out. She was wearing a tailored buff-colored linen suit with the trendy linen wrinkles in all the trendy linen places. A ruff of collar rose up almost to her chin, covering the not-so-trendy wrinkles on her throat. The smile she gave me was professional but hardly warm. It was, if anything, a conspirator's smile.

"Mr. Ward," she said. "So glad you could make it. I'm afraid we're a bit crazy here, what with Bertram gone missing." She gestured at the empty desk.

"Does he do this often?"

"Only when he's got boyfriend trouble," she said, speaking to me as though I were already one of the family. "Frankly, I thought he'd finished with all that a year ago. Birdie's *meticulous*," she said, "but he's not really *stable*."

"Can you trust him?" I asked.

She gave me a measured glance. "He worked for my husband before I took over," she said. "He's proved himself. Some of the information he handles is *extremely* sensitive."

I tried not to imagine the way Birdie would look by then. "I'm sure it is," I said. "I just need to know."

"Of course you do," she said with the barest of smiles. "Jewel's your ward and I'm sure you must love her very much." She managed to make the words sound as though they'd been coated in rancid baby oil, smooth, shiny, and foully suggestive.

I just smiled.

"Come in," she said, all business. "I've found your papers."

She turned her back and vanished through the door. Wisps of hair hung over her collar. As I followed I yanked a hand out of my pocket and sneaked a look at my watch: 4:05.

Mrs. Brussels was fast; she'd already seated herself behind her desk by the time I entered the room. The desk was clean and uncluttered except for a wad of stapled legal-size sheets of paper covered with very small writing. The computer console was turned part of the way toward me. My heart sank as I realized that its screen was dark.

That was something that had never occurred to me. In my projections of the scene, it had always been on. I developed an immediate stomachache.

"The contracts," she said, lifting one corner of the stack and then letting it flop back onto the desk. Then she sat back and threw one arm over the back of her chair, regarding me like a fisherman estimating the weight of his catch. Without the third-grade teacher's smile she looked older and considerably meaner. Gravity had done its work on her face; gravity and something else, something she supplied from within.

"We're going to need many signatures," she said, tilting the chair back even farther. "I hope your writing hand is in good shape."

"I even brought a pen," I said, pulling out one I'd stolen from Morris. I was trying to figure out how to get her to turn the damned computer on.

"Good, good, good," she said automatically. "But first, before you sign, I'd better tell you that I think we can put Jewel to work almost immediately. Will that be all right with you?"

"Anything that gets the cash flow going," I said, trying to keep my eyes away from the empty screen.

"It'll flow," she said. "You have no idea how it will flow. However, there are technicalities. I already asked you if she could travel, so that's out of the way. But there is one other point, and it's an important one."

"And what's that?" I was beginning to perspire.

"I need to know that you have the legal right to sign these papers."

"I told you," I said, working up a semblance of affronted indignation. "She's my ward."

"And you told me that her parents are dead." Her gaze was as steady as a dial tone.

I could hear my watch ticking and I fought down the impulse to check the time. Morris was probably keying in by now. "Dead as Marley," I said.

"Aunts? Uncles? Cousins two or three times removed? Anybody who might suddenly take an interest in the child? Anyone who might get someone looking for her?"

It had to be 4:10. I leaned forward and put my hands on my knees so I could see my watch: 4:09. "Forget it," I said. "I'm the whole story. It's just Jewel and me."

"We both know what we're talking about," she said. She was looking through me. This was a conversation she'd had many times.

"Honey," I said, licking my lips. They were drier than dry cleaning. "Even Jewel's not completely in the dark."

Now she focused on me and gave me the motherly smile. "Well," she said, "that simplifies things." She turned the contracts around so that they were right-side-up for me. "Everywhere there's a red X," she said, "just sign your name."

"Dwight Ward," I said.

The motherly smile broadened and turned slightly gamy at the edges. "Anything you like," she said. "Sign away."

"Wait," I said. "I've got a couple of questions of my own."

She lifted an eyebrow. Four-ten had come and was in the process of going. "You're not going to hurt her?" I asked, trying to keep the desperation out of my voice.

"Damaged goods," she said with a shrug. "Who wants them? The prettier she is, the better you'll do."

"That's the other question," I improvised. "What's my cut?"

"Thirty percent," she said.

"Only *thirty*?"

She gave a world-wise shrug. "Expenses," she said. "Security. This is not an inexpensive operation."

"Um," I said. "Still, thirty?" It was 4:11. I knew without looking at my watch because I'd been counting.

"Thirty percent of quite a lot," she said. "The average job, say two days, costs two thousand. She can do three jobs a week, sometimes four."

I squinted at the ceiling like someone whose idea of a complicated math problem was buying a new belt. "That's, ah . . ."

"Thirty percent of six thousand is eighteen hundred," she said coldly. "And you don't have to do piss-all for it. Just get the checks, deposit them, and spend it."

"I have to think," I said.

"Think while you sign," she said, shoving the contracts at me. "It's the standard deal. We don't make exceptions. Eighteen hundred a week is almost ninety-four thousand a year. That's a lot of money."

"Not enough," I said, stalling. By now Morris was slamming away at the keyboard, and anyone who happened to tune in was in for an interesting surprise.

"Thirty-five," she said flatly. "But that's it. And that's only because she's so pretty."

"Thirty-five," I said, chewing on the end of my pen.

"That comes to a hundred and ten thousand a year," she said, "and that's if we don't push her. This little girl, she's going to be flavor of the month. So figure it'll be more for the first year. That's enough to buy a new ward. Maybe we'll set up a long-term relationship."

"More than one kid?"

"You can field a baseball team, if you can find them." She leaned toward me. "Boys too," she said, dropping her voice. "Some boys do better than girls."

"Gee," I said, straining my brain to find some reason not to sign the papers. After I signed them, I'd have to leave. Why hadn't I anticipated the possibility that her computer wouldn't be on? "How many on a baseball team?"

"Nine," she said through tight lips. "That means rich, is what that means. Now, are you going to keep fucking around or are you going to sign your name?"

I gave up. "Fine." I scrawled "Dwight Ward" next to the first red X. She watched with satisfaction.

A phone trilled, a bright little soprano gargle. A button, one of six on her desktop instrument, lit up. Holding my breath, I flipped through the contracts, counting the red X's.

"Brussels' Sprouts," she said, watching me. "Yes, this is Mrs.— What?" she demanded. "What are you talking about? What're you, nuts? Hold it, hold it, slow down and tell me . . ." The phone rang again and another button lit up. I went on signing Dwight Ward's name as she put the first person on hold and punched the new button.

"Yeah?" she asked. "Who is this? Bullshit, that can't be right. Listen, I've got someone—" The voice on the other end squawked and squalled. "Hold it," she commanded. "Shut up and hang on." She swiveled the computer toward her and looked up at me. "Keep writing," she said grimly, flicking the On switch.

I invented names for each of the red X's as she punched her way across the keyboard and accessed the data base. I'd gotten to Alice B. Toklas and was halfway through Anna Q. Nilsson when she got through. Then I lifted my head as her computer whirred, and watched her, hoping she wouldn't look at me.

I needn't have worried. I could have sprouted wings and a full set of serpents' scales and turned into Quetzalcoatl right there in the chair, and she wouldn't have noticed. She'd worked her way through the menu and was staring at Morris' surprise.

First her eyes widened and then her jaw dropped. The fine hairs on her forearms stood straight up as thousands of tiny muscles did the job assigned to them millions of years ago, when the danger in the world was old-fashioned and predictable. What she was looking at was nothing that could be avoided by a prickling at the back of the neck. As the lines on the phone blinked in paranoid semaphore and as a third line started to ring, she sat back. The console was turned away from me, but as I watched the blood drain from her face I had no difficulty seeing what was on the screen. She was looking at a picture of a happy, hopeful Japanese girl in a baseball cap, and under the picture were the words: MY NAME IS JUNKO FURUTA. THESE PEOPLE KILLED ME.

"Hnaaahhh," she exhaled. She had turned to stone. I counted to twenty and signed "Darryl F. Zanuck," and a jolt of electricity snapped her upright. Her eyebrows were disappearing into her hairline. In front of her, I knew, were the curiously indistinct features of a Mongoloid girl, delighted at being the center of all the attention involved in being photographed, and below her heartbreaking smile was a legend: MY NAME IS ANITA MORALES. THESE PEOPLE KILLED ME TOO.

She picked up the ringing phone without looking at it and hung it up again. Then she knocked it off the cradle with an abrupt gesture. She was staring at the screen as though it were a marksman's pistol aimed between her eyes. "Fucking *hell*," she said. She'd completely forgotten I was there.

"No," she said to herself. The third picture had appeared on the screen. This, scanned from the *Actors' Directory* like all the others, was the image of the first little girl I'd seen in the morgue. I'M LIZABETH WORTHY, it said beneath her frail face. THEY BURNED ME BEFORE THEY KILLED ME.

"Lizabeth," she whispered involuntarily. I folded the contracts lengthwise and then opened them again. I signed the last one "John Hancock" and put an elaborate scrabble beneath it as Mrs. Brussels sucked in her breath at the sight of Ella Moss' face appearing on the screen. Another phone line began to shrill at her.

I'd written the line of print under Ella Moss' face. I couldn't see the screen, but I knew what it said: FOUR OUT OF FOUR. WE'RE COMING. Morris had done it right.

"Your turn," I said, pushing the contracts toward her.

"I can't," she said wildly to me. "I can't do it now. You'll have to wait. I've got an appointment. I've got . . . I've got . . ." She looked at the screen as the normal menu reasserted itself. ". . . an appointment." She forced herself to look at me. Her eyes were all whites. "Come back tomorrow," she said.

"Trouble?" I asked.

"No." She cranked her mouth into a smile. "Nothing. Just . . . just a little glitch." Her eyes dropped to the contracts. She looked a thousand years old, a perfectly preserved Queen of Egypt crumbling at the rush of new oxygen as the bandages were cut. "Leave the papers," she said, struggling for control. "Come back tomorrow."

"Sure," I said, getting up. I shoved the contracts into the back pocket of my jeans, but she didn't notice. She was staring with a kind of superstitious dread at the computer screen. The phone was still burring away.

"Tomorrow," she said mechanically.

"Your phone's ringing," I said, leaving. She didn't look up.

The parking lot was pitch dark. "We're on," I said to the Mountain as I got back into Alice. "We're rolling." Ten minutes later Mrs. Brussels' Mercedes fishtailed out of the lot and left onto Sunset. We were three cars behind.

27

Chicken Central

She went home.

That was a surprise.

Home was a house north of Sunset in Beverly Hills. Only downtown Tokyo was more expensive. I'd had to fall back a block or so after she turned her tidy little fifty-thousand-dollar Mercedes left off Sunset. There wasn't enough traffic to cover us. As extra insurance I doused Alice's headlights, hoping the Beverly Hills cops weren't anywhere around. No question whose side they'd be on.

As the neighborhood got better, the Mountain got worse. We were out of his element. "Maybe we should have bought a map to the stars' homes," he grumbled. We'd passed half a dozen kids flagging the night air with folded pieces of paper directing the credulous to the homes of people who'd been dead for years. "Long as we're up here, we could drop in on Jane Fonda. She could tell me how to get down to half a ton."

We were parked across the street and half a block up, still hoping for no cops. The Mountain was listing movie stars in no particular order, clearly disgruntled. He'd gotten to Leslie Nielsen, so it had been quite a while.

"Leslie *Nielsen?*" I asked in spite of myself. "Is he the one with the aqualung?"

"That's Lloyd Bridges," he said with infinite scorn. "His kids probably live up here too. There's all sorts of people live up here. What I want to know is, why the fuck are *we* here?"

"She's the one," I said. "Just shut up and sit back. Work on your cellulite or something." The air was ripe with Mountain's pong. "And roll down the window, if you don't mind."

"Can I smoke?"

"You can light fire to your feet if you want to." I hadn't known that the Mountain smoked. Now that I thought about it, it made sense. You didn't get to be his size without a lot of bad habits.

He pulled a crumpled pack of some unidentifiable off-brand cigarette out of his shirt pocket and lit up. Wreathed in smoke, he gave out a relatively comfortable sigh. "Why don't we just kick the door in?" he asked.

"They're not here," I said, my nose twitching toward the smoke. Ancient yearnings arose within me. "It doesn't make any sense for them to be here. She gave them to Birdie."

"Birdie?"

"Never mind," I said. "Give me one of those."

"You?" he said. "I didn't know—"

"Just give me the fucking thing." He tossed me a cigarette and I let it dangle uselessly from my mouth. "What am I supposed to do?" I asked. "Rub my legs together to make a spark?"

"Jesus, you're touchy," he said, handing me a book of matches. "Want me to kick you in the chest to get it going?" He coughed up a blubbery woof of laughter.

I lit the cigarette, my first in two years, and sucked in the smoke, feeling my uvula knocking in protest against the top of my tongue. The nicotine navigated my defenses without apparent effort and filled my lungs, and I got light-headed immediately. All the problems of the world fell away; it was a crossword puzzle and I was a dictionary. I was as definite as Noah Webster. "She'll come out," I said, blowing smoke, "and we'll follow her, and then we're home."

"So what's she doing in there?" the Mountain asked. "Lining up her shoes?"

"She's making calls," I said with absolute certainty. Until

that moment I hadn't known what she was doing. "She's freaking out, and she's getting the kids together so she can move them."

"Move them where?"

"Out of L.A. She has no idea what's going on."

"Me neither," said the Mountain, lighting another one. He had apparently eaten the first. "Maybe you'd like to explain."

I explained, finishing my cigarette and bumming a second in the process. I could quit later. In the meantime, nicotine seemed promising.

"Holy shit," the Mountain said after five minutes of concentrated explanation. "Let's french-fry her."

"What's the first thing you do when you make french fries?"

"Chop," he said. "First you have to chop up the potato."

"Dibs on that," I said. "I get to chop. You get to drop the pieces into the fat."

He exhaled enough smoke to guarantee chemotherapy to most of the Midwest. "So you're saying we wait." He tried to cross his legs under Alice's dashboard and failed. "The world is too small for me," he said. It was a statement of fact, not a complaint.

By the time she backed her car out of the driveway, it was almost nine. The sun was long gone, the moon was taking a nap behind the clouds, and the straight nine-tenths of the world was heading for bed. The little Mercedes scooted out backward and turned downhill toward Sunset.

I started Alice. "Told you," I said. "She's got to go somewhere. And where she's going is where they are."

"Hey," he said, "if I didn't believe you, why would I be here? Shit, I could be having a great old time mopping tables at the Oki-Burger."

"Thanks for Apple," I said, thumping his knee. "Let's turn it around, okay? If *I* didn't believe *you*, why would you be here?"

"So okay," he said. "We're both champs. Just keep her in sight."

In fact, I nearly lost her as she swung east onto Sunset. The light went yellow and I accelerated through it anyway, hoping she didn't have one eye on the rearview mirror. Some cowboy getting a jump on the red tooted a little Fiat's horn at us with a pipsqueak flatulent sound and swerved around us, making operatic Italian hand gestures out the window. I passed him on the left, hoping Mrs. Brussels hadn't heard the horn, and the Mountain leaned out of the passenger window, made clawing motions toward the guy's throat, and roared at him. The guy driving the Fiat took one look at the Mountain and braked abruptly, then made an immediate right to get out of his vicinity.

"Focus," I said as Mrs. B. made a right down Doheny. "The enemy is up ahead." I followed her, gunning Alice's engine to decrease the distance between us as the Mountain subsided into mutinous mutters in the passenger seat.

"Little wop cars," he grumbled. "Rinky-dinky little Tinkertoys. How come people don't buy American?"

Since the trade deficit was not the issue at hand, I concentrated on Mrs. Brussels. She drove fast and well, with an aristocratic disregard for lane lines and yellow lights. I'd had to run two more reds by the time she turned left onto Pico, heading east.

"My father works in Detroit," the Mountain volunteered out of nowhere as we crossed La Cienega. "Thirty-year man. For thirty years he's been putting the same fucking fender on the same fucking car all day long. Then he goes home and drinks two six-packs of Stroh's and falls asleep on the couch with his shoes on. Where do you think she's going?"

"As I already said, where the kids are." I braked to avoid a head-on as yet another Italian car, driven by someone whose driver's license probably noted that he'd had a prefrontal lobotomy, turned left in front of me. "But, Jesus, don't let me interrupt your autobiography."

"What I mainly remember about my mother," the Mountain continued serenely, "is that she could get his shoes off without waking him up. I thought it was terrific. Now I think about it, I realize she probably could have amputated his legs without waking him up. How many kids you think they'll be?"

"Depends on how many are in L.A. They're selling them in about four states." A spate of drizzle misted the windshield. Alice's wipers would only have made it worse, so I just locked on the red blurs of the Mercedes' taillights and kept driving.

"She's turning," he said.

And she was. She was making a right, turning south onto a little street with a name that might have meant something to the people who lived on it. There were more people on the sidewalks here, and more of the faces were black. The people gathered in front of immaculate four- and six-unit apartments and sat on the fenders of five-year-old cars and watched the world drive by.

"Heartbreak city," the Mountain said, glancing out the window. "Nobody going noplace."

"There's something to be said for staying home," I said. The Mountain greeted this hand-stitched homily with the silence it deserved, and Mrs. Brussels made a left onto Jefferson Boulevard. She lost a little traction on the newly wet road, and her taillights did a brief shimmy. With one of those abrupt transitions that make L.A. the world's most schizophrenic city, we found ourselves in an industrial area.

Here there was no one on the sidewalks. In some blocks there were no sidewalks. The streetlamps layered the damp landscape with a bluish light that turned the Mountain's lips purple. It was not an improvement. Warehouses hunkered down, dark and featureless, behind chain-link fence topped with razor-wire. Behind the fences Dobermans roamed, snapping at moths and waiting for something bigger.

"Nice neighborhood," the Mountain observed. "What happens when we get there?"

It was an extremely good question. "We park and wait and watch, and when we're sure that we can take the guys inside, we go in and take them," I said. "Then we set the kids loose."

The Mountain said nothing.

"Then we go home," I said lamely.

He lit a cigarette and passed it to me, then lit another for himself. "Boy," he said, "that's some plan."

I dragged smoke into my lungs. "It's a little short on details," I admitted.

"*Short?*" he said, exhaling a cumulus cloud. "It sounds like a political platform. What are all these guys supposed to be doing while we win the war? Multiplication tables?"

"That's where you come in," I said as Mrs. Brussels pulled into a driveway. "What we have here is a classic division of labor. You're going to sumo them, and I'm going to finish them off."

"Great," he said. "I hope some of them are fat." I passed the driveway and pulled over to the curb. The drizzle had let up, but the night was darker than Junko's eyes. On the whole, that was good.

"What we're going to do now," I said, dragging feverishly at the cigarette, "is we're going to count to twenty. Slowly. Then we're going to get out of the car and walk around the block, in the direction away from the gate she just drove through. We're going to count doors and windows. We're going to look for another gate, anything anyone could drive a car through. We're going to keep our mouths shut until we're back at the car."

"And then what?"

"Then we're going to figure out what to do."

"I was wondering when we'd get to that," he said. He waited a moment. "How far have you counted?"

"Sixteen."

He tapped the dashboard three times, very rapidly. "Twenty coming up," he said. Then he tapped again and opened his door. Before he got out, he turned back and held out a hand. I found it in the dark and took it. It felt like it was made out of asbestos. "It's been nice knowing you," he said. Light from somewhere glinted off what might have been teeth.

"Let's total the fuckers," I said. We got out of the car.

With the Mountain to my left, we paced the sidewalk. He broke stride to step on his cigarette, and his hand went automatically to his pocket. I slapped it away and took the box of wooden matches from his hand. I shoved them into the pocket of my shirt.

"No matches," I said. "Nothing that anyone might see."

"Okay if I suck on it?"

"You can jam it into your tear ducts. You can chew it and swallow it. Just don't light it."

"Falafel," the Mountain said aggrievedly. "You'd think the man had a plan."

The warehouse occupied a whole block. It was an extremely dark block. The streetlights had all been put up somewhere where they could keep rich people from tripping over the cracks in the sidewalk. We turned right onto a street named Detroit, a fact I suppressed because I was afraid it might prompt the next chapter of the Mountain's life. I was getting seriously worried.

"What you didn't ask me," I whispered, as though the oversight were his fault, "was who she was calling."

"Getting the kids, you said," he boomed. I made little lowering motions with my hands, indicating that he should put a damper on the volume. "Question is," I whispered, "who's delivering them? A bunch of shoe clerks or twelve Arnold Schwarzenegger clones?"

I stopped walking, wrapped the fingers of my right hand through the chain link, and turned to study the warehouse. There were lights visible through the five big transom windows I'd counted so far. The windows were about ten feet off the ground, not useful exit routes unless the floor of the warehouse were raised six or eight feet. As though it had been summoned on cue, a car turned in off Jefferson, pulled up to the warehouse door, and doused its lights. At a single toot of the horn, a door in the warehouse opened, emitting a rectangle of light, and someone who could conceivably have outweighed the Mountain got out of the car and walked around to the passenger door. Through the door of the warehouse came a short, skinny guy who stood behind the giant. The skinny one had something in his hand. The giant opened the passenger door, and two small figures emerged. They couldn't have been more than five feet tall. It was hard to see them, but they seemed to be wrapped in blankets. Thin, knock-kneed legs stuck out below. With the big guy in front of them and the little sharp one behind, the two kids went into the warehouse. The door closed again.

"One big one, one tweak, two kids," the Mountain announced to the night.

"And no other exits," I said, clinging to the routine I'd outlined. "So far." The size of the big one had unnerved me slightly. And what had the skinny one been holding? I began to think longingly of calling the police.

"The kids are on our side," the Mountain murmured. "We can take the other ones."

We scouted the remainder of the eastern side of the building and then hurried along the side facing away from Jefferson. There was one big airplane door that you could have driven a Sherman tank through, but I just registered it as the first possible exit and hauled the Mountain along. There was also a gate in the chain link, but it was chained and padlocked from outside, so I ignored it. From this side, you couldn't see who or what was arriving.

The next shipment, as far as we could tell, pulled up to the warehouse after we'd turned right onto the third side of the rectangle that made up the block. There was the same single toot on the horn, and another walking whopper clambered out of the car and waited. The sharp skinny guy re-emerged from the warehouse with the same indefinite object in his hand. This time three small loosely wrapped people were shepherded inside before the door closed.

"Five kids, two oxen, and the same tweak," the Mountain said, his face pressed up against the chain link. "Okay odds. Let's go get them."

"There could be more coming. We don't want to lose some of the kids because there's a firefight going on inside the building when the next car arrives. Let's give it ten minutes."

"Firefight?" The Mountain sounded surprised. "What firefight? I break their spines and you get the kids."

"Listen," I said, "we could wind up shooting." I reached down to touch the little automatic I'd tucked inside the front of my pants. I did it without thinking about it, just to make sure it was there.

"I told you," the Mountain said, "I hate guns. And there's kids in there."

"Then go home," I said. "What do you think, this is a movie? You think we're going to walk in and you're going to flex and they're all going to faint? People are probably going to get shot."

"Well, fuck a duck," was all he said. But he looked betrayed.

I pulled Alice's keys out of my jeans and held them out to him. "Go," I said. "It wasn't a good idea to begin with. You should be at Tommy's, not here. Take the car and beat it."

The Mountain took a step backward and looked down at the sidewalk. His face twisted and retwisted and then settled itself into an expression I'd never seen before.

"I can't drive," he said.

The drizzle began again. "What're you, Greenpeace? *Everybody* can drive. This is Los Angeles."

"I can't." He wasn't looking at me. He was looking at the warehouse, at the pavement, at everything except me. I held the keys out for a moment longer and then recognized the look on the Mountain's face. He was telling a lie. It was the first time I'd ever seen the Mountain tell a lie. He was terrible at it.

It was my turn to back away. I felt like the Marquis de Sade trapped into a conversation with Florence Nightingale. I felt like the personification of corruption in a political cartoon.

"Let's call a cab," I said. It was the best I could do.

"Skip it," the Mountain said, looking at his left foot as though it had just appeared at the end of his leg—shoe and all—through spontaneous generation. "Just tell me what we're supposed to do, that's all."

"We're going to wait," I said, suppressing an urge to hug him. Like Apple, I couldn't have gotten my arms around him. "We're going to wait and see who else goes in, and then we're going to decide. Okay?"

"Sure," he said without looking up at me.

"And I'll tell you what," I added as a car turned in to the warehouse from the opposite direction, sweeping us briefly with its headlights, "we're going to wait across the street and sitting down. Okay?" I touched his arm.

"You're in charge," he said negligently, trusting me with his life. Trusting me with his life was easier for him than telling another lie.

"And we'll count," I said as yet another bruiser climbed out of the car in front of the warehouse. The same little sharpie came out to serve as rear guard to the little girl who emerged from the passenger side. "We'll count very carefully. Right?"

The two of us crossed the street. I sat on a strip of grass that paralleled the sidewalk.

"Right," the Mountain said, still standing. "That's three fatsos, six kids, and the little coat hanger."

"Who has something in his hand," I said.

"It's probably a vitamin," the Mountain said, sitting next to me on the wet grass. "Weensy little guy like that needs building up, probably worries his mother sick. You could X-ray him with a squint."

A couple of urban crickets chirped in a ratchety fashion as we sat there. The drizzle continued. My confidence, such as it had been, was being washed away. We'd gotten them there, all right. If the ones we'd seen were the only ones coming, maybe we could handle them. Maybe. I'd have felt a lot better if the Mountain had been president of the local chapter of the National Rifle Association instead of a benevolent fat guy whose idea of mortal combat was throwing Jackie Gleason out of a six-foot circle.

Nonetheless, I worked on pumping my adrenaline. I'd

just finished a deep-breathing exercise that Eleanor had taught me, the New Age equivalent of "Whistle a Happy Tune," and was starting to stand up so I could go in and massacre everyone more than five feet tall, when the Mountain gave my arm a yank that almost dislocated it.

"Squat," he said. "Somebody coming."

Another car, the fourth that we'd seen, cruised through the gates and pulled up to the door of the warehouse.

"One fatty or two?" the Mountain whispered. "Five dollars says one." The car's horn honked.

"Two," I said. We shook. I lost. The coat hanger came out again, vitamin in hand, and escorted a single guy with the bulk of a mature elk, plus one child, into the warehouse. Same procedure: the fatty went first, the kid was in the middle, and the little guy brought up the rear, brandishing his vitamin.

"They've got it down," I said. "They've done this before."

"Give it three minutes," the Mountain said, assuming command. Maybe he heard the uncertainty in my voice. "Then we move."

Four minutes later we were running down the block and through the gate, heading toward the left side of the warehouse. We'd decided not to go for the door on the first pass. I didn't know whether it was locked from inside, and I also wanted to see whether there were people in there who might have arrived before we did. The finish line for our run was the second transom window, which had been propped open.

By the time we reached it, the Mountain was wheezing like a man in an iron lung. Nevertheless, he squatted down and held up his arms. I stepped onto his shoulders and he braced my legs with his hands, exhaled an imperial gallon of air, and stood up.

He rose so fast that I scraped my forehead on the stucco and almost toppled us backward by pushing myself away from the wall. Nothing bleeds like a cut on the head. I could feel blood running down my face as the Mountain steadied himself and I peered in through the window.

What I saw at first were trucks. There were three of them, big mothers, with the Cap'n Cluckbucket logo painted on their sides. They were standard refrigerated tractor-trailer semis, the same models that cart California lettuce to salad bars all over the continent. These trucks held kids: special orders being delivered in response to requests. The kids who traveled in the backs of the trucks were used to the cold. They'd been through obedience school.

It was hard to get a grasp of the internal geography of the warehouse. Bare bulbs under iron cones hung at the ends of wires here and there, creating islands of bright light that gleamed off the tops of the trucks. In the spaces between the splashes of light, it was dark. I felt the Mountain tremble beneath my weight as I waited for my eyes to adjust.

High up on the opposite wall was a large picture window. On the other side of the window was undoubtedly what had been the foreman's office when this had been a legitimate operation, a vantage point from which the highest-paid guy in the room had supervised the loading and unloading of the trucks. Lights were on behind the glass, but I couldn't see anyone. Then a child let out a shrill scream, and I followed the sound all the way to the right and found myself staring at a small circle of people gathered in a dark spot near the door.

There was a sudden disturbance at the center of the circle as people took a step back, and the child screamed again, and my heartbeat began to pound in my ears. Somebody laughed. It took all my willpower to ignore the screams and the laugh, and count the people.

Mrs. Brussels was the first one I spotted, still in her trendy wrinkled linen. She had her back to me. The children were probably in the middle of the circle, since I couldn't see them. I counted five grim giants on the circle's perimeter. That was one more than we had counted, so someone *had* arrived before we had. As far as I was concerned, that cinched it. We were outweighed, even with the Mountain in reserve.

I grabbed the edge of the transom window with one hand

and leaned down to tap the Mountain's wrist with the other. At the signal he crouched, and I stepped onto solid ground.

"There's another one," I whispered. "That makes five. I don't know how many kids. I didn't see the little one, but I think he's hurting a kid." Another shrill cry shivered through the window, and the features on the Mountain's face squeezed together, tighter than the knot at the end of a sausage. He started to move toward the door, and I put a hand on his arm.

"It's too many," I said. "We've got to call the cops."

"Forget it, asshole," Max Bruner said from behind me. "They're already here."

28

The Boys in Blue

The Mountain heaved himself around with such force that he grunted. Then he froze.

Framed in the pale pool of light falling from the transom window, Bruner's usual impeccable wardrobe looked damp. He made up for it, however, with the perfect accessory: a nickel-plated automatic aimed at the center of my stomach. Behind him, looking much wetter and more wrinkled, was a man who seemed only marginally smaller than Ship Rock, New Mexico. The man also held an automatic. His was pointed at the Mountain.

"Hello, Fat Boy," Bruner said to the Mountain. "You should've stuck with the burgers." To me he said, "I really didn't think you'd get this far."

"Max," I said, swallowing my heart to clear speaking room, "you shouldn't be out in this weather. You'll ruin your creases. Your dry cleaner is going to be furious."

He moved the barrel of the bright little gun in a tight circle. The top of the circle was my nipples and the bottom was my groin. Not much of a choice.

"Pissant," he said. He shook his head. "I tried to tell you. I tried to get you out of it."

"I've always had a hard time with advice," I said.

Bruner's mouth twitched into a straight line that made his upper lip disappear. "Fatal flaw," he said. "And contagious, too. You're going to take Tubbo here with you."

"You snotrag," the Mountain said between heavy breaths.

"You're supposed to help them." Ship Rock took a step forward and raised his gun so that it pointed at the Mountain's forehead.

"Help them what?" Bruner said, putting a restraining hand on Ship Rock's forearm. Ship Rock stopped like he'd been freeze-framed. "Help them go home to the people who chased them away in the first place? Home to all those hugs and kisses and sweet words? This may be hard for you to believe, Tubbo, but the people who write Hallmark cards aren't in charge of the universe."

The child inside shrilled again. At the top of its arc the sound tore itself into confetti and mingled with the drizzle settling around us.

"Neither are you, snotrag," I said, borrowing the Mountain's phrase. It had seemed to nettle Bruner.

"Over the long haul," Bruner said, "over the millennia, probably not. But what you're looking at here," he added, lifting his arm straight in front of him and training the silvery automatic directly into my left eye, "is the present."

The flow of time slowed to a trickle. I could feel a bead of cold moisture make its way down my cheek in agonizing slow motion. There was an itch in the center of my back. I knew that the moment I moved the smallest muscle I was dead. The hole in the end of the automatic looked wider than the Milky Way.

"The question," I said through rigid lips as the Mountain wheezed and snuffled beside me, "is what brought you out from under the plumbing?"

Bruner lowered the gun with a nasty little grin that told me he knew he'd scared the shit out of me. He kept it aimed casually at my middle. "Good question," he said. "You should have been a cop."

I wiped the moisture from my cheek and found that it was blood from the scratch on my forehead. "So should you," I said.

Ship Rock bared puffy gums and let out a truncated bark. It could have been a laugh or a particularly vehement scoff. His gun stayed trained on the Mountain.

"This is Sergeant Belson," Bruner said by way of introduction. "Sergeant Belson thinks you're funny."

"Yeah," I said, wiping the blood on my pants. My hand brushed over the hard barrel of the gun, and I immediately let my arms dangle at my sides. "Well, it's hard to get good help."

"Hey," Belson said. It was probably the longest sentence he'd spoken in a week. He was looking at me instead of the Mountain. Belson could be distracted. That was something to remember. Not much, but something.

Bruner shook his head again, pityingly this time. "You're not going to rattle me. You sure shook up Doris, though. It was a cute stunt, but any idiot would have known it was a setup."

"Doris?" I said. "You mean the Wicked Witch of the West has a first name? What'd you do, Max, slip into the Mister's used condoms? Were they still warm?"

"Keep trying if it makes you happy," Bruner said. "The Mister, as you call him, had to keep poking the merchandise. I handled the investigation on the Mister, which maybe you already know." I certainly hadn't. "He had a very sweet thing going. If he hadn't had his heart attack when he did, I would've attacked his heart for him. Now, let's go inside." He gave his gun a tiny jerk toward the door, and I turned obediently, hearing the Mountain snap into step behind me. To draw attention away from the gun jammed into the front of my pants, I laced my fingers together and put my hands on top of my head.

"So that's why you're here, Max? You're the new Mister? You figured the pictures on the computer were a draw play?" I asked, keeping as close to the wall of the warehouse as possible. It was darker there. We were about a third of the way to the door.

"Doris panicked," he said, full of male superiority. "Keep walking. Your little parlor trick got her all superstitious. She barely had the brains to call me. It was an obvious spook trick, and I was working on my list of possible spooks. When she described you and your adorable little ward, the list shrank to one. I didn't know about Tubbo, here, but I'd already decided that she should get the meat together and Belson and I should hang around and watch you show up. Tubbo just makes it better."

We rounded the corner. The door was only paces away.

"Why does he make it better?"

"He'll cook slower," Belson said in the resonant voice of someone who uses his skull mainly as an echo chamber. Then he barked again.

"Shut up," Bruner said.

"The sergeant has something on his mind," I said, "and it must be an exciting occasion for him. If you don't let him talk, he could have a stroke. There must be *some* blood pressure up there." I had slowed considerably, and the Mountain bumped up against me. I could smell the sour sweat of fear coming from him.

"Accelerate, please," Bruner said. "If you keep walking, I'll explain. Otherwise, I shoot you here, and not to kill. A man who's been gut-shot can live long enough to burn to death."

I accelerated.

"When they respond to the fire alarm," Bruner said, giving me my reward, "they'll find a bunch of dead missing kids and two dead adults. One of them is a private dick who decided to go for big money instead of a fee you could count in pennies, and the other is a tub of lard who works at the place where the kids hang out. I mean, you couldn't ask for more perfect suspects. Case closed."

The child's wail split the night again. I drove my fingernails into the palms of my hands.

"Don't slow down again," Bruner said. "You want to measure your life in minutes, or in half an hour or so?"

"Fire alarm," I said. "The kids are going to be dead. Then why are they hurting her?"

"Ahhh," Bruner said, "some people know what's going on, and some people don't."

We'd reached the door. It was closed.

"Hit the horn, Belson," Bruner said. Belson ambled obediently toward the nearest car.

"Why, Max?" I asked, trying to keep him talking instead of thinking about searching me. "What happened? Al always said you were a good cop."

"I *am* a good cop," Bruner said. The Mountain made a small choking sound. "That's the problem. I'd bust the pimps and see them on the street the next night. I'd save the kids' lives and send them home and then watch them come back and turn into pimps."

"This is bullshit," I said as Belson gave a beep on the horn of a car behind me. "It can't be the lady. I mean, she's okay for someone with a lot of wear on her, but nothing to abandon your life over. She's got a neck like a leg of poultry."

"Don't be silly," Bruner said. "I've seen enough sex so that I don't ever want anything to do with it again. Anyway, I'm not the Mister that way. We stay away from each other. I'm what you might call the fixer." There was a knock from inside the door.

"Knock twice," Bruner said.

"It was the money," I said, not knocking.

"It was a lot of things," Bruner said, "and none of them matter worth an ounce of spit. Knock on the door two times or I'll shoot you in the back." I hesitated. "Even better," Bruner said, "I'll shoot Tubbo, here."

The Mountain let out an involuntary moan. I knocked twice.

The door opened as Belson shuffled up behind us. It was like a dam bursting: light flooded through it and into my eyes, and I was blind.

"Well, Happy Easter," said a familiar voice. "I must of been a good little boy. And, looky, the Mountain too."

"Marco, you little shit," the Mountain said.

"Congratulations, Marco," I said, trying to focus. "Nice job on Junko."

"Nothing compared to what I'm going to do to you." He bared his cocaine-rotted teeth and waved the switchblade, his vitamin, under my nose. His pupils were the size of punctuation marks but less expressive. Marco was flying.

"Now that we've all said hello, Marco," Bruner said in a voice that would have frozen vodka, "maybe you can get the fuck out of the way so we can get inside."

Marco jumped back as though he'd been jerked on a wire.

"Max," Belson said, "I think we—"

"BELSON THINKS," I said desperately. "What a headline for the *Times*. On a par with MAYOR ABDUCTED BY UFO or ELVIS APPEARS AT SUMMIT MEETING. Do you pay Belson to think, Bruner?" What Belson was thinking, I was certain, was that he should search us. "When was the last time a crustacean had a good idea?"

"God *damn* you," Belson said. The Mountain hissed in warning, and a 747 flew into my right kidney. My head snapped back and I hurtled into Marco, knocking him flat on his back. I landed on my face next to him, feeling the concrete floor rip at the cut on my forehead. Something black and hot rose in the back of my throat and I turned my head and retched. In what seemed like the far distance I saw Belson blowing on his fist.

Marco scrambled away from me, swearing in a thin, chemically high-pitched voice. The next thing I knew, he was standing over me, grinding his foot into the back of my head and rolling my face back and forth in whatever it was that I had spit up. "Your turn, asshole," he said. Then he increased the pressure of his foot and said it again. The Mountain was making a blubbering sound.

"You little jerk," Bruner said viciously. "I'm telling you, get back inside and do what you're supposed to do. Or maybe you'd like to be on-line?"

Marco lifted his foot.

"I'm too old," he said in a pleading voice.

"Too old for what?" Bruner said. "Get Tubbo inside, Belson, and close the door. Too old for handcuffs and a plywood table? Too old for John Wayne Gacy?"

"Jesus," Marco said. The door slammed shut behind us. It sounded like a very heavy door. "You wouldn't do that."

"There's all kinds of customers," Bruner said.

"I'm going," Marco said. "I'm going." I heard his heels tap on the concrete, going away from me. Then I heard a door close.

"And you, Belson," Bruner said, "keep your fucking hands to yourself."

"But, Max—"

"You want marks?" Bruner said. "You want internal injuries? You want something to wake up some smart coroner who wants to run for governor? Or you want to go to work tomorrow and take early retirement in a couple of years and live to be a hundred?"

"Okay, sorry," Belson said, "sorry, sorry, sorry."

"You bet your ass you're sorry," Bruner said. I'd made it to my hands and knees. My forehead was bleeding freely and something vile dripped from my chin. "You're about the sorriest thing I've ever seen," Bruner continued remorselessly. "Just keep your ideas to yourself and your eyes on Tubbo. And you," he said to me, "get up. It wasn't all that bad."

I tried my legs. They worked, more or less. "It wasn't a weekend in Acapulco, either," I said, wiping my face. More blood flowed immediately from my forehead. We were inside and we still hadn't been searched.

"What'm I, your travel agent?" Bruner asked. "You're not going to have a weekend anywhere. Now, stop dicking around and walk." He reached into his jacket and popped some Maalox. I hoped he was digesting his backbone.

The Mountain was now weeping openly behind me. Great. All my life I'd fantasized having a sidekick, and the one I'd finally gotten had turned out to be the Cowardly Lion. I consigned him to the litter heap and walked.

There was a door inside the door, an arrangement like a low-tech parody of the airlock in a movie spaceship. Marco had closed the inner door behind him, or maybe it had closed of its own accord. The four of us—Bruner, Belson, the Mountain, and I—were now alone inside a brilliantly lighted room about twelve feet square. Now, if ever, was the time to make a move. Now, before we were inside the warehouse with a bunch of guys who looked like the offensive line of the Green Bay Packers.

My back was turned toward Belson, the Mountain, and Bruner. No one could see my hands. I forced a cough and then a chain of coughs, bent double, and put my right hand under my shirt. The grip of the gun felt cold and rough beneath my fingers. I was trying to tug it upward, free of my pants, when the coughs, to my surprise, became real and I bent forward against my will and retched again.

"Damn, you're messy," Bruner said from behind me. I ignored him: I'd worked the gun up an inch or so. I could have gotten it out if I'd been able to straighten up, but another spasm seized me and I doubled up and spewed some horrid liquid onto the floor.

"Hey," Belson said happily, "I hit the kidney."

"The trophy comes later," Bruner said. "Tubbo, open the door."

I was still jackknifed forward, fumbling hopelessly at the handle of the gun, when the Mountain went past me and pushed the door open. Bruner or Belson shoved me from behind, and we were inside the warehouse. Without the door to muffle them, we could hear the screams.

In front of us was a scene out of the elder Bruegel or Hieronymus Bosch. The trucks gleamed in the distance, wherever they were picked out of the darkness by the bare hundred-watt bulbs under their conical metal dunce's caps. Closer to us—much closer to us—in the center of a spill of light, was a circle of big men. They were spread apart holding hands like a beefy parody of a circle dance, forming a living wall to keep the children inside. The scream had come from the middle of the circle.

"Give her two more, Marco," Mrs. Brussels' voice said calmly. Then the door swung closed behind us and the men turned their heads to look.

"Where do you want them?" Marco's voice said into the

sudden silence. He was invisible, blocked from sight in the middle of the huddle.

"One minute." Mrs. Brussels came around the outside of the circle and regarded us. "We have visitors."

She looked cool and imperturbable. Except for the damp perspiration stains on her collar and beneath the arms of her jacket, she might have been behind her desk discussing some baby's future nightmares. "Mr. Ward," she said, "or, rather, I guess, Mr. Grist. What a shame you weren't who you said you were."

"One of the great themes," I said, wiping new blood from my forehead, "the difference between appearance and reality."

"Welcome to reality," she said. "You seem to have cut your head. Who's the fat one?" She wasn't talking to me. The Mountain whimpered.

"A clown," Bruner said behind me. "A walk-on, that's all."

"What's a walk-on?" She knew less about Shakespeare than Bruner did.

"He walks on and then walks off," Bruner said, "except he's not going to walk off."

"Well, good, Max," Mrs. Brussels said. "You were right. You said he'd show up," she said, meaning me, "and he did. One for you. Where's Jewel, Mr. Grist?" In the center of the circle, something choked out hurt little sounds.

"Where you'll never find her," I said.

"Don't bet on that," she said. "If I really want her, I know where to find her. Bring our friends in, Max. Maybe they'd like to watch."

"I'd like to watch you die," the Mountain said shakily.

"Good thing you didn't buy a ticket," Mrs. Brussels said. "I'd hate to give you a refund. This is a different kind of show. We've got a bad girl here, and she's learning what it means to be bad." She made an airy gesture with her hand. "Boys?" she said. "Boys, let our guests get a look at what happens to bad little girls."

The ring of steroid addicts parted reluctantly. One of

them looked at me, and recognition struggled with stupidity for possession of his face. Stupid or not, he looked dangerous. It was good old hearty Marty from Cap'n Cluckbucket's.

"I know you," he said, narrowing his eyes with the effort.

"That makes one thing you know," I said, swallowing my own blood through the corner of my mouth. "Give you the rest of the year, you might make it into double digits."

"I *know* him," Marty insisted to Bruner.

"Great," Bruner said. "Get out of the way."

Marty stepped aside, and the circle broke open as though he'd been the cue they were waiting for. Crowded inside were eight wide-eyed children, six girls and two boys, wide-eyed in a way that suggested nothing but vacancy within. They were wearing bedsheets, insurance, I guessed, against their trying to make an escape.

Aimee Sorrell wasn't among them.

In the center of the circle was a little girl. She might have been fourteen. She was wearing nothing but underpants, and long slashes across her rib cage and her tiny breasts and her thighs wept long red streaks. One of the giants held her by the armpits. Her hands were tied behind her. Her hair and face were wet with tears. Her eyes were enormous and crazed. In front of her was Marco, switchblade in hand. He looked annoyed. He'd been interrupted in the middle of the only thing he truly enjoyed.

"This is Marie," Mrs. Brussels announced in her third-grade teacher's voice. "What did Marie do, children?"

There was an agonizing pause. Children gathered their sheets around them and looked at the floor.

Mrs. Brussels clapped her hands twice. The children's heads jerked upward. Mrs. Brussels arched an eyebrow in the general direction of her hairline. "What did Marie do?" she demanded.

The children, as a group, emitted a confused sound.

"That's right," Mrs. Brussels said. "She tried to run away. She talked to the police." Behind me, the Mountain released a heavy, captive sigh.

"And what happens to children who talk to the police?" Mrs. Brussels said.

"They die," said a little boy, bolder than the rest. Like the rest, he was wearing a sheet.

"Good, Jamie," Mrs. Brussels said with horrible approval. "And is Marie dead yet?"

"No," the children chorused. Other than Marie, the oldest couldn't have been more than twelve. They chorused their answer in a demonic imitation of group spelling exercises. Their eyes were hooded, their last defense against total madness.

"Marco," Mrs. Brussels commanded, "finish it."

Marco waved the bright knife in the air. The side of his mouth that was still mobile curved upward and he took a step toward Marie. Marie closed her eyes and let out a scream that would have broken the windows in the Pentagon.

Something hit me on the shoulder, pushing me into the overdeveloped triceps to my left. The Mountain broke through into the circle, scattering children and Mr. Universe contestants alike, and threw his hands around Marco's middle from behind. With an inhuman roar he snatched Marco from the floor and picked him up. Before either Bruner or Belson could do anything, the Mountain had snapped Marco right and left, a terrier with a dishrag. There was a sound like God's fingers being snapped, and Marco's spine broke.

Marco yodeled his anguish, and the Mountain dropped him on the floor like so much garbage and turned to face Belson, who tried too late to stop himself in mid-charge. As Marco twitched on the floor, the Mountain roared again, bent double, and planted his shoulder into Belson's middle with the force of an Alpine landslide. Belson barked again, but this time it wasn't a laugh. He folded in half like a paper airplane, and the Mountain picked him up by the waist and, lifting him over his head, slammed Belson's head against the concrete floor. Belson's body went all loose and floppy, and something gray and puddinglike flowed out of his head. Marco was letting out little yippy moans. The top half of his body still worked. He writhed on the floor like a rattlesnake who'd been run over in mid-spine.

"Get him," Mrs. Brussels screamed. At the same time, a muscular arm encircled my neck. It belonged to the bozo I'd bumped against. I felt his biceps tighten as he lifted me off my feet. I could hear Mrs. Brussels screaming, a kind of atonal counterpoint to the Mountain's roars and the whimpering of the children. My air was being cut off. As spots began to appear before my eyes, I saw the Mountain put his fist all the way through the face of another of the muscle cases, breaking his neck like a wishbone, and I finally worked the gun out of my pants. Then Mrs. Brussels screamed again, and I saw that the Mountain had lifted another bodybuilder in a sumo hold, lifted him so high that the man's head struck the light hanging beneath the cone and set it swinging wildly, and I finally had the gun and I angled my hand and wrist around so I could shoot the guy with his arm around my throat, and his hold on my neck loosened and I fell to the floor with him on top of me, among the small bare feet of the children, and someone out of somewhere pried the gun from my hand, and I saw Bruner step forward and aim the shiny little automatic with both hands and blow the Mountain's brains out.

29

End of the World

B runer fired again reflexively even as the Mountain fell, and the second shot tore away most of the face of the man the Mountain had been about to kill. The two of them, the Mountain and the goon, toppled to the floor as the children scurried backward and Mrs. Brussels shrilled, as high and incoherent as a smoke alarm.

The light swayed and wobbled as it swung in a long, dizzy overhead arc, creating crazily elongated El Greco shadows that advanced and retreated, bringing alternate moments of brightness and relative dark. The children had bolted at the sound of the shot, and the goons were grabbing frantically at them. The instant the bulb swung past us and the light started to wane, I pushed the limp weight of the big man off me and scurried on my hands and knees away from the group, across the floor and toward the trucks. I'd managed to scramble under the first one before Mrs. Brussels saw me and called out, and Bruner snapped off a shot. The bullet pinged away from the concrete about two feet behind me and bounced upward before it slapped into the side of the truck.

Staying on my hands and knees, I crawled rapidly under the second truck and then under the third. Behind me I heard a confusion of voices: Bruner calling directions, children whining and keening, goons arguing. On the far side of the third truck was the large airplane door I'd seen from the street, and next to it was a gray metal light box containing

318

six thick black switches. This was where they'd driven the trucks in and out when the place was a real warehouse, and this was where they'd turned on the lights before they brought the rigs in.

Heavy feet slapped the concrete, heading reluctantly my way. "*Go*, goddammit," Bruner shouted. "Marty got his gun."

Above me and to the left was a big transom window, a single pane of rippled glass. Below it were wooden crates—the kind they ship produce in—stacked almost six feet high. It was plausible. I measured the distance mentally, committed the picture to memory, closed my eyes for a head start, and snapped off the lights.

Shouts sounded out. I counted five and opened my eyes. The darkness was absolute, except for a rectangle of light high at the far end of the warehouse: the window of the foreman's room. On both sides of the warehouse, the footsteps came to a halt. The goon on the left shuffled indecisively. A voice I didn't recognize—possibly Marty?—called out a panicky question, and I slipped off my boot and threw it at where I thought the window would be. It hit the wall with a smacking sound and thumped down on top of one of the boxes. I'd missed. I had exactly one more chance.

"Over there," someone said, reacting to the noise. Almost certainly Bruner. Someone else, someone closer to me, lit a match, a tiny point of light about thirty yards away. It was no help, either to him or to me. I pulled off my other boot and threw again, harder and higher this time. There was a resounding shiver of glass.

"The window," Bruner shouted. "Marty, find those fucking lights. Pete. Get outside and see if you can catch him. Son of a *bitch*. Jackie, you go with Pete."

Find the lights. Of course. There would be a light box at the other end too.

The nearest truck bulked up above me, only slightly darker than the room itself. I heard the door at the far end close behind Pete and Jackie as I felt my way around the side of the truck, moving quietly in my socks and keeping my hands pressed against the hard, chilly side of the truck. After what seemed like an eternity I came to the front end of the refrigerated section, which was shaped like a squashed tube, and found the cab that towed it. I stepped up onto the running board and fumbled around for the window. It was open.

I spread my hands flat on the top of the cab for friction and managed to get my right foot high enough to put it on top of the rolled-down window. Then I heaved myself up and scrabbled across the roof of the cab to the refrigerated section. Mrs. Brussels was saying things that no lady should think, much less say aloud, as I flopped on my stomach on top of the truck.

The bulbs snapped on. They created a lot more light than I wanted.

I hugged the truck, wishing myself thinner than I was. I would have liked to be as thin as a coat of paint. "Marty, keep the kids together," Bruner said. "Hurt anybody who moves." His voice echoed in the empty warehouse. "The asshole could still be inside."

"He went through the window," Mrs. Brussels said in a voice that was elevated by adrenaline. "You heard him."

"I heard a window break," said Bruner, ever the cop. "You take the right. Marty, watch the kids."

"Me?" she said ungrammatically. "Me take the right?"

"Who do you think you are, Snow White? If you see him, shoot him in the stomach." So she was armed too.

There had been five of the muscle boys originally, plus Bruner, Marco, and Belson. The Mountain had killed Belson and another one, and put Marco out of commission, and Bruner had shot one of the muscle boys by mistake. I'd taken care of another, although I wasn't sure he was dead. That left Bruner, Jackie, Pete, and Marty. Jackie and Pete were outside looking for me.

"Look under the fucking trucks," Bruner shouted. I could hear the two of them working their way slowly through the warehouse in my direction. Bruner was being careful. More careful than he'd advised the expendable strong-arms to be.

He and Mrs. Brussels met up directly below me, between the truck and the airplane door. "That's the window," Mrs. Brussels said, looking up. The shoe had taken out almost all of the glass. "He's gone."

"Not if Jackie and Pete get him," Bruner said. "Marty?" he yelled. "Got the kids?"

"All except the one upstairs," Marty shouted back.

Upstairs had to be the foreman's office.

I debated dropping down on Bruner and Mrs. Brussels and smashing their heads together before either of them could shoot me. It didn't seem promising. Besides, Marty had the kids.

The two of them moved back toward the other end of the warehouse. Bruner put a reassuring arm around her waist. They were talking in low voices.

". . . have to move them after all," I heard Bruner saying.

"You're so fucking smart," Mrs. Brussels said bitterly, knocking away the reassuring arm. " 'We'll get him,' you said. 'No problem,' you said. Now, look: he's gone and we haven't even been to the bank." She reached up and tucked in a flyaway wisp of hair.

"There are still Pete and Jackie," Bruner said. "And there's cash upstairs."

Since they were both walking and talking, I guessed they wouldn't be listening too. Without any idea why I was doing what I was doing, I climbed down from the truck and stood on the running board. The springs of the truck groaned. I was still reluctant to put my feet on the floor, where someone might see them beneath the trucks.

As the babble of voices receded, I found myself looking into the cab of the truck. It was about what you'd expect: two cracked and worn leather seats, an oversize steering wheel, and a stick shift half the size of the pole used for an Olympic pole vault with a big transparent plastic knob on top. Something bright caught my eye. Lodged between the seats was a yellow plastic bucket with the word BUTTS stenciled on it.

Whoever usually drove the truck wasn't a smoker, but he

caught a lot of colds. The bucket was full of used tissues. I reached in, picked it up, and upended it, scattering wadded Kleenex across the driver's seat. What I had was too crude to be called an idea. All I knew was that they were going to move the children, and I couldn't let it happen.

In my urgency, I knocked the bottom of the bucket against the steering wheel with a hollow-sounding *whuump*. I held my breath, but the noise had been covered by the opening and closing of the door at the other end of the warehouse. "He got away," either Pete or Jackie said.

"Fucking hell," Bruner fumed. "What are you fruitcakes good for, anyway?"

"He had a head start," either Pete or Jackie said plaintively.

"He had a head is what he had," Bruner said. "You assholes haven't had a new idea since you learned to jerk off."

"The children," Mrs. Brussels said. For an insane moment I thought she was reprimanding him for swearing in front of them, but then she added, "We've got to get them out of here."

"Keep your pants on," Bruner snapped. "We'll be gone in ten minutes."

Ten minutes. Clutching my newly empty bucket, I stepped lightly onto the floor and slid on my back underneath the truck. The concrete floor was cold.

"Marty," Bruner said, "get your ass outside and circle the block. Maybe these cretins missed him." The cretins murmured dissent in injured tones. "Look for a low-rider's Chevy," Bruner continued. "If you see it, slash the tires."

"I haven't got a knife," Marty said as I stared up at the underside of the truck. It hadn't been maintained, and rust was rampant. Also, there was blood in my eyes from the cuts on my forehead. I wiped it away with my sleeve.

"Take Marco's," Bruner said acidly. "I don't think he'll need it."

"You should kill him," Mrs. Brussels said. "Poor baby."

Somebody, and it had to be Marco, let out a gabble of pain and protest. It was cut short by the spanging sound of

Bruner's gun, echoing between the warehouse's bare walls. End of Marco. "Now," Bruner said, "now will you get the fucking knife and get out of here?"

The door closed behind Marty. I stared up at an expanse of rust.

"Children," Mrs. Brussels said. She clapped her hands. "We're not going to hurt Marie if you behave. You all like Marie, don't you?" There was something that might have been assent. "For right now, you stay close to Pete and Jackie. They're going to take care of you. Marie, you're group captain. I've saved your life, and I'm depending on you to make sure that everybody's good."

I'd worked my belt partway off, arching my back so I could tug it through the loops in my pants. The tongue of the belt was sharp between my fingers, but not sharp enough.

"We're all going for a nice drive," Mrs. Brussels continued in the same implacably insane voice. "If we're all good, no one will get cut. If we're not good, Marie will get cut first, and then we'll cut whoever was bad." Now I had the belt all the way off. I sharpened the cheap metal tongue on the concrete floor.

"I'm going upstairs," Bruner announced.

"Not by yourself, you're not," Mrs. Brussels said curtly. "You just wait. Pete, Jackie, keep them together." Feet shuffled as Pete and Jackie pushed the children into a tight group. At the far end of the warehouse I could see fat black shoes and small bare feet. "What do you say, Marie?" Mrs. Brussels asked, Miss Manners gone berserk.

"Thank you," said a tiny voice.

"And what else?"

"We'll be good."

"I only hear one voice," Mrs. Brussels said threateningly.

"We'll be good," the children chorused raggedly.

"Let's go, Max," Mrs. Brussels said. A moment later I heard the two of them climbing the circular iron stairway to the foreman's office.

That left Pete and Jackie, and they had their hands full with the kids. They mumbled resentfully at each other and herded the children toward a corner, and I found what I was looking for.

It had to be right. Nothing else could be that big. Trucks the size of this one took lots and lots of whatever the hell they ran on.

After I'd rubbed the tongue of the belt against the concrete a few more times, I tested the point. It was sharp enough to puncture my left index finger, which it promptly did. I sucked on the finger, swallowed yet more blood, and shoved the new point at the end of the tongue against the bottom of the fuel tank. This was my week for petroleum products. I was sweating and bleeding at the same time, and my eyes kept clouding over.

Rust or no rust, it wasn't easy. While I was working the spike back and forth, trying to make a hole, the door swung open and closed. Marty had come back in.

"I found the car," he announced proudly. "It was right in front." Then he paused. "Where are they?" he asked.

"Upstairs," either Pete or Jackie said. "Scamming the loot, probably."

"We'll see about that," Marty said quietly. "Anyway, I slashed his tires. He's not going noplace."

"I thought he was already gone," either Pete or Jackie said.

"Ummm," said Marty, sounding less certain, and at that point I punctured the bottom of the tank, and diesel fuel poured out onto my face.

"You saw the car?" Bruner boomed at Marty from the top of the stairs.

"Right where he left it," Marty said. "But it's totaled."

"Then he's still around," Bruner said. "Jackie, you dipshit, get out there and find him." I heard Bruner's shoes click as he came down the circular stairway.

I positioned the yellow plastic bucket beneath the stream. The gasoline hitting the bottom of the bucket made a sound I hadn't anticipated, a rattling noise like someone pissing on a tin roof.

"What's that?" Mrs. Brussels asked.

"Oh, for Christ's sake," Bruner replied. "Stop imagining things. We'll need the truck at the end." That was the truck I was under.

"No, listen," Mrs. Brussels said insistently.

I hoisted the bucket until it touched the bottom of the tank. Now it sounded like someone pissing into a pond. The bucket was getting heavier, and the smell of petroleum made me choke.

"He's here," Bruner said wildly. He'd given up on poise. "Son of a bitch, he's here. Get Jackie back. No, skip it. Go get him. Kill the motherfucker."

The bucket was full. I hoisted it away from the hole in the tank and shoved the tongue of the belt into the hole as hard as I could. The stream stopped and the belt dangled down from the tank like a rattler anesthetized in mid-strike.

They were so busy looking around the other end that I could climb back on top of the truck without being heard. It was harder than it had been the first time because I had the bucket in my hand. I gave up and heard the children crying, and then I didn't give up. Back on top, bucket in hand, I waited.

Marty was the first one I saw. From the far end I heard the children being organized again. It had to be Pete. My breath was coming in ragged gasps, and I put one hand over my mouth to silence myself.

"Nobody," Marty said after a cursory look around, his bald spot gleaming. He sounded relieved. He wasn't being paid enough for this. Heaving a sigh, he moved away from beneath me and into the darkness.

"Bullshit," Bruner said from some distance. "You didn't look carefully enough. He's here."

"Get the kids into the truck," Mrs. Brussels said. "Open the door."

The door she meant could only mean the airplane door, and the truck she meant could only be the one I was on top of. It was the closest to the door.

"What about *her*?" Bruner asked.

"We'll get her before we roll," Mrs. Brussels said. "It's

not as though she could go anywhere. Or maybe we'll just let her burn. Now, open the damn door."

A quiver ran through the metal skin of the truck, and I looked down to see Pete pulling open a hatch at the back of the refrigerated compartment. The children huddled there in their sheets, small heads bent downward. Pete pulled the hatch open, and the children, with Marie bringing up the rear like a good group captain, started to climb in. I ducked back. There was nothing I could do without hurting the kids.

Then I heard a ratchety sound and looked to my left. Bruner was pulling on a chain that connected two iron pulleys, one above the door and one below. The pulleys were anchored to the wall with heavy bolts. The chain ran from the floor to the ceiling.

The chain didn't move easily. Bruner was hauling himself off his feet to pull it downward, and he shouted something that I couldn't understand. A moment later, Mrs. Brussels came around the front of the truck and joined him. She'd stopped looking chic some time ago. She added her weight to his, and the door began slowly to rise.

Pete was pushing the kids into the back of the truck. Jackie was outside, looking for me, and God only knew where Marty was. Things weren't going to get any better.

I steadied the yellow plastic bucket with one hand and used the other to fumble in my pocket. When I had the little box I wanted and when I had slid it open, I said, "Hey, Max," and tossed the contents of the bucket over his head.

He looked up at me as though I'd risen from the dead. Mrs. Brussels backed away like she was on wheels, and I grabbed five of the Mountain's wooden matches all at once, lit them, and threw them at Max Bruner.

He exploded into flame with a scream like a jet landing. I smelled the cashmere burning as he wheeled around, still screaming, and flailed his immaculately tailored arms in a useless attempt to beat out the fire. With his hair on fire he gave me a horrified look and stumbled against Mrs. Brussels. She was his last hope in life, and he wrapped his flaming arms around her, spending his final breaths on a confused mix of prayers and curses. The skin on his face was beginning to melt, and he clung to Mrs. Brussels in an embrace of desperation and fire. There was a little pattering sound, like rain on a roof, as they toppled to the floor and Maalox tablets from Bruner's pocket skipped over the pavement.

She clawed at his eyes with her long nails, but he didn't feel it. The spots where the diesel fuel had splashed onto her linen jacket blossomed into blue flame, and the two of them rolled over the floor like the man and wife in a Hindu funeral pyre. Her screams mingled with his, an octave above, and more profane.

They crackled and fizzled as I climbed down from the truck. Their tortured voices punched holes in the sound barrier. Pete was long gone, running for dear life toward the other end of the warehouse. Bruner and Mrs. Brussels had stopped rolling and were burning like a bonfire of autumn leaves as I wrenched open the door in the back of the truck and said to the kids, "Go. Get out of here. Wait outside. Damn you, *scram.*"

The far door of the warehouse opened and closed. Marty and Pete were gone. The kids stared up at me with eyes that had seen everything. I was nothing new. I had blood dripping from my forehead and vomit all over the front of my shirt, but I was nothing new. They had seen two of me every day. Marie, closest to the door, shook her head and summoned up a word. "No," she said.

"It's over," I said, fighting a rising sense of futility. "They're dead. Beat it. The door's over there."

Marie extended blood-streaked arms to restrain the others.

"Please," I said. I could smell fire in human hair and Bruner's burning jacket. Bruner's lungs emptied with something that was too late to be a word. It was the rattle at the end of the world. "Go," I said. "Get out of here. Damn you, it's over. You're safe now." They looked up at me with the hopeless eyes of sacrificial lambs. They knew what happened to someone who ran away, and they weren't budging.

"Fine," I said, giving up, "if you're not going to go, wait right here."

I left them there and headed for the circular stairway leading to the foreman's office. As I climbed the iron stairs I found myself replaying a conversation I'd had with Jessica a century ago and wondering what had become of the softy who wouldn't light fire to Junko's pimp.

30

The Girl in the Cage

The stairs were steeper than they'd seemed, or maybe I
was just weak. I had to stop part of the way up and
catch my breath. The sound of cars starting outside told me
that Marty and Pete and Jackie had abandoned ship and
were heading for whatever hidey-holes they thought they'd
be safe in. Bruner and Mrs. Brussels were flaming away,
producing an extravagant amount of foul-smelling smoke. I
hoped the tongue of the belt was securely wedged into the
bottom of the truck's fuel tank. Otherwise, my next surprise
would be an explosion that could spread both me and the
kids over the neighborhood like peanut butter.

At the top of the stairs was an iron door. It was ajar. I
shouldered it open and found myself in an office that was
awful in its normalcy. A gray metal desk faced the window
overlooking the warehouse. With an almost hallucinogenic
sharpness I saw the paper blotter positioned dead center on
top of it and a wicker wastebasket at the left corner. There
was a Pirelli Tire calendar, at least ten years old, on the
wall. A naked girl hugged a large black tire as though it
were the second coming and she hadn't had her first.

Bruner must have been left-handed, I thought irrelevantly
as I stepped into the room. The son of a bitch had wadded
papers up with his left hand and tossed them into the basket
to the left. Two of the desk's drawers were gaping open.
Both of them had locks and keyholes, the worthless residue

of past security. That was where the cash had been, the cash that was now burning in Bruner's and Mrs. Brussels' pockets.

Other than the desk and the wastebasket and the calendar, the office contained nothing more than an old wooden coat rack, a map of the U.S. pinned to the back wall with brightly colored thumbtacks, and four pairs of rubber galoshes lined neatly against a yellow line on the floor. Beyond the galoshes was a door. Like the one I'd already come through, it was made of iron.

She, they'd said, *she* was up here. The one missing child. Well, she wasn't here, so she had to be on the other side of the door. And maybe *she* was Aimee and maybe she wasn't, but there was no way to find out without opening the door.

My hand was shaking so badly that I had to pull it back and flex it before I turned the knob.

The room on the other side of the door was bigger than a closet, but just barely. It was also dark. I slapped at the wall to the right of the door and finally hit the switch. That was when I saw the cage.

When you want to ship a dog on an airline, they give you a cage. If you don't have a very big dog, the cage is large enough to let it sit down without scraping its head against the top. Or maybe not. The cage I was looking at was of the latter variety. Woofers might have found it spacious.

Actually, I smelled it before I saw it. Even before the light flooded the little room I smelled the stench of abandonment and desolation. My eyes adjusted to the light and I found myself staring through wire mesh at the crouched figure of Aimee Sorrell.

Her mother wouldn't have recognized her. Bent double on knees and elbows, she wore a diaper that was fastened with an oversize safety pin, a final humiliation. Her knotted hair obscured her face even though she was looking up at me. There were three bright orange dog dishes in the cage. One held what looked like dog food, one held water, and the third was overflowing with human waste. Aimee obviously hadn't been a good girl by Mrs. Brussels' standards, and my heart overflowed with a jumbled mixture of grief and pride.

"Aimee," I said to the yellow-haired thing on its hands and knees, "we're going home."

Aimee narrowed her eyes and yelped in panic. I remembered what I looked like. Aimee's eyes through the bleared tangle of yellow hair were as blue as a summer sky and as empty. She backed away into the far corner of the cage, her hands clawing at her face, at her eyes, trying to banish me to the land of nightmares.

"I'm your friend," I said. "I'm going to take you home." I got down on my hands and knees so I wouldn't be taller than she was: it's a trick you do with dogs. Very slowly, so as not to frighten her further, I unfastened the catch on the outside of the cage and pulled the door open. "Come on out," I said very softly.

Instead of coming out, she squeezed herself more tightly into the corner. Her mouth was wide and open, and a high, sustained tone came from it, like an organ with a dead man's nose pressed against the highest key in the treble clef. There was no vibrato in the tone at all.

"Aimee," I pleaded into the horrid, unwavering sound, "I'm your friend." I reached a hand into the cage, opened it, and turned it to show her that it was empty. "Come out," I pleaded, "come out. We'll go home to Kansas City."

She swiped at my hand with claws I hadn't known she possessed, and my wrist began to bleed. "*Good* girl," I said, resisting the urge to yank my arm back. "Come on. Please, please, come on. Aurora's waiting."

For the first time something happened inside the blue eyes that might have passed for understanding. She looked rapidly from my bleeding hand to my eyes and then back again. The glance she gave me drilled holes through the back of my head.

"You're such a good girl," I said, babbling on automatic pilot. "No one else has been so good. That's why they had to put you into the cage. Come on, Aimee. Aimee, let's go."

I extended the raked, bleeding hand toward her. She looked at my face and then back down at the hand and then at my face again.

"Take it," I said, turning the hand palm-up. "Take my hand, and get out of the cage."

She hissed like a snake, but she didn't claw at me. I was smelling fuel again, and some clear, rational square inch of my brain was thinking about an explosion. "Please, darling," I said, "Mrs. Brussels is dead. Birdie is dead. Max is dead. They can't hurt you now."

She had stopped shrilling. "SaSaSaSa," she said. In her mind it might have been a sentence. She saw the blood on the back of my hand and recoiled and then looked from my open hand to my eyes again and realized that she had done it. *"No,"* she said. She locked her eyes onto mine and reached up very slowly with one hand, took her hand in mine, and pressed the place where I was bleeding against her cheek.

"Come," I said, drawing my hand away, but keeping hers in it. The blood was a bright smear on her pale cheek. "Come. They're dead. We're leaving." The smell of fuel was growing stronger.

"Aimee," she said, not letting go of my hand. Her voice sounded rusty. But she'd said the word that meant "her."

"Aimee, Aimee, Aimee, yes, Aimee," I said. "I'm Simeon. Please, let's go. There's a fire down there. I have to get you out of here, out of here so I can take you home."

She crawled six inches toward me, upsetting the dish with the water in it. Then she stopped cold. "Aimee's a good girl," she whispered fiercely.

"Aimee's the best girl in the world," I said. I was crying. "Aimee's the best girl in the whole wide world."

She watched me cry for a moment. Then, with great deliberation, she nodded. "With you," she said, "I'll go with you."

More quickly than I would have believed, she'd crawled out of the cage. When she stood upright, her legs trembled and gave way beneath her, and she had to grab at my waist to keep from falling. I put one hand on her head and said, "All we have to do is go down the stairs." I dropped my hand to her shoulder and steadied myself to turn and take her with me.

Her shoulders went as rigid as iron. She pushed at the hand on her shoulder. "Eeeeeee," she said, dropping to her knees again. I pulled my hand from her shoulder, but she wasn't paying attention to my hand or to me or to anything to do with me. She was backing into the cage on hands and knees, her eyes on something behind me, mad and wide and clear and empty as water, and the skin-splitting *Eeeeeeeee* sound flowed from her mouth in a rippling ribbon of anguish. I turned and saw that I'd betrayed her.

A flap of burned skin hung from Mrs. Brussels' chin, and her hair was gone. What was left clung to her head like the charred remnants of a burned-over cornfield. The left side of her face was a water balloon, a single enormous, distended blister. Her designer clothes were blackened and shriveled by the fire that had consumed Bruner, but the gun in her hand was steady and her eyes were ancient and fierce and lashless and remorseless. They were an alligator's eyes. Aimee's scream had decayed into a kind of dog-kennel whuffling.

"Sweet," Mrs. Brussels said between blistered lips. "Very sweet. Aimee. Come out of there."

Aimee, eyes closed, crawled out of the cage. Once out, she froze on her hands and knees, her forehead pressed to the floor in abject submission.

"Over here," Mrs. Brussels commanded. "Come to Momma, you little bitch." And Aimee crawled past me as though I weren't there and went to Mrs. Brussels.

"So it *was* Aimee," Mrs. Brussels said. The words were slurred with pain. "That was what Max said." She reached down and twined her fingers into the matted hair and pulled the child upright. Aimee's eyes were squeezed shut.

"We can make a deal," I said, wondering wildly what it might be.

"You already made one, Jack," Mrs. Brussels said, "and

you won't like it." Her free arm encircled Aimee's throat. Aimee's eyes opened and rolled toward the ceiling. She was gone again.

"You're going to go down the stairs," Mrs. Brussels said with difficulty. "Backward. Aimee and I will follow you." With the gun hand she pressed against the massive blister on her face and winced at the pain. The gun remained pointed at me. "Do it right, and we'll see what happens."

All I wanted was the gun I'd lost. Or Bruner's gun. Or fucking anybody's gun. "And if I do it wrong?" I asked.

"First, she dies," Mrs. Brussels said, meaning Aimee. "Then, you. And then, little Jewel, when I find her. And I'll find her."

I put my hands helplessly into the air. "Tell me what you want me to do."

"Don't turn your back," Mrs. Brussels said thickly. When she talked, the fluid in the giant blister bobbed up and down. "Keep your hands up there, and back up. Back around us. Back out of the room."

I did as she said, bumping against the door. Mrs. Brussels made a catching sound in her throat and pushed the gun toward me. I eased myself around through the doorway. She followed me into the main office, trundling Aimee in front of her. The stench of diesel fuel was very strong, and so was the smoke. Bruner was still burning.

"This place is going to blow up, you know," I said, backing toward the door that led to the circular stairway, my hands still in the air.

"No shit," Mrs. Brussels said, "and you're going to be in it. Just like Max planned." Her arm was tight around Aimee's throat as she forced the little girl forward.

"What about the kids?" I said. I'd backed through the door and my foot had hit the first stair.

"The livestock? They'll be with me. There are other states, you bugger. California's played out anyway." She was suffering exquisite pain and her world was crumbling beneath her feet, but she had a contingency plan. She had the concentrated focus of the truly desperate. She sighted over

Aimee's head and trained the gun directly at my forehead. Her hand was as steady as Gibraltar. The only thing that mattered to her was getting down the stairs, and she was going to do it no matter whom she had to kill. I was beginning to realize why Birdie and Marco had been so afraid of her.

From below I heard whimpering: the children. Petroleum fumes rolled up at me. I was forced down two more steps.

"Kansas City," I said experimentally.

"Keep going," Mrs. Brussels said. "Shut up and keep going." There was no reaction from Aimee. Her life had deserted her. I went down some steps, but I was too fuddled to count.

"Aurora," I said, "the harbinger of dawn. Remember Aurora?" I stumbled and turned my ankle on the next step. Pain shot up my leg and I had to clutch the rail to keep from falling.

Aimee was an automaton. Her eyes were three-quarters closed, like some bogus East Indian mystic meditating on a profitable future life. She moved in perfect consort with Mrs. Brussels, a little girl who had learned long ago to let her partner lead.

"Just roll," Mrs. Brussels said. "Keep going, and maybe I won't put Jewel up for auction. You haven't seen an auction, have you?"

We were most of the way down the stairway. "What about Prince Arthur?" I asked, dealing what I figured was my last card. Aimee's eyes flickered.

"I've told you to shut up," Mrs. Brussels said. "I could shoot you here and step over you. I don't even have to worry about my nylons."

"You can frighten me," I said doggedly, waiting for the gun to blow a hole through my skull, "but you can't frighten a little girl who's worn a pig suit." The gun came up toward my forehead. Her hand wasn't shaking. "A bright pink pig suit," I said, closing my eyes. "Everything but the squeal."

There was a sharp noise that might have been a bullet snapping into place, and my eyes jerked uncontrollably open.

Aimee was staring up at me through suddenly lucid eyes, and as the muscles in Mrs. Brussels' forearm contracted to pull the trigger, Aimee reached up and knocked her hand aside. The gun boomed, and Mrs. Brussels cursed, and Aimee wrapped both hands around the arm circling her neck and went limp.

Mrs. Brussels flailed at the railing, trying to keep her balance as Aimee's deadweight pulled her forward, and she hit the railing with the gun. The gun flew from her hand and even before the two of them collapsed on top of me I heard the gun clatter and skitter on the concrete floor below. Then Aimee and Mrs. Brussels hurtled down on me, and I fell backward down the stairs, trying instinctively to turn and save myself, but something went very wrong with my left knee and I skidded down the circular stairs on my nose and chest in a tangled ball of arms and legs, Aimee screaming and Mrs. Brussels swearing, all of us enveloped by the smell of fuel from Mrs. Brussels' clothes.

We hit the floor in a sandwich: me on the bottom, Aimee in the middle, and Mrs. Brussels on top. My head slammed against the concrete and I was trying to get my eyes to focus as the weight on top of me lessened. Mrs. Brussels was crawling on her belly away from me, scrabbling toward the gun.

I attempted to roll onto my side to go after her, but Aimee was still on top of me, and my knee sent an urgent signal of pain straight to my brain. I did my best to get Aimee off me gently as Mrs. Brussels squirmed toward the pistol, and then Aimee began again to emit the shrill flat sound, and it was echoed from the corners of the warehouse.

First there was one siren, then another, human sirens produced from small, tight throats, and then there were three and then four, and then too many to count. And Aimee pushed herself off my chest and got to her feet. Like a robot she walked slowly after Mrs. Brussels, still shrilling, hands hanging loose at her sides, and then I saw Marie, and behind Marie two of the other girls, and then the other children, all closing in on Mrs. Brussels, all with their mouths hanging loose and all tearing the air with the same inhuman sound.

Mrs. Brussels shouted a hoarse command, but the children kept coming. Her hand was only inches from the gun. I tried to roll onto my hands and knees but the pain overwhelmed me and the last thing I saw before I gave up and let the darkness take over was Mrs. Brussels, flat on her back and taking hopeless swipes at the children, trying to knock aside the sharp little fingers converging on her eyes.

31

Dust to Dust

The Mountain's funeral took place on the first sunny day in weeks.

It was surprising because of the size of the turnout, the width of the grave, and the presence of Donnie in the company of a large woman who wore bright orange hair and half an inch of makeup, makeup thicker than the average circus clown's. From the way he looked at her, she had to be his mother.

Two enormously fat people, the Mountain's parents, stood next to the minister. Tommy stood in the place of second honor, on the other side of the minister. He and the Mountain's mother were weeping freely. The Mountain's father was dry-eyed, staring stolidly at the horizon. He wore a dark suit, buttoned over a plaid shirt of the type the Mountain had favored. The Mountain had worn his father's old shirts.

The minister seemed to be at something of a loss as he surveyed the crowd. I didn't blame him.

Other than Jessica, Morris, and Hammond, who'd insisted on coming as a kind of penance for Bruner, the crowd was largely made up of Oki-Burger regulars. The Young Old Woman and the Toothless Man clung to each other in the presence of death, probably the only remaining item on their once-long list of fears. Tammy and Velveeta were decked out in full Hollywood mourning. Velveeta had even found a black feather boa, while Tammy had to settle for a black leather motorcycle jacket and a miniskirt to match. They were wearing almost as much makeup as Donnie's mother, and it was running copiously, creating long black streaks down their cheeks.

Hammond stomped out his cigar as a gesture of respect as the minister began to speak. The minister obviously hadn't known the Mountain. He did some spiritual boilerplate about the tragedy of a young life cut short, but the only time he caught the crowd's attention was when he revealed the Mountain's real name, something no one but his parents had known. At some point in his life, the Mountain had thought of himself as William Edward Dinwiddie the Third.

William Edward Dinwiddie the Second stared at the dead grass in front of him as his wife clung to his arm, her oversize frame shaken by sobs. Only Tammy and Velveeta cried louder.

But then it was Tommy's turn to speak.

"He did what he hadda do," Tommy said in a combination of Okinawan English and pure, deep grief. "He sent da kids home. He was a big fat guy, but he sent da fuckin' kids home." The minister blinked. "Nobody else done it. Lotta times I hadda take care of da tables because he was workin' da pay phone, gettin' da kids home." Tears rolled down his cheeks. "There's kids all over da place, they'd be dead if da Mountain hadn't sent them home." He stepped back, squeezing his eyes into fierce little slits. Salt water dripped from his chin.

The minister mumbled the appropriate concluding mumbo jumbo and backed away as the Mountain's mother threw a handful of dirt into the grave. Then she collapsed against her husband, slipping an arm inside his suit jacket, against his plaid shirt. He looked down at the arm as though it were an anaconda curled around his middle, and the crowd started to disperse. Some of them were chattering, working on first-draft gossip that they'd refine and share later with those who hadn't been there.

There wasn't much left to do: Aimee was home and undergoing therapy in Kansas City. The Cap'n's restaurants had been closed down. Mrs. Brussels was in a jail hospital, burned and blind, and the other kids were in Juvenile Hall, waiting for someone to turn up to claim them. So far, according to Hammond, only two had been claimed.

"Your son was a hero," I said to the Mountain's parents as the others turned their backs on the grave. Two guys with shovels were filling it up on union time, disgruntled because the service hadn't lasted longer. If it had, they might have gotten time-and-a-half.

"He was a big fat dope," William Edward Dinwiddie the Second said. "My whole life. My whole life I worked so he could go to college." Despite her formidable bulk, Mrs. Dinwiddie seemed cowed by the fierceness in her husband's voice. "So what was he? A fucking two-bit waiter."

It had never occurred to me to wonder why the Mountain had hit the streets. Now I knew.

"With all due respect to your loss," I said, "you're an asshole."

He called something hoarse and obscene after me as I turned away from them and caught up with Tommy. Jessica, Morris, and Hammond followed.

"I've got some money," I said to Tommy. Aimee's mother had sent me a bonus of five thousand dollars. I'd cashed the check, deposited half, and had the other half in my pocket.

"So?" Tommy said, wheeling on me. He was ashamed that we'd seen him crying.

"So here's twenty-five hundred bucks," I said, pressing the roll of bills into his hand. "Use it to hire someone who does what the Mountain did."

Tommy curled his hand around the wad of hundreds and then opened it again. He pressed the bills back into my hand.

"Already did," he said. "Whassa matter, you don't think I know what's important or something?" He sounded indignant.

"I don't mean to clear tables. I mean to send the kids home."

He glared at me as though I were subhuman. "So do I,"

he said. Then he turned his back to me and stalked off toward a waiting car.

In front of me, Donnie and his mother were heading toward their car. She was hanging back, complaining that she didn't know why she'd been brought all this way to attend the funeral of someone she'd never met. Donnie kept darting ahead of her. He was restraining his impulse to run. The next time he really ran, I was wondering, who would catch him?

"For Chrissakes, hold on," Hammond grumbled behind me, and I realized that I'd increased my pace, limping on my bad knee to keep up with Donnie. Hammond was following, pissed off and shamefaced and sucking on a new cigar. Behind him were Jessica and Morris.

They had their backs to the grave and they were holding hands.